SPIRITS C ⸻ **NAJEN**

Sethi's Song - BOOK 1

By Ginger Salazar and Jasmine Shouse

Cover art designed by Ginger Salazar, edited by Jasmine Shouse

PAULINE,
HOPE YOU ENJOY
THIS WORLD WE'VE CREATED!

Acknowledgements

Special thanks to Laura Salazar for her long-standing dedication to reviewing and proofreading for us, no matter how many or how small of changes we made.

Thank you also to Anthony Crump for his contributions to what became his fictional alter-ego in this world we built.

We'd also like to thank everyone who took the time to read and preview, and to our families and friends for their (sometimes begrudging) support and encouragement while we gushed on about what we were working on for the book.

Pronunciation

PLACES:

Beccilia	*BEH-sill-ee-ah*
Essenar	*Eh-seh-NAHR*
Falajen	*Fah-LAH-jen*
Lantheus	*LAN-thee-uhs*
Micinity	*MIH-sin-ih-tee*
Pahl'Kiar	*Pahl'KEE-ahr*
Resarian	*Ri-SAHR-ee-ahn*
Res'Baveth	*REZ'BAH-vehth*
Sariadne	*SAHR-ee-ad-neh*
Trycinea	*TRY-sin-ee-ah*
Vipurg	*VEYE-puhrg*

PEOPLE:

Aderok Simtel — *AHD-er-ahk SIM-tehl:* Kiaran Navy officer, Ekani's childhood friend

Antuni Crommik — *Ahn-TOON-ee Crohm-ik:* Resarian Dominion enlisted, Etyne's childhood friend

Arquistas Nal Enan — *Ahr-KEY-stahs NAHL EE-nahn:* Emperor of Sariadne

Brisethi Sen Asel — *BRI-seth-ee Sen AH-sell:* Resarian Dominion enlisted, daughter of Naiana and Tirinnus

Deseria Holt — *Deh-SEH-ree-ah Holt:* Resarian Dominion Elite Soldier

Drienna Vorsen — *DRIH-ehn-ah VOR-sehn:* Etyne's mother

Gasani Nin — *Gah-SAH-nee NIHN:* Sulica's older sister

Ekani — *EE-KAH-nee:* Kiaran Ambassador, Simtel's childhood friend

Elion Hadsen — *EE-lee-on HAD-sehn:* Resarian Acolyte, Livian's music instructor

Etyne Vorsen — *EE-teyen VOR-sehn:* Resarian Dominion enlisted, Crommik's childhood friend, son of Drienna

Ibrienne Sestas — *EE-bree-ehn SEHS-tahs:* Resarian Dominion enlisted, orphaned

Jenibel Teer — *Jen-ee-BEHL Teer:* Resarian Dominion Elite soldier

Jiridian Vorsen — *JIHR-ih-dee-ahn VOR-sehn:* Ekani's father

Kanilas Trenn — *KAH-ni-lahs TREHN:* Resarian Dominion

	enlisted, scout
Korteni Pyraz	*CORE-tehn-ee PEYE-raz:* Resarian Dominion enlisted, close friend of Brisethi
Li'lii	*LIH-lee:* Prelate of the Citadel
Livian Reej	*LIHV-ee-ahn REEJ:* Citadel trainee, orphaned
Maerc Nessel	*MAYRC NEH-sehl:* Resarian Dominion officer
Milia Kon	*MIHL-ee-ah KAHN:* Resarian Ambassador
Naiana Sen Asel	*NEYE-ah-nah:* mother of Brisethi, wife of Tirinnis
Petin Kayula	*PEH-tihn kay-U-lah:* Resarian Chief
Roz	*ROHZ:* Resarian Acolyte
Sentiar Asellunas	*SEHN-tee-tahr AH-sell-loon-ahs:* Ancient emperor, founder of the Dominion
Serythe	*Seh-REETH:* Resarian university student
Sulica Nin	*SUHL-ih-kah NIHN:* Resarian Dominion enlisted
Tirinnis Sen Asel	*Tihr-UHN-uhs Sen AH-sell:* Resarian Dominion Navy Admiral, father of Brisethi, husband of Naiana
Tuvalyn Bryns	*TWO-vahl-in BREENS:* Kiaran Marine
Yulana Terrez	*YOU-la-nah TER-ehz:* Resarian Dominion Navy junior officer
Vimbultinir Shani	*Vim-BUHL-tih-NEER SHAH-nee:* Kiaran Emperor

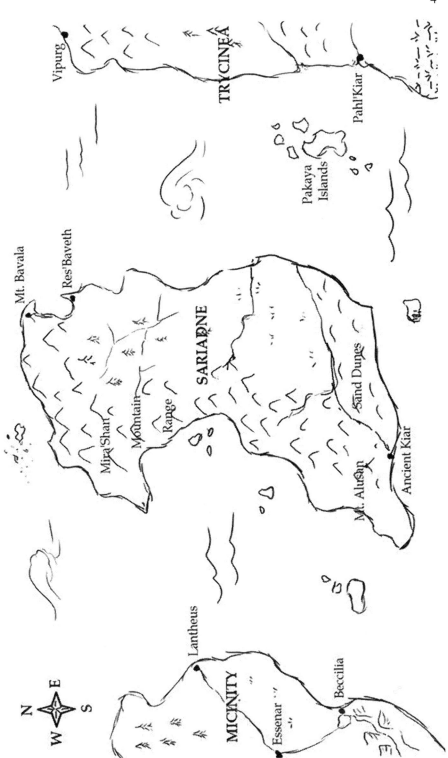

4

-:- -:- -:-

Prologue

*"For three-thousand years the Resarian Dominion has been at war
with us, ensuring we never return to our native land on Sariadne.
They continue to practice sorcery and witchcraft against us, melting
entire fleets and summoning demons just as their first emperor did at
the Dominion's inception. If we continue to fall before them, no one
will be able to stop them when they decide to conquer other nations.
It's time we ally with the rest of Falajen to throw our deadliest war
machines against them. You, my dear, are one of our deadliest war
machines. With your help, Pahl'Kiar will prevail."*

Kiaran Emperor Vimbultinir Shani

The chill of the autumn night mixed with the ocean breeze felt like icy glass against his skin. Captain Tuvalyn Bryns and his Marine squadron of ten men approached the heavily patrolled Sariadne coast in a lightly armored watercraft. They were fortunate enough to have terminated a small group of Resarian Dominion soldiers just hours ago near the icy island where their ship was anchored, but at the cost of two of their own. It had taken thirteen Kiaran Marines to extinguish four Dominion soldiers in the skirmish. Between Resarian Dominion mystics and Kiaran guns, the battle was quick. That particular group of unfortunate Resarians was without a healer or a shield summoner. Even their destructive mystics were minimal with very little power and diminished energy use.

Captain Tuvalyn and his team were sent to scout the Northern Coasts of Sariadne, just a day's ride from the main Resarian City, Res'Baveth. The reconnaissance mission to determine how many enemy soldiers patrolled and how often was meant to find a weakness in their defenses. The Kiarans usually kept to the warmer southern route, farthest away from the main Resarian city but thought to try a new, colder area.

"I don't see the logic in scouting just outside their main city. Of course it's going to be heavily patrolled," whined Sergeant Jonsen.

"They won't be expecting us in the north - they know we hate the cold," Tuvalyn replied, attempting to stifle a shiver. "They know the East and South is where we always strike from -"

"Then why did we only bring one ship? Why not an entire fleet?" asked another Sergeant.

"I told you why days ago, Valin, lay off the tressel mushrooms, they're messin' with your memory," Tuvalyn ordered. "The fleet will come along with our new allies once we've determined the Dominion's armory and posts up here. Our potential new allies will be in need of this information if both of our nations are to take on the Resarians from two sides."

"I don't trust our new 'allies', these *Lantheuns*," stated Sergeant Jonsen, breathing into his gloves to warm his hands.

"You don't trust anyone with pale skin," chuckled Tuvalyn. He readjusted his wool cap when strands of his thick, black hair fell to his eyebrows.

"I barely trust half of our own," Jonsen sighed. It wasn't until he enlisted into the Kiaran military that Jonsen had seen the first person with skin that wasn't as golden brown as his. He'd also never seen someone that actually had pupils in their irises unlike the Kiarans. But meeting a Resarian who wielded magical powers had made him more astonished and resentful that his people had been stripped of their own mystics and exiled from the same continent thousands of years ago.

It was an hour before dawn when the men reached the shore, quietly disembarking to scout the area. Tuvalyn knelt down to one knee and longingly pressed his fingertips into the wet sand.

They were home.

However, the Kiarans were forbidden by the fierce regime known as the Resarian Dominion to remain on their own land.

The familiar sound of horse hooves trotting along the nearby dirt road alerted the Kiaran men to hide behind a cluster of boulders. With their backs to the calm sea and under the reflecting light of the two moons, Tuvalyn could see six horses approaching, each manned with a Dominion soldier dressed in black and red uniforms trimmed in gold. One of them broke away from the others to examine what had arrived on shore. Tuvalyn listened to the men speak in Resarian, addressing their officer in charge. A woman's voice replied.

"Why do they let their females have combat roles-"

"Quiet," whispered Tuvalyn to silence Jonsen.

They were so preoccupied with the three Resarians who were gathering at their watercraft that they hadn't noticed the Dominion soldier behind them.

"Surrender your weapons!" said a female Resarian Dominion soldier in fluent Kiaran tongue from behind them.

Instead of surrendering, the Kiarans readied their flint lock rifles, aiming at the woman who gave the order.

"It would behoove you to return to your boat and your ship. Failing to do so will result in your death. All thirteen of you," she stated calmly as her five fellow soldiers surrounded them. Her pistol remained in its holster. Their laws of war stated that she would not need to fire it against an intruding adversary.

"We didn't return to our native land just to die to you!" Tuvalyn shouted and fired his rifle at her, grazing her neck. The others followed his lead and also fired their rifles at the six Dominion soldiers.

At seeing their commanding officer take a shot to her neck and falling off of her horse, ice shards, shockwaves, and fire fell upon the unfortunate Kiarans from the mystics conjured by the Resarians, whose firearms were only used for even numbered fights.

Tuvalyn heard the screams of his enlisted comrades as they were either frozen instantly, set afire, or launched back into the sea behind them. Jonsen was one of those thrown into the water. Profoundly shaken, he swam to shore to retrieve his rifle. The water droplets on his skin became ice when the Resarian targeted him. Jonsen's labored breathing intensified as he felt the beginnings of frostbite on his fingers and toes. He screamed when his limbs froze, followed by his blood vessels and organs. Death swiftly followed.

Tuvalyn stood and dropped his empty rifle to unsheathe his dagger, regret filling his nerves when his uniform caught fire, melting to his skin. He dropped back to the ground, shouting his surrender as he rolled in the wet sand to douse the flames. Through his agonizing pain, he was dimly aware that he was the sole survivor of his team as the remaining five Resarians closed in on him. Dazed, he wondered why they hadn't finished him off with more powerful flames as he watched them whisper to one another.

"Leave this land," the female commander demanded. Blood was still seeping out from the wound caused by the Kiaran captain, but she seemed to have recovered enough, though her voice was raspy.

Tuvalyn cradled his side, breathing sharply from the pain made worse by the salty water. His dark blue uniform had melted into his skin in places. As his eyes fell upon his fallen men, he groaned audibly, the burned unrecognizable. His mission was one at a familiar end, the same as most Kiaran missions when attempting to infiltrate their rightful home of Sariadne. Very few ever survived Dominion wrath. On his knees, he tried to straighten his posture when the Resarian woman walked close to him. Her uniform was drenched in her own blood.

Masking her own pain, the woman observed the young captain, assuming this was his first scouting mission away from Pahl'Kiar, the nation of the displaced Kiarans. She placed a bloody hand on his face to look into his hazel, pupil-less eyes - a distinctly Kiaran trait. "Do not allow your arrogance to force us to destroy your entire ship, Captain. We're giving you the chance to go away."

"Why? Why not end me now?" Tuvalyn pleaded as he hunched over from the unbearable deep skin tissue burns.

"We always send someone back with a message, Captain." Her voice was remarkably calm and soothing. "As I state to each one of you that steps foot on Sariadne, our peoples will never co-exist on this continent again, Kiaran." She turned from him and gave an order to the Resarian healer in their group tending to their fallen comrade. "Sergeant Wenders, heal his nerves so that he doesn't die of shock on his way back to his ship."

"Yes, Ma'am," he replied and shuffled to the Kiaran.

Tuvalyn remained on his knees and elbows, enraged at his own weakness, his failure to keep his men alive. He watched the Resarians carefully place the bodies of his men into the watercraft they arrived in. The pain was so intense, he could have sworn to seeing a hint of remorse in their weary faces. Their healer knelt to touch him, and Tuvalyn considered refusing but wanted nothing more than the throbbing pain of his burns to subside. Within seconds of the healer's mystic aura reaching him, the pain was gone.

The Dominion soldiers mounted their horses after carefully tying their one corpse to his horse to follow behind. Tuvalyn watched them fade out of sight into the night through the grassy plains before solemnly returning to the watercraft.

"We were once brothers, the Resarians and us. Living peacefully as small tribes among the dragons. When did it come to this?" Tuvalyn shivered, rowing the watercraft through the ice-cold ocean waves. "I'm sorry, boys," he muttered as he moved, "We've heard the stories, we've seen the log entries of every defeat. War is not the solution if we ever want to return home."

Spirits of Falajen

Part I – Progenies of the Dominion

Chapter I

Pushing away any and all second thoughts, she held her hand up as ordered. "I, Brisethi Sen Asel," she began.

"...Vow to support and defend Sariadne against all adversaries..." First Lieutenant Ubrey continued to recite the oath to her.

Brisethi repeated his words and hoped that the Dominion officer didn't notice her trembling hand.

"I will obey the lawful orders of those appointed over me," Brisethi said after Ubrey.

The officer concluded the final words of the oath.

"According to the Uniform Code of Dominion Regulation," Brisethi declared.

They took a seat at her family's dining table where her mother had prepared tea for them. Brisethi skimmed through the contract one last time, knowing this was what she had wanted since she was a child. Using the fountain pen imprinted with the Dominion symbol, Brisethi nervously signed the contract. For the next four years, she belonged to the Resarian Dominion Armed Forces.

Naiana gasped after reading the morning bulletin. "No! 'Sethi, my baby, you're not going!"

The Dominion recruiter arched a brow from his cup of tea as Brisethi leaned in toward her mother. "What is it, mother?"

"They were just outside the city last night!" Naiana shrieked.

"I assure you, Mrs. Sen Asel, we took care of the Kiarans rather hastily. Your daughter may never even see a Kiaran in her short time in the military. Unless she decides to stay in," the recruiter replied.

"I intend to stay in!" Brisethi grinned.

"You won't be able to handle the expedition, 'Sethi," Naiana discouraged her. "Recruits have died during the basic training! Your father warned you."

"The weak and reckless have died, yes," First Lieutenant Ubrey replied rather lightheartedly and stood to his feet. "It is time."

"Sethi, please reconsider, stay at home!" Naiana pleaded.

"Mother, I already signed the contract, I took the vow! I'm leaving..."

Naiana drew her daughter in for a final embrace. "Please don't leave me," she weeped as the recruiter made his way to the door. He waited outside the carriage to let the mother and daughter say their goodbyes.

Brisethi told herself she wasn't going to cry. Dominion Warriors in training were supposed to be stripped of emotions. But witnessing her own mother hysterically plead for her to stay formed the tears. She wished her father wasn't at sea all the time to calm her mother's nerves.

Brisethi placed one foot onto the carriage steps and stole one last glance back at her home. She never meant to break her mother's heart by shattering her dreams of her daughter becoming an artist or housewife to raise children. But she had no desire to become as emotionally unstable as her mother, nor did she aspire to be as salty and drunken as her Navy Admiral father. "I'm sorry, mother," Brisethi whispered. "Your dreams for me, they are not my dreams."

-:- -:- -:-

Brisethi Sen Asel nervously remained on her knees, glancing over at the three brash women chopping off the hair of anxious Resarian Dominion recruits. Word spread quickly of last night's attack so close to their city as each recruit whispered worriedly to one another.

Brisethi had just reached her twentieth year of life in the world of Falajen and like most of the recruits alongside her, she enlisted immediately into the Dominion Military to defend her nation against the relentless Kiarans. She had higher ambitions in life, however, than to merely defend her continent of Sariadne.

Gloomy clouds threatened to drop snow in the crisp fall air above the courtyard of the Dominion Command Citadel in the city of Res'Baveth. Brittle amber and rust-colored leaves scattered in the breeze along the cold, cracked dirt beneath her knees. Brisethi watched her breath steam out before her while braiding her lengthy, burgundy hair one last time, dreading this day of stripping away her eccentric life to be a soldier. All one hundred recruits in her division would have the same haircut for the Four-Year Expedition that was used as the Dominion Armed Forces basic training.

"Chin down, keep still," one of the women said gruffly as she grabbed Brisethi's thick, long braid in one hand and brought up a sharp knife in her other, cleanly chopping off the braid. Brisethi guessed the middle-aged Resarian woman was nearing five hundred years old as she continued to cut at layered strands until her hair was no longer than her smallest fingers. Brisethi exhaled deeply when the woman was done and raked her short hair. It was as symbol of stripping away their individuality to become one team. Every six months, she and the others would have to cut it to the same length until their four years of basic training were done.

Brisethi looked at the petite girl next to her who had stifled a sob after her long, blonde hair was chopped away as well. To spare the poor girl any reprimands from the fearsome commanders glaring at each recruit, she decided to attempt to cheer her up. "Last night was the closest the Kiarans had ever come to our city. They won't ever be that close again. We will prevail. They won't touch you, or your family."

"My boyfriend's going to cheat on me!" the girl sobbed, burying her head in her hands.

Brisethi exhaled loudly, staring blankly at the back of a recruit's head in front of her and wishing she hadn't said a word. Thankfully, Brisethi had ended her young relationship just before enlisting, knowing that she would be away for four years, training and patrolling the continent.

The first week at the Citadel had the new recruits shuffling from one section of it to another, obtaining their new gear and sizing for uniforms. While they waited on their names to be stitched onto their uniforms, the drill instructors began testing the recruits' physical abilities by working them in countless numbers of squats to push-ups to squats again. Sweat dripped down her face as Brisethi tried not to stare in awe at the ornately decorated swords and pistols attached to the hips of the instructors. The same petite girl next to her made no attempt to conceal her admiration of the physique of the men training them.

Brisethi's training division, known simply as Division Forty-One, consisted of one Army officer and three higher enlisted Navy and Army instructors who would oversee their Four-Year Expedition. Due to how arduous and lengthy the basic training was, the average graduation rate was about eighty percent. Those eighty or so who completed the training were allowed to choose to serve in the Dominion Navy, Army, or return home to serve in the lifelong reserves. To begin with, however, the division would remain at the Citadel's barracks for the first month of their preparation of further physical processing and paperwork.

Finally, the instructors called a halt to the physical training and barked orders to organize their packs. A lanky, dark-haired girl accidentally bumped into Brisethi during the shuffling chaos of recruits. "Oh, I'm sorry," she quickly apologized.

Brisethi ignored the clumsy girl even as she sat beside her and turned her pack inside out. They were instructed to ink their last names onto everything issued to them from hygiene kits and underclothes to winter garments. Each time one of the drill instructors walked by to inspect each recruit's stenciling, Brisethi was called out with a few others for their terrible penmanship. Their reprimand was the intensive feet shuffling move while resting on their hands known to them as "mountain-climbers".

Brisethi returned to her items, frustrated that she couldn't make straight enough lines of the Resarian alphabet of her own name. "I didn't join the Dominion to spell my name on items," she muttered.

The clumsy girl next to her kept glancing over at her while neatly placing her items back into her pack. The girl felt bad for her and wanted to help if only to spare her from more intensive training. "Hey, Sen Asel, is it? I just finished with all of my items, would you like assistance?"

Teamwork was encouraged in Dominion training as Brisethi Sen Asel sighed, nodding to her. "I, uh, I'm tired. My hands and wrists hurt from those push-ups and mountain climbers. They keep shaking when I try to spell my name."

The girl pursed her lips in almost a pout and shifted some of Sen Asel's items in front of her to begin neatly stenciling.

Brisethi was grateful for her help. She viewed the name sewn on to the girl's black and red uniform. "Pyraz?"

"Yep, Korteni Pyraz. Where are you from?" She asked while focusing on the task at hand. The cold, stone hall was alive with the chatter of a hundred recruits getting to know one another.

When she finally looked at the girl's face, Brisethi was taken aback by her seafoam eyes that contrasted sharply with her pale skin and sable hair. She was probably the most beautiful girl she had ever met. "Here, Res'Baveth," Brisethi said.

"Ah, a city girl. I'm from Worgale," Pyraz replied, ruffling at her thick, freshly-cut hair. "You ever been there?"

"I've never really traveled south of here. I grew up in northern Res'Baveth, closer to the sea." Brisethi considered how it might be a good idea to have at least one friend for the next four years as she continued small talk with the cordial woman. "Were you on a farm or something?" Considering how pale the girl's skin was, Brisethi realized how silly her question sounded.

Pyraz chuckled. "Nope, my family specializes in weaponsmithing."

"I'm intrigued, what kind of weapons? Swords? Rifles? Everything?" Brisethi asked with renewed interest in the conversation.

Before Pyraz could answer, the recruits were ordered to gather their packs and fall into ranks. They were led inside one of the Citadel's many entrances and escorted to the recruit barracks, located in the basement. The recruits quickly placed their issued items neatly away in individual small lockboxes located near their racks. In reality, the barracks was just one large room, dark and cold, which could snugly house one hundred recruits. The females only took up a quarter of the room yet had their own wash room, with the same amount of privacy as the males, which meant none. The Resarian Dominion had been known for having the only military in all of Falajen that allowed females to enlist into combat roles. But not all people of the world of Falajen had the advantage of living nine centuries that Resarians did, while only having a maximum of two children. The Resarian population valued each of their own too much to segregate genders.

The first month of training passed quickly by, filled with the most basic of instructions and orientation. The division only lost one member due to her failure to adapt. Nobody was going to miss the tiny, depressed, female who couldn't obey the simplest commands. Korteni Pyraz had been the only person to attempt to help the girl, but even she had lost her patience after three weeks when the girl wouldn't stop crying about her lover, worried he would leave her for someone new.

Then the day came to pack up and head out. "We're finally leaving, isn't this exciting?" Korteni elbowed Brisethi.

"When do we get our own swords? I want a pistol, already," she replied.

"They have to make sure your spirit is synchronized before they give you physical weapons," answered a kind male standing behind them in formation. "Did you not talk to Prelate Li'lii yet?"

"I did," replied Brisethi coldly. She wouldn't say out loud what the Prelate had revealed to her of her spirit. She'd already known most of what was lectured to her.

"Ah, well, I guess she valued my brain more than yours. We'll get them at our first camp," the sinewy, dark-skinned man teased. "I'm Antuni Crommik, by the way. Nice to meet you-"

"Stop talking in formation, Antuni, you're going to get us reprimanded again," his comrade nudged him.

"I'm just trying to inform these," he paused to look both of them up and down, despite their bulky uniforms, "nice ladies of why we don't have weapons yet," he quipped then turned his attention back to the girls. "And this impediment of a half-Resarian swine is Etyne. We grew up together in the inner city," Antuni grinned, placing his arm around his childhood friend who had joined the Dominion Expedition with him.

Etyne nodded politely to them, giving no real consideration to the two women he would purposely try to avoid for the next four years. He and Antuni had been given the lectures from their recruiter about females in training expeditions and the drama that followed. Befriending anyone more than his childhood friend was the last thing Etyne Vorsen wanted out of the expedition.

Korteni hadn't realized she was staring at the half-Resarian's eyes. Never before had she known a pair of aqua colored eyes that resembled tropical waters. What was more alarming were his missing pupils. "Do you mind if I ask-"

"I am half Kiaran; our pupils reflect the same color as our irises," he austerely replied, apparently accustomed to the question when someone stared at his face for an uncomfortable amount of time.

"Oh, I see it now - although, I've never met a Kiaran, before," Korteni bluntly stated, staring closely at his sharp features, black hair and bronzed skin.

"Soon, we may meet more," he said, once again anxious about having enemy blood running through his veins.

"Just remember whose side you're on when it comes time to fight them." Brisethi held in a laugh then murmured to Korteni, "I've always wanted to say that to someone, just like in the stories."

Etyne ignored her, annoyed from hearing that line half a dozen times in his first month of training. Antuni chuckled, "I tell him the same thing at least once a year." He elbowed his half-Kiaran friend, earning a glare in return.

"Crommik! Vorsen! Pyraz! Sen Asel! Since it appears the four of you have so much to chat about, step out of formation and commune with one another while mountain climbing!" Shouted Master Chief Synsun.

The four recruits muttered a curse, blaming Antuni, mostly, for their hour-long physical reprimand.

Master Chief Synsun was the highest enlisted division commander and gave most of the orders. He represented the naval warfare portion which the recruits would train in during their fourth and final year of the expedition by taking part in ship patrols. His voice bellowed, silencing all recruits throughout the drill hall as they formed up with their gear on their backs, standing at attention. "Recruits, this is your last chance to back down. Once we leave the city, we are all on our own. If you don't think you can handle marching, fighting, hunting, and sailing in extreme climate for the next four years, then Captain Tallien doesn't want you in her Army and I don't want you in my Navy." Complete silence followed. "Attention to the Dominion Creed!"

In unison, every recruit shouted the creed they were instructed to memorize their past month.

The spirit of our land resides in us
through the breath of dragons.
Our fire from the sky scarred the nations.
From the scars of Sariadne, the Dominion was born.
I will defend her from her enemy.
I will die before I commit treason.
I represent the antecedents
who have passed their spirits unto us,
And I will use such spirits to honor our nation,
never against my brethren.

After a moment's pause, Master Chief shouted, "Forward, march!"

The four division commanders led wooden wagons full of tents and supplies, pulled by stalwart horses, followed by the ninety-nine recruits. The absence of chatter continued as they marched toward their first destination due south across the plains under the blanketing late autumn snowfall. They would learn to adapt and enjoy the soft footfalls of a hundred and two pairs of leather combat boots that broke the silence during their next four years.

Chapter II

Within six months of marching, camping, learning defensive techniques, and basic survival skills on the grassy terrains of middle Sariadne; under cloud cover, sunny days, blizzards and thunderstorms, it was time for the commanders to choose their first corporals. Just under a third of the ninety-nine recruits had already been promoted to private first class, and it was time to choose the top four of those thirty to help lead the division in an ancient tradition from before the Dominion was even created.

The sun was set and the freshly hunted boars were cooking in the earthen firepits. Torches were lit around the field at the foot of the lone laccolith mountain on the grassy plains.

"There was a time," Captain Tallien began with the recruits surrounding her, "when the Kiarans and the Resarians lived peacefully with one another on our beloved, enchanted continent," Everyone, including herself, had removed their black leather uniforms, trimmed in scarlet and gold, to don native, natural leathers and hides just as their indigenous ancestors had in the time of tribes and clans. Designs and ancient text had been painted on their bodies to mimic the warriors of their past. They wanted to instill into the recruits that the rank of corporal was once considered "Chief" among small Resarian and Kiaran tribes.

"As the centuries went on the tribes became bigger," she continued, "new ranks were added and eventually, the rank of corporal had become the stepping stone to becoming a Dominion recruit leader while on the expedition. Tonight, thirty of you will take part in 'Destination Devastation': The primordial, difficult ascension to the top of Mount Devastation. The first four to make it to the top, will be our first corporals of the division." She purposefully elected to not mention the ropes, ladders, bridges and loose steps that covered the entire steep, twelve-hundred foot mountain, nor the fact that they would all be without their shoes.

As exciting as the climb sounded, Brisethi was in no hurry to get to the top. She would pace herself behind the other recruits, finding the mistakes they would make in their efforts to overrun each other.

Captain Tallien fired her flintlock pistol into the air, sounding the start of the race.

"I can't see three feet in front of me," Brisethi groaned as she carefully walked barefoot around the mountain, trying not to follow anyone. Antuni Crommick was at her heels, especially when he noticed her light a small flame in the palm of her hand. There wasn't a rule stating that mystics were prohibited, considering most Resarians their age couldn't summon mystics without a proper trainer.

"Do you even want to rank up, yet?" Antuni asked her, startling her from her concentration.

"Considering I'm going to be the General of the Dominion one day, yes, but this barbaric task isn't how I imagined I'd get there," she scoffed. Although it was dark, she still felt as if the two pieces of leathers that barely covered her thighs and chest were very revealing. She had Korteni paint various ancient Resarain symbols on parts of her body that weren't covered by the skimpy clothes.

Etyne Vorsen was following his friend, listening to them both ramble on about how simple the first six months of basic training had been. He was fortunate that they had followed the one recruit who had learned mystic summoning as a child, and happened to have been that of fire. She had saved their already calloused feet from several protruding rocks strewn about the grassy ground.

"I just have this solid feeling about her, man, she's stronger than most people, already conjuring flames at will so young. She's already igniting a fire in my heart! And we both know how I love strong women," Antuni retorted to his curious half-Kiaran friend.

"You're going to move on from her before the year is up," Etyne sarcastically replied. "Just try not to get us into anymore trouble."

"Oh piss off, you old cloudy-eyed bastard! It wasn't even my fault last time," he riposted.

"Hey! Do you two bumbling boar butts mind? Go follow someone else!" Brisethi chided.

"At least I don't look like one," Antuni retorted back to her.

Etyne broke away from the two and found his footing on an unstable ladder built into the sheer mountain wall. Antuni noticed his friend had deviated and followed after him. Brisethi kept on her own path, starting to climb with the assistance of a rope a little further on.

Private First Class Kanilas Trenn had already climbed halfway up, shoving his fellow recruits out of the way. He had removed the makeshift leather gauntlets from his forearms and wrapped them around his bare feet. Early promotion to him meant more frakshins and power. He thrived on competitions and would ensure he was the first to the top. He noticed that more than half of the recruits around him were already tiring, slowing down and resting longer than they wanted. His strength and endurance was outlasting everyone he came across.

Etyne Vorsen and Antuni Crommick felt as if they were the only ones pairing up to help one another out. They had paced themselves and reserved their energy by helping pull each other up over ledges and cliffs. The only reason the two of them bothered to take place in this competitive race to corporal rank was to ensure that those with terrible leadership skills weren't going to be in charge of them. If Brisethi Sen Asel had followed behind them, they would have assisted her as well.

Chief Renast chuckled as he casually climbed to start healing the unfortunate recruits who had taken a fall, sprained an ankle, or pulled a muscle. He was within a few paces of Brisethi who was flawlessly climbing another rope to a ledge that led to an ascending bridge.

"It's always cute when female recruits actually think they'll succeed at Devastation," he slandered. "You're a follower, Sen Asel, get back to the bottom."

"That's terribly rude" Brisethi apathetically replied as she pulled herself over the ledge. "What's the matter, Chief? Your mother beat you as a child and now you're afraid more women will become stronger than you?" She knew that would earn her a reprimand by morning but she was without discretion when it came to him. She hated Chief Renast's impudence.

"Maybe your father should have beat you for that mouth of yours. If I could reach you I would throw you off from that ledge, female." He spat the last word like an insult.

"Why don't you try to catch me then?" Brisethi taunted and sprinted across a rickety bridge, disappearing into the shrubbery of the mountain. Her burst of energy quickly depleted, she leaned against the mountain face to examine her blistered feet. She moaned when she prodded them, testing how much more her feet could take. She mentally berated herself when she finally thought to wrap her arm hides around them.

Sergeant First Class Vilkinsen stood to greet and congratulate the first Corporal of the night to reach him. "Well done, Corporal Trenn," he patted Kanilas on his bare, painted shoulder.

"That was too easy, Sergeant, give us an actual challenge next time," Kanilas Trenn countered.

Half an hour later, Antuni climbed the final ledge and pulled Etyne up after him. They were numbers two and three to reach Sergeant First Class Vilkinsen.

"Ah, I knew the two of you would make it up here, Corporal Crommick and Corporal Vorsen," Vilkinsen greeted, shaking their hands. Kanilas Trenn was the least bit thrilled to see them.

"Is anyone even left down there?" Vilkinsen asked after another half of an hour went by with no one else turning up.

"Yes," replied Vorsen.

"Nope!" shouted Trenn.

"Yeah, everyone I'm going to be in charge of," said Crommick,

"Three yeses," Vilkinsen grinned, pacing about the flat top of Mount Devastation. A single post atop the mountain hoisted the black Dominion banner, trimmed in scarlet with the ancient insignia stitched in gold thread. The Dominion symbol consisted of three falling stars crashing down to Falajen.

"A volcano is just a mountain with hiccups," joked the weary, intense voice of a female, peeking over the ledge of the dormant volcano. The sweat dripping down her face smeared most of her tribal paint. The intricate designs painted on her body were mostly smudged off or mixed with blood from various cuts of the climb. She pulled herself up with the last of her energy, straining her swollen muscles.

"Ha, I thought Chief pushed you off the mountain!" shouted Crommick as he walked over to congratulate Brisethi Sen Asel climbing onto the plateau with them.

"Are you serious?" asked Trenn incredulously at the woman. "How?"

Vilkinsen chuckled at her innocent joke, taking her hand to help her stand. "Congratulations, Corporal Sen Asel," he smiled.

Breathless, she thanked him, attempting to straighten out her fabricated native vestments. The sliver of both of Falajen's moons shone enough light to portray Brisethi beaming with pride. She looked at the other three recruits that had made it before her, each of them shirtless but painted in black and white markings. Antuni's dark skin had more white paint to stand out, while Etyne's sienna skin was a mixture of both colors of paints. *The paint and hides contrasting their skin colors have them looking as if they time-traveled from the second century,* she thought, trying not to stare in reverence. Even Sergeant First Class Vilkinsen with his shaved head, sun-touched skin and slightly more elaborate hides and paints depicted a perfect image of their ancestors.

The four new corporals followed Sergeant First Class Vilkinsen down the "easy" path to join the rest of the division down below. He was the only one who wasn't weary and engaged conversation during the forty-five minute hike down. The historical tidbits the Sergeant First Class gave them were fascinating, but the recruit Corporals still had a hard time paying attention to him while navigating the path.

The ceremony continued, prompting the new corporals to scavenge for whatever food had been left for them from the feast. Korteni ran up to her first friend, Brisethi, handing her some meats she had saved for her.

"Thank you," Brisethi gleefully told her.

"Nope," Chief Renast swiped the food from her hand, letting it fall to the ground. "You owe me," he leered.

Brisethi had to hold back the tears attempting to form in her eyes from such humiliation. She was famished, and wanted only to eat the spiced boar meat and drink refreshing water. Her blistered feet were throbbing and her muscles were sore from not only the climb but the past few days from every week they had intensely trained.

"Down! On your fucking face! Female!" Renast shouted to allow everyone to hear.

Brisethi dropped to push-up position, holding back an annoyed groan.

"One-two-three!" he began the four-count exercise where two pushups only counted as one.

"One!" she hastily replied lest he speed up the count.

"One-two-three!"

"Two!" she counted off. Before she could even reach the number thirty, her arms were giving out. Sweat poured down her face, with the remaining paint mixing in and stinging her eyes. Some recruits gathered to stare, while others walked away in fear they would be told to join her.

"I said, two!" Renast repeated. "Give me number forty!"

Brisethi refused. The failed muscles in her chest and arms would not oblige. She planted her face in the dirt and grass, breathing heavily from her fast-pacing heart. She said nothing even as the chief kept screaming at her.

"Looks like we only got three corporals tonight!" Renast snickered, standing over the defeated recruit.

"Chief, that's enough," Sergeant First Class Vilkinsen scolded as he helped Brisethi to stand. He would ensure she stood in the middle of the circle the division was forming to take part in the promotion ceremony. He guided her to stand between Antuni and

Etyne but behind Kanilas with their backs all to one another to face the division.

Master Chief Synsun began the ceremony by stating the Dominion Creed. Captain Tallien then tacked each new corporal in the chest their metal pin of a four pointed star and a pointed curve beneath it, representing their new rank.

When the ceremony concluded, Brisethi was ready to collapse.

-:- -:- -:-

"We'll set up camp here," Captain Tallien stated to Master Chief Synsun. "Chief Renast and his scouts should return before morning with news of Division Thirty-Nine. Have the recruits prepare evening meal once the camp is set up. Do not let a word of this get out to them."

"Aye, Ma'am," Synsun replied. He briskly walked away and shouted orders to set up camp. The recruits sighed with relief. They had marched into the early evening that day to make up time lost for an extended training session.

"I thought we were meeting up with Division Thirty-Nine?" Brisethi Sen Asel whispered to Korteni Pyraz as they began to unload the wagons.

She shrugged. "Etyne said he overheard Captain earlier questioning Master Chief about the exact location. I think we're lost," she chuckled.

"Who's Etyne?" Brisethi had trouble keeping up with the amount of friends Korteni had acquired in the division over the past few months.

"Etyne Vorsen, the half-Kiaran one, how can you forget?" Korteni laid their tent across the ground, waiting for Brisethi to hand her the ropes.

"Ah, the dreamy one," Ibrienne Sestas chimed in as she helped with pitching the tent.

Brisethi shrugged, "Oh, Corporal Vorsen, I didn't know his first name."

"Do you even remember *my* first name?" Korteni teased. She waited for Brisethi to pound in the poles they would attach their six-person canvas tent to.

Ibrienne Sestas helped prop their tent up, "I was his combat partner once. It was the only time we had any kind of conversation, and he was so friendly-"

"I'm sorry, are you two still going on about Corporal Vorsen?" Brisethi interrupted.

"*Maybe* – how come you never tell us about anyone you like, Sen Asel?" Ibrienne innocently asked

She intentionally ignored the childish question only because there were more important matters to be discussed. "Anyways, I doubt we're lost," Brisethi said. "They use this same route every expedition." She lowered her voice. "I think something happened with the other division. Chief Renast took Corporal Trenn and a few other recruits with him to scout."

Sergeant First Class Vilkinsen had explained to the Corporals that a division integrates with another one during the first and second year of the expedition due to the crossing of the paths. Except this time, the division they were supposed to meet with had not shown up.

Brisethi's heart sank when she realized it had already been almost a year since the day she enlisted into the Resarian Dominion Military. She hadn't even replied to her mother's last letter in three months. All of her waking moments were dedicated to helping lead the recruits under Sergeant First Class Vilkinsen. Her audacity in challenging authority found her punished by the other commanders, most especially Chief Renast. Sergeant Vilkinsen, on the other hand, had noticed that she possessed the leadership skills required to assist him while motivating and encouraging her fellow recruits to work as a team to overcome the obstacles already placed in their paths the past few months. Her willingness to stand out had earned her the rank of private first class, but it was her tenacity in the "Destination Devastation" that earned her corporal rank while most of the division were still privates. He especially valued her talent to ignore the attention some of the males were giving to her and the gossip the females would speak of her. Every division had the similar drama that most recruits struggled to resist staying out of.

"Go ask Sergeant Vilkinsen, I'm sure he'll tell you," Korteni nudged her friend.

"That's borderline fraternization," chimed in Sulica Nin snidely, the fourth recruit who shared the tent with the three females since leaving the Citadel eleven months ago. "How can we *not* notice the way you two look at one another when speaking privately?"

Brisethi let out a sigh, now ignoring the girl who thrived on spreading rumors. "The more I talk to him, the harder he is on me. Or have you not noticed that the division doesn't receive intensive training as often? That's because the Corporals are taking the beating for you all. Vorsen, Crommik, Trenn and myself – every other night, reprimanded for something you idiots did. My muscles hurt," she complained, stretching her arms over her head. Each time she or the other three Corporals were called on by any one of the commanders, they would inspect their uniform and military bearing. If any of them found the Corporals to be less than perfect, or if they replied with a wrong answer to the commanders' military questions, they would make the four recruits drop to the ground to do as many push-ups as they could, or any other type of strength-training, muscle failing routine. As the recruit Corporals were corrected on issues they were previously unaware of, they in turn would correct the other recruits so as to spare them the admonishment.

Six campfires were lit among the eighteen tents while recruits prepared their meals for the night. They had been trained to hunt their own meat and forage for their own fruit and vegetables while some recruits even gathered spices. Everyone had a part in preparing meals. They would fry flat bread, cut meat, mix the stew or boil beans. Water was the only beverage they were allowed to drink daily which was gathered from streams or the rain. Once they hit their first year mark, the recruits would be allowed one day a month to drink ale, wine or any other alcoholic beverage they could afford from any small village or town they passed. It was the one day a month the recruits could look forward to, but also the one privilege that would quickly be revoked if they became insubordinate. Fortunately for the other recruits, the four leading corporals ensured that none of their privileges would ever be revoked when taking the blame for others' mistakes and mishaps.

The evening meal was relatively quiet without Chief Renast's barking. Ever since the "Destination Devastation," he had found some reason to put Brisethi in the midwatch rotation as often as possible. That night, she looked forward to a full night's sleep for the first time in days.

Chapter III

The sound of cannons, rifles, and distant shouting followed by the clanking of steel and pistol fire startled Brisethi awake. She bolted upright, taking in the raucous noises. Boots shuffled outside while orders were belted, indistinct over the cannons.

"What's going on?" Korteni asked blearily, sitting up.

"I'm not sure," Brisethi replied, "but we should probably go out there. It might be a drill." They woke the other two recruits and urged them all out of their bedrolls, donning their black and red uniforms.

Exiting the tent, Brisethi stopped to let her eyes adjust to the darkness, then hastily made her way towards the shouting. She stumbled upon something on the ground, causing her to lose her balance and fall to one knee. She mumbled a curse and looked down to see what had tripped her. Her eyes took in the canvas uniform on the body in front of her: one of her own division soldiers had been slain. She gasped and covered her mouth, looking away in realization that there was no exercise. They were being attacked.

Her breathing rapidly increased. In a small panic, she grabbed at the dull training sword at her hip until she felt Korteni squat down beside her. "Brisethi, what's going on?" she asked again. Brisethi heard her friend's sharp intake of breath upon seeing their fallen comrade. "Who is that?" Korteni exclaimed, her voice higher-pitched than usual.

"It's Finik," Brisethi sadly answered. "Go back to the tent and gather Sestas and Nin. Find the medics and healers and be ready to tend to the wounded that I'm about to go find." Brisethi had given her first official order.

She inhaled slowly, attempting to calm herself of the fallen comrade before racing to the edge of the camp. She hurried from tent to tent, summoning her spirit's mystic to light a red flame above each wounded soldier as a beacon to guide Korteni's company. "Sergeant!" she shouted when she saw Sergeant First Class Vilkinsen running toward her.

"Sen Asel, get back! We're retreating!"

"But the wounded need-" She quickly whipped her arm forward to conjure a flicker of flame behind the Sergeant. The man that was about to fire his pistol at Sergeant Vilkinsen from behind let out an agonizing scream as he was engulfed in red flames. Within seconds he was flailing on the ground to extinguish the flames, but they only grew hotter until he turned to ash.

Brisethi stared in horror. It was the first man she had ever killed. She hadn't realized her mystics would actually kill him, only meaning to disable his wielding arm, not take his life. But some inner rage and panic inside forced her to spread the flames and increase the heat upon the man threatening to take her commander's life. She stood in shock, unable to hear the blasts around her. Sergeant Vilkinsen grabbed her arm, jarring her, and forcing her to run with him.

She had questions, so many questions, but struggled to find the words. Finally, they fell out in a rush. "Where will we go? They'll follow us, we can't outrun them…Who are they?"

Sergeant Vilkensen kept silent for a while, dragging her through the camp. Dozens of recruits fell in behind them, grabbing supply packs that were easy to reach and light to carry while others paused and helped the wounded stand and keep up. The only horses accompanying the division on the expedition had been taken by their specialized healer, Chief Renast, and his ten recruits who were still scouting in search of Division Thirty-Nine.

"Who do you think they were, Corporal? Is this your first day in the Dominion? Who's our only enemy!" Sergeant Vilkinsen vented his frustration at her questions.

Even in her panicked state, she bristled at his reaction. "Why is no one else using their mystics to fight the Kiarans? They're taking our people out one by one with those arrows and rifles!" she shouted back.

"Because, not every Resarian discovers their spirit's mystic at your young age! We're outnumbered and out armed-"

"No, we're not!" She pulled away from him and quickly turned to run toward the back of the group. Suddenly she stopped, and, facing the enemy, she summoned hundreds of bursts of small, scarlet fireballs, each one aimed to consume every shot and arrow headed in her direction. She peered through the rain of fire to glare at the ground beneath the enemy before her. They were approaching rapidly, charging with swords raised now that they had exhausted their projectile weaponry. She thought about the mystic she needed to summon and exhaled slowly. Within a blink of an eye, cracks in the earth formed at their feet, followed by molten lava spewing forth in the form of fiery geysers. She could have just as easily summoned a small brush fire to chase the enemy off, but the sight of one of her fellow soldiers dead on the ground back at camp fueled her hatred. She wanted these attacking men to recompense for stepping foot on her continent. As her deadly mystics conceded to her will, she heard grown men scream in agony at the sight and pain of their bodies melting; first their feet, then their legs, followed by the rest of their bodies. Men tried to run out of the pool of lava beneath them but were quickly felled.

The smell was sickening.

Brisethi instantly wanted to stop the lava from pouring out; she wanted the men to stop wailing from pain but couldn't remember how to desist her mystic. She closed her eyes and fell to her own knees, covering her ears to drown out the sound of dying men. "Stop screaming! Just die!" she cried aloud, bemoaning the massacre she had created and suddenly regretted using her mystic.

Where over a hundred heavily armed enemy marines had once been, now lay smoldering earth, leaving nothing and no one identifiable. Corporal Brisethi Sen Asel had obliterated an entire enemy squadron into dust and ash.

Her shards of fire turned to embers as Sergeant Vilkinsen approached her. She was unable to stand to receive him. Her legs refused to move, and her stomach rolled every time she thought of what she had done.

"How the fuck!" He stared down at her in awe. "Only the highest ranking officers in the Dominion can summon that much power in that short amount of time. I don't even think the Emperor can conjure that kind of devastation."

Brisethi looked up and gazed blankly at the dwindling magma. Finally, she stood and looked with empty eyes into Sergeant Vilkinsen's astonished expression. The despair she felt in her heart re-ignited her mystic at the sound of the suppressed cries from the other recruits. Embers fell from her fingertips like the tears she couldn't shed.

I took the life of a Kiaran man. He was attacking Sergeant First Class and all I could think was to protect him. And then I killed all the rest of them. I couldn't count all of them, but it had to be more than a hundred. I didn't leave any bodies, not even skeletons. There was just...nothing. Brisethi decided that her thoughts would be more of a suitable letter to her father, rather than her mother. *Everyone is afraid of me; I'm afraid of me. Sergeant First Class Vilkinsen hardly includes me with the other corporals anymore. Only Korteni remains my friend, always smiling and trying to find the good in everything as she always does. We salvaged as much of our stuff as possible, but we cannot return to the city, yet. We have to stay nearby to wait for our scouts and find out what happened to Division Thirty-Nine. I'm sorry that I took this long to reply to your letter. I know this will worry you, but I assure you that I can most certainly take care of myself and, if need be, the rest of the division. I promise to you that nobody will come to your door with a folded up Dominion flag.* She wrote at least three pages describing her life in the expedition, how she had ranked up faster than her other fellow recruits for having the same bellicose personality as her father, and how his raising her had allowed her to make use of her spirit's mystics before anyone else. Moreover, how it had saved so many lives. *Thank you, Dadi, for the early mystic training.*

"Four years old?" Korteni repeated to her friend after finishing her own letter to her family.

Brisethi nodded as she crawled under her blanket. "My earliest memory of summoning fire was four years old. My father would throw broken branches into the sea on the cloudiest days and challenge me to summon a mystic from them. He knew I was born a fire mystic - it's what the acolyte told him, but refused to let me know. Finally, on the day before my fifth birthday, I felt my spirit make use of its mystic. Expecting to see the branch in the sea turn to ice, I watched it ignite."

"That makes no sense, it was wet, how can you set wet wood on fire?" Korteni suspiciously asked.

Sulica remained silent on her bedroll, too tired to argue with Brisethi, and very much still grieving the loss of so many recruits. Ibrienne listened intently, never having had a father, let alone a mother, to teach her to use the mystics she taught herself to use at the orphanage.

"Because my mystic evaporated the water inside and outside of it to allow me to ignite it. But the entire stick had evaporated - vanished into air after bursting into flames for a very short second," Brisethi paused a moment, smiling at the memory. "My father was so proud of me, he took me downtown to buy me a birthday dress." She lowered her head and smirked. "But I didn't want a dress. I wanted a Dominion Navy uniform like his. We settled on a pirate coat and hat instead," she giggled.

Korteni chuckled and turned the lantern low. "How did your mother react?"

"Oh she was infuriated at my father. She was hoping I'd be a healer or shield summoner. She very much despised destruction mystics and for good reason," she replied, letting her voice trail off into a yawn. She had also left out the fact that it was already the second time in her fours years of life to bring disappointment to her sullen mother.

It took the entire next day to gather each fallen Dominion Soldier and lay them to rest in a burial, including Captain Tallien and Master Chief Synsun who had been among the first to fall from the surprise attack in their attempt to defend the recruits. Messengers were sent out to the nearest towns to have their orders and briefs sent through local horse riders back to Res'Baveth where Dominion Command resided.

Many recruits grieved for the loss of their comrades, the close friendships they had gained over the past year that quickly ended overnight. It was one of the most difficult tribulations the remaining recruits were currently facing, having to bury their very young friends.

Korteni walked up to Brisethi, each of them covered in dirt from digging dozens of graves. She looked down at the makeshift wooden memorial with the name, Ilikan Finik, painted across. "He adored you," Korteni softly told her.

Brisethi nodded. "I know, and I gave him no regard," she remorsefully replied. She walked throughout the other graves until she came upon Captain Lora Tallien's. "And I adored her," she continued. "I hope to be as confident and graceful as she was."

When the remainder of the recruits returned to camp after their evening bath and washing of uniforms in the ocean, Brisethi stayed behind. She sat on the shore, needing to listen to the peaceful splashing of waves crashing upon the rocky beach under the starry night, painted with Falajen's two neighboring planets. The fire she created was destructive, but water was cool and soothing. It would be colder this time of year had she been in the northern part of Sariadne, in Res'Baveth, but because they were further south, it remained warm during the winter months.

She hadn't slept much since the attack. The images of her devastation couldn't be put from her mind. In all of her training with her father, Brisethi had never been prepared for using mystics on people. She always imagined that war was fought equally with swords and retractable shields and figured that slow flintlock pistols and rifles were obsolete by now. She thought she would be trained better by now to kill a man before he killed you in a fair fight. But the recruits only trained in the minimum of defense techniques during the first year, learning cannons, archery, and slow, inaccurate rifles. They were taught how to defend against an ambush of an equal enemy, not the heavily armed, overwhelming numbers of big, experienced soldiers.

Brisethi regretted her first failure: using mystics in a panicked state to take down the enemy. Although her first instinct had been to draw her sword, she knew she wouldn't have reached the man before the bullet hit her superior. Her flames would easily reach him before her sword. It was horrible enough igniting the single man who had wanted to kill Sergeant Vilkinsen. His tormented scream echoed through her head each time she closed her eyes at night.

And then she heard all of them, watched all of them suffer again and again. They were men with wives and children and parents. Now they were dead. Brisethi had never imagined that she could bear witness to such a horrific scene, let alone be the cause of it. She had become her own horrendous nightmare.

Prelate Lii'Lii had warned her from the very first month in the Citadel to wait until year three to experiment with her mystics. She had warned her that hers was of the most destructive spirits she had seen in all seven-hundred years of her life. However, Brisethi had already been trained by her father and knew how to use them and stop them at will. But she failed to control them while panicked. Her arrogance had become her downfall.

"Sen Asel," Sergeant First Class Vilkinsen approached her, startling her from her nightmarish reverie. "Until Chief Renast returns, you, Crommick, Vorsen and I are in charge of the remaining fifty-two recruits. If the scouts don't return by sunrise, we're packing up and moving on with our expedition. They'll find us eventually."

She realized he was telling her to return to camp immediately. She jumped down from the rocks she sat upon then nodded at him. "I understand." She didn't mean to linger her glance to him, and finally understood what Sulica meant by the way they looked at one another. But it wasn't a shared notion of attraction, the way lovers long for one another. She admired him as she did her father, and Sergeant Vilkinsen adored her as a daughter. He was better at hiding his admiration of her after decades of professionalism training.

Before she could walk off, he tapped her shoulder. She turned to face him, expecting another order. He met her gaze with unwavering eyes. "I wanted to tell you – it was a brave thing you did that night. You saved us all with your mystic when mine was depleted, when most of the recruits were still untrained to use their own mystic. You deserve to know what happened. All of it.

"Captain Tallien was our shield summoner. The moment her shields were terminated, she didn't have the energy to summon them again." He paused, clearly remorseful of the losses. "The adversary realized she was the one with that power so she was quickly targeted. Master Chief used his remaining mystic of water manipulation to sink the vessel they had sailed on. As soon as I saw him overrun by a dozen men I had to fall back. I had to save everyone I could."

There's no bravery in using mystics to send over a hundred men to their grave, Brisethi thought. Then she realized he was silently asking for her forgiveness for retreating. She nodded and they began walking back to the camp. "What is your mystic?" she asked.

He remained silent a moment to contemplate his answer. "My mystics summon ice and snow anywhere for as far as I can see. But I can only use it once every few weeks. My spirit's regeneration rate is incredibly slow. Sometimes, I fall unconscious for days if I use too strong of a spell. When the Kiarans ambushed us, I summoned a simple chilling fog to hinder them, not to kill or weaken for fear I would black out."

Brisethi didn't know how to respond. It seemed almost cowardice that he had the potential to halt the entire company that attacked them, but held back just in case he wouldn't recover in time to save himself. "Why would you tell me this? Why would you admit to me that you didn't fully take up arms?" Her self-hatred spilled out at him. "Do you think I wanted to bestow annihilation on an entire squadron of Kiarans? Half of our division is gone because you were afraid of blacking out during a battle that you single handedly could have ceased before it even reached you!"

"Somebody had to stay alive to look out for the rest of you!" He didn't expect the volume of her voice to escalate so suddenly. Nor did he expect the lump in his throat to form. "This is the reason I lead training expeditions instead of experienced patrols. The Dominion doesn't need training leaders with useless mystics, they need destructive leaders like you."

She vehemently shook her head. "No, it doesn't! This war needs to end, this bloodshed needs to stop."

"What did you think you were going to do in the military? Did you think it was just all hiking and camping and sailing around the continent? The Dominion has endured for over three thousand years and will continue to endure until the Pahl'Kiar Empire has crumbled into dust." Sergeant Vilkinsen gripped the hilt of his sword as if challenging her to say otherwise.

Brisethi sighed. "I imagined that if I had killed anyone, it would be by this sword in self-defense." She laid her own hand on her sword. "But, somehow, I knew we wouldn't be able to outrun them, not all of them, not all of us. The fire of my spirit was invoked by a sort of rage. How dare they attack us? But I only meant to disable them somehow. I lost control."

Sergeant Vilkinsen, wanting to console her without giving the wrong impression, nudged her arm with a fist. "You're only in your twenties. It will take you at least a hundred years to master every spell you can conjure. Just hold off on the mystics for now until we meet up with Acolyte Roz in year three down south. There is much you can learn from him."

Chapter IV

After two weeks at camp and still no sign of the scouting party or Division Thirty-nine, Sergeant First Class gave the order to pack up and move out. The hike to their next camp took the entire day, covering less land than usual without the help of horses to pull the two wagons, which had been destroyed in the battle. Each recruit had to carry extra packs and take turns carrying the tents and ammunitions. Everyone was solemn, still mourning the soldiers they had lost. That night, after camp was set up, Sergeant Vilkinsen randomly paired up the recruits to train their combat skills. It was a welcome break from routine.

Brisethi faced her partner, the half-Kiaran Corporal Vorsen. His aqua-colored eyes almost appeared to illuminate while his dark hair fell just below his ears. It was the same length as her own hair, same as the rest of the recruits. Everyone had recently developed mixed feelings about him since the night of the attack, including herself. She knew it wasn't fair to judge him based off of who one of his parents was, especially since she was more or less being ostracized as well. But she was still too young to understand the complications of the War of Eras.

Sergeant Vilkinsen shouted the command to ready their weapons, followed by a second command for everyone facing the east to commence one fighting style, while those facing the west defended using a skill they had been taught three months ago.

Brisethi swung her sword the way she had been taught as a child. The instructors had trained in a similar manner. Vorsen wasn't surprised at how ferociously she fought though he defended himself flawlessly, even through her changing techniques. He deflected every one of her swings, encouraging her to hit faster and harder. Brisethi's last few combat partners were actually timid against her so she found a calm against someone who could take her hits.

Vilkinsen soon halted the fighting and had the recruits switch stances, leaving Brisethi as the defender. Brisethi muttered to Vorsen, "Do *not* go easy on me just because I'm female. I need to learn to fight a real man. Not someone who's afraid to hurt me." She grew frustrated with every partner she had in the past who wouldn't push her limits for fear they might injure her.

Vorsen nodded and, when the command was given, he held nothing back, knowing she was capable of defending herself properly. Before beginning his onslaught, he analyzed what he knew of her. Vorsen knew that she was strong from the physical training she endured with him and the other Corporals when they were being held responsible for the rest of the recruits' problems. He respected the woman for her ambitions but had concerns about her recklessness and arrogance. He believed that she was the type of leader who would risk as many lives as needed to accomplish the straight-forward goal rather than seek out an alternative. Although her mind was resilient for the Dominion, it was her heart that lacked the compassion of others.

After several minutes of combat, Brisethi grew weary of the constant strikes Vorsen had been swinging at her. Already tired from being the first one to attack, she wasn't used to someone actually challenging her. They hadn't eaten since that morning, and she could feel her hunger taking its toll. Her breathing was heavy and her blocking became sloppy.

"If you need me to lighten up-"

"No," she panted. "The enemy wouldn't 'lighten up' just because I'm tired."

He gave a mighty swing of his sword, making Brisethi throw up her retractable shield. She blocked the attack but was knocked to the ground. Her weary arms threw the shield to the side. Keeping her sword in one hand, she quickly rolled to the side when Vorsen's sword came crashing down in another attack. She used both of her legs to trip him and, as he fell to the ground, he barely deflected her sword in time. She became the attacker once more. When Brisethi pulled her sword back for a second thrust, he kicked her in the stomach, forcing her to double over and fall back down.

No one had ever kicked her before. She threw her sword down, holding her stomach as she caught her breath. When she noticed that Vorsen had a slight look of concern, she leapt forward, throwing punches toward his face. He blocked the first few, but her small knuckles did little damage to his face. Vorsen tripped her once more and finally held her down by her throat with one arm. She always had trouble getting out of a chokehold. It was the one move her father had never been able to get her to master. But because of the arduous training she had received recently, she finally had the muscle strength and leverage needed to grab Vorsen's arm to push his entire weight off of her.

Sergeant Vilkinsen halted the skirmish, realizing half of the recruits had stopped training to watch Sen Asel and Vorsen fight. Brisethi lay on her back, gasping for breath.

"Sergeant," she struggled to speak as she slowly rolled onto her knees. "I want him as my training partner for the rest of the expedition," she coughed.

Vorsen wasn't the least bit thrilled when the sergeant agreed to her request. He didn't want to fight only a woman for the next three years; he needed to fight men stronger than him which from his experience thus far, was only Antuni Crommik. "Do I not get say in this?" he asked Sergeant Vilkinsen.

"If she's too powerful, I can find a smaller girl for you," Sergeant Vilkinsen laughed. Though, he understood Vorsen's need to strengthen, and he would allow him to partner with Crommick every few fights, simultaneously letting Sen Asel train the other girls.

The recruits put away their gear and worked on cooking the meal. The mood of the division lightened up while they had chatted about the way Sen Asel and Vorsen fought hand–to–hand. Neither Vorsen nor Sen Asel spoke to one another for the remainder of the night.

"How are you not dying from taking his foot to your abdomen?" Korteni exclaimed. "Even *he* hesitated for a moment to make sure you didn't lose a rib," she added, pouring a ladle of stew into her bowl.

"Our armor's thicker than it looks. Very shock absorbing," Brisethi said with a grin that turned into a grimace before she leaned over from the pain in her abdomen. It would take a few days to stop feeling tender.

Brisethi, Ibrienne, and Korteni walked away from the food line and sat down near the fire. Brisethi moved very carefully, trying to keep her soreness from showing on her face.

"Did you see the look on his face when Sergeant Vilkinsen agreed to let him be your partner until we're out of here?" Ibrienne laughed as she soaked her flatbread in the broth of her stew.

"I did not, I was too busy puking the nothingness in my guts out," Brisethi replied, taking a massive bite of the steak bits in her stew.

"I don't think he likes you," Ibrienne replied with slight concern.

"Good. I don't need a partner that's going to flirt with me like the others did. I want to go against someone who actually wants to kill me," she grinned.

"Something's wrong with you," Korteni jested. "Sometimes I wonder if you even like anyone beyond friendship - male or female."

"It's not something I want to talk about," Brisethi interrupted. "I just have goals in life that don't involve a significant other holding me back or asking for my time. I don't have a sibling so I'm used to doing a lot of things by myself. It doesn't bother me to be alone so often." Brisethi yawned then stood to signify the end of the conversation. She queued up in line to wash her bowl and spoon.

"You're so peculiar, Brisethi," Ibrienne teased as she and Korteni followed the example. The women finished cleaning their cookware and went back to their tent.

Tired as she was, Brisethi lay awake for some time, replaying the fight in her head. She needed to get better, and Vorsen was going to help her.

Chapter V

Livian Reej sat upon the creaky, small bed, re-attaching the arm of her plush puppy. Although she was the oldest child in the orphanage at age thirteen, the other kids near her age were prone to forming alliances against her. They didn't like it when she had to pretend to be their mother and tell them what to do each day, not realizing the reason she was so harsh with them was so that they could all be rewarded with better food from their caretaker. She was tired of being one of only three children to participate in the daily chores and constantly had to scold the boys for not helping. That day, the boys had stolen her favorite plush toy and ripped it into pieces to try warning her to never yell at them again.

Like the other thirteen children, Livian didn't have much, so when the one thing she loved had been torn away from her, she no longer held her mystic back from the boys who hated her. For punishment, she was locked in her own room, as was customary when the rules were broken. She protested at first, saying none of the boys were even hurt from her shockwave, that they were just faking their achy muscles. But after their caregiver inspected them and discovered bruises forming, she had no choice but to lock Livian away after dinner.

She wiped the last tear from her eye and smiled at her dilapidated plush, holding it close to her chest. For eleven years she had lived at the only orphanage of downtown Res'Baveth and knew no other home. For as far back as she could remember she had watched nearly every other child in the orphanage get chosen to go home with Resarian parents. As she grew older, the less likely it was that she would even receive a passing glance from a couple looking to take a child into their care.

Livian ran her achy fingers through her tangled, blonde hair before lying down in the bed. She thought of her miserable life and how much longer she would have to remain in substandard conditions with barely enough food to fill her tummy twice a day. She stared at the ceiling, daydreaming of the times when the Dominion Military volunteered at the orphanage and took the children out in town to buy them food, clothes and toys every few months. Those were the happiest days of her life because it was usually a kind man who would treat her like a princess for a day. The last time, the sailor who had chosen her for the day was a female, however. Livian loved Chief Balia Suin because, instead of buying her a dress or fake jewelry, she bought her an actual knife and the plush puppy she had just sewn back together. The Chief made her promise to never tell anyone she had bought her the small, elaborate knife until after she left the orphanage.

"I'm buying this for you," Chief Suin had explained, "because I also grew up an orphan for most of my childhood." She told Livian that their orphanage had been robbed a year before she was able to move out and live on her own. But before the thieves left, unspeakable actions had been done to her by the two robbers and she hoped no girl would ever have to suffer as she did. Livian kept the knife on her always, whether in her boot or in a hidden pocket of her shirts, always careful to not let the other children or the caretaker see it.

It had been over a year since she last saw Chief Balia Suin or any of the soldiers or sailors. She wondered if the War of Eras had ramped up and that's why the Dominion couldn't afford the time or money to spend on the children anymore. As much as she thought about Chief Suin and admired her for the strong woman she was, she never relished the thought of ship life. She did, however, linger on the thought of becoming a Dominion soldier if ever she left the orphanage. With her luck, Livian was sure she would be doomed to become the new caretaker when she was old enough. She drifted off to sleep, dreaming of glory.

Livian woke in the middle of the night, immediately coughing as smoke filled the air. Glowing orange light could be seen through the cracks of her door. Her hand had barely touched the handle when she leapt back with a yelp. Whatever was happening on the other side of the locked door, she was trapped in the room. Livian started banging on the door, hearing the other kids screaming, panicking when she realized the orphanage was on fire. Quickly, she dropped to the floor and crawled over to the window. She tried to unlock it, but it wouldn't budge open. Using all her might to try breaking it with her fist, she cried in pain when her weak hands couldn't break the glass.

"Help me! Somebody get me out of here!" she screamed, pounding on all the walls, door and window. Her lungs burned from the effort of yelling through the smoke. She forced herself to calm down and finally grabbed her plush to focus meditating on summoning her small spell. Within seconds, the window before her shattered, forcing her to shield her eyes from the flying glass. She grabbed a blanket from her bed to protect herself from broken glass on the window sill as she hastily climbed out, jumping onto the cold grass.

Livian stood and turned to see that several nearby buildings were also on fire. She no longer heard the screams of her fellow orphans, nor did she see them among the few guards and townspeople that were trying to douse the fire. In that instant, she made a split-second decision. Before anyone could spot her, she made sure she had her knife and her plush and took off toward the dark alleyway. She didn't want to be transferred to another orphanage, though she didn't think another one existed in the city.

She ran as fast as her legs would take her, as far as she could go. Finally, she could move no further. She paused, panting, and fell to her knees in a narrow alley. She knew she wasn't in the nicest part of Res'Baveth and tried to remain quiet, using her plush puppy to stifle the lingering smoke-induced cough. She shifted off of her knees and leaned against a building, still trying to catch her breath.

The bell tower in the distance struck the third hour of the early morning. She had nothing. All of her basic necessities of shelter, food, clothing, even soap, had all been taken from her, just like the family she'd never known. She hadn't even had time to put her shoes on. The two girls she barely considered temporary friends in the orphanage had surely been killed. The caretaker who was the closest thing she'd ever had to a mother had probably died in the fire, too, for all she knew. And the one person Livian considered a sister would be impossible to reach. Tears welled in her eyes at the thought that she had suddenly become homeless, vulnerable. She shivered from the cold spring air and sobbed into her plush puppy.

The humid chill of morning and the distant bell tower sounding the sixth hour startled her from a short, restless nap in the alley. Livian's muscles ached from sleeping on the hard ground, and dirt and ash covered most of her clothes and skin. The rising sun was peeking through the towering buildings of downtown Res'Baveth, slowly dissipating the spring morning chill.

An ache of despair hit her heart heavily when realization hit her again that she was homeless. The city didn't have beggars and homeless people; a Resarian who didn't work was unheard of. If someone was caught stealing food, begging, or living in the streets, they were sent to the fields to work for minimum wage, hired by noblemen as servants, or sent to the Dominion Armed Forces. She was too young to join the military, but would gladly earn pay and shelter working in the fields or as a maid for someone looking to hire her. Anything had to be better than the orphanage.

Livian walked out of the alleyway to find herself near the busy main circle of merchants and vendors setting up their shops for the daily market. Sweet and spicy aromas of baked goods filled the air, causing her stomach to rumble. She ignored the hunger and approached the produce stands first, asking the merchants if she could work for them. They saw how young and small she was and told her to go back home to her parents and ask for their permission. Other merchants simply ignored her, thinking she was probably just lost. When she finally told one of the other merchants that she didn't have parents, he instructed her to return to the orphanage.

"It's been burned down," she said.

"By the spirits, girl, where are the other children?" the man asked.

She shrugged. "I'm the only survivor. I need a job. I need a place to stay."

He glared at her small figure. "I've got no extra jobs or money to give to a child. Go to the Citadel, they hire children to clean the sanctuary."

"How do I get there?"

"Take the North road for about six miles, you can't miss it." He walked away from her to tend to an actual customer.

Livian had no shoes to casually walk the six miles and no frakshins to hire a carriage. She hadn't eaten since the night before and the bell tower had tolled eight times in sets of two, notifying the people of the sixteenth hour of the day. She was more thirsty than hungry, and she felt out of place among the clean, well-dressed Resarians. She, on the other hand, smelled like the horses that pulled their carriages. After the horses had survived a barn fire.

For a while, she rested beneath the shade of a tree before being able to summon the energy needed for the trek to the Citadel, despite her blistered feet, aching stomach and weakened muscles.

"Kid! Hey kid!"

She turned her head to see a city guard trying to get her attention. He quickly caught up to her. "Where are your parents?"

Livian held her puppy tight, fighting to hold back the tears she'd refused to shed all day. After a few seconds, she gave in, feeling the sting from her eyes as the tears fell. "I'm from the orphanage that burned down," she began. "I just want to get to the Citadel but I'm in so much pain, I'm so hungry." She planted her face in her plush, red with shame and exhaustion.

The guard knelt down beside her. "I heard about the fire. Thank the spirits someone survived." He patted her on the back to console her. "You remind me of my own daughter when she's begging me to get her something. Except your tears are actually genuine." He tried to grin, but it didn't cheer the girl. "What's your name?"

"Liv," she mumbled in a sob.

"I'm Constable Oto," he shook her hand. "Come now, let's get you a proper meal and we'll be on our way to the Citadel before you can say hopjacks."

She gave the constable a teary smile, and he led her to a few of the stands, buying her a couple unfamiliar fruits and a pastry.

Maybe my luck is changing, she thought to herself as she ate the delicious food.

He brought her to a parlor just as it was closing. As the owner was the constable's very own wife, she helped to clean Livian up, bandage her blistered feet and cut hands, and give her proper clothes, along with walking shoes. Livian was overly grateful for their care.

The Citadel was larger than any structure she had ever seen in her life. A courtyard sprawled in front of the main building, complete with a beautiful fountain. Its design was foreign to Livian's young eyes. The Citadel was not only a sanctuary to honor the Spirits, but also a fortress for the Dominion Armed Forces. It served as barracks for initial recruits, quarters and schoolhouses for officer training, held dining halls, war rooms, armories and housed acolytes serving to uphold the faith of the Spirits. Although the Resarian palace was taller, the Citadel was wider, covering more land. It was the sole defensive fortress inside the mystic walls of Res'Baveth.

Livian felt very grateful to the constable and his wife who fed her, clothed her, and hired a carriage to take her to the Citadel. When the constable and Livian arrived, they walked through the courtyard, up a flight of marble stairs to the great hall. They were met by the head Acolyte working directly under Prelate Li'Li.

"Livian Reej," the man addressed her. He had a young face but his eyes seemed full of kindness and wisdom. She was unusually speechless in front of the spiritual man in his impressive robes. "I am Acolyte Roz. I'm terribly sorry about what happened to your last place of residence and hope you will find our establishment as a suitable home. Allow me to show you to your room so that you can settle in before I give you a tour and a description of your duties." The acolyte was dressed in red robes with simple black cording to trim the belt, hood and cuffs.

The constable stayed long enough to ensure Livian would be welcomed and taken care of before saying good-bye and disappearing the way they'd come.

As Acolyte Roz and Livian walked, he asked her some basic questions - her age, skills, the name of her stuffed puppy.

When she felt comfortable, Livian asked, "Do you always take random children off the streets into your care?"

"Children don't live in the streets, "Acolyte Roz pointed out. "They live in the orphanage, which is already being rebuilt." He noticed the despairing look on her face out of the corner of his eye. "But, seeing as how you're a bit older than most children who typically stay in an orphanage, I agreed to the guard's request of allowing you to work for me. You're younger than most people I hire, because you should still be in school. Not to worry, though, we have a schoolhouse here for the children of those who work for Falajen's Spirits or if both parents serve in the Dominion military." Roz came to a stop in front of the door that led to her new room.

She opened the door and stepped inside. Roz lit the candles and lanterns of the small, cozy room to reveal paintings of ancient gardens of Sariadne blessed by the Spirit's presence. The room held a single bed, a dresser and a desk with a simple wooden chair. The blankets, pillows, curtains and rugs were dark red and, even though the fortress was made of stone, the walls were lined in finished wood panels to give the effect of a cozy lifestyle. She glanced out the single window of her room, high above the city below. She didn't remember climbing four flights of stairs to get to her room.

"It's perfect, thank you," she said to the acolyte, briefly remembering her manners.

Roz smiled kindly. "The robes in the dresser are your daily attire for school and work, but you will be paid frakshins by the Citadel to purchase your own clothes and goods. Down the hall on the right is the bathing room, women to the room on the left once you enter. I will return in one hour to take you to supper, then we will do a tour and discuss your duties and contract in the morning." Roz stepped out of her room and closed the door.

In all her daydreams, Livian had never imagined leading a spiritual life, but then again, the Resarian's faith wasn't a strict one, let alone demanding. She had a strong mystic from her spirit, she might as well at least thank them for that by working for them.

"Why are there paintings and statues of dragons everywhere?" Livian asked Roz later as they walked to the smaller dining hall.

"Have the schools stopped teaching our ancient history entirely?" he answered with a question.

She shrugged, unsure of what he meant.

"Before the War of Eras, it was once believed that our spirits came from dragons, hence why only our people live for centuries and summon mystics. As millenias passed, the thought that dragons ever existed became a myth. These few statues and paintings survived the obliteration of ancient Resari from the Kiaran attack and have become merely ancient relics of a civilization before Res'Baveth," Roz explained.

"Dragon spirits?" she asked with a hint of disbelief. "Kiarans used to be here, why don't they live centuries and have mystics?"

Roz sighed, internally fuming at the current state of Resarian public education. "As punishment for hunting down every last dragon, then attacking their northern brethren, the Resarians, they were exiled to the continent of Micinity. As each generation of Kiarans were born, they were too far from the Sea of Renewal to be born with a dragon's spirit. Perhaps as further punishment, or as a reminder of what they did, no one knows why, but their eyes have also been removed of their color - by being born with pupils the same color as their irises."

"Serves them right," Livian muttered, suddenly intrigued by ancient history. In the dim lantern light, she lightly touched a dragon statue, taller than her.

"Until someone finds a way to allow both races to co-exist once more, this War of Eras will never end. The massacre the Kiarans conveyed to our people three thousand years ago was wrong, yes, but that generation is long dead. I believe that someday, there will be peace, and they will live among us once again," Roz explained.

"I hope to meet a Kiaran one day," she confidently stated.

"Why is that?" he asked, leading them out of the sanctuary. "What would you say to him or her?"

She contemplated the questions, genuinely wondering if she would welcome one, or fear one. "I don't know," she finally answered.

Chapter VI

Sergeant Vilkinsen blew the reveille horn to wake the recruits just as the sun was about to peek over the horizon. "Rise and shine, everybody, it's run time!" He sang as he walked about the camp.

Brisethi and Korteni dreaded run days. They moaned while dressing into their light weather uniform. The other two women in their tent were just as unhappy.

"We haven't run in nearly five days, it was due," snapped Sulica Nin finally.

"You're tellin' me," replied Ibrienne as she patted her belly. She hated running as much as Brisethi and Korteni, but needed it more than the other girls. She struggled to keep as lean as everyone else even though she never ate any more than the other girls. Ibrienne sometimes envied the others' fit bodies, but she tried to not let it show. "Come on, ladies, let's go!" she said brightly.

The recruits formed up in four rows at the edge of camp. "You're not hiding in the back, are you, Sen Asel? You're running up front with me and the other two Corporals!" shouted Vilkinsen.

Brisethi muttered a curse under her breath as she sprinted to the front of the line where Sergeant Vilkinsen, Corporal Vorsen and Corporal Crommick were waiting. *At least,* she thought, *Corporal Trenn had gone with Chief Renast. Two less people to get on my nerves.*

"Yeh, go, Sen Asel! Keep the pace nice and slow," chuckled Ibrienne.

"No, sprint as fast as you can," Sulica shouted. The four women had shared the same tent for nearly a year, but Sulica was the only one hating her life with them. She took every advantage she could to make everyone else as miserable as she. Korteni was far too optimistic to let Sulica bother her. Ibrienne followed Korteni's example, while Brisethi flat out ignored everything the mean-spirited woman spat.

"Whenever you're ready, give the command," Vilkinsen gestured to Sen Asel.

"Oh, right." She was still waking up. Clearing her throat, Brisethi called out, "At a double time, forward, march!"

"Call the cadence," Vilkinsen ordered as they began running at a steady pace.

She had only memorized the one cadence which fortunately required the recruits to call back as often as the cadence caller.

"From the ashes; *he proved them wrong*

As he summoned; *stars from above*
the clouds broke; *igniting the skies*
and the stars crashed; *to Falajen*
Sariadne! *Home of Resaria -*
Sariadne! *Res'Baveth reborn*
Sentiar; *Asellunas*
Creator of; *the Dominion*
With spirits from; *creatures of lore*
We will keep all: *others away*
Sariadne! *Home of Resaria -*
Sariadne! *Res'Baveth reborn*

Sergeant Vilkinsen called the remaining cadences, picking up the pace of the recruits who had gone a bit soft since the night of the attack. He told Brisethi to return to the back of the formation to keep a steady pace for those who struggled to keep pace with the front runners.

The cadence Brisethi had called made her wish they were in their third year of the expedition when they would finally reach the southern volcanoes. It would also be when the acolytes were scheduled to join them and would help the recruits seek their spirits and learn how to summon their mystics.

The run continued on for a couple of miles, from the edge of the forest where the camp was to the beach shore. Their feet pounded the sand in rhythm, voices calling out cadences in unison. The spray from the surf splashed the recruits' faces, giving them renewed energy to push on.

"Come on, Ibrienne, you can do this." Brisethi slowed her pace to match Ibrienne's slowing run. "Stop looking down at the sand, look at the sun rising above the ocean, hiding behind the clouds, it's so beautiful! Now take a deep breath, through your nose. Exhale through your mouth. That's it, you're doing outstanding. If you need to take your boots off, I'll take mine off with you, it'll feel much better running in this sand with bare feet, wouldn't you think?"

Finally, Sergeant Vilkinsen led the recruits back to the camp. The hot sun had made them perspire. They arrived back at camp drenched and exhausted. The rest of the morning was spent washing at the shore and preparing for hunting and gathering.

Brisethi hiked about half a mile away from the camp that afternoon. She notched her arrow as quietly as possible, slowly drawing the string back. Slowing her breath she took aim at a majestic hooved beast. She was the only one in the division that still slept under her issued thin fabric blanket whereas the rest of the division had been taught to make theirs from fur and leather of bears, boar and deer brought down during hunts. One recruit even took down a mountain feline but refused to eat the meat since he hadn't killed it in self-defense, a personal choice but one that some considered wasteful.

Soldiers in the Dominion were trained to hunt only what would be eaten or only kill in self-defense. Brisethi was capable of hunting birds, trapping rabbits, and fishing, but she had yet to kill her first large mammal. For months, she had been saving the down feathers from the amount of chickens she had eaten to make herself a down blanket. Unfortunately, her sack of feathers had been stolen, and she had to start over in saving up feathers.

She stared the buck in his eyes and took another deep breath. Instead of letting the arrow fly, she released the tension of her bow string and placed the arrow back in her quiver. She simply didn't want to kill a beast that wasn't attacking her, especially one that she would have to butcher and skin on her own. She rarely ate deer meat unless it was dried and overly spiced.

"Sethi!" Korteni's voice called out in the distance.

She left the thick brush and ran into a clearing. "Yes?"

"Sethi," Korteni repeated her name, stopping in front of Brisethi, "they're about to kill Etyne," she panted from sprinting around looking for her.

"Who's Etyne?" Brisethi knew the name but couldn't fit the face as she furrowed her brow.

"Your combat-partner, Vorsen!" Korteni shouted out of frustration.

"Oh, no, I need him alive!" She followed after Korteni as her friend began sprinting back the way she had come.

Korteni led Brisethi to a group of six other recruits. They were gathered in a circle, each taking their turn kicking or punching at a man in the middle. As the girls approached, they saw him fall to the ground.

"Hey! What's going on here? Where's Sergeant Vilkinsen?" Brisethi's breathless shouts went unnoticed by the men.

"I couldn't find him, I'll go search again," Korteni said, already running back toward camp.

Brisethi struggled to push through the tight circle surrounding the half-Kiaran, noticing two other men unconscious to either side.

She finally squeezed through and fell upon her beaten partner. The recruits attempted to pry her off of him, kicking and punching at her as well. She shouted from the pain of the hits and warned the recruits to back off. When they didn't, she summoned her power to conjure her scarlet flames in her hands, arcing all around her and Vorsen and scorching the hands of the recruits who didn't back away in time.

Three of them wailed from the burns as Brisethi shouted, "Get back to camp and report to Sergeant Vilkinsen! If you cannot find the Sergeant, you will remain in your tents until I bring him to you, understood?" Her ability to summon such powerful mystics so suddenly and meticulously struck fear into the six men, encouraging them to obey her order.

She diminished the flames as Vorsen coughed blood, forcing her to lean off of him. "Gross, what the fuck, Vorsen? What the fuck happened? You're not going to die, are you?" She examined the cuts on his face as she wiped blood from his cheeks and jaw with her sleeve. "Mother of Spirits, is the rest of you as bad as your face?" She then lifted his shirt to examine his wounds.

"It's partially your fault, Sen Asel," he tried not to show pain when she touched his bruised ribs.

At feeling her own face throb from the few fists she took she raised her voice. "Do *not* put the blame on me for you failing to overcome six stupid recruits-"

"Eight," he nodded to the two he had taken out.

She stared blankly in their direction then continued to prod to ensure he had no broken or fractured ribs, mostly wanting him to give in to the pain. A small pain in her side caused her to examine her own injuries. "Where's Corporal Crommik?" she asked.

"He's with Private Nin on a hunt, somewhere," he told her.

After ensuring both of them were devoid of serious injury, Brisethi glanced sideways at him to continue her interrogation. "Go on then, why did you nearly kill everyone just to get yourself nearly killed?"

He slowly sat upon his knees. "You know how men can be. They didn't approve of your decision of 'permanent partner', wondering what I did to 'deserve' your attention. Then suddenly it became my fault for the Kiarans attacking us nights ago. I guess one of them lost their 'boot beau' that night."

"Their what?" She asked.

"Bootcamp girlfriend, because it's true love when you meet in the expedition."

She tried not to laugh at his blatant sarcasm. "They're going to live, right?" she nodded toward the two unconscious ones.

"Unless you want to end them yourself for what they said about you and the other girls. They lack honor," he replied, rubbing his head.

Any other day, she couldn't care less what people said about her, but today she saw two men knocked unconscious because of what they had said. She narrowed her eyes. "Just what exactly did they say?"

Etyne Vorsen deliberated for a moment on how much to tell her, but his desire to see her reaction won out. "You know how most men brag about who could be the most creative in what they could do to a woman? Those two bragged about what they had already done to you and what they had you do for them," he said, leaving the sordid details out.

Her gray eyes pierced through his and could almost feel her anger scorching. He listened to her breathing intensify. She clenched her teeth then finally relaxed enough to speak. "Why would *you*, 'defend my honor' by beating two men for me? I thought you hated me."

"I don't hate anyone. I dislike you," he smirked, "but I still respect you as a fellow recruit leader, you've earned that much. Besides, as I said before, I was already infuriated at them for blaming me for the Kiaran attack and, of course, what they said about my mother." He stood on one knee, examining his torn uniform. "I just repaired this uniform from the attack the other night," he sighed.

She helped him to stand, also observing the small rips and tears. "I'll make you a new one if you have extra hide big enough to also supply a blanket for me."

He stifled a painful laugh, "That's right, *you're* the one terrible at hunting. We're about to head into the mountains during winter, you know?"

"I'm not *terrible* at hunting; I can shoot birds down just fine! I just refuse to kill such a large beast that I don't particularly want to eat or butcher."

"Corporal Vorsen, are you well?" Ibrienne ran up to him with her medical kit, limping slightly from the strenuous run that morning.

"I just need to wash off; those two need all the healing you can give them," he said, gesturing to the two men who were just beginning to regain consciousness. He thanked her for the salve then walked back to camp with his combat partner.

They slowed their pace when they were in view of Sergeant Vilkinsen screaming at the six men who had beaten Vorsen. Korteni stood behind at parade rest, watching the two approach camp.

"Sen Asel! Vorsen! Get your asses over here!" ordered Sergeant Vilkinsen.

Brisethi quickened her pace but Vorsen remained at his limping slow walk.

"The fuck did I tell you about using mystics near the recruits? Get down on your face with the rest of them!" Vilkinsen shouted to Brisethi.

"Sergeant, with all due respect, she was defending the two of us from the six of them," Vorsen replied.

"You think I don't know that, Corporal? Get your ass to the infirmary tent and then wash that dirt and blood off you. Take Pyraz with you, you're all pissing me off today," he shouted. He glanced back down at his recruits who were strenuously shuffling their feet simultaneously back and forth with their hands on the ground. He then shot a particularly vicious glare at Brisethi as she joined the other six and yelled. "Stop flaunting your fucking mystics, that's not why the spirits embody our vessels!"

"Aye, Sergeant," she voiced. She was genuinely terrified of the Sergeant First Class every time he snapped to reprimand mode. She was already downtrodden from the recent distance he kept from her and now he was furious at her.

"Repeat after me, males: I will not attack other soldiers of the Dominion. Female, repeat after me: I will not use my mystics against soldiers of the Dominion," he watched sweat pour down the seven soldiers' bodies.

"I will not use my mystics," Brisethi started to say, "against soldiers of the Dominion." Her voice was hoarse as she struggled to breathe during her mild panic attack.

"It's in our fucking creed, morons!" Vilkinsen shouted once more.

He waited until his pocket watch read the eighteenth hour to finally halt the intensive training. Brisethi remained collapsed on her face after the males hesitantly stood and walked off. Her body was beyond aching from the activities over the last few days.

Sergeant Vilkinsen knelt down next to Sen Asel who had rolled on her side, trying to breathe. He placed his hand on her collar and ripped her Corporal rank insignia from its post and placed it in his pocket.

She didn't realize she would lose a rank over helping someone. She should have just allowed Vorsen to keep taking the beating until Vilkinsen appeared. But she knew deep down that she'd never allow that to happen.

After removing his hand from his pocket, Sergeant Vilkinsen added her new rank insignia to her collar then patted her on the shoulder. He reached down to help her stand up, but she wanted only to lay for another minute. "Congratulations on your promotion, Sergeant Sen Asel."

She pulled at her collar to awkwardly look at her new rank. "You just reprimanded me for the last hour and now you're promoting me?"

Sergeant Vilkinsen grinned. "You risked breaking the rules just to protect your combat partner," he replied.

"Oh," she exhaled, wiping sweat from her face with her sleeve. "And I would do it again, for any of them." She thought about what Vorsen had told her regarding what those guys said. "Well, almost any," she muttered before placing her head back down in the dirt.

"Also, I can't run the division on my own, I need someone to do all of my paperwork." he said with a laugh.

Chapter VII

Recruit Training Division Forty-One was given one additional day to hunt, trap, harvest and gather before leaving the coast to hike to the mountains. Brisethi had still not gathered enough food to last two days' worth of hiking and wasn't looking forward to eating off rations. She searched desperately for large enough fowl, but only found crows and other small birds about. Giving up on birds, she traced her steps back to camp to grab her fishing pole and scavenge for fish bait.

When she reached the shore, Brisethi turned the rowboat right side up and placed the oars, her pole and her pouch into it. She removed her boots and also placed them in the boat then rolled her pants up and pushed the boat into the sea. Her body still ached from the day before, making her groan as she leaped into the boat and dug the oars into the water. The cloud cover brought with it some choppy waves and mists of salt water flying into her face.

Her arms grew weary when she finally reached water deep enough. Scraps of entrails she had collected from hunters the night before made for sufficient bait as she hooked some sort of rabbit organ to her hook and sinker then tossed it into the sea. The waves calmed enough for her to lean back against her boots and wait for a bite.

Brisethi examined the remaining fish hooks that she made within the first few months of the expedition. She had excelled in the art of fish hooks and sewing needles made of fish bones, allowing her to trade her craft for leather and boar meat. She had even carved small trinkets out of the bigger bones and arrowheads along with tools and daggers. One of the older recruits requested a necklace to send home to his wife. Most of the men enjoyed hunting, and many of the women took one of those men as a lover so they would be taken care of for the rest of the expedition. Some women, such as Korteni and Ibrienne, were better at trapping and gathering. Sulica, meanwhile, was one of the women who got a male recruit to hunt for her. Since Korteni was the only other recruit able to get along with Sulica, she had made decent trades of Brisethi's bone wares for the meat and hides of some of Sulica's lover's hunts. Korteni would then share with Brisethi and Ibrienne her successful trades of the day.

As far as Brisethi knew, no one else enjoyed fishing as much as she did. Her mind traveled back to her childhood, when her father had taken her out on fishing trips. She remembered them with a smile, thankful for the tricks she learned from him on braiding fish hooks and how to test for better fishing spots.

The slightest tug of her fishing pole brought her back to the present as she quickly yanked it up to hook the fish's mouth. Once again she silently bemoaned her fatigue as she fought with what felt like an eternity until she wore it down and started reeling it in. She proudly grinned at a fish the length of her thigh as she quickly ended its life and placed it in her fishnet. She considered its weight and decided she would need only one more to last two days if she were to share with her friends. The decision made, she hooked another piece of bait and threw it over the side of the rowboat once more.

When the division left the shore she would have to fish in the mountain streams and lakes. Those fish didn't grow as big as the ocean ones. She contemplated catching a third fish if the second didn't take too long. When she hooked the second fish, smaller than the first, within a decent time, she decided to try for a third.

Brisethi noticed storm clouds beginning to creep toward her on the horizon. Feeling a little antsy, she rowed a bit closer to the shore. She hoped a third fish would quickly bite so she could have enough time to gut and descale all three fish at the shoreline before taking a quick bath and washing her uniform. Just as she had finished her thought, the line tugged once more, and she quickly pulled up on it again. Her third catch was as big as her first one, ending her day with something to smile about.

She made it back to camp before the rain began falling, even after her bath and uniform cleaning session. Firepits had already been lit, and the smell of roasting boar and deer filled the air.

"Sethi, what did you bring us?" Korteni greeted her companion. "I mean, Sergeant," she corrected herself, jokingly standing at parade rest.

"Gigantic fish!" Brisethi exclaimed. "I hope you have some seasonings for it. Or side dishes."

Ibrienne held up a few small red peppers as well as some green herbs that helped flavor meats. "I also traded some of these for dried deer meat for us," Ibrienne said.

Brisethi's eyes widened, "Lava peppers are my favorite!"

Korteni had been mixing her find of cauliflower and garlic with flour to grind into dough that she would fry up with her portion of fish. "I'll trade you some of my dough for some fish? Make fish cakes out of it!"

"Deal!" Brisethi agreed while Ibrienne bartered with Korteni for some of her mix as well.

Although the Dominion recruits were paid monthly to patrol and train for four years, they were also taught the value of the ancient bartering system. They saved their coin for spending on alcohol, spices, and cheese in villages. Some soldiers would even spend their coin on the pleasures of women of the night at the towns when they couldn't attract or risk the attention of the female soldiers they trained with. Brisethi preferred spending her coin on exotic oils, soaps, books and the occasional new fishing line and reel. She also had an odd collection of compasses with different designs engraved in the back of them ever since her father brought one home for her from the faraway nation of Vipurg.

Trading finished, the girls began cooking over the campfire outside of their tent. Ibrienne watched Korteni as she made the fish cakes. "Where did you learn to cook like that?" she asked.

Korteni smiled fondly as she continued working with the food. "I had to help my mother in the kitchen sometimes. Didn't your mother teach you?"

She shook her head. "No, she wasn't around."

"Korteni," Sulica's voice interrupted their idle chit chat. "I have some extra apples and cinnamon spice. These two apples and two cinnamon sticks are yours for two fish cakes."

Korteni glanced at Brisethi who nodded with a smirk and an arched brow. She then replied, "On one condition: You have to sit and have dinner with us."

Sulica sighed and conceded to Korteni's request, sitting on the far side of her. She only spoke when spoken to but listened intently to each of her tent-mates.

"Is Crommick on watch tonight?" Korteni was curious as to why Sulica wasn't with her male friend.

"Yes, he is," she replied, raking her fingers through her short blond hair.

"That's too bad, I rather enjoy chatting with him. He's always fun to banter with," Brisethi replied. She didn't see Sulica narrow her eyes in her direction. The girls continued talking quietly while they finished their meal.

Sergeant Vilkinsen walked around, snuffing out the fire pits and ordering everyone to their tents for the night. Only the three soldiers on watch would be awake to guard the ten tents.

In the dim light of the lantern, Brisethi stared at the odd bundle of fur on her bedroll, hoping to the spirits it was a cat. As she leaned in closer, she realized it was just a fur blanket. She laughed to herself as she picked it up and looked up at Korteni.

"Oh, that! Etyne stopped by just before you came back from fishing and dropped that off for you. And since I'm so very protective of you I asked him what it was for and he said he owed you," Korteni replied.

"Who the fuck is Etyne?" Brisethi casually asked and inspected the neatly sewed and freshly cleaned blanket in the lantern light.

"*Corporal Vorsen*," Korteni corrected herself with a smile. "I know you're not that stupid to not know his name by now," she teased.

"It's Mira Snow Cat fur, like the one Lenken killed," Brisethi stated dismissively of Korteni's jab.

Korteni nodded. "Vorsen requisitioned it from Master Chief a few weeks ago when no one wanted to eat the cat meat. Since it spoiled, he agreed to use the cat meat for traps or fishing bait. He was going to save the fur for his lover back home, but he said he was done carrying it and taking care of it," she finished with a shrug.

Brisethi ran her hand across the soft fur. "I like cats, especially the Mira Snow Cat. Although, I would never kill one unless it was trying to kill me first, nor would I actually buy its fur." She spread the fur blanket across her bedroll. It was light gray with black ring shapes. "I won't let it have died in vain and treasure this much needed gift," she said, admiring the beautiful fur.

Ibrienne joined them and was completely infatuated with Brisethi's acquisition. "I admit I'm really envious of you right now. You convinced the most charming man in the division to give you his cat blanket that was meant for his girlfriend in Res'Baveth."

Brisethi laughed. "Ew, he's hardly charming. And I didn't *convince* him, we were bartering! I told him I would repair his uniform if he gave me enough hide for both uniform and blanket. We're heading into the mountains for the winter tomorrow and I still only had that stupid issued fabric blanket."

"Maybe you should have hunted down your own beast like the rest of the soldiers did," Sulica interjected.

"Are you really one to talk, Sulica?" Brisethi wasn't in the mood to ignore Sulica's comment, to have her one grateful moment torn down so fast. "Nobody believes you killed a wolf in self-defense, it was Crommick! He only lied for you because he's too nice for his own good! He'll do anything and everything to impress you so he let you keep the wolf fur."

"Oh how righteous of you to keep up with division gossip, *Sergeant*. I'm sure you've heard the one about how you really earned your rank." Sulica sat on her knees and motioned placing an object into her mouth.

"Whoaaaa!" Ibrienne shouted in disbelief.

"Bitch!" Brisethi snapped and pounced upon Sulica, not wanting to leave a mark on her, but still wanting to inflict some sort of pain. The cheers of Ibrienne nearly drowned out the screams of Sulica.

"Assault! Assault!" Sulica shouted until Brisethi covered her mouth and held her down.

"Dammit, Sethi!" Korteni finally managed to get a hold of Brisethi's arms and pried the Sergeant off of the Private First Class.

Sulica wiped her bloody nose. "How can someone as immature as you possibly think you can lead anyone?"

"Stop!" Korteni shouted, placing herself in between the two women. "Go to sleep, all of you. I'm tired. We have a long day of hiking ahead of us in the morning."

Brisethi unbuttoned her top layer of uniform and angrily threw it on top of her pack. She crawled into her bedroll and underneath her new fur blanket. At least she would no longer wake up weary from keeping herself warm with her fire mystic all night.

Chapter VIII

The nearby thunder and lightning woke the division before the light of day. Lanterns were lit as Sergeant Vilkinsen ordered everyone to pack up quicker than usual so as to leave before the rain left them stranded. They broke camp and formed up to begin the hike. They hadn't gone half a mile when the drizzle started.

He had told Sergeant Sen Asel to remain in the front of the formation with him in order to give her, Crommik, and Vorsen training on leadership and Dominion core values. When he had a break from all his chatter he randomly mentioned something odd. "They weren't Kiarans."

"Who weren't?" Brisethi wiped the rain from her face with her wet sleeve.

"The men who attacked us a few weeks ago could not have been of the Pahl'Kiar Empire," Sergeant Vilkinsen continued. "We have set rules of engagement ever since they were first exiled thousands of years ago. No attacking civilians, no attacking training commands. Battles are to be fought by experienced soldiers and sailors only," He explained.

"You didn't get a look at their uniforms?" she asked, repositioning her oversized rucksack on her back. She was starting to regret purchasing two books in addition to her issued language training book weighing her rucksack.

He glared at her. "Well first off, it was dark; secondly, you charred every single one of them before I had a chance to see what they were wearing after the fact." She lowered her eyes from his.

"Something is wrong," he muttered. "How did we lose track of an entire division that's a year ahead of us in training? Where is Chief Renast and his scouts? Who ambushed us and why? Never in the history of the Dominion has a recruit training division been attacked by Kiarans. Either they've thrown out the pact to become more desperate and aggressive, or we're dealing with armored bandits. Possibly, a whole new nation that wants in on our land. The only aggressors recruits usually ever see are pirates during the fourth year."

Brisethi remained quiet as she thought about the War of Eras started over three thousand years ago. Since the men of Sariadne first established civilization, the Kiarans of the South had always disputed with the Resarians of the North.

In the beginning, Kiarans had also been born with the same spirits as the Resarians. Kiarans had used their mystics to engineer majestic architecture and destructive war machines in fear that the

Resarians had power over the ancient, aggressive dragons. When the war broke out, they had used these powerful cannons and ballistic missiles against the Resarians and their dragons, nearly sending them both into extinction. The Kiarans were determined to rid the world of Falajen's aggressive creatures, unbeknownst to where their mystic spirits had even come from.

Less than four hundred Resarians had survived the final attack. One of the survivors was the unbroken Emperor of Res'Baveth, Sentiar Asellunas. He had retaliated with such impeccable might that he had summoned the stars from the sky to crash down upon the armies of the Pahl'Kiar. It was then that he exiled every Kiaran off of Sariadne, never allowed to return. He had deemed the Resarian Empire as the Dominion of Sariadne and named himself the sole emperor of the continent. Since three thousand and forty years ago, no other Resarian had ever been able to conjure the stars to carry out his or her bidding. Even the Dominion emblem was his creation; three stars crashing through the atmosphere in the color of gold against black and red banners and uniforms to remind the rest of the world of his summoned destruction. He would rule and protect Sariadne for five hundred more years until his death from the natural cause of Mystisomnia.

The lightning in the distance stirred Brisethi from her history review. The storms reminded her of her childhood spent along the sandy shore of the North Coast. A child of only four winters stood before the raging sea, its waters dark and foaming. Her father had just made the naval rank of Captain, meaning he would be at sea more than at home. While he was home, he spent most of the time teaching Brisethi to summon her inner spirit.

.Although it was fire that her spirit had manifested, it was lightning Brisethi had become obsessed with. She was drawn to thunderstorms over the sea and particularly any time Mt. Bavala erupted, which was every few years. She would climb the nearest foothill of the Mira'Shan Mountain Range to watch the lightning strike above the eruption. The three times she had witnessed the natural phenomena, she imagined that she was the one summoning both the lava and the lightning.

Sergeant Vilkinsen interrupted her thoughts when he halted the division at a meadow, routinely used for camp, and had the recruits set up. They had marched a quick pace throughout the day, despite the puddles and mud they trudged through, stopping only once for a quick, small meal. The recruits would only stay one night at the designated post then wake up before dawn again to march further north and west.

They had spent their first year out of the Citadel barracks training along the eastern coastline of Sariadne. The soldiers had learned to live near the plains to hunt, and the sea to fish and bathe. They would spend the next year living in forests and mountains to experience all seasons. It was the mountain winter training that broke many Resarians each expedition and encouraged some of them to return home, never completing their Dominion training.

Division Forty-One had a long night's rest to prepare them for the following day of marching through chilled weather. The sun never broke through the clouds during their trek through the cool forest, and, when they came upon their next destination, flurries had started to fall.

It wasn't until their sixth consecutive day of trudging through snow and mud, ascending in elevation, that the division finally approached their base camp. They would remain near the lumber yard, building their own garrison of log barracks then taking them back down when they left. Sergeant Vilkinsen told them it had something to do with building teamwork, survival skills, and field training, but Brisethi often felt it was just another way to tire out their bodies.

It took only one week to complete the garrison of the command quarters, four huts that would serve as barracks for the fifty-two soldiers that were left, a bathing house, and a kitchen area for storing and cooking their food. Winter nearly caught the recruits unaware as the Resarians quickly learned to layer their uniforms with extra leather, fur and wool. Some of them even made cloaks. Many considered making coats a wasted effort that required a skilled needle, not easy to come by with gloved or cold hands.

Snow began falling nearly every day, piling onto the ground, the trees and their huts. The flurries would settle on the branches, weighing them down until they were sure to break. The sky rarely was seen as anything other than shades of gray, bright when the sun should have been out and dark at night. It would have been a winter wonderland for anyone not having to go outside and train all day. Despite the heavy snowfall, Sergeant First Class Vilkinsen still had the recruits marching double-time through ice and snow while carrying their full armor, weapons and shields for the strength and endurance training.

Now that Vorsen and Crommick had also been promoted to Sergeant, Brisethi unintentionally spent the majority of her days with them and Sergeant Vilkinsen, learning how to plan the next week's activities. Some days were dedicated to survival techniques, how to turn the ice into an ally instead of an enemy. Others were devoted to strategy development, how to attack and defend against armies. The recruits continued to pair up every other night for combat fighting. Vorsen tended to ignore Brisethi unless the task at hand required him to speak. He was no more eager to talk than she was after each spar.

Brisethi reluctantly approached Vorsen before their training one evening. He was sitting on a fallen tree, working on his gear. "Hey, Sergeant, you never did bring me extra materials for your new uniform," she said.

He looked up from sharpening his blade. "Ah, I ended up repairing it on my own."

"Well I still felt like I owed you so I made you this," she handed him the wool bundle.

He stood up to take the gift from her hands. "I thought we were already even, you saved me from a brutal beating, and I saved you from cold winter nights. I can't accept this, Sergeant."

"Take it, please. It's the least I could do since you gave me something meant for your loved one back home," she looked down at the bundle, silently cursing to herself. She hadn't meant to bring that up. "Besides, I made one for myself already and my two closest friends. I had a lot of extra wool from all my fishbone trinket and jewelry trading," she smiled, proud of her crafts.

He finally accepted the gift and unraveled it. She had crafted for him a black wool cloak, its hood lined with bear fur. The clasp was made of fish bone and carved into the shape of the Resarian Dominion insignia. He fingered the neatly carven stars surrounded in various shapes of ancient mystic symbols painted gold. He placed it over his makeshift fabric blanket cloak. "I have to admit I needed this. I appreciate it very much, Sen Asel." He shook her hand in thanks.

"Try not to get too much blood on it?" She jested.

Hunting and fishing were considerably more difficult when it constantly snowed. The lakes and rivers froze over, compelling Brisethi to ice fish. She trekked a few yards onto one of the nearby lakes, slowly moving forward until she was sure the ice would hold her. Then she took her gloves off and squatted down. Closing her eyes, she concentrated on the fire within until her hands felt very warm. Her index finger traced a circle in the ice in front of her. Brisethi opened her eyes, seeing the ice begin to melt away, leaving a hole just large enough for her purposes. She grinned smugly, satisfied with her growing ability to control and direct her mystic.

She placed the baited hook into the hole until it reached the water down at the bottom. Her stomach complained loudly from hunger. The dried flatbread she had eaten the night before was just not as substantial as meat. Her hands began to get cold and her toes were getting numb. She was obliged to summon her mystic again in order to warm her skin.

She had been sitting there for quite some time when the sound of crunching snow signaled someone's approach. When the footsteps stopped she finally looked up to greet either Korteni or Sergeant Vilkinsen. To her surprise, it was neither of them.

"Sergeant, you need to kill something with meat on it," Vorsen said and placed his bow and quiver of arrows beside her.

"Well, I'm not just doing this for fun," Brisethi quipped. She winced at the thought of slaughtering a big animal.

"Don't give me that look. You need to eat, you need to move around. Kill us an animal, and I'll do the gross work." He held his hand out to her.

"Why are you helping me?" She cautiously took his hand to stand up.

"Because I don't want a weak combat partner, is that so wrong?"

"Oh, of course." She picked up his bow and arrows then followed him off the ice and into the woods.

"Also, I need a trinket made. I'll pay you for it," he added quickly. "Something simple, like those star boxes you made for a couple others. You paint them, too, right?"

"Painting costs extra. Paints aren't cheap and neither is my time," she gloated, earning an eye roll from Vorsen that went unseen as she picked her way into the forest.

They hiked deeper into the forest using small deer trails. The thick pine branches overhead kept most of the snow off the ground, making it easier to stay quiet so as not to spook any animals. Dozens of other soldiers hiked and hunted in the area surrounding camp, but Vorsen led Brisethi on a different route, taking them climbing up a cliff and crawling through a couple of glacial tunnels. The usual afternoon snowfall arrived, making the air around them almost deafening. He taught her to walk quieter, using the forest bed to cushion the sound of their feet by walking deliberately from heel to toe. She was a bit unnerved that he had taken them so far from the garrison and nearly voiced her concern until he squatted down and motioned for her to do the same.

She slowly crept toward him to see what he was looking at. As quietly as possible, she notched the bow and took aim at the large buck scraping his antlers against the cherry blossom tree trunk, barren in the winter cold. She knew exactly where to aim but still hesitated on releasing the arrow. Even though Vorsen said he would help her take care of the bloody pieces, Brisethi briefly wondered how they would carry such a massive beast back. She took a deep breath and cleared her mind of everything around her. At the end of her exhale, she released the arrow, sending it to the heart of the buck.

"Good shot," Vorsen complimented as they both headed towards their kill.

She retrieved the arrow, cleaning the blood off of it with snow. "How are we going to get this all the way back to the garrison? That was some pretty rough terrain we hiked through."

"I was just going to do the work here so there's less for us to carry," Vorsen removed his cloak and handed it to her. He then removed various knives and bags from his backpack.

"Ah," she remarked. She stood awkwardly, his cloak she had made for him in her arms, not wanting to ask if he needed help. She didn't want to deal with the amount of blood pouring out from the belly that Vorsen had just sliced open. "I would help, but-"

"I understand. But if you're bored, build us a fire before we get frostbite." He busily cut at the animal. Its body was still warm enough to keep him from freezing, but that wouldn't last long.

"You mean before *you* get frostbite," she smirked, casting a small fire through her gloves. It was a wasted effort. Vorsen was preoccupied with the deer. "I wish I'd known you were going to abduct me or I'd have brought my paints and log book so I'd have something to do. I want to paint the forest."

"You should let me see your paintings some time," he casually replied.

"I sell them, too, by the way. In case you were interested," she said, never one to turn down a bartering opportunity.

She gathered twigs and used her mystic to cast fire to melt the snow before her. She placed the sticks into the dry patch and once more allowed her spirit to summon a flame to light the damp wood. She couldn't have used ordinary fire to ignite such useless kindling.

Brisethi watched Vorsen empty the guts and then skin the animal, and quarter up the meat of it. He took a break every so often to wash the blood off his hands with snow and re-warm his hands by the fire. He asked if she wanted any of the bones for her crafts and she nodded, telling him to save her any of the easy to carry bones. As he set them aside, she used the snow to clean them a little more. She would finish the job when they got back to camp.

The awkward silence was destroying her sanity, even when she hummed her favorite songs. She brushed at the snowflakes that fell upon her. "Sergeant Vorsen," she glanced sideways at him, "what's your first name?" she innocently asked.

Without pausing or taking his eyes off of his task he shortly replied, "It's Etyne. You take muster every single morning during formation and read our names more than once a day when filling out paperwork and log entries. Surely, you've memorized most of us by now."

"I knew that. I was just making sure I was pronouncing it correctly," she made a face at him before he could look up at her. "I'm Brisethi-"

"I know your name," he met her eyes.

She held his daunting gaze until it was awkward once more. "Good talk," she finally ceded to silence once more and crouched back in front of her fire to listen to her thoughts. She wasn't quite sure what her friends saw in the man. *You're cold, stand-offish, and barely attractive,* she thought to herself.

The light of day began to dwindle when they finally packed up the goods of their hunt and headed back toward the garrison. The trek back was more treacherous now that they were descending in the dark. They had both already slipped on ice once and didn't want to risk falling off a cliff so she lit a red flame to light their path.

They were near the garrison when they came upon the small cliff they had climbed that afternoon. Vorsen took off his pack and scaled down the cliff the same way they had gone up. He looked up at her still holding a red flame in her hand. "Throw me our packs then I'll help you down."

She did as he told her but she was reluctant to climb over the edge as swiftly as he had. "I don't think I can. I'm just going to find another way down."

"This is the smallest part of the cliff, Sen Asel. You'll be going the opposite direction from the garrison for a while if you do," he assured her. She could almost hear the smirk in his voice.

"I'm going to fall and break my ankle," Brisethi whined. She never realized she had a fear of heights. Maybe it was the ice and snow that terrified her, or the darkness. Or the combination of all of them. She went to her knees to peer over the edge once more.

Although she was only about ten feet high, it felt like twenty feet in the dark.

"I won't let you fall, you won't break anything. You're useless to me if you hurt yourself. Like a horse. I'd have to put you down," he teased.

Too terrified to retort, she slowly got down onto her belly and crawled backwards to dangle a leg over the edge. Her foot found a hold, and she lowered herself onto it. The edge was slippery where she held her body weight up. She began to panic, keeping herself pressed tightly against the cliff's walls.

"Just relax, take deep breaths," Vorsen called to her. "Lower yourself down slowly to the next foothold." He kept his voice calm to ease her fears.

Brisethi grunted as she used the strength of her arms to lower herself down. She found another foothold, but it wasn't level enough to allow her to let go of the ledge. She slightly turned her head down to look at Vorsen. "I can't reach, I don't remember climbing this!"

"You're doing fine, just maneuver a little to the left, there's a small ledge to put your foot on," he realized it had been easier for him because he was slightly taller than her.

As she attempted to shift to the left, she lost her grip from the slippery ledge and felt herself falling back. She imagined falling on her neck to her death as she let out a startled scream. *This is how it ends,* she thought.

Vorsen quickly braced for the impact of catching her as he fell backwards when she landed on him.

"Shit, are you alright?" Brisethi asked. She jumped to her feet and helped Vorsen up before checking herself for injuries. There were none.

"Just the wind knocked out of me. Catching you was like catching a bear falling out of a tree," he joked. He picked up their packs and led the way back to base.

"What is that supposed to mean?" she asked.

He smiled, "You're clumsy and oddly heavy."

"Maybe you're just weak," she replied.

"Well I don't typically lift bears," he teased.

Later that evening, before the division could enjoy meal time, they were formed up with their combat partners for the usual round of spar training. Fighting in heavy, wool and fur armor was extremely difficult for the recruits, but the snow cushioned the falls.

"Mind if I ask you something?" Vorsen faced his combat partner.

"Sure?" Brisethi didn't know what to make of his sudden desire to converse.

"It's about what happened that night of the attack – I don't mean to bring it up, but I've often wondered about your destructive powers. Was it an accident that you were summoning that much devastation all at once? Have you done that before?" He dodged her fist as they practiced the hand-to-hand combat they were training to perfect.

She remained in her attack stance to think before answering. She knew most of the division viewed her as either a monster or a savior since that night, but she wasn't sure what Vorsen thought, nor was she keen to find out. "I have caused Mt. Bavala to erupt. Though that was an accident, because I didn't know I had that power."

"How do you know you caused it to erupt? It happens often enough to be a coincidence." It was his turn to attack. He quickly attempted to pummel her but she was quicker to deflect.

"Because," she said, giving him another couple of swings, "as quickly as I had summoned it, I was able to stop it. And then I did it again a few minutes later to confirm my suspicions. Then I did it to another, smaller mountain for a shorter amount of time. I can do much more than spark a few flames, Vorsen." She didn't mean for her voice to sound as callous as it came out.

"That was the first time you've ever taken someone's life, though, right?" He blocked a kick from her then tripped her.

She leveraged the weight of her legs to hoist herself up from her back to stand up faster, a move incredibly difficult in snow. "You think me some sort of contract killer?"

He laughed and braced for her attack. "Well, you *are* more aggressive than most people I've known in our short life thus far, just like a bear. Sergeant *Bear*sethi Sen Asel," he chuckled.

She was certain it was the first time she heard the man laugh since meeting him at the citadel a year and a half ago. She tried to hide her smile.

Chapter IX

The recruits were ordered to pack their warmest layers and bedrolls the night before. Sergeant First Class Vilkinsen planned to lead the recruits on a two-day hike to the northernmost mountains for the first official day of winter. They would experience the shortest day of the year near the north volcano, Mt. Bavala.

The recruits began the hike before dawn. Light of day had barely brightened the snow clouds when the division reached their first lethal ascension up an icy cliff. It was a wall mixed with jagged rock and ice ascending sixty feet above to the next trail.

"This is the day I fall to my death," Brisethi dramatically declared staring up at the mountain above.

"Nah, there's plenty of snow to cushion your fall," Korteni cheerily replied.

"This snow is packed solid – it never melts," Ibrienne added, trying to force her boot through the hard snow.

Sergeant Vilkinsen demonstrated to the division how to operate their climbing gear. He strapped ropes and clasps to himself along with Sergeant Sen Asel, Sergeant Crommik and Sergeant Vorsen. Hooked together by the ropes, they would be the first four to scale the intimidating rock face.

"Once we reach the top, we'll come back down. Then each of us will guide ten of you at a time," Vilkinsen told the division.

Vilkinsen found his footing first, followed by Crommik. Sen Asel was next to follow their guidance while Vorsen closed in the rear. Although Vilkinsen had climbed this same rock nearly a hundred times, he paced himself to allow the first-time recruits to adapt to pulling up their own weight.

"You're not going to fall on me again are you-"

"Probably!" Brisethi abruptly and nervously shouted, cutting off Vorsen's cynicism.

The thin air of the peaks made it difficult for everyone to breathe. They had to fight through the light-headedness if they were to make it to the top. The weight on their backs from the gear added extra difficulty to their climb. Sergeant Vilkinsen's voice echoed through the air, shouting words of encouragement that they were almost there, while adding insults of how disappointed he was for them taking so long.

Brisethi felt her rope tug after taking too long of a rest in a somewhat comfortable position. She looked up at Crommik who was now halted and signaled up to Vilkinsen. The Sergeant First Class took the opportunity to pound in an anchor lest someone lose their footing. A chunk of ice that Sen Asel grasped at, came loose and fell below.

"Could you, uh, calm the fuck down there, Sen Asel?" Vilkinsen lightheartedly shouted. "Take deep breaths through your nose."

She peered up and couldn't see him on his own ledge. She looked down and instantly regretted it. Panic set in when she realized how far they had already climbed. She took deep breaths through her runny nose as instructed, closing her eyes to erase the image of the tiny dots below her that she knew to be the recruits.

Vorsen patiently kept his eyes on her, praying to the spirits she wouldn't lose her courage and take them down with her. His own heart started to pound, not only from the lack of oxygen, but also from seeing his combat partner above him starting to tremble. He wasn't in the best position to rest easily, mostly holding himself with his fingers and toes. He started to worry that he would be the one to lose his strength and take them all down.

"Sen Asel, please," he whispered, closing his eyes. He wasn't looking forward to doing this again with the rest of the recruits, although he finally realized why they had spent the last two months out here training their upper bodies. It was no easy task to pull their own body weight up, let alone on the icy ledge. He found it silly at first, that they had spent two days a week climbing trees and the same sheer cliff near the garrison he had helped Sen Asel on. He never imagined having to climb anything taller than that twelve foot ledge.

He felt the rope tug and thanked the spirits that Sen Asel had finally moved on. It was now his turn to take a short break where she once rested.

"No way, Vorsen, you don't need a rest, you're my strongest recruit," Vilkinsen shouted down.

"I didn't realize that I've been busting my ass to achieve this magnificent form of mine to not be the strongest recruit!" Crommik corrected him.

"You're my second strongest recruit, Vorsen," he corrected.

Vorsen remained leaning against the cliff and glanced up, seeing only Sen Asel. She was glancing back down at him, holding herself up wearily. He could see the despair on her face as he reluctantly held her back from climbing onto the ledge she nearly dangled from. He finally regained his strength and signaled to her that she could move on.

After what felt like an eternity, the four finally reached the top of the cliff. Brisethi wearily sat on the ground, putting her head on her knees. When she recovered, she joined Crommick and Vorsen at the cliff's edge, bracing for the gusts of cold mountain wind. Above the treeline, they could see plumes of smoke rising from Mt. Bavala and merging into the leaden sky. Although the snow-covered volcano was visible from Res'Baveth, the recruits had never seen the west face. The peak that towered over it yielded the perfect view. Their treacherous hike would eventually take them around to the southern face where even Res'Baveth could be seen.

Sergeant Vilkinsen hammered multiple pulleys and anchors for them to repel down. He put in a couple more for additional safety lining. "Drink water, snack on rations and head back down when you're ready," he ordered.

Brisethi felt safer going down the cliff than climbing up thanks to the support of the pulleys and anchors. Getting ready to repel down was just as terrifying as the smaller cliff had been, but she was reassured by the equipment. After the first jump, she found it to be much easier, even fun.

Brisethi placed her feet in the solid iced-over snow below. The other girls flocked to her side.

"How many times did you slip?" Korteni asked, beginning to help Brisethi out of her harness.

"Is it really that hard to breathe up there?" Ibrienne asked, quickly examining Brisethi for cuts and bruises.

"Is there more mountain climbing after this?" Sulica added.

"It's actually not that bad," Brisethi replied. "But my group's going last in case Ibrienne needs to heal or revive anyone that falls. And you three are in my group." She looked at her list that Vilkinsen had prepared for the sergeants and darted off to find the other six who would be climbing with her.

Since the strange disappearance of Chief Renast and his scouts, Ibrienne Sestas had been promoted to Corporal and given the title of the division's official healer. Ibrienne took her new responsibility very seriously. She felt as though the well-being of the recruits was her burden to bear, much like when the younger kids at the orphanage had been left in her care, though she said this to no one.

The recruits were soon sorted into their assigned groups. Sergeant First Class Vilkinsen had set out enough anchors to allow Sergeant Crommick and Sergeant Vorsen to lead their groups simultaneously. He had directed them to begin scouting ahead once they reached the top and had sufficiently recovered. He gave the Sergeants a smaller area to scout than was standard, not wanting to risk losing any more recruits. His own group, slightly larger than the other three, would scale the wall solo to keep Ibrienne in reserve.

When it came time for her group to finally approach the wall, Brisethi focused on everyone else's safety, which took her mind off of the formidable ascension. In her experience thus far, she had learned that the more confident she appeared, the more willing others were to trust her. Having an extra rope tied to her from the anchor above also helped to boost her confidence.

They were about halfway up the cliff when Brisethi suddenly felt a sharp pull on her harness, causing her to grunt and nearly lose her balance. A few screams shortly followed after.

Someone had lost their footing.

She grabbed the anchor spike tightly, praying to the spirits that the rock, or her hands, wouldn't give way from the added weight. Her feet were planted onto the small ledge as she tried to distribute the additional body weight using the extra line she was attached to.

"Korteni!" she shouted, trying to angle her head to look over her shoulder.

"I got her!" Corporal Jymi Wylis called up. He was next in line after her. Holding onto a wedge of cliff, he used his other hand to grab Korteni's arm and pull her close to him.

Brisethi had to wait for her pounding heart and trembling body to calm before continuing. It was the worst feeling when the image of her parents receiving a folded Dominion flag flashed before her eyes. *"She fell off of a mountain, her head was split open on impact,"* was what she imagined the officer telling her mother.

The rest of the climb was uneventful and passed fairly quickly. When they finally reached the top, they were greeted by the rest of the division at the ledge, helping them get onto the top of the cliff.

"My arms are like noodles," Brisethi whined, dramatically lying on her stomach, face in the snow. "I have a craving for noodles," she whispered to herself.

"Ah, it wasn't that bad," Korteni teased, starting to remove the gear she wore.

"You almost got us all killed!" Sulica shouted, her blond hair frizzing, giving her the appearance of a crazed woman.

Korteni shrank back from Sulica's dark stare and harsh words.

Sergeant First Class Vilkinsen chuckled to himself at the quarrelsome women, unclasping the ropes from Brisethi's limp body.

"Don't mind me, I'm just trying to hurry this along," he told her. He lifted her by her harness to turn her over and unbuckled the belts, letting her fall back to the snowy ground. He would allow her and the other two sergeants a short rest for their added strenuous climb.

"Between you and Sestas, it's a wonder we ever made it to the top at all," Sulica was saying to Korteni.

"I definitely was not the one slowing us down!" shouted Ibrienne.

"Please, Ibrienne, the only thing you never slow down for is mealtime," Sulica retorted, trying to perform damage control on her hair after Crommick had helped her from the harness.

"Shut up, all of you," Vilkinsen finally snapped. His tolerance of their volleyed insults gave way. As far as he was concerned, that was his job. "Form up, dummies!" he ordered everyone else.

Korteni held out her hand to help Brisethi out of the snow. "Sorry I slipped," she said. Her heart was still beating fast from her close call and the exchange with Sulica.

Brisethi simply gave her a quick hug. "I'm just glad we all survived."

The recruits shuffled into two lines, side by side, for the initial path that Vilkinsen would guide them along. Apparently the scouting report had come back clear. He sent Vorsen and Sen Asel to the back of the formation to ensure no one fell out.

Vorsen couldn't help but stifle a laugh at the sight of Sen Asel hastily eating more rations while they marched. "Are you preparing to hibernate?"

"Stop with the bear comments!" she shouted through a mouthful of dried fruit and nuts.

"It's not an insult, bears are kind of intriguing," he lightheartedly teased.

"Will they still be intriguing if they bite your head off?" she growled.

"Wait, are we talking about actual bears or Sergeant Bearsethi Sen Asel?" he countered, holding his hand out for her to give him some of her rations.

She stared at his hand, contemplating on whether she was going to eat the rest or not. "Did Sergeant Crommick put this Bearsethi idea in your head? You don't strike me as witty enough to come up with it on your own." She finally poured some of the mix into his hand.

"Crommick teases because it's the only way he knows how to get a girl. I tease because you haven't been much of a conversation starter," he said with a smirk.

"That's not entirely true," she softly replied, no longer interested in the conversation.

Etyne was slowly starting to realize that Sen Asel wasn't quite the same as the other girls he'd known in the past few years. He was accustomed to chatty girls that never left him alone, always asking him for help lifting or reaching items for them; finding any reason to converse with him. Resarian women were spellbound by the uniqueness of his Kiaran eyes. The night Brisethi had asked their Sergeant First Class to make Etyne her permanent partner, he assumed it was for the same reason most girls wanted to be close to him. *You genuinely wanted to better yourself,* he thought, smiling sideways at her. *By the end of our expedition, I will ensure that you're better than all of us,* he stated in his head with finality.

The rest of the division had fallen silent soon after. Weary from their first cliff climb, many of the recruits simply marched listlessly forward. To take her mind off the familiar soreness settling over her body, Korteni's eyes wandered around, taking in the beautiful snow all around. Icicles hung from tree branches, glistening in the dwindling sunlight. She marched automatically, lost in the serenity of the world around her. So much so, that she nearly ran into Ibrienne in front of her when the columns came to a halt in front of a massive wooden lodge.

Evening came quickly that day, given the time of year and mountainous location. Temperatures dropped just as fast with the light when each group of recruits huddled around dozens of heated lanterns. Everyone wore their fur coats, cloaks and blankets to cover their entire bodies from head to toe in the permanent building that had been built centuries ago.

"Damn, I thought for sure we were going to sleep outside," Brisethi mumbled.

"Are you crazy?" Ibrienne asked, shivering under her blanket. She had been kept busy during the preparation of the evening meal, checking everyone for the blue-gray signs of frostbite and reversing it on those who were affected.

Brisethi shrugged. "Not the first time I've been asked that." She left the group suddenly and walked outside, not forgetting to warm herself with her mystic. Fresh snow crunched beneath her thick boots. She kept her eyes on the orange glow of Mt. Bavala's peak in the distance, almost hypnotized by it.

"Don't forget to look up." Sergeant Vilkinsen's voice startled her.

Brisethi hadn't seen him sitting on a pile of logs outside the lodge's entrance. She followed his instructions and looked up into the sky. Neither of the two moons or neighboring planets were showing in their sky that night as she gazed into the blue and green strands of luminescent anomalies. "The Sea of Renewal," she smiled. "I haven't seen it in years." The two remained silent, taking in the glorious sight.

The recruits left the next morning. Ibrienne stared in awe at the towering clouds rolling over the western mountains. She was fascinated that the pink and orange clouds reflecting the sunrise behind her looked like a giant tidal wave frozen in place. The strands of clouds reaching down to Falajen's earth was thick, heavy snow.

At first the sun had warmed the recruits as they began their march, even melting some of the snow. A few hours later, however, frigid wind froze the water, which made hiking the single file trail more treacherous than it already was. The trail wasn't alongside a mountain like the day before, but rather on the actual peak that connected two mountains. It was a sheer drop off of thousands of feet below on either side of them. Not even those who had been gifted with the sharpest vision could see the base of the mountains due to the clouds below them. When the flurries of snow began, they never touched the recruits once Sergeant Vilkinsen used his mystics to keep the snow from hindering them.

Vorsen and Sen Asel were the last to reach the wider paths of the final peak. The division had arrived at their destination while there was still light.

Snow clouds surrounded the division, setting a gloomy mood on those recruits who thought they had hiked all this way to see something other than snow. Sergeant First Class Vilkinsen smirked and parted his hands towards the west as if he were parting shrubbery. The clouds followed the bidding of his mystic, clearing the majestic view of Mt. Bavala with Res'Baveth just in view behind.

"I need to paint this." Brisethi shuffled through her pack for her log book and fountain pen.

"I hope we're not staying up here, I'm freezing." Sulica gritted her teeth against the cold.

A sudden explosion startled the recruits as Mt. Bavala erupted. They immediately crouched down with their backs to the volcano to embrace the rapidly approaching shockwave. Vilkinsen began casting a mystic of heavy snow to absorb some of the impact. Brisethi had remained standing, rooted to the spot in awe. She couldn't think of anything to cast that could help alleviate the force and, instead, was brought down by Vorsen who summoned his own mystic to shield the entire division from the debris and impact of the explosion. Vilkinsen dove under the mystic shield with no time to spare.

It suddenly felt eerily silent and as though time had stopped when Brisethi looked up at Vorsen. He was crouching over her, holding a single arm up with a crystalline mystic shield absorbing everything that touched it. Somebody else had to be slowing time for him.

"Are you doing this?" she whispered up to him.

Within seconds, everything went calm. Vorsen's shield lowered, and the recruits stood to observe the lava flowing out of Mt. Bavala in a molten stream into the sea. Vorsen wearily stood then helped Brisethi to her feet, apologizing for nearly crushing her.

"Huh," Sergeant Vilkinsen casually said. "That wasn't supposed to happen." He commended Vorsen for his bravery, silently thankful that spirits of support mystics were impulsively learned. He ordered his recruits to double-time down the dangerous hike to outrun the darkened skies from the ash of the volcano. They were fortunate that a subtle high-altitude breeze had kept the fatal clouds behind them.

Ice and narrow paths atop sheer cliffs made for a terrifying escape. Etyne and Brisethi were once again left to the rear to ensure no one was left behind. There wasn't a recruit who hadn't lost their footing but fortunately, no life had been lost to a fall.

"What the fuck was that, Vorsen?" Brisethi asked him when nearing the end of the narrow path.

"What the fuck was what?" he innocently asked. Gusts of chilling wind distorted the soundwaves of their voices.

"You tackled me up there, then summoned that shield faster than the shockwave-that's impossible! Are you a...time-shifter?"

"We both know that time-shifters are a myth-"

Brisethi glanced back to see Etyne miss a step and lose his balance. She quickly turned and fell forward to grab his hand before he could grasp at ice that would surely send him to his death. The grip he had on her forearm was starting to send her into a panic, trying to keep herself from being pulled off the ledge with him.

He didn't mean to keep a death grip on her arm, but he wasn't going to let her go until he could safely pull himself up onto the ledge. He was suddenly thankful that her body structure was dense and heavy from her muscles, able to anchor herself to save his life.

"Shit, you're heavy," she grunted, trying to pull him up enough to allow his leg to reach the edge.

He was finally fully on the ledge, breathing heavily and shaking. Embarrassed at his clumsiness, he couldn't look at Sen Asel. It was a part of Vorsen she had never seen before. The tough, strong and conceited half-Kiaran was frightened, unable to let go of his tight grasp of her hands.

Brisethi remained lying on her stomach just as he was - if only to make him feel less intimidated. She was just as frightened that he would have inadvertently taken her with him if she hadn't found a stable position. But selfishly, she was terrified of almost losing someone that was helping her become a warrior.

"Hey, Vorsen. You alright, man?" Seeing him in such a frightened state had her worried for him. She tried to pry one of her hands from his grasp. Once freed, she laid it on his shoulder. "I got you." She wanted only to calm him.

When his racing heart had finally settled, Etyne summoned the courage to meet her eyes, still holding her gloved hand. "Sen Asel...I'm glad our strength-training sessions haven't been a complete waste - you never would have caught me, otherwise," he smirked.

She pushed at his hands and hastily rose to her feet. "You're a fuck, Vorsen."

He chuckled, albeit nervously if only to hide his genuine sincerity to her.

Chapter X

The division spent more than a week in the highest parts of the mountain pass, honing their survival skills. Combat practice continued, but the sessions were much shorter in the harsh weather. By the time Sergeant Vilkinsen had directed the recruits back down the mountain, many felt as though the chill in their bones would never leave.

Everyone was grateful for the slightly warmer weather upon returning to the garrison. Compared to the peak, it nearly felt like autumn again. Once again, they were within a day's march of Res'Baveth. Fourteen of their number took advantage of the proximity to leave the training and return home, citing the harsh weather, intense training, and the trauma of the one battle they'd been in. They bid their fellow soldiers good fortune and left for home under escort of several seasoned soldiers.

The three Sergeants were instructed to patrol the garrison, helping recruits patch holes in their gear and ensuring the division's log buildings had survived during their absence. Brisethi had just finished helping Ibrienne tend to one Corporal's twisted ankle when she noticed Sergeant First Class Vilkinsen heading towards the gate. He caught her eye and motioned for her to follow.

Vilkinsen approached the guards with Brisethi on his heels. The sergeant on duty nodded to them. His whole body was covered in armor and a coat, and he kept one hand on his sword. He removed his helm to speak with Vilkinsen. "How was it?" he asked.

"No deaths, no frostbite, not even a serious injury this time," Vilkinsen replied.

Brisethi's eyes widened. Despite her father's drunken stories, and even after her own close encounters, she hadn't really considered it a real possibility that harm could come to the recruits in ordinary training conditions.

The other sergeant nodded, smiling slightly at Brisethi's reaction. "That's good," was his only reply.

"Sure helps having a healer around, eh, Roderick? Speaking of," Vilkinsen continued nonchalantly, "any word on what happened to our scouts? Or Division Thirty-Nine?"

Roderick's expression darkened, and he glanced at Brisethi, clearly unsure on whether she should be present for the conversation. He looked back at Vilkinsen for confirmation before giving his report. The base commander had informed all personnel about Vilkinsen's letters detailing the attack and the missing recruits. "There hasn't been any word that's traveled this far about them," Roderick said. "Though I did hear that the next recruit expedition was stalled."

Vilkinsen thanked Roderick for the news and led Brisethi back to their compound. "Sergeant," Brisethi began. "What does it all mean?"

He sighed heavily. "It means something very bad indeed happened."

The descent through the mountains and to the south took the expected three months to complete. Compared to the previous two years, it was considerably less eventful. Division Forty-One arrived on time to begin year three - desert training.

The recruits gladly put their winter clothes into their packs upon leaving the chilly mountains, returning to the summer uniform. They spent a few days in the forest before crossing the river that flowed out of the mountains and separated them from the desert. Row upon row of sand dunes spread across the land as far as the eye could see. Even Brisethi and the other few recruits who thrived on heat dreaded the coming months. When the command came to break camp, it was with great reluctance that the division complied.

The soldiers marched for days, carrying more water than they thought they would ever need. The river they had camped at would be the last abundance of water they'd see for quite some time, and they were soon thankful for Sergeant Vilkinsen's foresight.

Marching through the heat of the desert had Brisethi wishing she was in the cold mountains again. Sweat poured down her face, neck and back as she thirsted for the precious water they carried. As they pushed on, she suddenly realized that the four-year expedition wasn't just physical training, but mental training as well. She had gone two years without the comforts of family, a cozy bed, the touch of another person holding her, hugging her, kissing her. The strict rules of Dominion training were meant to physically and mentally break a Resarian down until even their spirit was broken. The division became the only family needed. They were meant to endure the longest, harshest training in order to be ready to overcome obstacles of the enemy in the future. The recruits had to allow the Dominion to dismantle and rebuild them so that the enemy couldn't.

Still, Brisethi thought, her throat parched, *a little water would be nice.*

The desert of Sariadne was no different from any other desert in the world of Falajen – dry and intensely hot. The recruits had long since exchanged their thick leather uniforms to don their light, airy, woven uniforms which had hoods to protect their skin from burning. Instead of wearing black leather with red trim, used for attracting as much sunlight as possible in colder conditions, they now wore red fabric with black corded trim.

As the sun was setting on their fifth day, the division finally reached the desert garrison, which would be their base of operations for the next several months. Brisethi walked around the barren recruit camp that evening. Only thirty-nine were left. Thirty-seven recruits plus the Captain and Master Chief had been lost to the still unknown enemy. The ten scouts were still missing, and fourteen recruits were sent home in addition to the one who had left the first month.

The division started with sixteen women; now there were only four - herself, Korteni, Ibrienne, and Sulica. She was a bit surprised that Sulica Nin and Ibrienne Sestas had remained through the second year. Sulica had serious issues with authority while Ibrienne physically struggled at times to keep up. But Brisethi learned that no matter your personal struggles, if serving the Dominion was priority in your heart, the challenges were worth the feeling of pride in the end. She knew Korteni had a strong soul, intelligent and willing to help anyone with anything. She admired her friend for always being by her side and sometimes being the one to challenge her to push through mental and physical difficulties of the training. Korteni had even made peace with Sulica again following the incident on the mountain peak.

The garrison of large canvas tents had strategically been set up far enough away from the river on the northern edge of the desert that the recruits would spend all morning running to it before the peak of day. The division whooped with excitement when they laid eyes on the water the first time.

On sight, Korteni recognized it as the same river they had left the bank of a week before.

"That's impossible," Sulica said when Korteni mentioned it. "Do you know how far we've come?"

Korteni considered arguing but decided against it. "It's just not worth it," she muttered to herself, forcing Ibrienne to stifle a giggle.

When the formation reached the river, sheer discipline prevented them from jumping right in. Sergeant Vilkinsen held the formation in place, facing the inviting water. "Some of you may have already realized it," he said, prolonging the torture, "but this is still the Devali River, the very one you enjoyed a short time ago." Korteni couldn't resist smirking at Sulica.

Finally, Sergeant Vilkinsen released them. They spent several hours into the late afternoon washing uniforms, trapping fish, bathing, and replenishing water flasks. From then on, every other day, the division set out in formation to double-time march to the river. Sergeant Vilkinsen allowed the recruits to return to camp in groups of four or more, advising them to be well on the way back by the time the sun began to set.

The division was supposed to receive haircuts every six months or when at a village with a hair specialist. However, complications with the small division had often stood in the way of it, particularly the lack of someone to do the job and make it look halfway decent. Korteni decided to take up cutting the men's hair, while the four women decided, with Sergeant Vilkinsen's permission, to let theirs grow out until it reached their shoulders. Figuring there would be plenty of time for enforcing hair regulations, Sergeant Vilkinsen decided to bend the rules for the remainder of the expedition, or at least until they reached the fleet.

The division was paid a small amount at each Dominion base they visited every four months. They wouldn't receive the remainder of their coin and frakshins until their final return to Res'Baveth. It was impractical to carry so much with them during their expedition. Brisethi spent nearly a third of her last pay at the last village they had stopped in for luxurious soaps, hair oils and the one book she wanted from her favorite author. Most of the recruits who read books had bought educational books on history, politics or war. But she purchased a fictional adventure book about wizards and dragons, which she enjoyed reading on the riverbank when all of her other tasks were taken care of.

Sulica sat on the ground next to Brisethi and began brushing her hair. "How can you read such childish literature?" she criticized.

Brisethi didn't even bother to look up from her page. "When a dragon swoops down and grabs you with its claws, don't forget to thank me when I take it down with my arrow to its most vulnerable spot." Her response earned a giggle from Ibrienne.

Although the dragons of ancient Sariadne had been hunted to extinction eons ago, she wanted to believe they still existed somewhere in the world of Falajen.

On one of their excursions to the river, Antuni Crommik took an interest in learning how to fly fish from Brisethi. Since Etyne Vorsen's only friend was Antuni, he relished the opportunity to learn a useful skill since their own fish traps were empty. Sulica remained close, looking bored, to stay near Antuni while Ibrienne vainly stood by, hoping to get to know Etyne, despite the many times he had shrugged off the advances of any female.

"Ibrienne, he has a lover back home, let him be," Korteni had once told her after Ibrienne's umpteenth complaint of his ignorance.

"As if she's going to still be waiting after four years," she had retorted. She wanted to be remembered by Etyne when he came to that realization.

Brisethi handed out her tiny, crafted fish hooks then taught Etyne and Antuni to make fake flies out of thread and pieces of feathers. At this, even Sulica seemed to lose her haughty air, so Brisethi included her in the lesson. Brisethi had replenished her fishing lines at their last village stop and shared it with the two men as well. Sulica declined, more interested in making the flies than using them.

Brisethi made her way to the shoreline, the men following her. She warned them to keep to the side of her before she cast the line and tiny fly replica into the river then quickly yanked it back out, mimicking the flight of an insect. When she sent it out a fourth time, a decent sized fish grabbed the bait as she set the hook and reeled it in.

Before the sun could set on the western horizon she acquired over a dozen fish while Etyne and Antuni managed half a dozen between them. They were thankful of her patience and time to teach them. The group of six recruits headed back toward camp for the evening, laughing and joking along the way. Even Sulica was tolerable that afternoon, almost friendly.

They were still a good distance from camp when Etyne, with his impeccable vision, spotted something half-hidden in the sand, glistening in the fading light. He broke away from the group to hike toward the edge of the dune to investigate the source of the shiny object. He knelt down and wiped sand away from the object before him. "By Falajen's spirits," he whispered.

"That's our insignia," Brisethi observed, having followed him up the dune. The gold emblem of a Dominion leather uniform glinted.

Etyne swept more of the sand away, uncovering a uniform still worn by a dead soldier. The sand and uniform preserved much of the body, but they couldn't recognize the face. The desert heat and wind had given it an almost mummified look. They searched for the division patch instead. "It's not our scout's, but it is a member of Division Thirty-Nine," he concluded.

He stood up to climb the rest of the dune up to its peak, the rest of the group joining him. His jaw slackened with horror when he discovered the dozens of half-buried Dominion Soldiers in the small valley of the dunes. The others froze at the sight. Etyne shuffled down the sand to investigate the scene, covering his mouth and nose with his hood to alleviate the smell of decay. "I think this is all of them. But if they're in the desert, why are they in their leather uniforms?" he asked no one in particular.

"They weren't supposed to be here, they were supposed to meet with us near the Veretian Shore over a year ago," Brisethi reminded him. "Have they been dead a whole year?"

Ibrienne pulled her growing light brown hair back from her face to observe a few of the bodies. "I'd say they have," she said. "They've been scavenged badly, so it's hard to tell what killed them." She gave one a closer examination. "None of the bones were fractured, though, and the skull is still in place, so I don't think it could have been battle." She waved a hand over the body, closing her eyes in concentration. "It wasn't natural causes or starvation, or heat exhaustion," she continued.

Sulica scoffed and crossed her arms. "How can you tell that at all? They're nearly skeletons." She twisted her mouth in disgust.

"It's what healers do," Ibrienne replied patiently. "Just like Sergeant Sen Asel, I had to learn at a young age to summon my spirit's mystic. I can determine what pains a vessel. After death, our spirits leave the vessel with a sort of… impression of why the spirit left. This one here," she continued and squatted down, "was boiled from inside."

"How? By who? All of them? And why are they down here? Is this the entire division?" The questions poured from Brisethi's mouth before she realized no one else could even begin to solve the mystery.

"Does it look like any of us know any more than you, Sethi?" Antuni replied.

Ibrienne studied another corpse. An image left by the dead female's spirit sent Ibrienne into a fearsome shock. She let out a small shriek and fell backward, covering her eyes. "How can that be? They don't exist anymore," she mumbled.

"What don't exist anymore?" asked Etyne, crouching next to Ibrienne.

Ibrienne sat up then stared blankly ahead before relaying one word, "Dragons."

Brisethi's eyes lit up at hearing that word. "A dragon did this?" She tried not to sound too excited lest she come across as unsympathetic for the loss of an entire Dominion division.

"That's impossible, you're very much mistaken, Ibrienne," Sulica retorted. "We wouldn't embody their mystical spirits if they were still alive today. They died tens of thousands of years ago. They're all dead."

"Except that they're not," replied Brisethi. She impulsively believed what Ibrienne saw. She unhinged her bow from her back piece and removed an arrow from her quiver. "Do you know what this means?" she didn't give them a chance to reply before answering her own question, "we're going to hunt down a dragon!"

"Uh, yeah no, 'Sethi. Last I checked, I'm not fire proof, nor invulnerable to being mauled. And you know what mythical dragons do? Burn and maul shit. You're on your own for that," Antuni remarked, scurrying back up the dune in the direction toward camp with Sulica at his heels. Korteni and Ibrienne quickly followed.

"We're not chasing dragons. We need to get going and report this to Sergeant First Class. If he wants us to hunt down this mystical creature, then we will," ordered Etyne.

Brisethi shared a look with Etyne as they both shivered when the sun dipped below the horizon. The chill of the desert night enhanced by the thought of a predator dragon in their vicinity sent them racing one another up the dunes. The night was clear without moons or neighboring planets. Though the sand was rough to run in, their light and airy uniforms and added adrenaline made sprinting a rush to their senses. They sprinted over dozens of sand dunes, slowing to catch their breath. Both sergeants paused when stars shot across the clear night sky.

"Quick, make a wish!" Brisethi panted.

Any other day, Etyne would never oblige to such a childish request. But the crisp night air sheltering endless desert sand dunes made him in no rush to sleep in his tent. He thought of a wish, then waited for her to stop staring at the sky. He watched her face completely spellbound with the stars above.

"What did you wish?" she finally pulled herself away from staring at the sky.

"If I tell you, it won't come true," he replied, continuing their journey back to camp.

"You don't strike me as someone that believes such nonsense," Brisethi retorted.

"You first," he said to her.

She understood what he was asking of her and smiled. "I wished to become the ruler of the world."

Etyne stifled a laugh. It was horrible of him to doubt her ambitions and instantly felt a pang of regret for portraying it. "I wished that I could live forever, so that I can overthrow you as an even better ruler of the world."

"Ha, good luck!"

-:- -:- -:-

Immediately after hearing the news, Sergeant Vilkinsen assigned Brisethi to write everything down so that he would be able to send the memorandum out the next time a messenger found them, or if they traveled near a village. Resarian military officials and agents would then be sent to remove the bodies for proper investigations and burials.

"We should avenge their deaths, Sergeant!" Brisethi persisted.

"Sen Asel, if that much bigger group of recruits couldn't survive these so called dragons then what makes you think we can?" Vilkinsen asked.

Brisethi knew he was right but pressed on anyway. "They clearly didn't have a powerful enough mystic to overcome them."

"They had Lieutenant Sarion, an air mystic who could create thunderstorms. Your lava from the earth won't do much against a flying beast," Vilkinsen replied once more.

She finally ceded to his logical decision.

"Don't write that we're assuming a dragon did this. Though I don't doubt Ibrienne's mystics, I can't have reports based off of visions. Once the division learns to use their mystics, maybe we'll go after this dragon," Vilkinsen reassured her.

"Promise?" she grinned.

"No," he shortly replied and ordered her to get back to her tent.

"I don't think I'll ever sleep again knowing there's dragons out there waiting to eat us," Korteni whimpered later as she dimmed the lantern light of their tent.

"I'll protect us," Brisethi mumbled, already falling asleep in her bedroll as if it were just another normal day.

-:- -:- -:-

The daily routine consisted of a morning run, strength training, and language or military history lessons, after which the recruits were placed into groups of four to refresh training in group combat. Vorsen and Crommik led their own groups, each person in the team taking turns to take on the other three. Brisethi happily took up the opportunity to team up with Korteni, Ibrienne and Sulica to show them Vilkinsen's new techniques. The teams would remain fighting each other for one month, then go against other teams the following month. First, they would learn each other's strengths and weaknesses, then use those against other groups to work as a team. Vilkinsen informed them that once they learned to use their mystics, the teams would form again and repeat the process, but with focus on mystics.

Vorsen had no trouble motivating the men in his team to attack him - two of them still had bitter feelings about him as the only half-Kiaran. The third recruit in his team was a quiet type, timid, and often had to be prodded to attack anyone.

The men took the opportunity of the heat to remove their shirts. Fortunately for the half-Kiaran, his skin wasn't as susceptible to sun burns as the Resarians' fair skin, nor was Crommick's dark skin which only became darker in the sun. Sweat dripped down their entire bodies from the desert sun as Vorsen sidestepped in the sand, dodging the two men's vicious attacks. He had memorized the specific tactics taught to him by Vilkinsen when each recruit had a chance for one-on-one training for four consecutive days since their sixth month in the Expedition. Vorsen successfully defeated the two attackers by disarming their swords, daggers, then finishing one with a blow to the head, and the other in a headlock. They were in need of a break as Vorsen took his time with the third recruit, Zinny.

"Come on Zinny, imagine I'm a full-blooded Kiaran who just attacked your hometown," Vorsen teased.

"Sergeant…" Zinny's voice cracked. The grip on his sword was turning his knuckles white. As if fighting his drill instructor last year wasn't terrifying enough, he now had to fight the second biggest man in the division, the half-Kiaran with a heart of gold. "I can't attack you, Sergeant…it's, not right."

Vorsen leapt toward him, shoving him rather hard. "I said fucking attack me!"

Zinny raised his sword in an attempt to block, only to drop it in fright. The other two recruits chuckled at the unfortunate man, leaning back in the sand dune and taking in the sun rays.

"Zinny, what is your biggest fear? Pretend I'm that fear and face me, dammit!" Vorsen was losing his patience. He had sparred with the thin man before, back when they first learned basic defensive skills and everyone was lower than corporal. Now that Vorsen was one of three sergeants, he felt it was his duty to ensure any recruit he teamed with would successfully fight against him.

Zinny would never reveal to anyone what he feared. He had already lived it and felt he would never recover from the trauma of his childhood. He had a difficult time trying to imagine that Vorsen could ever relate to anything similar to the man who had assaulted him at the age of twelve.

"Poor little Zinny can't keep his sword up - probably can't keep his pecker up either," laughed the other recruits of his team. For once, Vorsen was encouraging them to keep the insults coming if only to fuel Zinny's inner rage.

The insults kept rolling in, helping Zinny to see his childhood attacker in them. The other two only wanted to see him cry, but Vorsen wanted to see him angry.

"Haha, look at him, he looks like a child about to get raped by the big, scary Kiaran!" shouted the other recruit.

Zinny was triggered. With a battle roar, Zinny charged after Vorsen. But instead of attacking him, he used a move that slid him into Vorsen, landing him to his face as Zinny twisted to the other two. They saw him coming at him and leapt to their feet into a fighting stance. Zinny swung his dull, training sword at them. Had it not been a training sword, the men would have been decapitated. As it was, they would still need treatment from Ibrienne when the session was over.

Wiping the sand from his face and remaining on his knees, Vorsen cheered on Zinny. He had succeeded at getting him to attack and even properly conduct combat moves they were trained to use.

Korteni had no trouble attacking Brisethi. She loved the challenge and enjoyed learning new tactics thrown at her. She knew that her dear friend took advantage of a good spar as well and could take the beating.

Sulica, slightly intimidated by Brisethi's strength, took advantage of the three versus one by standing back to observe each of the other three young women. Ibrienne was a good distraction, allowing Sulica to land in a few hits to Brisethi's flawless face. It took all three of them, but they were finally able to disarm Brisethi nearly an hour after they had each lost their weapons to her first. Ibrienne was the first to tire and sit out as she watched Korteni start to slow, finally joining Ibrienne a half hour later.

Since Sulica was storing her strength and energy while the other two tired Brisethi out, it was her chance to attempt to defeat her.

"Let's dance, Sulica, show me what you got," Brisethi taunted, breathing heavily. The girls were drenched in sweat and had removed their sun-protecting outer layer, wearing only their sleeveless undershirts and airy pants. Sulica charged, but was met with Brisethi's bare foot to her abdomen. "Again!" she shouted to her.

"I hate you so fucking much," Sulica replied with a quick recovery. "Why don't *you* fucking charge at *me* for once, you twat!?"

Without a word, Brisethi burst into motion. She knew that Sulica would imitate Brisethi's last move, anticipating the bare foot she brought up in an attempt to kick her. She grabbed her foot, twisting it, forcing Sulica to twist her leg and her body the way she was taught to prevent injury. She fell to her back and turned her legs, tripping Brisethi. She heard her laugh, actually enjoying falling to her face. Sulica could tell Brisethi was weary and kept her attacks on her.

Every evening of combat training that month ended the same way - Sulica reserving her energy while allowing Korteni and Ibrienne to exert their own against Brisethi. The three could not take her down. Finally, the last day arrived of inner group sparring before the groups would face off against each other. Sulica was determined to defeat Brisethi.

The sun had long set when the two were still fighting. Both women were sore, weary, dehydrated and hungry. Most of the division flocked to the girls to watch such a vicious, blood-drawing spar. Vilkinsen had Ibrienne standing by in the event one of them would seriously hurt the other. Neither Brisethi or Sulica held anything back.

Brisethi felt one of her ribs crack when she foolishly misjudged a quick fist, followed by an even quicker foot to her torso. Half excited that Sulica mastered that move while half in cringing pain, she grinned, trying to deflect her adversary's rage. Both moons, in addition to both the red and the blue planet reflected the sun's light to shine bright in the first hour of night's morning. Every recruit was wide awake atop the dunes watching the two still going at it. Sulica's wrist and ankle were surely dislocated, but she was certain she had fractured Brisethi's ribs and shins. They couldn't tell if they were numb from adrenaline or shock, or if Ibrienne was secretly numbing the pain for them. Blood mixed with sweat covered them from head to toe. Sand stuck to their wet skin. Brisethi could go on no more. She wasn't fueled by rage the way Sulica was. She fell into sand, dampened by blood, when Sulica with all of her rage and adrenaline, landed a final blow to the side of her head.

Sulica fell to her knees. She had finally defeated Brisethi.

Ibrienne rushed to them both, using her mystic to set their bones, repair their fractures, and seal their open wounds as quickly as possible. She had Vilkinsen order them both to stay in their quarters the entire next day to allow Ibrienne's mystics to fully heal both Brisethi's and Sulica's wounds. By the time she had finished with them, even Ibrienne was ordered to remain in quarters to rest.

Etyne and Antuni were allowed to visit the girls in their bedrolls in their ventilated tent the next afternoon.

"Antuni!" Sulica shouted in excitement at seeing her man. He gave her a gentle hug, congratulating her on defeating Brisethi. He held her hand, landing a kiss on the top, but she brought him in for a more passionate kiss despite her busted lip, black eye and darkened cheek.

"Awwwww," Brisethi exaggerated with mock tone. "So where the fuck is my kiss, Vorsen?" she joked. The already hot day suddenly felt hotter to her when she realized what she'd said.

Etyne let out a small chuckle as he sat beside her, unsure of how to actually greet her. He tried not to stare at her black eye, her swollen lip and bruised side of her cheek, appearing to be almost a darker-haired twin to Sulica. He didn't view her defeat as a failure, but as a victory, that she had been able to train her friends the way Vilkinsen trained them. He wanted to let her know that much. "How are you feeling, Sen Asel?" He casually asked with sincere concern, the corner of his mouth curling upwards.

"Ibrienne's healing is impeccable - I'm barely sore," Brisethi revealed, holding her bruised knuckles up to him where one was once fractured.

He took one of her hands into his, gently running his fingers over her knuckles, testing her current pain threshold. "I'm proud of you," he softly said. "Does that hurt?" he asked, pressing ever so gently on the darkest part of her hands.

"Psh, no," she stated with confidence.

He pressed harder and watched her flinch. "Sorry," he smirked, "not really," he added. The moaning of Sulica and Antuni behind him was distracting and awkward. He hoped to the spirits their clothes were still on and didn't want to risk turning and seeing something he couldn't unsee. Instead, he watched Brisethi's eyes glance over to them, also hoping they were ready to stop.

"Do you guys fucking mind?! I'm trying to heal over here!" Brisethi blurted out in hopes Etyne wouldn't leave her so soon.

Antuni chuckled and picked Sulica up to sneak her to a private spot - if there was such a thing.

"I almost got Zinny to defeat me," Etyne continued. "I showed him some new strength training techniques that Antuni and I perform weekly, and hopefully he'll stick to them."

Brisethi's eyes diverted to his shoulders contoured through their thin, red uniforms. "I'd like to learn this technique of yours," she smiled, attempting to sit up. She gasped at the sharp pain in her side.

"Of course, I'll teach you everything I know to strengthen every muscle of yours in that broken body," he teased.

"Thank you, Vorsen. I appreciate all that you've done for me so far, since the night we first fought," she said sincerely, "I've learned so much between Vilkinsen and you and can't wait to become as strong as either of you," she beamed.

"You're already faster than me," he added. "I can't imagine the beast you'd become, nay, the *bear* you'd become, if you were as strong as me, too."

Brisethi chuckled albeit painfully. "You have a strange obsession with bears."

They were awkwardly silent for a moment, unaccustomed to her uncommon small talk, but he wasn't ready to leave her alone for the remainder of the afternoon so soon.

"Oh, I nearly forgot," Brisethi continued and attempted to reach for a small pouch. Etyne grabbed it for her. She pulled out a tiny trinket box carved from bone, with small purple flowers painted on the lid. "As you requested," she grinned and handed it to him.

Etyne had nearly forgotten he requested her skill for the gift meant for Marinelle. He ran his fingertips along the smooth surface and admired the intricate flowers engraved and painted on it. "It's very nice work," he said. "I think my mother would appreciate this more, though. How much do I owe you?"

Brisethi chewed at her lower lip in thought. Charging him frakshins suddenly didn't seem like something two friends would do. She eyed her empty water container. "Uh, since Korteni went out with one of her new friends, I'm kind of in need of a caretaker for the day, as in, I'm incredibly thirsty."

Etyne nodded, took her water container and stood, "I shall return."

She couldn't understand why her heart was racing. *Must be an effect of Ibrienne's lingering mystics,* she assumed, knowing her friend's fondness for Etyne. Her throat was dry and couldn't wait for

Etyne, or anyone, to return with her container full of water. He had been gone longer than she expected, hoping the camp didn't completely run out of water for the evening. She attempted to crawl toward the opening of the tent to see if anyone was on their way to check up on her, bumping into Etyne, causing him to nearly spill what he was carrying. She threw a curse word at him.

"I'm sorry about the wait, I was hungry and had a feeling you would be as well," Etyne said as he placed the bundle of food between her bedroll and him. He unfolded the cloth to reveal fried bread and fresh seasoned chicken his tent-mates had been cooking up when he went to retrieve her container of fresh, cool water.

Brisethi was overjoyed at the sight and aroma of the meal he shared with her, fueling her small talk into ongoing conversations about the odd dreams she'd had while healing and various other experiences relating to her vivid dreams.

"And this dragon - he was an indigo color, so pretty, swooped down and took me in his talons to teach me to fly! But then suddenly I was just standing on top of a snowy mountain and he was gone, I was so angry that my dream switched just as I was enjoying it," Brisethi finished her recollection of one dream.

"That sounds incredibly fun - I think my favorite dream had to have been about a year ago, when we were about to head into the mountains, I dreamt that I was talking to the wolves! They were all my-" Etyne's story was cut off by the sound of recruits shuffling about, shouting, followed by gusts of heavy winds.

They were all shouting, "Sandstorm!"

"Aw, I want to see!" Brisethi whined as Etyne jumped up and hurried out of the tent.

Etyne shielded his face from the rapidly approaching winds carrying a massive cloud of sand. He couldn't see in front of him and barely heard other recruits shouting and heading into nearby tents. The safety of his fellow recruits was his only concern but feared he was only putting himself in bigger danger when he could no longer see his hands before him. He retraced his steps back to Brisethi's tent but was disoriented by gusts of sand blowing in all directions. He lowered himself to his hands and knees as unsecured debris flew all around.

Sergeant First Class Vilkinsen spotted Antuni and Sulica struggling when the first gust of wind had toppled over tents that weren't properly secured. He directed them toward the command tent then searched for anyone else nearby who hadn't sought shelter.

Ibrienne crawled, holding one arm out in hopes of finding somewhere to wait out the storm. Sand violently pounded at her face and whipped the hood off her head. She cried aloud in hopes that someone would shout back and guide her to their tent. Her shouts went unanswered. She crawled a few paces more until she bumped into someone.

Etyne grabbed the arm of the recruit that had bumped into him. He felt another hand grab the side of his arm to the right of him.

Brisethi pulled both Etyne and Ibrienne into the tent, thankful that both of her friends were safe. "It's a good thing Ibrienne made sure to double post our tent!" She exclaimed while tying the flaps of the canvas tent.

Panting, Ibrienne replied, "Sounds like I was the only one who paid attention to his sandstorm lecture!"

A nearby tent flew into theirs, startling them all, but their shelter still held.

"I believe you were," Etyne agreed.

Brisethi crawled back to her bedroll, still wincing from small pains in her body. Ibrienne followed her to relieve some of the pain where her mystics were wearing off.

"Ohhh, thank you Ibrienne," Brisethi moaned in relief. "Hey, Vorsen, you sore anywhere? You should feel this," she took his arm to drag him closer to them both.

"I don't want you using up all your energy-" Etyne was cut off by the euphoric feeling of Ibrienne's mystics relaxing his muscles. "But if you happen to have spare..." his voice trailed off as he laid his head down in between them both. Ibrienne smiled and laid her head down as well, letting her mystics flow to calm them all.

Soon, the sandstorm passed, and the recruits stepped out of the tents to begin recovering the items that hadn't blown clear away from camp.

Chapter XI

Livian flawlessly ended the sweet melody with the draw of her bow across the strings, her fingers finding the correct strings with no sign of the struggle she'd shown initially.

Acolyte Elion Hadsen applauded his student's violin solo at the end of the musical score. "Well done, class. Tomorrow, we will begin a final score for next month's performance. Dismissed!"

The small class of students began to pack away their musical instruments. Livian placed her violin on her chair and hesitantly approached the acolyte composer. She cleared her throat and asked, "Mr. Hadsen, will you help me understand what I'm doing wrong?"

Elion Hadsen greeted Livian with a smile. He kept his long hair, dark as a raven, pulled back from his face and fastened with a pin, but a few strands always managed to escape during his exuberant displays when conducting. He brushed them back with his hand as he answered, "Of course, but I haven't heard anything wrong with your skill."

"That's because you haven't heard me attempt to play 'Descension'," she sighed.

"Dear spirits, Livian, why are you trying to learn such an advanced score?" Hadsen asked as he sorted through various sheets of music to find the piece.

"It's one of my favorite songs and I was hoping - well I was hoping someone more skilled than myself could partner with me, to play the main melody," Livian nervously asked, her eyes cast to the floor. She would have asked one of her fellow classmates, but, even after a year, she still could not seem to connect with them. However, she admired this particular acolyte instructor of the Citadel as a mentor, awed by his natural ability with the violin. Where many of the other instructors constantly demanded nothing short of excellence, Mr. Hadsen coaxed students to learn for themselves in a way that most of the time never even felt like learning. He was a favorite among many.

Hadsen found the score and reviewed it quickly, mentally noting the advanced key changes. He then reached for his violin case and opened it. "My dear Livian, I would love nothing more than to play this duet with you," he sincerely replied, beaming. Livian's heart raced with excitement.

Every evening for the next few weeks, Livian met with Hadsen in the sanctuary, for better acoustics, he had explained. When she needed to end early to carry on with her chores, he would offer to help her with them if they could practice another hour.

It was during one of those later sessions that Prelate Li'li had been searching for Hadsen to address a matter with him and discovered where he had been disappearing to. Prelate Li'li was enchanted with the duo's performance of the dark score. After discussing the matter with Hadsen, an invitation was sent to perform for the emperor.

"What shall we wear, Livian?" Hadsen asked in mock seriousness after reading the invitation.

Livian shrugged wide-eyed. "I own absolutely nothing fit for an audience with Emperor Arquistas!" She flushed, thinking of the extremely modest wardrobe she'd been given upon her arrival to the Citadel.

"And General Satnir and Admiral Onilak," Elion added, amused.

"The triad of the Dominion," Livian whispered ecstatically. To every Resarian who held any regard to the military, General Riez Satnir and Admiral Sarina Onilak were the two most exemplary military leaders of the world. Livian could only ever dream to be half as powerful and graceful as Sarina.

"Tomorrow, we will spend the day downtown in search of the perfect outfits. How does that sound to you?" Elion suggested.

Livian nodded with a grin. Her life couldn't be more perfect.

The thirty minute carriage ride to downtown Res'Baveth was filled with anticipation. Elion and Livian couldn't decide what color or what type of fabric they should wear for their performance before the Dominion Triad. She was sure that she'd had enough frakshins saved up to buy something that could pass as regal.

"Ugh, black and red? Why don't we just wear Dominion dress uniforms if you're trying to match everyone in the council room!" Livian teased.

"Well this violet color you're so keen on isn't exactly my type," Elion retorted. "We will go to every clothing shop downtown until we find what suits us both as a pair, agreed?"

Livian nodded. Elion led them to a coffee and tea shop before starting their mission. He paid for their hot beverages and sat across from Livian on the patio along the canal. Though the sun was bright and shining, the spring breeze was crisp, making Livian grateful for her light jacket. They sat in silence at first, Elion absentmindedly watching the citizens pass by on their various errands. Livian kept sneaking glances at him, and he pretended not to notice.

"Elion," Livian began. "Do you have a best friend?"

He swallowed his sip of tea and sought an answer in the sky. "Most of us acolytes spend a lot of time in solitary contemplation. We're always in meditation to commune with the spirits to strengthen our own. When we're not alone, we're instructing other spirits to summon their mystics." His dark green eyes met her piercing blue ones, and he smiled, "Since you've come along, I hadn't spent this much time with anyone in years. I suppose that would make you my best friend."

Livian's face flushed as she grinned. "I consider you my best friend, too." Mentally, she was kicking herself for sounding so lame.

In the first two shops they entered, they were immediately drawn to black and red silk dresses and suits. They shared an exasperated look with one another the second time. "It's like we can't get away!" Livian said. They finally entered a shop that had just opened up recently. The building had a beautiful ornate archway for the entrance, and the colors of the fabrics in the window were a wide variety of pastels. Livian favored the satin touch as she searched for a style and color she wanted.

After a moment, Elion approached her holding a suit and a dress of the same color and fabric. He held the dress up to her.

Livian's jaw dropped in astonishment at the white satin dress that flowed to the floor. They smiled at one another and tried on his findings.

When she finished putting on the dress, she walked out to seek approval.

"Great divine spirits," Elion whispered. "Do you know what an angel is?"

Livian arched a brow. "I remember learning about other nations that believed in them, yes. Winged spirits or something?"

"Celestial, beautiful, graceful." He took her hand into his. "That is what you look like, Livian, an angel." She glanced in a silver plated mirror nearby and was amazed at the transformation from her normal attire. Her platinum hair was still pinned up but strands had come loose from the effort of donning the dress. Still, she could almost believe his words.

After sharing dinner at a cozy restaurant, where Elion insisted Livian try a spiced drink he claimed originated from a distant land she'd never heard of, the two retrieved their altered garments. They carefully climbed into the carriage to begin their journey back to the Citadel.

"Livian," Elion said suddenly. "What is it you desire most in life?"

Livian thought about the question for a moment. She gazed out the window at the various buildings they passed. "When I was a child, I wanted a home, I wanted parents. When that never happened, I wanted only to join the Dominion military to be a part of that family."

"Is that still your life ambition?" he asked.

She let her eyes set on his again. "As I mentioned a year ago when I first joined your class, I've never been a spiritual person. I've slowly accepted this life, and respect the acolytes and your way of living. Prelate Li'Li has been nothing but kind to me. When I think about a four-year expedition training for the Dominion, I worry that I won't make it." She looked out the window again. "Sometimes, you create the most beautiful scores I have ever heard once we have mastered it. And then it makes me want to join a symphony. You alone have opened my mind up to many aspirations, Elion."

"I'm glad that my music has at least touched one person," he replied. "But whatever decision you make, whether military, spiritual or musician, I will be there to support you."

Livian smiled graciously to him. "Thank you."

The next few days passed in a blur. Before she knew it, the evening to entertain the Dominion Triad had arrived. Elion and Livian stood outside the ornately carved palace doors, giving one another compliments on their elegant dresswear. Elion's dark hair was pulled back behind his ears while Livian's blonde hair fell in curls to the middle of her back.

"Would you mind terribly if I said a prayer?" Elion asked, portraying anxiety before her for the first time since she had known him.

"Of course not, please, ask for their blessing," Livian obliged.

They placed their violin cases on the ground to hold each other's hands. They bowed their heads respectfully.

"Divine spirits of the Sea of Renewal," Elion began. "Two spirits below seek out a simple blessing this night. Your descendants of Sariadne's sovereign dragons ask only for the courage to calm our nerves, and the precision to perform the score created by your own, centuries ago. With sincere gratitude, your humble caretakers."

Upon completion of the prayer, Livian lifted her head to steal a glance at her mentor, her best friend. "Good fortune, Elion."

"Good fortune, Livian."

Prelate Li'Li, followed by the Emperor's trusted political advisor, Milia Kon, led Livian and Elion through the door and down a long hall towards the council room of the triad. The hall was adorned with masterful artwork, even by Citadel standards. Every so often they would pass a door presumably leading to some room or other halls. At the end of the hall was a room with a high vaulted ceiling and a grand mahogany staircase that swept up to the council room.

Livian couldn't calm her pounding heart as they ascended the grand staircase. When she felt Elion take hold of her hand, her nerves suddenly settled. She briefly wondered if his very soul had inhabited her own to fill her with confidence.

Ambassador Milia Kon was the first to enter the chamber of the triad. He swept in ahead of them and bowed gracefully, his thinning brown hair briefly visible to the triad. "Good evening, Emperor Arquistas, General Satnir, and Admiral Onilak. On behalf of Prelate Li'li and the acolytes of the Citadel, I present to you, Acolyte Elion Hadsen and his pupil, Livian Reej."

Livian and Elion were both spellbound by the elegance displayed in the large room that served as an office and a council room of the Dominion leaders. Sconces along the wall burned brightly but the chandelier above gave off the most mystic light that seemed to somehow reflect into the room, and the heat emanating from the torches was light, playful almost.

Emperor Arquistas stood to walk to the front of his desk. Still considered to be in the prime of his life, the weight of keeping Sariadne safe had clearly taken its toll. He leaned against the desk as his two military leaders joined him to quietly talk to one another.

"They're absolutely stunning," Sarina softly spoke to Riez and Arquistas, strands of her strawberry blonde hair falling over her forehead as she leaned in.

"Indeed, they are," Arquistas agreed, his cerulean eyes twinkling as he beheld the pair.

General Riez Satnir gently motioned to their guests. "If there's anything you require of us?"

Livian was spellbound by the mighty leaders. Emperor Arquistas was lightly tanned with dark long hair neatly tied back. General Satnir had the biggest muscles she had ever seen, perfectly toned with his dark brown skin. But Admiral Onilak, in all her beauty, was fair skinned with hair nearly as blonde as Livian's, tucked away into a styled bun.

"Thank you, Sir, but we have everything we need," Elion confidently stated. With their violins at the ready, Elion gestured to Livian and began the dark melody of "Descension".

Within seconds of beginning their score, Elion used his mystics to turn every burning flame from its natural yellow-orange to a deep blue. He then summoned blue sparkles of light to slowly fall around them, even swirled strands of light throughout the chamber. Their dulcet notes fell pleasantly on the ears of their small, yet powerful audience. Livian concentrated on moving her fingers and bow across the strings, feeling more at ease with the performance than she ever had in practice.

They played two more mesmerizing songs until they reached their final score. It was a score that Elion had created specifically for Livian. They began the introduction of the song, then, when reaching the bridge, Livian lay her instrument in her lap and took a deep breath. Her voice came out in a clear, mezzo-soprano tone, quiet at first then building as she regained confidence. "Eternal spirits guide us throughout Falajen. Descending from the Sea of Renewal, we're not worthy of immortality." Although they were very few words, they were drawn out in a most melodic opera. She continued her violin melody to Elion's harmony. After a verse, it was her turn to sing again. "Follow your spirit's path, you cannot guide yourself, although we create our own destinies. Call upon the stars, summon your spirit's strength, design your reality." She held the final note for an extra beat as Elion's faded away.

Emperor Arquistas, General Satnir, Admiral Onilak, Prelate Li'Li and Advisor Milia Kon wildly applauded the duo.

"Very beautiful, Elion and Livian," Emperor Arquistas declared as he approached them. He held his hands out to each of them, displaying his gift of a collectible coin in each one. "I rarely hand these out, please accept these as my gratitude for your time."

The General and the Admiral had also presented the duo with coins of appreciation followed by the highest compliments. Milia Kon invited Elion and Livian on a private tour of the palace, escorting them to various halls, kitchens, libraries and balconies with grand views of all of Res'Baveth.

"Milia," one of the council members approached him. "The emperor requires your assistance."

"Ah, of course he does," Milia sighed. "Do either of you remember the way out?"

Elion nodded. "Just down the stairs and to the left?"

"Yes, please try to take your leave by the twentieth hour so as not to become interrogated by the guards," Milia kindly suggested.

"Will do, thank you, Mr. Kon," Elion replied.

As Milia and the councilmember departed, Livian leaned against the balcony railing. The night air felt cool on her cheek as she looked out to the city lights twinkling below. "Oh spirits, we're so high! At least a hundred feet!"

Elion smiled and stood beside her. "Try three hundred feet."

The night sky was absent of the light of moons and planets. The stars pierced the sky in an attempt to make up for the lack of planetary reflections. The massive city before them glistened its own twinkling lights back as if to reflect the night sky. In the distant east, the sea was in view. "I've never seen Res'Baveth from this angle. Thank you, Elion, for giving me this opportunity," Livian said and wrapped her arms around him.

Elion froze. As much as he wanted to return the embrace, it seemed unwise for someone of his age to hold someone as young as her so closely.

"Are you unable to hold me?" Livian asked when she broke away. Her eyes searched for his for reassurance but didn't find it.

Elion furrowed his brow. "Forgive me, Livian, I cannot."

Livian diverted her gaze. "Is it because I'm so young?"

Elion nodded. "Yes, my dear sweet Livian. Even if I were only nineteen years old, you are still under the age..." He trailed off, letting the implication sink in.

Livian returned her glance back to him. "If I were two years older? In two years, would you...?"

Elion smiled sincerely. "I'm still a hundred years older than you, but if it's what our spirits desire in two years time, I will stay reserved for you."

Livian hugged him once more. He returned the embrace, shortly, but tightly. Though, he was an entire century older than her, their spirits preserved their youthful appearance for centuries. Elion would not begin to age any further until Livian was nearing her seventh century of life on Falajen.

Chapter XII

Violent ocean waves collided against the ancient lava rock of the dormant Mt. Alusan. The water was a deep blue with frothy white crests that could smash an unwitting soul against the rocks with no remorse. The southern shore was the most tropical region of Sariadne. Extravagant resorts and upscale huts lined parts of the coast for vacationing Resarians. In between the small towns lay open fields with rolling hills.

Acolyte Roz meditated upon a grassy knoll beneath flat top trees, away from the busy resort sector. The sound of Division Forty-One approaching reached his ears as his assembly of six disciples and seven horses stood by to welcome the small band of approaching recruits. Acolyte Roz and his counterpart, Acolyte Krain, rotated the responsibility of guiding a division on the mystic training portion of the expedition. The journey south was long and arduous for the acolytes, causing the Dominion to consider shifting the mystics training up by two years when the Divisions would be closest to Res'Baveth. The military's stance on the subject was that they wanted their recruits to 'earn' the privilege of learning to summon their mystics by completing the more physically demanding portions first. Finally, Acolyte Roz made an agreement with General Satnir that, in eight years, the military would move naval training up by six months, and the recruits would spend their final six months in the Citadel again, learning to summon mystics west of the city.

"Sergeant First Class Vilkinsen," Roz softly spoke to the man walking toward him after halting the division. They shook hands in greeting. "Let me first offer my sincerest condolences for the loss of your men and women during the unfortunate attack during your first year.

"As for your soldiers finding the lost division; our medics have recovered each body of Division Thirty-Nine and are still researching the source of the fire that took their lives."

While the two men finished quickly debriefing one another on their accounts, the recruits were partitioned into six groups; one team for each mage disciple. They would remain with their mage for six months to properly learn the skills required for summoning their spirit's mystics.

"Sergeant Sen Asel," Roz called out when he was finished speaking to Vilkenson.

"Yes?" Brisethi turned her head from the group she had been sent to.

"You're with me," he ordered. He began walking away.

"Oh," she replied, hurrying after him and swatting at insects flying around her head.

"Retrieve an overnight bag," he said over his shoulder. "We'll be gone until morning."

She did as she was told then joined him by the tree that was being used as a hitching post. They both mounted horses to start their journey in the direction of the dormant volcano. Neither spoke during the three hour ride toward the top. Brisethi was content with the silence, distracted by the strange lava rock formations and lost in her own thoughts.

"Mt. Alusan hasn't erupted since the two-thousand and fifty-fourth year of Sariadne's people's existence," Roz began when they neared the top. "It was the year of the Kiaran exile; the year that Sentiar Asellunas brought down the stars from the skies; the year the Dominion was born in the ashes of ancient Resari." Roz's voice had a soothing yet ominous pitch to it as he went on. "Your great ancestor had awakened a beast that previously lived only in the under-earth. As the beast settled in to Mt. Alusan to make it his nest, he managed to stop the flow of lava. Dangerous poisons began to fill the air, making it impossible for any Resarian to investigate it." He paused, studying Brisethi's reactions.

Her eyebrows furrowed in confusion. "We're pretty close to the rim of the volcano, why aren't we affected yet?"

Roz signaled for them to stop and dismount. Brisethi looked around when her feet hit the ground, focusing her gaze on the jagged green mountains north of the volcano as they tied their horses to a lone tree. The majestic mountains were steep and ridged, covered by trees and plants, unlike the gray, snow-capped peaks of the north.

"Not to worry, I have cast a shield around us that filters the air to deflect any putrefying gases. It's a rare spell that only blesses a spirit every few millennia." The man was completely calm when speaking to her. He sounded factual, not boasting.

She glared at him momentarily, considering how heavily to stock her faith in the young acolyte before taking a deep breath. "Why are we here, anyway? I'm not a scientist. I know nothing about rocks."

The acolyte smirked knowingly. "In the last two hundred years, Mt. Bavala has erupted more frequently and the lava flow has increased. It will eventually flow to Res'Baveth if a way to relieve the pressure is not found."

Brisethi narrowed her eyes suspiciously. "How exactly is that going to be accomplished?"

"You're going to restore this volcano's natural lava flow," Roz said as though it were the most natural thing in the world.

"Ah, of course. That sounds easy enough, nothing could possibly go wrong." Brisethi sighed, wondering if it really could be as simple as her summoning lava from the crater.

They hiked to the crater's edge, scanning for the least formidable path toward the opening. The crater was smaller than Brisethi imagined; barely a quarter of a mile in circumference. Roz carefully led her to a lower area where they could easily step down and make their way to the center. Plumes of smoke surrounded the area, but Brisethi had the feeling that it wasn't natural. Roz pointed to the ancient crust and ordered Brisethi to summon her mystic.

Brisethi's eyes widened. "If you're asking me to create lava, it's going to kill us both," she said quickly. "This is too small of an area for me to keep it under control-"

"It won't kill you because it's your own mystic adding to it, silly girl. And you're not 'creating' lava, you are pulling the magma from beneath the mountains. I won't die because I am constantly healing even when I'm not hurt. I'm nearly invincible, dear child." He chastised.

Mildly resenting his comment, she decided to stop arguing with the acolyte and quickly summoned a geyser of liquid fire that spewed up directly in front of where they stood, twice their height.

Chills shivered up her spine when an eerie sound echoed from within the crater. It was a sound she had never heard before and could only be certain it was the angry roar of a beast. "I'm no scientist but I'm pretty sure volcanoes don't make that sound when releasing its energy," Brisethi murmured.

"Less talking and more summoning, we need to clear the lava tubes of whatever is in there," Roz stated, sounding mildly irate.

Brisethi did as he bid, trying not to panic when the roar became louder, closer. She called upon her spirit's mystic to push more magma up from beneath the surface. She was sweating from the heat of the liquid fire but when embers fell on her clothes or skin, she felt nothing. She looked back to see if the same was happening to Roz, but he seemed to have had a sort of reflection shield protecting him.

The ground began to shake slightly under her feet. A huge rumble forced Brisethi to turn back to the volcano's opening where she saw a dark, massive form crawling out of a lava tube. Her heart began to pound at the sight, as if it would beat a hole out of her chest to escape, and she involuntarily screamed at the sight of the black winged dragon leaping toward her. She turned to run, but Roz held her in front of him, forcing her to face it.

"What the fuck, Roz, we have to get out of here! We're going to die!" she shrieked as the dragon landed heavily before them, shaking the crater's fragile crust. Brisethi was nothing she imagined herself to be if ever she faced a dragon. Her bravery and confidence diminished at the frightful sight.

Roz remained silent, staring in awe at the majestic creature. Bits of lava fell from the dragon's body like water. On all fours, it was as tall as one of the smaller buildings in Res'Baveth. Its tail flipped back and forth as its head snaked toward them, its blazing eyes seemingly focused on the acolyte and recruit.

A deep, low-pitched voice resonated loudly in Brisethi's head, causing her to fall to her knees and cover her ears as though it might dampen the sound. She had the fleeting amazed thought that the dragon was speaking to her, albeit in a language she had never heard before. His head drew back back, conjuring fire within his throat. As he exhaled the flames, Brisethi summoned her own flames in a force more powerful than the dragon's fiery breath to push his flames away from her. Simultaneously, she rose to her feet and summoned a sphere of red flames, adding the lava from her geyser to it, and then hurled it at the dragon.

Brisethi assumed that the dragon hadn't expected a quick bolt of fire to come back toward him, but he took the hit easily and merely shrugged off the embers from his onyx scales. The voice bellowed in her head once more, but in a slightly more familiar language. His piercing red eyes glared at her until she replied in the small amount of Kiaran words she had learned during her Dominion training.

"*Verikas, mok da ne shan.*" She shouted her surrender and that she meant no harm.

The resonating voice replied but this time in the Resarian language, allowing her to speak in her native tongue.

She dissipated the flames in her hands, momentarily awed of her capability to communicate with the ancient beast. She inhaled deeply then asked in Resarian, "*Bestivak tak nogh ves talivak megh tach?*" She wanted to know if the dragon was responsible for the deaths of her people over a year ago.

"I was avenging the death of my mother," the dragon's voice rumbled in her mind. His claws dug into the lava rock as he 'spoke'.

"That specific group killed your mother?" she asked, still marveling at how it was possible that one dragon was alive, let alone two.

The dragon's horned head gave a short nod. "They should have just left us alone," he growled. "She was ailing, but they hunted her. I chased them down into the desert and burned each one from the insides so that they would die a slow, agonizing death."

Brisethi had no response. If a group of people had killed her mother, she would have obliterated them all, too. Knowing the history of her own people thrived on vengeance, she viewed it as a justified cause.

"Leave me, or I will hunt you down as well," the voice threatened in a growl.

Not wanting to gamble their lives by asking more questions, Brisethi and Roz finally fled the crater, careful not to fall into the newly created lava pools.

"Is this a dream?" Brisethi asked when she finally caught her breath. They arrived at the tree where their horses still stood, restless and struggling to put as much distance between them and the strange noises at the volcano's peak. The last light of day was quickly fading away. "I mean, a nightmare?" Brisethi corrected herself. She attempted to soothe their mounts by offering them each a sugar cube. They slowly quieted under her touch.

"No," Roz said passively, "but he will forever haunt our dreams just as the ancient dragons once haunted the men of past who had seen them." His voice was calm and unconcerned as he spread out his bedroll to sit upon.

"Oh good." She stared blankly then readied her bedroll as well. Laying down, she stared up at the two moons that were growing brighter as the sunlight dissipated. "I thought dragons didn't exist anymore," she said after a few moments.

"Just because no one alive has evidence, that doesn't disregard its existence," he replied. Roz's voice had never changed from his calm state, even in the presence of a dragon. Brisethi couldn't decide on if that was reassuring or annoying.

"What happens now? Do we tell everyone what we just witnessed?" She sat up and unfolded her thin fabric blanket.

"That depends. Do you want to be removed from the Dominion and placed in the asylum for your mental health?" He took out a piece of dried bread from one of the saddle bags he had packed.

Brisethi ignored the question, assuming Roz fully knew her answer. "How will you record the deaths of Division Thirty-Nine if you're not going to mention the dragon?" She sipped at her water container.

"Unless our dragon friend makes himself known to more people - and if people did believe us they would hunt him down, by the way – I will have to make something up. Perhaps they drank contaminated water when rainfall hit Mt. Alusan, seeping its poisonous debris into the river. They were so delusional from this poison, that they forgot to change into their summer uniforms when crossing the desert." Roz finished eating his small amount of bread then laid down in his bedroll, clearly done with conversation.

Unnerved at the acolyte's ease with lying, Brisethi lay back on her bedroll and looked up at the two nearly full moons. The light reflecting from them made most of the stars invisible in the night sky while the two nearby planets had not yet come into view. Her body was exhausted from the day's adventure, but her mind was still wide awake from the rush of the dragon encounter. She contemplated the acolyte's last words. The recruit division ought to be avenged, but she couldn't bring herself to wish the incredible dragon harm, despite the fear he had struck in her. *What if he is the last of his kind? We'd be responsible for the devastation of an entire species.*

Her mind wandered back to her friends. She wished she could confide in her closest companions, Korteni and Ibrienne. Even Antuni Crommick would take interest in the story and then make fun of her for it out of jealousy. She even contemplated telling Etyne Vorsen, just to have something to talk about with him. There was something admirable about her combat partner that she couldn't easily dismiss from her thoughts. Even though she didn't pay much attention to looks, Brisethi couldn't deny that Etyne was probably the most attractive man in the division. She was mostly fond of his consideration toward others even if he had unjustly become an outcast because of his half-Kiaran roots. She breathed deeply then exhaled, hoping it was only her loneliness during the past three years that was driving her to have the most infinitesimal thought of infatuation, though the thought was a welcome distraction from her recent encounter. An infatuation that couldn't be as insignificant if his touch kept sending her heart into flutters. Since her combat partner was not available, the thought to become close with him was out of the question. It only furthered the notion that it would pass if she focused her thoughts on anyone else, or anything else.

"I told you to leave me, why have you returned?" the thunderous voice boomed in her mind once more.

I thought I did leave…How did I end up back here? Her thoughts ran wild in her confused mind. Shimmering scarlet eyes gleamed at her. The dragon's onyx scales reflected the moonlight. He had two black horns just above his small ears that were as thick and as long as her legs. His bared teeth were longer than her hands.

"Get out!" he shouted and then spread his wings wide to summon red flames.

When Brisethi cast her own burst of flames, nothing appeared. She panicked as she suddenly found herself engulfed in the dragon's flames. Realizing she was no longer under the protection of Roz's filter shield, she began coughing violently. Roz was nowhere to be found. When the fit subsided, it dawned on her that the smoke and heat was irritating her lungs, not his fire.

When the dragon noticed that his flames didn't harm her, he opened his jaw wide and lunged forward.

Brisethi woke from the sound of her own voice attempting to scream. She bolted upright, examining herself quickly. As her breathing began to slow, she could see her hands glowing red from the mystics she hadn't been able to summon in her nightmare. When she looked up at the moons, they had barely moved to the west. She hadn't even been asleep for an hour.

Chapter XIII

"I don't understand the constant special treatment she keeps getting," Corporal Sulica Nin griped as she helped prepare the morning meal of strips of boar meat and fried potatoes. She was peeling potatoes with a knife. It slipped and barely missed cutting her finger. She muttered a curse under her breath.

"Are you talking about Brisethi?" Corporal Korteni Pyraz asked. "I wouldn't call 'advanced training' or 'intensive training' as special treatment. She just gets more challenges to test her leadership skills - the same goes with the other two sergeants. If any one of us had stepped up in the beginning, we'd be in their place instead." Korteni was quick to defend her friend.

Sulica wanted to continue her rant but knew that she would get more grief than empathy from Korteni, Ibrienne, Etyne and even her own loved one, Antuni. Sergeant Antuni Crommick had respected Sen Asel since the beginning. He had told Sulica more than once that she could always befriend the group of recruits who were anti-Sen Asel. Sulica often considered abandoning her current acquaintances to make new ones. She probably would have if she thought Antuni would join her.

"Since we're on the subject of Sen Asel," Antuni chimed in, looking at his own friend, "Are you and her more than just combat partners? Just want to, you know, stamp out the rumors if they're only that."

Sergeant Etyne Vorsen stopped chewing his food when he realized the group was staring at him. "I'm sorry, what was the question?"

Corporal Ibrienne Sestas giggled. "You heard him, quit feigning ignorance!" Though she had always been interested in Etyne, she could see him settling with someone more confident and strong like her dear friend, Brisethi. She was silently hoping for them.

He swallowed his food and washed it down with a swig of water before answering. "Sergeant Sen Asel and I can barely tolerate one another as combat partners let alone anything more. I will thank you lot to not fuel those rumors. Also, I still have a girl back in Res'Baveth that I will remain faithful to."

"Marinelle hasn't replied to your letters for nearly a year," Antuni pointed out followed by a chuckle. "And you two are definitely good friends by now, stop pretending you hate her."

"Speaking of mail," Ibrienne nodded toward Sergeant First Class Vilkinsen walking toward the center of camp with dozens of letters in his hands.

Sergeant Vilkinsen began calling out the names of everyone who had letters, flinging each envelope into the air one at a time. Recruits scurried all around looking for their letters. After the local messenger gathered the outgoing mail, he mounted his horse to ride back to the closest town.

When Etyne's name was called out, he waited until everyone else gathered their letters before going to retrieve his. Before he was able to stand, Ibrienne suddenly appeared at his side and, smiling kindly, handed him both of his letters. "Thank you, Sestas," he politely replied.

To his surprise, one of the letters was from Marinelle, his patient lover. The corners of his mouth turned up slightly as he opened the envelope. But when he read her words, he realized she hadn't exactly responded to anything he had asked or written about. The slight semblance of a smile faded. Her rushed letter was mostly filled with complaining about her family putting her to work in their fabric business. The only happy sentence she wrote was about a new friend at the family shop. Etyne's heart had reluctantly skipped a beat and his face flushed when she didn't write "I love you" in the end as she usually did. He convinced himself that Marinelle had probably been rushed now that she was busy working.

The small circle of companions were silent while they read their letters from home. The men struggled to hold back tears when reading their mothers' letters while Korteni let hers flow. Sulica, having received the first letter her father had cared to write, stifled a sob. Antuni heard her and wrapped his arm around her shoulders, not looking away from the paper he held. Something about a mother's tender words and a father's encouraging quote could break even the strongest soldiers.

"Brisethi, welcome back! Here, I grabbed your letter for you," Ibrienne smiled, handing her an envelope.

Brisethi stared blankly, still recovering from her restless night and early morning's ride back to camp. She shook her head to clear her thoughts. "Thank you, Ibrienne," she said and took the letter from her.

"How did your training go? You look miserable," Antuni jested. "Did the acolyte throw you off the mountain?"

"I *feel* miserable, thank you." She ignored Antuni's questions. Instead, she grabbed one of the meats from the pan in the pit and took the only available seat on the bench next to Etyne. Both her mother and father had each written a letter, sent in the same envelope. She took each word to heart. Tears welled in her eyes from her mother's loneliness, but it was her father's sad and kind words of missing his little girl that made the tears run down her face. "A year and a half to go," she muttered, wiping her face with her sleeve.

Ibrienne had received a few letters throughout the expedition, usually from friends she grew up with in the orphanage and sometimes from one of the children she had looked after while working there before enlisting. The envelope she held, however, was stamped with the red marking of the Citadel. Confused, she opened it and began reading.

We regret to inform you...

Her eyes quickly scanned the rest of the letter. "No," she whispered. "It can't..." The note fell to the ground as she buried her face in her hands.

Korteni looked up, shocked to see her normally cheerful companion so distraught. "What's wrong?" she asked, her voice full of concern.

Ibrienne broke out crying and headed off in the direction of the girls' tent.

Amazed, the others stood around, trying to figure out what had happened. Finally, Etyne picked up the dropped letter and read aloud its contents. Wordlessly, the other three girls moved as one to find their friend, leaving the men behind.

"Did you know she was..." Antuni broke off.

"An orphan?" Etyne finished. "No, I don't think she's ever mentioned it."

"Ibrienne," Brisethi called out as they approached the tent. Korteni looked inside, but it was empty. "We need to find her," Brisethi said. "She can't be left alone right now."

Sulica closed her eyes momentarily, trying to reach out with her mystic. "I think I found her," she told the others.

They followed her past the edge of the camp, across the clearing, to just inside the line of trees at the beginning of the marsh. There, they found Ibrienne sitting on a fallen tree, her light brown hair disheveled as though she'd been pulling at it. Cautiously, the three girls approached her, like they would an injured animal. When

Ibrienne didn't bolt, Brisethi and Sulica sat on either side of her while Korteni moved to the back of the log.

Sulica, mimicking Antuni's earlier reaction to her own sadness, put her arm around Ibrienne's shoulders. Brisethi grabbed her hand, and Korteni carefully began working on Ibrienne's hair.

A couple of minutes passed before Ibrienne spoke. Her voice cracked with the words. "They're all gone," she said hoarsely. "The only home, the only family…" she trailed off.

"We are all so sorry," Brisethi told her, knowing the words were pitiful.

Ibrienne suddenly glared at her. "Fire," was all she said. She immediately broke down again and apologized profusely. "I know you had nothing to do with it," she cried. "I just-"

"I know, it's ok," Brisethi said, patting her back. It was a painful reminder of why her own mother resented her fire mystics.

When Ibrienne had calmed down again, Korteni leaned in and hugged them all.

"What was that for?" Ibrienne hiccuped.

"It's awful circumstances, of course, but I'm so glad that we're all together and no one is arguing for once!" Korteni said happily.

All four of the girls laughed a little and headed back to camp. Etyne and Antuni were waiting near their tent.

"We took care of the clean-up," Etyne said when they were within earshot.

Antuni handed a pouch to Ibrienne. "Here, it's not much, but, you know."

She opened it to find an assortment of perfectly ripe berries, a rare treasure. "Thank you," she said, looking around at them all with a smile. "I lost one family, but I feel like I've gained another."

-:- -:- -:-

Learning to summon their Spirit's Mystics was, by far, the easiest six months of their Dominion Training. The recruits weren't yelled at as often by the disciples and even the physical training from Sergeant Vilkinsen became more about teamwork and coordination during their favored sport of *Chel'kan*.

When playing *Chel'kan*, the division was split into two teams - one wearing two red banners at their waist, the other wearing blue. The ball, made of padded leather and sand for added weight, was tossed to members of their own team from one end of the field to the other. Each time the ball was caught, that person was allowed to only take two steps before handing it off or throwing it to their teammate.

The opposing team was encouraged to block or intercept the ball and if the ball was dropped, the opposing team would retrieve the ball in an effort to take it back to their end. The game consisted of continuous sprints as the ball was constantly tossed from player to player. The physical exercise, coordination, and teamwork made it an excellent game for a division to take part in it during their training. It also served to boost morale, particularly during the annual games held in Res'Baveth when the forty permanent divisions and squadrons across all of Sariadne and its fleets competed against one another.

"Don't throw that shit at me!" Brisethi shouted when Antuni tossed the ball at her. She deflected it with her elbow instead of attempting to catch it.

"I bet if the ball was a sack of candies you'd catch it," Antuni teased.

"Nah, Bearsethi would catch it if it were a honeycomb!" Etyne said, laughing at her failure in team sports. Because of her inability to catch, the other team took advantage of the opportunity and scored.

"Over here!" Ibrienne shouted to Etyne, who was also on his team. She caught the ball with ease and quickly threw it surprisingly far down the makeshift field to their teammate, Korteni, who barely managed to catch it while taking a fall. Ibrienne thoroughly enjoyed the sport and was even better than most of the men on both teams.

As Korteni threw the ball, it was intercepted by the opposing team before reaching its intended target, Sulica. She was just as bad as Brisethi at team sports and was grateful that she didn't have to suffer the humiliation of failing to catch the ball.

Both teams sprinted to the other end of the field. When the recruit that Brisethi was supposed to be guarding was about to catch the ball, she screeched at him to distract him and, to her surprise, it worked. It fell just to the right of him, where Brisethi waited to scoop it up. She scanned each of her teammates in their blue bannered belts, but each of them had a red-bannered team member trying to hinder them.

"Sen Asel-Sen Asel! SEN ASEL!" Sergeant Vilkinsen mockingly shouted her name continuously when he sprinted past her with one of the red team members on his heels, trying to encourage her to pass the ball to him. When he was just out of her range, knowing she wouldn't be able to throw the ball that far, he shouted her name again if only to frustrate her.

One of the red team members started to run at her in an attempt to tackle her and strip the ball from her. Panicked, she flung the ball as high and far as she could until Antuni broke through the two-man guard on him and jumped up to catch the ball, pulling it securely down to his chest. He took his two steps and swiftly threw it halfway down the field to Etyne for the score. The two childhood friends had always been attuned to the sport when playing it in the streets with the other kids of lower-income families.

"There she is, our most valued player," Antuni teased Brisethi when she limped up to the group after the game had concluded.

"If it weren't for me giving the other team scores, the game wouldn't be very challenging," she played along with him.

"If you were on the other team we'd all be deaf from your constant screaming at us. You're like one of those harpy bats up in the cliffs, screeching at anyone," Antuni then wailed to imitate her.

-:- -:- -:-

Even though Brisethi Sen Asel had mastered her skill of summoning flames and lava, Roz continually tested her on any other mystics that her spirit might have been hiding from her. He referenced a logbook of every Resarian in the division stating the mystics they were born with. Each Resarian was born with a specific spirit with the potential to summon powerful mystics. It was up to each acolyte to train the soldiers how to summon their mystics if their parents were unable to succeed.

"How did your father teach you to summon fire if he's a water mystic?" Roz interrogated her.

"Uh, he's persistent? Tenacious? Probably paid someone off to teach him?" Brisethi guessed.

"I'm going to guess that he pulled some strings to have an acolyte nearby when your father 'trained you' to summon them. Many high ranking officers like to abuse their powers for their offspring," Roz assumed.

"Are you going to turn him in?" Brisethi voice unintentionally dropped to a threatening manner.

"No, but I will seek out this acolyte and acquire my share of his frakshins," Roz smirked.

"Why do I instantly regenerate, enabling me to summon every spell over and over?" she asked a few days later, searching for an excuse to take a break but also eager for the answer.

"Some spirits are just faster at regenerating than others," Roz nonchalantly replied. "Now do it again."

Roz pulled the five most powerful spirits of the division and taught them a life-saving mystic that was never to be taken lightly. He instructed them to only use it in the most dire of situations. Only those five, including Brisethi, Etyne Vorsen and Ibrienne Sestas, were shown how to perform the ancient mystic that, Roz had warned, very few spirits could survive. The sacrificial, honorable skill was known simply as Soul Reclamation.

During Ibrienne's intensive training, her healing abilities enhanced drastically, to include saving a failing heart or any organ, purifying infections, stopping inner hemorrhaging, and clearing air passages if they weren't breathing. "Hey 'Sethi, if you fall into cardiac arrest during your panic attacks, I can stop it and get it back to normal!" she laughed.

Sulica Nin was extremely disappointed to discover that she had the ability to only enhance the spells of other spirits and hasten regeneration rates of powerful mystics of others, but not to cast anything particular at an enemy. Hers was a support spirit that would only ever be used to partner up in battle with someone who possessed a destructive power. "I would have been better off paying a thousand frakshins to an acolyte to learn of my mystic in two weeks instead of spending four years as a Dominion slave," she complained.

Acolyte Roz remained silent at her frustration. Before his departure, he had been informed of Sulica Nin's disturbing mystic from Prelate Li'lii. It was within the acolyte's sworn duty to never reveal to Sulica the full extent of her unsettling, powerful mystic.

Korteni Pyraz had attuned to the mystic of water summoning. She could create clouds to bring about rainfall, or manipulate the sea around her, calming rough waters or causing them. She was even able to turn the water into ice. "Well, this influences my decision to re-enlist as a sailor, instead of a soldier," she told Brisethi.

"Oh gross, you want to live on a ship?" she asked her friend, already dreading their final year to come out at sea.

Antuni Crommik's spirit was of a rare dark mystic. "It's because I'm black, isn't it?" he asked the acolyte upon the revelation.

"Spirits do not recognize skin color, Antuni," Roz sighed.

Despite his rare dark skin, people like Antuni were the race of Resarian, or whichever nation they were born into. During the ancient eons in the beginning of time, the world of Falajen had been separated by skin color or eye shape. As humans became seafaring, races became nations, settling amongst one another in these continents and adapting to one another's cultures and faiths.

Antuni tested his mystic. He was able to transform himself into a mere shadow, obliterating nearby objects, but at a high cost. His spirit's mystic required a high amount of reserved energy to cast, and he didn't replenish his power within a few days like the average Resarian. It would instead take him weeks. He would benefit the most from Sulica's ability to speed up his regeneration rate.

Etyne Vorsen had also inherited a unique spirit. He had the ability to transform his own human vessel into the spirit that empowered him, much like Antuni's, in order to become invisible to human sight. While in his incorporeal state, he could traverse across great distances in a short amount of time. He'd already known that he could summon protective shields, but he learned that the shields he generated around others distorted the air nearby to make them difficult to detect. "Unless we're infiltrating the adversary's homeland, which we never do, I don't see how my mystic is useful," he sighed to his trainer.

"You have no idea how useful you will be to your comrades," Roz muttered, under his breath.

The remainder of the recruits had similar, though comparatively weaker, mystics of healing, summoning elements, enhancement, or manipulating air to create shock waves of force. Although acolytes were for hire in Res'Baveth to teach any Resarian how to summon their mystics, only the Dominion Military paid them to train their recruits for half of a year so as to maximize the potential for ultimate defense and destruction against their many adversaries.

"Now that we've all been trained in our mystics, did you still want to go hunt your dragon?" Korteni asked. The girls were readying their tent for night routine.

"No," Brisethi quickly replied. "Sergeant Vilkinsen won't allow it," she saved herself the factual explanation. The dragon didn't deserve to die for avenging his mother.

"But you *always* get your way, Sen Asel," chimed in Sulica.

"Not this again," sighed Ibrienne.

Ibrienne, Brisethi thought to herself. They nearly forgot they both had watch that night and raced to don their uniforms and relieve the watch.

"I don't even want to imagine what reprimands we'd be receiving right now if you hadn't remembered," Ibrienne said to Brisethi as they roved the camp.

"I would have taken the blame, not to worry. But, I'm thankful you're on watch with me and not someone who isn't sociable," Brisethi added.

It meant a lot to Ibrienne to know she was appreciated by someone held in high regards to most of the recruits. She smiled and readjusted the rifle on her shoulder. They engaged in various, personal conversations throughout their entire watch. Their trust in one another displayed their loyalty to the point that Brisethi finally revealed to Ibrienne about her peculiar mother.

"I suppose the first time I had ever disappointed her was the day I was born," Brisethi spoke with a sigh.

"I don't believe that!" Ibrienne said incredulously. They took a break and sat on a downed tree trunk on top of a hill overlooking the entire camp lit by only the light of two moons.

Brisethi nodded. "I was supposed to have had a twin brother," she continued. "Two of us were in her womb, but only I took a breath when born."

"Oh," Ibrienne quietly said. "Twins are incredibly rare, considering we're only able to give birth twice."

"The physician said it was because of the amount of smoke she had inhaled just a day before - " Brisethi stammered. "My mother had been abducted by former Dominion sailors-turn-pirates; trusted friends of my father, who wanted frakshins from him. Apparently he owed them from a bet he lost - I'm not sure, he will never tell me the full story. His is a dark past," she paused momentarily. "Mother was already at her eleventh month of pregnancy with my brother and I by the time the Dominion caught their ship. But the pirates decided to set their own ship on fire since they were about to be caught anyway. My father and his acquaintances had saved her just in time. That is why she despises destructive mystics, most especially fire. Hence, the second time I had disappointed her with my 'gift' of fire mystics."

Ibrienne was speechless. She placed her arm around Brisethi's shoulders to draw her in with comfort. "You're the strongest person I know, 'Sethi. Growing up, I always wished I had known my parents. But I couldn't imagine living with guilt for events that were out of my control, that had caused pain to my mother. I'm very sorry for what she went through and the guilt she is unintentionally putting you through."

Brisethi shrugged and smirked. "That's life, Ibrienne. Everyone is struggling in their own mental, silent battles. All we can do is try not to let others be affected by them. It's one of the reasons I want to help the Kiarans - they were stripped of this gift of ours thousands of years ago. I understand why they war with us. It is my intention to gain the trust of both nations and bring them back to end both our losses."

Ibrienne smiled, "That sounds like a lot of work. But you're tenacious, I know you can do it."

"You're too kind, Ibrienne," Brisethi continued. "You grew up without the love and affection of parents, yet here you are, the kindest soul I've ever known. Korteni can only wish to be as kind as you," she teased. She was incredibly fortunate to have made friends with such uniquely gifted spirits.

Chapter XIV

The harbor that the division marched to for the final leg of their training was just outside the ancient city of Kiar, once home to the Kiaran Empire. Although the Kiarans had been exiled from their city over three-thousand years prior, some Resarian archeologists spent their lives taking care of the ruins. Mystics of preservation and repair helped them maintain the ancient ruins. Dominion guards were also rotated out to patrol and protect the city from bandits and pirates.

When the division arrived, they remained on the outskirts of Kiar, grouping up in tens. The recruits were to be escorted by one guard and one archeologist through the ancient city for study and knowledge of their adversary. They were only going to spend one day exploring before marching to the docks in the evening.

Etyne entered the immense city of his ancestors, trying not to show his excitement, lest his loyalties be questioned. He had never met his father, since Kiarans weren't allowed on Sariadne; but Etyne vowed to one day seek him out and tell him of his people's ancient city. Etyne had a trifling feeling of resentment toward his mother for not staying with his father on the continent of Micinity, where the Pahl'Kiar Empire had been rebuilt. But she promised him that one day, she would save enough coin to sneak them both to visit his distant father. He then wondered what his life would have been like living in the Kiaran Empire with Resarian blood, never learning the power of his spirit's mystic. *Would I have served in the Kiaran military, attempting to breach Sariadne's defenses for them?* He shuddered at the thought of living life as the enemy of the Dominion.

Every primordial, colossal building was made from the red stone found in a nearby quarry of the southern mountains. Built over six thousand years ago, the Kiarans, even then, were an advanced race for their time, and it showed through their massive, daunting architecture. Palm trees were placed geometrically along the cobblestone roads. Vines of yellow and red flowers grew along the stone walls of the estates, sanctuaries, council halls, and even their elaborate arena where games of ancient sports including *Chel'kan,*were hosted. That had been during the ages where the Resarians and Kiarans were allies and competed against one another in friendly athletic competitions. The main palace was as tall as the current Resarian palace, but also wider and bulkier. The shimmering rooftops, made of copper and scarlet gemstones, shone in the morning sunlight, well preserved by the archaeologists.

The recruits walked through the streets, admiring the architecture and beauty of Kiar. Archeologists were only too happy to narrate their walk, explaining how the Kiarans had supplied the Resarians with much of their current engineering and laid the foundation for further studies.

Brisethi noticed Etyne had stayed at the rear of the group and hung back to speak to him. "Does it sadden you at all, Etyne?" Brisethi asked, then suddenly realized she had never called him by his first name before.

He shrugged. "I'm grateful that the Resarians have kept the city looking the same as it did before the Kiarans were exiled. But yes, I am saddened that the Kiarans are too violent to ever return."

Brisethi crossed her arms across her ribs and stated confidently, "When I become leader of the world, I'll let them come back. They'll be heavily policed at first, but, once they prove to be peaceful, I'll eventually withdraw my military from there and let them live their lives peacefully again."

"*Leader of the world?* You are barely co-leading a dilapidated division and you're already shooting for world domination?" he teased.

"Hey, I can dream. Dream for the world or not at all, I say," she smiled.

He considered the thought of Sergeant Sen Asel ever advancing higher than an army captain in the Dominion. *Any more power than that and no one would take someone as eccentric as you seriously*, he thought.

In the ancient palace, Brisethi had become entranced by one of the extravagant art pieces. It was an oil painting dating back four thousand years depicting what appeared to be Mt. Alusan erupting. In the distance, dragons circled the peak in the ash and embers of its aftermath.

Sulica and Ibrienne walked up beside her to see what she was fixated on. "Ugh, you and your dragons," Sulica scoffed and hurried away with a flip of her hair.

"Do you think other dragons still exist?" Ibrienne asked, an air of wonder in her voice.

"Yes," Brisethi replied. She quickly amended her statement. "I mean, there's no way we could have found and killed every single one of them. Maybe they migrated to the other continents, or just an island we haven't yet discovered."

"I suppose it could be possible that the dragon who killed that division had flown from a distant island," Ibrienne said, remaining optimistic.

Korteni and one of the recruits she recently befriended, Jymi, joined the girls at the painting.

"Dragons," Corporal Jymi Wylis enthusiastically blurted out. He was just as fascinated by the piece as Brisethi and started a conversation about the illusions he would have of them every time he ate a particular type of mushroom.

Brisethi smiled at his story, but she was unable to tear her eyes from the picture. The more she studied it, the more she felt that one of the flying forms seemed disturbingly familiar.

The daylight hours passed by all too quickly exploring the city. Soon it was time for the division to ready their gear, don their sailor uniforms, and march down to the harbor.

The port of Kiar had once been very large and prosperous, the southern center of trade. After the Kiarans were banished, the port became a small naval base for the Dominion. Only three wooden docks remained, stretching from the sandy shores out into the crystal water where the dwindling sunlight played upon the small waves. Moored at the farthest dock was a large, majestic galleon. Three masts reached high into the air, their black and red sails furled tightly. The ship itself was deep red in color, as though made of mahogany. *DSV Reliant* was stenciled in gold letters on the side.

The recruits formed up on the pier where they were greeted rather brusquely by Naval Commander Maerc Nessel and Master Chief Mattias Braul.

The sun had long since set behind the mountain when the Master Chief finally ended his lecture about Dominion Navy in the most dramatic tone Brisethi had ever heard from a person. "Lack of attention to detail will get someone killed in the fleet. The moment I catch any of you not doing your job, I will have you removed from the Dominion. Your last three years will have meant nothing. Is that understood?"

"Yes, Master Chief!" the division shouted in unison.

Master Chief gave the order for dismissal, and Division Forty-One boarded the *DSV Reliant* the way they had just been taught-saluting the Dominion flag, and requesting permission from the watch officer to board. Brisethi Sen Asel was pulled aside by Sergeant First Class Vilkinsen as soon as she boarded. "She's all yours," he told

Master Chief Braul as she was shoved next to Vorsen, Crommick and a third unrecognizable Sergeant.

"Are you serious, Vilkinsen? You promoted *her*? Vorsen and Crommick could have taken care of the division just fine without her." The familiar voice of Chief Baljien Renast echoed on the deck.

"Renast! Where the fuck have you been?" Vilkinsen called, patting his fellow senior enlisted commander on the shoulder when he was within reach.

"Clearing the way for your pathetic group to catch up to us," he sneered.

"Considering you had our horses for the past two years, I'd hope you did something productive." Vilkinsen's tone quickly darkened. "You cleared nothing for us – we were ambushed the night you left."

Renast lowered his voice, low enough that Brisethi and the others had to strain to hear him. "I heard about that, man, you lost nearly half the division in the attack? Then the crazy mouthy bitch executed the enemy squadron without even questioning them, right? So you promoted her? Are you out of your fucking mind, Vilkinsen?"

"Hey, fuck *you,* man," Vilkinsen retorted, making no effort to keep his own voice down. "You left us for three years on some 'scouting' tangent of yours, failing to find the lost division which *my* people found. It was *my* recruits who defended themselves against an experienced, large group of the adversary. It was me alone who trained them to become the warriors they are today and will be for the rest of their lives." He glared at the Chief. "So fuck you. We thought you were killed in action but it appears you were just absent without leave, you fucking coward."

Renast flushed at the harsh words. "You could have sent for a replacement, you know."

Vilkinsen scoffed, "Didn't really need three more commanders for half a division. I knew my recruits were competent enough to help lead." Vilkinsen didn't add that he'd instructed close to forty expeditions already and hardly needed the help of fellow commanders.

Commander Nessel finally interrupted and took control of the two division commanders, escorting them to his cabin for debriefing. Master Chief Braul was left with the four highest ranking recruits left to him by Vilkinsen and Renast. They were no longer Sergeants of the Dominion Army, but Petty Officer Second Classes for the Dominion Navy.

Master Chief Braul was already familiar with Petty Officer Kanilas Trenn since Chief Renast had shown up a couple of days prior with his group of ten recruits, implying they had scouted ahead for two days, not two and a half years. He stood in front of Petty Officer Crommick to inspect his uniform, then looked over at Vorsen and Sen Asel, who was adjusting her neckerchief. "You three have half an hour to cut your hair back into regulation standards and make sure everyone else does the same."

"Aye, Master Chief," they replied in unison.

"Dismissed," Master Chief responded.

Chapter XV

Sleeping in the small rack of the ship felt like a cloud compared to the thin bedrolls the division had been using on the ground the past three years. The ship's berthing at least had thin mattresses, with each rack stacked three high against the wall, or bulkhead. The small amount of room in the compartment seemed that much smaller after the open wilderness. The smooth, rocking movement of the ship listing upon the waves brought sleep to even the most anxious of recruits. Unfortunately, the amount of sleep they were allowed was much less than they were used to.

It was still dark when the crew mustered at the fifth hour, standing in formation to await the officer of the deck. The division inspected each other in their new sailor uniforms to ensure no one would receive unwanted reprimands. Their uniforms were still black and trimmed in crimson but their gold insignia was now on their sleeve, opposite the arm of their ranks. The cloth was made of the same light and airy fabric as their desert garb, but more fitted with intricate designs at the inseams and on the red neckerchiefs. Men wore snug garrison caps while women wore bandanas over their head to keep their hair from falling into their face while mooring lines, handling sails or dropping anchor.

"I feel like a pirate," Brisethi jested under her breath, causing Korteni to giggle just as Master Chief Braul and Commander Nessel approached the front of the formation.

"Attention on deck!" Shouted the sailor who was first to see the ship's captain.

"What's the joke? Do share, Petty Officer Pyraz," the Master Chief said, coming to stand in front of her, his arms crossed.

Brisethi answered instead. "No joke, Master Chief. I muttered something comical, not thinking anyone would actually hear me."

"What was muttered?" His eyes narrowed further with each word as every other recruit tensed up. They were quickly learning that their new leader didn't have the same sense of humor as Sergeant Vilkinsen.

"I…I only remarked that I felt like a pirate, Master Chief" she stammered. Immediately, she felt that she should have lied, but she was never good at lying to people.

"*Centuries* of Dominion Navy tradition are instilled into these uniforms!" Master Chief Braul began. A lantern's glow revealed a single vein in his forehead growing larger and his face turning red. "I will not allow my petty officers to mock navy customs onboard my ship!" He grabbed Brisethi by her neckerchief and forced her to walk forward to the railing. "Do you want to be treated like a pirate, Sen Asel?" he hissed.

"No, Master Chief!" Her voice cracked. She kept her hands on her neckerchief to keep from strangling which only allowed him to use his other hand to pick her up and easily dangle her over the edge above the restless sea. She was terrified of drowning and gripped the master chief's arms to alleviate the pain and pressure around her throat.

He brought her toward him briefly, "Go be a pirate elsewhere, shipmate!" Pushing her back away from him, he released his grasp on her. His laugh was as loud as her scream.

She hit the saltwater hard and unevenly, unable to take a breath long enough before hitting the surface and sinking. Panic started to set in as she struggled against the waves. Just before she lost hope, her hands found the surface once more, fighting to stay afloat. The sky had finally turned a lighter shade of blue to welcome the morning sun as she stared up at the ship's sails. She splashed around and attempted to swim back to her temporary home.

"Petty Officer Trenn, retrieve your shipmate before she drowns," Master Chief ordered off-handedly.

"Aye, Master Chief," he replied and dived flawlessly into the ocean after his shipmate.

Small waves kept splashing Brisethi's face, making it difficult for her to breathe properly. Her limbs grew tired with each movement. She saw the recruit petty officer dive in and made every effort to swim toward him.

"*You* are the dumbest of all the bitches, you know that?" Trenn yelled over the sound of the water, over the sound of their fellow recruits stating the Dominion Creed. He yanked on her uniform to drag her across the waves toward the ship.

She ignored him and allowed herself to float on her back while he swam them toward the rope ladder that was being rolled down for them. He let go of her to pull himself onto the ladder with ease and left her to take care of herself. The added weight of her soaking uniform and the force of the waves pulling her against the side of the ship made it difficult for her to hold onto the ladder, let alone pull her body up high enough for her feet to catch the bottom of it.

The order for the sails to be let down had been given as soon as the two recruits reached the ship. The sails caught wind immediately and the ship's sudden acceleration caused the wet rope to slip from one of Brisethi's hands. She held on using the remaining hand with all her might, too frightened and exhausted to even scream for help.

Ibrienne and Korteni stood at the railing, trying to untangle the top of the ladder to lower it further. Korteni attempted to climb over the railing and onto the ladder. She realized she wouldn't have the strength to pull her up. The best she was able to do was use her mystics to part the ocean waves away from her. "Vorsen!" Korteni yelled, beckoning to him. "She can't reach the rest of the ladder, come help her!"

Etyne rushed over from where he was helping set the sails. Glancing over the side, he quickly hauled himself over and descended the ladder until he was close enough to grab Brisethi's hand. He shouted at her to let go of the ladder so he could pull her up. When their eyes met, he could see the fear reflected in her gaze but only gripped her hand harder. He imagined that she must have seen the same fear in his own eyes the day he nearly fell off the side of a mountain. "Come on, Sen Asel, it's just like climbing the icy cliffs! All that extra water weight is equivalent to all that gear we carried on our backs!" She finally did his bidding and managed to get her foot on the lowest step once he pulled her up towards him. Slowly, they made their way up the ladder. Etyne glanced down occasionally to make sure Brisethi was still moving.

Ibrienne and Korteni were standing by to help Brisethi haul herself over the railing where she remained seated on the deck, coughing up water. Korteni used her mystic to pull the water from Brisethi's lungs. Ibrienne tended to her as well and helped her below decks, but Etyne stormed past toward Trenn.

"You piece of shit!" Etyne shouted as his fist flew to Trenn's face. "Why didn't you help her onto the ladder?"

Trenn touched his face briefly then tried to throw a punch in return but was easily deflected by Etyne. "It isn't my problem that silly whore can't pull herself up. She shouldn't have gotten herself thrown overboard in the first place!"

Etyne made as if to hit him again. Instead, he shoved Trenn and walked away, his fists clenched. *They really missed out on the combat training,* he thought dully when he realized how easy it was to hit the other recruit.

In the female berthing, Brisethi was still slightly trembling, her body cold and worn out as she removed her wet uniform to change into a second set.

Sulica walked into their compartment. She said with a laugh, "He flung you off of the ship like a rag doll. Funniest thing I've ever seen!"

"I'll throw you off if you don't stop laughing," Brisethi snapped.

Sulica remembered their previous engagement and didn't doubt her threat for a second. She crossed her arms and leaned against the doorway. "Master Chief wants to see you on the bridge. He's probably going to send you to captain's mast," she smirked.

"I couldn't care less if I'm demoted during expedition training." Brisethi rolled her eyes then laced up her wet boots and walked out. She wished she could stop shivering. If she had better control of her fire mystics, she would be able to instantly dry her clothes. It was a skill she planned on mastering soon enough, especially if being flung overboard was to become a common occurrence. She knocked on the door of the Commander's cabin.

Brisethi had expected Master Chief and the Commander to take turns yelling at her, but, because it wasn't an open mast where all the recruits could watch, the two men were suspiciously calm.

"I know who your father is, Sen Asel," Master Chief was saying in a very different tone than the last she'd heard. "I wouldn't have thrown you off the ship without his permission. I understand you have taken after your father's sense of humor, but when you're in formation, I expect you to remain professional. I won't give you special treatment just because your father is an admiral. In fact, I may even go harder on you because he told me I should." Master Chief glanced at Commander Nessel who nodded in agreement.

"I accept the challenge," she said, not even realizing the words had escaped her. She didn't know why she was smirking or why she had blurted out such a horrible response. Silently, she cursed her father for his countless sea stories of courage and insubordination.

Master Chief Braul slowly brought his palm up to his forehead, clearly exasperated with her conduct.

Commander Nessel spoke, "I still keep in contact with Admiral Tirinnis Sen Asel. I wouldn't want to send him bad news of his daughter acting up to her chain of command," the mild-mannered officer threatened quietly. "With that being said," he continued, "I'm demoting you. I want you to prove to me you deserve to graduate in one year as one of the highest ranking recruits."

Master Chief Braul took a knife from his boot to cut the sewn on rank from her sleeve. "Carry on," the Commander said in dismissal.

-:- -:- -:-

In the mess hall, Korteni was quick to help Brisethi sew on her new demoted rank. She could see in Brisethi's gray eyes that her morale had been diminished.

"I could go kill him for you, if you'd like? For a fee of ninety-nine frakshins, that is," Antuni Crommik jokingly commented.

"I have ninety-nine frakshins if you can take care of someone else for me," Etyne added while cutting into the overcooked meat they were eating. He was still heated from Kanilas Trenn's actions earlier that morning, not realizing how defensive he had become of his combat partner.

"While I appreciate the 'generous' offer, Antuni, I'll have to decline. Our training has been a bit relaxed in the past few months and I'm actually looking forward to this challenge," Brisethi said in a tone that convinced no one.

Ibrienne finished chewing her food before stating, "You're out of your mind."

Briethi kindly smiled her gratitude for the compliment in Ibrienne's way.

Thunder startled the entire crew in the galley as shouts were heard in the passageways. "Secure for sea!" shouted passing sailors. The ship had approached a storm.

Brisethi was giddy with excitement as the companions rushed to put their dishes away. Storms filled her spirit with joy as the ship heavily listed from the fierce waves, causing her to nearly walk on the bulkhead of the passageways.

It was almost impossible to strap down everything when the storm had rapidly brewed. Brisethi, Etyne and Antuni rushed to the upper deck to help with the sails. Most were already tearing from the winds. Brisethi ran in the rain to the bow to assist in securing the foremast. As she helped a fellow shipmate in tying the ropes, she looked behind her when the sailor shouted. Her face was pale at the sight of a wave taller than their ship rapidly approaching.

"Korteni!" Brisethi shouted upon seeing her friend on the bow. She was braced for impact, but staring at the wave before them. She could not hear anyone.

Brisethi's heart pounded at the thought of drowning but ran to her friend anyway. "We have to get below decks!"

"You do, but I can part this wave," Korteni calmly stated.

Brisethi refused to abandon her dearest friend and watched, spellbound, as Korteni brought up one hand toward the peak of the wave. It divided itself from the top to the bottom, allowing safe passage of their ship.

"By the spirits, what a sight!" Brisethi exclaimed.

The following waves were slightly smaller as the helmsman confidently guided the crew through them until the end of the storm.

Division Forty-One spent the following few months learning to efficiently extinguish ship fires, tie knots, moor lines, and how to properly raise, lower and replace sails and anchors. They navigated the ship day and night, charting maps and plotting courses to nearby islands while patrolling the seas around Sariadne. They had circumnavigated their entire continent twice, even pulling into the Res'Baveth harbor, only to train on mooring the ship. The crew was not allowed to enter the very city they were so close to, the splendid capital city in their sight. Much of the crew spent their idle time that day watching as fresh supplies came aboard. Some had the brief thought of sneaking out to explore, but anyone who was caught lingering more than a moment was given a task below decks, out of sight.

But the worst two months for Brisethi were spent diving off the ship and swimming to the shore of the islands. The recruits were trained to swim calm seas and rough ones, shark and jellyfish-infested waters and tropical lagoons.

Brisethi had always been a terrible swimmer and was even worse at holding her breath. Each day of swim training began with the recruits submerging themselves nearly thirty feet below the surface using dense rocks the size of their heads and walking with them along the seafloor to the shore. Slowly, Brisethi saw improvement in her progress, and, by the fourth week, she was able to advance farther than she ever had.

She could see the waves breaking above her and only needed to move a few more paces until her head would reach the surface. Her head pounded from the lack of air. Suddenly, she exhaled but couldn't bring herself to drop the rock. Her foot took another step, but she was unable to resist the urge to inhale. Dropping the rock, she leapt from the sandy floor and inhaled just a second too soon. Water filled her lungs as she coughed and inhaled more water, suffocating, drowning, and watching the light above her fade.

Etyne had already reached the shore and was waiting for his combat partner to either come up for air or finish the trial. He sprung into action the moment he saw her lifeless body breach the surface. Along with Koteni, they dived into the sea, racing to retrieve her. She was the third Resarian in the division to drown since swim training had begun.

Korteni reached her first, half a second before Etyne. With the use of her water mystics, she was able to bid the tide to push them to the shore faster. Master Chief Braul began shouting for Petty Officer Sestas to heal Brisethi as Etyne performed the resuscitation process each of them had all been taught. By his second attempt of blowing air into her mouth, Brisethi suddenly began coughing up sea water while Korteni extracted the remaining water from her lungs with her dwindling energy, forcing as much out as she possibly could. Ibrienne used her mystics to accelerate the oxygen back into her body.

"Did I make it?" Brisethi asked, still coughing as she crawled to her knees. The salt left a bitter taste in her mouth.

"You were about as successful as Trenn and Crommik," Etyne chuckled with Korteni and Ibrienne.

"But they drowned – oh." She stopped mid-sentence, realizing she had been saved just as the other two were in the first week. However, Crommik and Trenn eventually passed by the fifth week, leaving Brisethi and a half-dozen others still unable to pass the endurance test. It was an achievement medal she desperately wanted to add to her collection of certifications. Although she only had a medal for her archery, pistol, and rifle marksmanship, she wanted the navy underwater endurance one as well. Only two weeks remained to achieve her goal.

Brisethi sat on the sandy beach holding her knees up to her chest. Her black swim top and shorts were covered in sand. She shook her head once to get some water out of her ear that Korteni had missed.

Brisethi's thoughts darkened. She wasn't used to disappointment and failure. She normally excelled in everything she did. But running underwater wasn't meant for Resarians. Especially not for Resarians whose spirit mystics specialized in fire.

"This is a nightmare," she muttered to her friends while Ibrienne finished examining her. Etyne had finally sat down next to her to watch their division finish up the morning endurance training.

"Drowning? I'm sure it is," he elbowed her. "I can't imagine inhaling water instead of air. Please don't repeat that, I don't want to taste your salty face again."

Nearly out of breath from exhausting her mystic energy, Korteni added with a wink, "You sure rushed to resuscitate her before I could have the chance, unlike with Trenn and Crommick."

Brisethi peered sideways at her combat partner. "Oh really?" she licked her lips and winced from the salt of the ocean water.

Etyne glared at Korteni. "I was underwater still trying to qualify, too!"

Chapter XVI

"Fire!" Master Chief Braul shouted.

The recruits lit the sixteen canons instantaneously, creating deafening reverberations and flashy explosions. Each Dominion vessel was designed to be infused with the mystic of the commanding officer at the time. Commander Maerc Nessel's mystic enhanced the accuracy, speed and distance of each projectile in the cannons.

Their target was a massive cliff of a desolate island in the south, rising a thousand feet above the mists, too barren for civilization. After the entire morning was spent on target practice with the cannons, the crew was sent to repaint the cliffs with more targets for the next round.

Since no proper dock had ever been built for the massive ship at the island, the crew had to row small boats to the opposite shore of the island. From there, they hiked through a dead forest ascending toward the cliffs, and repelled down the face of the tall cliffs on a single rope with their canisters of paint.

Brisethi had been all too eager to be the one to paint the cliffs while Vorsen secured her rope. The crisp autumn air and slight overcast sky with her feet on firm ground far away from water put her in a good mood. As soon as she stood at the edge of the cliff, however, her heart sank at the sight of waves crashing fiercely against the sharp rocks below.

"Vorsen, I changed my-" she began.

"No, Sen Asel," Etyne interrupted, joining her at the edge. "We've already established this. You're the better artist. Now go down there and paint the best red and black circles anyone will have ever destroyed with mystic-propelled cannon balls." Etyne secured the straps around her waist and thighs. He wasn't about to admit that he was slightly still traumatized from the last cliff he dangled from nearly two years ago.

"How unfair!" she pouted. "We should have made the decision when we got to the peak and tested who was better at grasping the other," she jested but her confidence quickly dissipated. She placed the large paintbrush in one of her pockets and took a deep breath.

"I've already been in your grasp, remember? It was terrifying!" More seriously, he added, "I won't let anything happen to you, you trust me, right?" Etyne rested his hands on her shoulders to reassure her.

Brisethi slowly nodded, though she still glared into his startling pupil-less aqua eyes. When Etyne had fully secured both his and her straps to one another and to the stationary pulley on the ground, they both knelt down and crawled to the edge. She breathed heavily, trying not to panic at the thought of leaving the safe surface of the ground.

"You need to work on these panic attacks of yours," Etyne teased, grabbing her hands and nudging her toward the edge. "Don't look down;" he was mostly telling himself, "keep your eyes on your footing, feet on the cliff, hands on the rope. I'm going to let go of your hands, now, alright?"

As she hung on the edge, he released his grip on her clammy hands to pick up the canister of paint. He handed it to her, but she was reluctant to remove her hands from the rope. With a grin, he used extra twine to tie the canister to her belt.

"Are you ready to be lowered?" he asked when he was done.

Brisethi finally regained her courage and smiled, "Let's paint some cliffs already, you're holding me back!"

"Ha, literally," he jested back.

She was the last of twelve sailors to repel to the middle of the cliff. She only needed to paint four large targets as big as her own body and as far apart as she could reach whether above, below or side by side. When she wasn't thinking about her life dangling in Etyne's hands, she concentrated on painting large, perfect circles within circles, which she found to be surprisingly calming.

Before joining the military, she had passed many hours painting the landscapes surrounding her parents' home. Even on sunny days, she changed the atmosphere in her paintings to stormy, dark skies over rough seas, erupting volcanoes behind an abysmal lake, or approaching snowstorms over ancient ruins and dead forests. Everything about her seemed to thrive in destructive weather. Despite her gloomy paintings, she always enjoyed humming lively songs to herself. As she continued her work, she began to softly sing a ballad she'd overheard years ago.

Etyne remained sitting on his knees to counter the weight of his partner below. He gazed about at the other recruits involved in the project, noticing where the majority of stronger men held the ropes for their lighter painting partners. The half of the division not assigned to painting today remained on the ship for routine maintenance and cleaning of the cannons.

As the group worked, a violet overcast sky above created a misty ambience over the sea. Behind them, the dead forest helped set a gloomy mood on the tiny desolate island. The only wildlife that could be heard were the seabirds that seemed to inhabit every coastline.

The task at hand required very little mental presence, and Etyne found his thoughts wandering for the first time in months. Normally, every thought and action was focused on the present task. He rarely wondered about other people or thought about his future. Marinelle, his lover back in Res'Baveth, had barely crossed his mind since the last letter he had sent out to her. However, the more time he spent with his combat partner, the more he caught himself thinking about the wrong woman. Never one to talk much, he wasn't particularly interested in keeping most people around, and he had never needed more than a handful of close companions. But Brisethi Sen Asel challenged him with her thought-provoking banter on why she felt the need to travel the world and gain influence. She balanced her humor and recklessness with authority and tactics in every challenge or task she faced. Etyne had especially enjoyed listening to her and Antuni trade quips with one another, often sending their whole group into an uproar of laughter. Although she had a hard time recollecting factual knowledge from school, her common sense and quick decision-making had been more influential than repetitive text-book intelligence. He had begun to admire their unique friendship, often seeking her company. *When did I start to consider you my friend?* He asked himself.

Etyne ceased his daydreaming when he noticed the other sailors had already completed their tasks and were heading back down to the shore. He peeked over the edge to shout at Brisethi, but the sound of her voice caused him to pause. The song she was singing was one he only heard once at the Citadel's Sanctuary and had been longing to hear again. He was reluctant to disturb the peace she had found.

"I've seen my destiny; it's far greater than one can imagine,
"To the gray with the fates,
"Spirits guide me, empower me, give me the courage
"To take sovereignty among the gods of men."

She looked up when she realized she was the only one still painting. Etyne nodded at her and began to pull her back up.

"You do know what that song is about, right?" he asked, helping her climb onto the edge.

"Of course I do," she replied. "Sentiar Asellunas created the Dominion and intended to rule the world. Someone needs to finish what he started," she grinned.

"Why are your hands wet?" He looked at his hands after letting go of hers to find them covered in red and black paint. Before he could move, she quickly patted his face with both of her hands, laughing hysterically. Etyne attempted to return the favor, but she saw it coming and quickly sidestepped his hands. "Real professional, Sen Asel," he sarcastically remarked as he attempted to wipe the paint off with a rag.

When she was done laughing she finally spoke. "We can't always be serious or we'd forget why we're even fighting to stay alive. If the small things in life that make us smile are suddenly taken away forever, then why even fight for a life if not to live it?"

They hiked down to the shoreline, and both began washing paint off of their skin.

"I'll remember those words next time we're doing another project together," he smirked.

"I hope you do, Vorsen. You need to lighten up once in awhile. Everyone's so serious all the time." She climbed into the row boat where Korteni and Antuni had been waiting for them. The other dinghies had all left already.

"Everyone's serious because nobody wants to follow your example and end up getting launched off the ship by Master Chief Braul," Vorsen quipped.

Korteni and Antuni dissolved into laughter.

"You're never going to let me live that down, are you? It was seven months ago." She pouted and took a seat next to Korteni to allow the men to take the oars.

"It will be five hundred years from now when I'm still reciting the story to my grandchildren of the day Petty Officer Sen Asel was hurled off the deck of the *DSV Reliant* by the most malicious Master Chief to ever enlist into the Dominion Navy," Etyne said with a grin. He and Antuni effortlessly began rowing the boat back to the ship.

"Will any of us even talk to one another in five centuries?" Korteni asked, shivering a little from the autumn breeze.

"Nope," Brisethi abruptly replied. The sad look on Korteni's face instantly had her elaborating. "As General of the Dominion, I'll not have time for petty banter with you lot when I'm trying to occupy other continents."

"I hope you're kidding," Korteni replied, re-adjusting her uncomfortable headpiece to take her mind off the cool breeze.

"I'll be Emperor Crommik in about three centuries, trying to prevent Sen Asel from becoming a power-hungry dictator, which means I'll also have no time to talk with the rest of you lesser-than's," Antuni said loftily.

"Resarians aren't insane enough to vote you into the throne, Crommik," Korteni mockingly glared at him. Their boat peered around the edge of the island allowing their ship to finally be in view.

"Hold on," Etyne stopped rowing and silenced the others. He stood up slowly to keep his balance, glaring at a ship that had pulled up alongside theirs. "That's not a Dominion ship," he muttered.

"Is it Kiaran?" Korteni squinted to get a better view of the banners on the foreign ship.

"I'm not certain; I've never seen a Kiaran ship, have you?" He didn't wait for her reply. "I'm going to summon a distortion field around us so they can't see us approaching." Etyne brought his arm up to cast his spell on the row boat and its occupants. The air around them suddenly shifted, as if they were looking through faceted crystals. Etyne's spirit mystic had created particles forming a shield that appeared on the outside as a blurred diffraction. Although Antuni, Korteni and Brisethi couldn't see clearly through the shield, Etyne's vision was enhanced and magnified. He peered at the two ships.

"Falajen's spirits," Etyne whispered. "They're taking the commander and everyone else into binds and leading them down the main ladder well. They just look like pirates, probably taking our people to the brig. Why aren't they fighting back, though?"

"You seem awfully calm about a 'few pirates' holding our people hostage," Korteni murmured.

"What's the plan, Petty Officer Second Class Vorsen?" Brisethi asked with the slightest hint of bitterness. She had still not earned her rank back.

"Hey, he's not the only second class here," Antuni reminded her defensively.

"Since becoming Navy, you haven't exactly excelled at leadership, Crommik," Brisethi remarked when she remembered how much he complained about swimming.

"You are so salty right now, you lowly third class!" Antuni chuckled.

"Damn right, I'm salty," Brisethi crossed her arms.

"Children, focus!" Korteni interrupted. "This could be as bad as that night we were attacked. Except, this time, you can't just summon molten lava through the decks of *DSV Reliant* to save us, 'Sethi."

"We don't need her lava, we can use actual weapons, and the training Sergeant Vilkinsen gave us," Etyne interjected. "I'll keep us under illusion while we row to the aft of our ship. I can reach the deck and lower the ladder for the rest of you once I've scouted the area and taken care of any threats."

"How are you going to reach the deck? Climb the hull?" Brisethi asked.

"Mystics, how else?" Etyne gave her a funny look.

Antuni lost his composure and laughed abruptly. "Damn, 'Sethi, even *I* knew not to ask such a *stupid* question." He took every advantage to give his friends grief.

Etyne silenced everyone with a finger to his lips to initiate their stealthy reclamation of the *Reliant* and her crew. When the row boat was within arms' reach of their ship, Etyne used his spirit's mystic once more and vanished.

"That skill would have been useful when he was getting his ass beat three years ago," Brisethi murmured while staring in awe with the others.

"I fucking heard that," Etyne whispered loudly when he rematerialized on the ship.

Etyne remained under the cover of his distortion shield, unsheathing his dagger to ready his attack. The overcast sky had darkened as storm clouds formed unnaturally fast overhead. Etyne assumed that Korteni was using her mystic of water to create helpful distractions. He began to wonder why the Commander and Master Chief didn't defend themselves against a group of bandits by activating the ship's defenses.

Although he had been on the way to assassinating the pirate captain, he changed directions, thinking it better to investigate his crew so as to avoid putting them in more danger. He descended the ladder well until he was on the third deck where he'd seen the captives taken. There were only two pirates guarding the prisoners, chatting to one another. Etyne stealthily ran up to the closer guard, dematerializing from behind and knocked him out with a blow to the head. Before the other guard could move, Etyne swiftly jabbed the man's throat with the side of his hand then bashed the man's face into his knee, knocking him unconscious. His intent wasn't to kill them just yet, only to render them useless.

He grabbed the keys then hastily walked over to the cell where Master Chief Braul and Commander Nessel were restrained. "Master Chief, what happened?" He was glad there were only three keys to try and naturally, the last key he tried opened the cell door.

"Vorsen, before you do anything else, I need you to go rescue your six shipmates on the other ship. They were taken hostage. Their lives are in danger," Master Chief Braul quietly yet sternly explained.

"Aye, Master Chief," Etyne replied.

"Who do you have with you? Crommik, Pyraz and Sen Asel?"

"Yes, Master Chief. They're still on the boat until I secured the area enough to bring them onboard."

"Send Crommik and Pyraz here to help with defense. Take Sen Asel with you to the enemy ship as firepower while you rescue the others," Master Chief Braul ordered with the consent of Commander Nessel.

"Aye, Master Chief," Etyne nodded. He handed the keys over and re-activated his incorporeal form to swiftly travel throughout both ships. He counted how many pirates were on both the enemy ship and their own. He disengaged from his spell on the top deck, where he disposed of two more pirates with a dagger to their throats, tossing them overboard. Rain began to fall from the clouds above as he mentally thanked Korteni for the cover. He dashed to the aft of the ship where the row boat had remained.

Etyne deactivated his distortion shield from the row boat and its crew and lowered one of the ladders nearest them. He directed Korteni and Antuni, repeating Master Chief's orders to them. They quickly ran off, then Etyne told Brisethi of her orders.

"Firepower?. Let's do this. Turn us into spirits," Brisethi quietly ordered.

Etyne hesitated. "Wait. I've never used my incorporeal mystic on someone else. I don't even know if it's possible."

They were both standing under a partial overhang of the cabin's roof, out of sight of the windows. The wind picked up, blowing rain sideways, drenching the two recruits.

"Well, try it anyway. What could go wrong?" She was in a hurry to incinerate some pirates before the rain made it impossible.

"Sen Asel," he said as though addressing a young child, "when I use my power to become 'spirit-form', I de-materialize my vessel. That's how I was able to instantly transport to the deck from the boat.

I take apart my physical structure and store the particles into my spirit, practically becoming vapor. I'm almost certain that your spirit would be unable to do the same if I were to cast the spell on you. I can't fathom storing your dematerialized body into my spirit, either."

Brisethi bit her lip to hold back a suggestive remark that would have made her laugh, but not him. "You're right. I don't want to be your first victim to accidentally die from your dematerialization mystic. Just shield us with distortion, then?"

"You can't turn yourself into a small flame or something?"

She gave him the same funny look he had given her earlier. "That's probably the dumbest thing you've ever asked, Vorsen." She then looked up to the sky when a thought came to her mind. "I can create a diversion, however." She concentrated briefly. A burst of lightning struck the mast of the pirate ship as the sound of thunder reverberated throughout the air.

"*Lightning*? You can summon *lightning*?" He tried not to shout, impressed by her quick decision and astonished by yet another of her skills.

She smiled innocently. "The fire isn't going to spread, though, thanks to this rain," she stated. She had to fuel her own flames all around the pirate ship's mast to overcome the damp boons, sails and ropes with her powerful mystics.

"It will keep them from noticing the blur of our silhouettes running across the gangplank. It's not the complete invisibility I'd like to use on us, but it's better than having you seen out in the open," Etyne said, taking her hand in his to keep her close under his mystic's shield.

In the stealth of his mystic, the two Resarians swiftly crossed the slippery deck and the narrow gangplank that connected the two ships. The storm's growing ferocity made the sea rough and the going tricky. The moment Etyne and Brisethi reached the brig, after dodging out of the sight of panicked bandits who were trying to escape falling, flaming debris raining down upon them, Etyne dissipated his shield to allow Brisethi to target her attack.

Only one guard had remained in the area of the brig when the alarms sounded. His expression was slack-jawed as he tried to figure out what had just materialized before his eyes in the passageway.

Before the pirate could come to his senses, Brisethi let loose her crimson flames upon the guard, instantly melting his skin and sinew down to his bones. Etyne retrieved the keys, nearly burning his fingers on the metal after the heat of Brisethi's fire. He cursed to himself for not taking the flames into consideration and dropped the keys. Ibrienne and two others shouted their thanks, knowing they had been close to going down with the ship if the fire wasn't extinguished.

Petty Officer Second Class Trenn gave a slow clap with a bored expression on his face. He wanted the others to know he was not impressed. Brisethi half-heartedly considered leaving him behind. The Dominion Creed tugged at her in the back of her mind to not "accidentally" set him a flame.

"How'd you end up in here? Why didn't you use your mystics to defend against a few dozen pirates?" Brisethi asked Ibrienne.

"Don't tell her!" Sulica interjected. "She'll snitch and get the whole division reprimanded."

Brisethi rolled her eyes. "That's completely false. No matter, though. I'm sure at least two of you have conjured quite the elaborate story to debrief to Master Chief and the Commander."

Ibrienne was terrified of the unforeseen reprimand. They hadn't devised a fabrication and knew she would pour out the truth to Master Chief Braul. *If I tell 'Sethi, she will take the blame as she always does. She seems to welcome the physical reprimands. I wonder if she's a masochist?*

Etyne checked to see if the keys were cool enough to touch and finally unlocked the cell door, allowing the six recruits to escape. Ibrienne gave them both a tight hug, overjoyed to see them again.

"Everyone, stay behind me. Sen Asel, fire away at the front," Etyne ordered while summoning his distortion shield on the rest of the group.

"Aye, Petty Officer," she muttered out of respect. She moved to stand in front of the others, further distorting the air around them with the heat from her hands readying her mystics.

Most of the bandits were still in a state of alarm, scrambling about in attempt to save their burning ship. Embers and flaming debris continued to crash to the deck from above, so that even the Resarians had to move quickly while staying out of sight. The more alert of the pirates fired muskets in Brisethi's direction. She was forced to duck and roll behind Etyne's shield as she countered by sending a ball of fire back at them. She continued igniting any pirate in her line of sight, shooting fireballs at the deck near their feet, forcing several of the enemy crew to jump overboard to avoid the flames.

Etyne guided Brisethi from behind to the opposite side of the heavily trafficked gangplank so that the recruits could board one of the pirates' row boats. Trenn and Etyne lowered the boat while Brisethi continued causing chaos and destruction to keep the foes away. The ladder was lowered with the row boat as Trenn oversaw his five shipmates safely descend to the rough ocean waves below.

Trenn was the last to go as he shouted, "Come on, Vorsen, waiting on you!"

"I can't leave Sen Asel!" Etyne shouted back.

"She can take care of herself against pirates! She's lighting them up!"

"I agree, but she's still my responsibility." He left the area to seek out his combat partner. It was easy to find the battle so long as he followed the bursts of red flame shooting through the sky, igniting the remaining masts.

"Sen Asel, what the fuck," Vorsen knelt down beside a puddle of blood that Brisethi was kneeling in, one of her hands propping her up against a crate. "This better not be your blood."

She held her side with her other hand and looked up at him. "I'll live, I'm just hiding out until the ship sinks," she grimaced.

"You're terrible at holding your breath," he reminded her. "You'll definitely drown, silly." He took off both of their neckerchiefs and tied them together around her waist and hip, applying pressure to her puncture wound.

She groaned at the pain. The musket shell had pierced through her skin, and she prayed it would only be a flesh wound. "Ugh, it hurts, I'd rather be stabbed!"

"Can you walk?" Etyne helped her to her feet.

She nodded as she leaned into him but couldn't keep up with Etyne's speed. He ended up picking her up like a child and running faster to dodge the last of the three masts coming down on the ship. She held onto his neck and summoned a flurry of flames behind him, though she was certain all pirates had been killed or already abandoned the ship.

The sound of sixteen canons simultaneously firing reverberated through the air and shook the ship they were trying to escape from. The *DSV Reliant* had fired its first round of canons.

"Why are they firing now? The ship's already gone and we're still on it!" Brisethi shouted in Etyne's ear.

"Master Chief probably assumed we were done here," he replied. When they finally reached the ladder, he wasn't at all surprised to see that Trenn and the others in the row boat were gone. There was no time to lower another boat. "Hold your breath!" he shouted then tossed Brisethi into the sea. He jumped overboard after her, diving with ease.

Brisethi coughed up some water when she surfaced. "I'm a bit tired of getting thrown off of ships," she muttered, using all of her willpower not to scream in pain from the salt water on her wound.

The thick storm clouds above obscured any light from the evening sky as Etyne swam through the rough waves, dragging his wounded partner behind.

Even though Trenn couldn't have been bothered to wait for Vorsen and Sen Asel, he took all the time he needed to raise the ladder and properly stow it. *At least he left the row boat*, Etyne thought, irate, sore and tired. The rain had abated by the time they reached it. He climbed in first then pulled Brisethi in and examined her wound.

"Get it out of me," Brisethi whined through rapid breathing.

"You couldn't do it yourself when you were first hit? That's the first rule of gunshot wounds," he glared at her, knowing full well she couldn't see.

"It was too painful!" Her breathing was labored. "Just do it!" She gritted her teeth.

He pressed firmly with both hands on either side of the entry wound, glancing back at her to monitor the level of pain in her eyes. He felt the shell and used his fingers to dig it out of her. He smirked a little when she screamed in agony.

"Did you have to be so aggressive?" She panted, trying to hold back the tears.

"You're incredibly whiny for a superficial wound," he teased, washing her blood off his hands in the sea. "Do you think you can use your mystic to get someone's attention on the ship? I'm not sure how they couldn't hear your oh so tragic scream."

Keeping her eyes on his, she waited for the pain to subside to a dull ache and slowed her breathing. She looked up at the indigo sky and fired an illuminating scarlet sphere that pierced the leaden mists. It detonated with a sound of a dozen cannons, millions of scarlet sparkles emanating from the blast like the red stars of an entire galaxy falling through the universe.

Master Chief Braul was the first to peek over the ship's railing. He began shouting orders as soon as he saw Vorsen and Sen Asel. Seconds later, the ladder was unraveled for them.

Despite the throbbing in her side, Brisethi laboriously climbed to the top, with a significant amount of help of Etyne, and stumbled onto the deck. Ibrienne was first to greet her, immediately tending to her wound.

"'Sethi," Ibrienne whispered close to her ear as she worked her mystics. "I have a favor to ask."

In the commotion of the ship's crew readying the sails, Brisethi whispered back. "What is it?"

"The reason we were captured by those pirates earlier today, was because of Sulica's father," Ibrienne began. "Sulica thought she recognized the pirate ship as one that her father would sometimes work on. She was severely mistaken and we were quickly detained. I'm sorry, 'Sethi. I don't know if I can withstand the beating we're all about to get for this."

Brisethi bit her lower lip in thought and relief that her wound was no longer throbbing. "I will talk to Master Chief, and exaggerate your story a bit."

"Thank you," Ibrienne smiled to her.

Clean-up was already well underway. Corpses of the bandits were thrown off the side as the crew of *DSV Reliant* watched the fiery pirate ship sink into the restless sea.

Master Chief Braul approached Sen Asel. She rose to her feet when she felt stable enough, despite Ibrienne's disapproving look.

"Master Chief," Brisethi began, standing at attention. She wondered how much intensive training she could bear with how much blood she had lost. "I was the one who gave permission for Petty Officer Sestas and Petty Officer Nin to seek out Nin's father-"

"Spare me your bullshit, Sen Asel. I already beat Trenn for feigning ignorance and passing the blame on Nin and Sestas." Master Chief shook her hand, commending her for a job well done. She felt something pass from his hand to hers and looked down to see the rank insignia of Petty Officer Second Class.

Chapter XVII

When the Recruit Training Expedition Ceremony finally came to an end, after speeches from an admiral and a general, the Division commanders, and a final drill march formation, Brisethi's parents rushed to her from the audience outside of the Res'Baveth Citadel's grand entrance, fully decked out for the occasion.

"My little girl!" Brisethi's father, Admiral Tirinnis Sen Asel, yelled, wrapping her in his arms like he did when she was a child. "I'm so proud. You even earned your navy endurance medal - you were so worried about failing. And only four of you made it to second class petty officer rank, worse than my division," he chuckled. She didn't bother to tell him that she had drowned the day before passing the certification or that she had taken a shot to her hip which had earned her the last rank.

Her mother, Naiana, was in tears when she finally embraced her Dominion Soldier of a daughter. "This was the worst four years of my entire four centuries in this life," she sobbed. "I'm so happy to see you!"

Before they walked to their dinner table, Brisethi introduced her parents to Commander Nessel, Master Chief Braul and Sergeant First Class Vilkinsen. Each division commander told her parents they had raised an outstanding soldier and sailor, commending her once more for her achievements, for which she respectfully thanked them. She then introduced her parents to Korteni and Antuni, who had been about to introduce their parents to the commanders, as well as Ibrienne.

Thousands of tiny lanterns were strewn over the closed-off main street in front of the Citadel for the semi-annual Dominion ceremony. Decorated trees and lantern posts lined the massive cobblestone street while lit candles brightened each of the forty tables that were reserved for the recruits and their families. An orchestra of skilled Dominion soldiers and sailors played nostalgic notes of symphonic melodies.

Livian Reej stared in awe at the majestic celebration and the soldiers dressed in their ornate, decorated uniforms. Each year of her service in the Citadel, the ceremony seemed better than the one before, whether it was from more complex music, heart-felt speeches, prettier lighting or lavish table cloths. She enjoyed helping to set up and take down the festive decor, counting the days until she was old enough to enlist into the Dominion. For the next four years, however, she would audition to partake in the small orchestra for each ceremony.

She walked to each of the four tables she had been assigned to, serving glasses of wine and water to each guest, replenishing their fruit and breads and making small talk with the soldiers and sailors who hadn't come home to a family member. Livian could easily relate to those whose parents had been lost in some battle or another during the endless war with the Kiarans.

Although she wasn't in the military, the serving girls all wore form-fitting black dresses with burgundy overcoats flowing behind them. The gold Dominion insignia was embroidered on their right arm, nearly giving Livian the feeling of wearing a military dress uniform.

As she turned from one table to the next, she suddenly stopped in her tracks. "Ibrienne? Is that you?" Livian questioned uncertainly. The young woman who stood before her was much thinner and more confident than the one she remembered, but the warm smile was still the same.

"Liv!" Ibrienne quickly jumped up to hug the younger girl. She wrapped her arms tightly around her. When Ibrienne pulled away, tears were in her eyes. "Look at you! You're so beautiful, just as I remembered."

"I didn't know you joined the Dominion," Liv returned the tight embrace. "How was it? Are you staying in?"

Ibrienne smiled sweetly at her young friend from the orphanage. "I haven't decided if I'll continue staying in. I struggled quite a bit, and I wouldn't want to hold my division back in any way. But what about you?" she exclaimed. "How did you leave the orphanage?"

Livian bit her lower lip before responding to keep it from trembling. "It burned down, Ibrienne! I was the only survivor." The words fell out of her in a rush. "I had to sleep in an alleyway and then found my way to the Citadel. I've been working for Acolyte Roz for the past few years. I can't wait until four more years when I'm finally able to enlist."

"I'm so glad you made it out alive! When I heard what happened…" Ibrienne's voice trailed off for a moment. "Ah, never mind, I know you'll make a great soldier and sailor someday," she finished, beaming at the young woman who had been like her kid sister in childhood.

"Do you have friends? Is it true what they say that the people you meet in the Dominion are like family?" Livian sat down next to Ibrienne, not wanting to leave her friend alone again.

Tears welled in Ibrienne's light eyes again. She glanced down at the division photographs each recruit was given that evening that had been taken their first month at the Citadel. "Yes, it's true. Brisethi, Korteni, even Sulica – we endured the training together and helped one another out. If I don't stay in, though, I'm afraid I'll lose contact with them. But, Sulica said she wanted to help her father's merchant company with one of the others and asked if I would help her with the administrative and accounting part of it. I might take her up on it."

"Do it," Livian encouraged her. "Do whatever you think would make you the most happiest in the end."

Brisethi's parents took their seats while she remained standing by her chair a moment longer, glancing a few tables away where Etyne sat with two gorgeous women. She assumed one of them was his mother, but couldn't tell which. Resarians didn't age the way the rest of the world did. Their hair didn't gray and their skin didn't wrinkle until well into their eight-hundreds when their spirits grew weary and needed to return to the Sea of Renewal.

Etyne's eyes met Brisethi's, and he watched her smile awkwardly at him. He stood, excused himself, and walked toward her.

"Sen Asel," he shook her hand.

"Vorsen, this is my father, Admiral Tirinnis Sen Asel, and my mother, Naiana," she introduced them.

Vorsen saluted her admiral father who wore his navy dress uniform and shook Naiana's hand. "It was an honor to compete with your daughter for advancement the past four years," he told them respectfully.

"Liar," Brisethi muttered.

"Well, obviously you were no match for me in the beginning," he said with a faint grin.

Tirinnis chuckled, "As long as you made her work hard for those ranks you both achieved. She's quite the handful."

"Rude," Brisethi pouted jokingly.

Etyne guided Brisethi to his own table to meet his mother and the other woman sitting next to her. "Sen Asel, meet my mother, Drienna, and this here is Marinelle, my lovely other half." They both stood to greet her as she tried not to stare at both of them. *These must be the most beautiful women in all of Falajen. No wonder he barely looks at me if he has Marinelle to stare at forever,* she thought. Her normal confidence faltered as she suddenly felt unattractive in her gaudy uniform and muscular build with her uneven hair, standing before two soft, skinny women in silky, frilly dresses and flowing, curly hair. Her face flushed as all the previous sentiments she'd had for her former partner flashed through her mind. She made the appropriate salutations then excused herself to return to her own table.

Brisethi devoured her fruit and bread while waiting for her steak. She answered the dozens of questions from her mother that she was certain had already been answered in letters.

"'Sethi!" Hands gripped her shoulders, nearly startling her.

She looked up to see a familiar face. "Joss! What are you doing here?" She stood to embrace her childhood friend.

"Naiana invited me, of course. Sorry I'm late; my father wouldn't let me close the shop early to watch the ceremony," Joss replied.

"It's been over six years since we last spoke. I'm surprised you showed up at all, but I'm grateful," Brisethi said as she sat down once again, inviting him to sit next to her.

The two had been friends since the first day of school at age four, and they remained friends for the next twelve years until finally giving in to their desires of one another. Briefly, they thought they would stay together for centuries, but Brisethi always had different plans for her life. Joss hadn't wanted her to join the Dominion because of the risk, the danger, and the four years he would be without her. She said her goodbye to him two years before enlisting to make it easier on the both of them, thankful she was transferred to another school for her last two years. A pang of guilt swept over her when she looked into his longing eyes. He hadn't deserved to have his heart broken.

The dinner came to an end as lanterns slowly dimmed out and serving personnel initiated the take-down of the tables, chairs, and decorations. The Dominion Military personnel had officially been released for their month of leave. Some would return for a second enlistment of four years into the Navy or Army, some would pursue more training to earn a commission as an officer, while the rest would return to civilian life as a lifelong reservist.

As the families left one by one, several of the new graduates bid each other goodbye. Antuni grabbed Sulica's arm gently and led her to a quiet section of the street. They stood awkwardly for a moment, neither knowing how to say what was on their minds. Antuni gave Sulica a lopsided grin and took her hand.

She smiled in return, pushing a strand of her silky blonde hair behind her ear. "Thank you for helping me through the last few years."

He shrugged. "Well, you're joining your father's crew, right?"

Sulica nodded. She began to reach for Antuni's face but changed her mind halfway through the gesture and brought her hand up to play with the necklace around her throat, a gift he had given to her after bartering with Brisethi. "And you?"

"I'll probably re-enlist. I'm going to see how I feel after the month off, though. I want to spend some time at home for a while."

She nodded again. "Well, if you ever..." She didn't finish her sentence.

"Thanks. You take care, okay?" Antuni pulled her close one last time.

"You too," she whispered in his ear.

They broke their embrace when Korteni's voice reached them. "Nin, Crommick, where are you?" she called.

The two rejoined the rest of their friends who were all busily exchanging contact information in case anyone wanted to meet up during the break. "You'd think this was a summer camp farewell," Sulica said in a bored tone, but she joined the others easily. Another half of an hour later, the group finally parted ways amid shouts of fortune and promises of future gatherings.

Joss and Brisethi sat on carved log chairs at their old meeting place along the northern shore. The sky was absent of moons and clouds to allow the clusters of stars to shine brightly. Only the red planet nearby graced Falajen with its presence, casting its glow on the water below.

"Do you have to remain at the Citadel for the entire four years of officer training?" Joss asked.

"Yes. It's going to be a long time until I finally purchase my dream home downtown. Above a bakery, perhaps, or a trinket store. And then I'll get a cat to keep me company," she said with a grin.

"If it's company you want, you should get a dog. They're happier creatures. And why downtown? Why not a big house with multiple rooms for children along the shoreline and enough land for multiple dogs? City life is harsh, noisy," he lectured.

And so it begins, she thought sadly, *trying to convince me that his life decisions would be more suitable for me.* "Because, Joss, I don't want to spend hours commuting on horseback from the shoreline to the Citadel when I can take a carriage for only half of an hour. And I wouldn't make some poor dog suffer by living in a tiny flat." She tried to force a laugh.

"What about your children?" He persisted.

"What children? I have hundreds of years to go before I even think about taking the time to raise a child. I don't understand why so many Resarians feel the need to rush into making a family before the age of one-hundred." She was becoming irritated.

"And then you'll move out of the city?" he asked once more.

"In a few hundred years I'll be ranking up to general. Do you know where the high ranking officers get to live? In the palace! They get their own grand chambers in one of the six towers because they need to be within summoning range of the emperor in the event that Sariadne is under attack. That's the life I want, Joss. Roaming the palace halls and spending hours in the libraries, reading and painting, learning to play the piano or violin so that I can take part in grand orchestras on my off time. I want to lead the Dominion and influence the militaries of the rest of the world to unite with Sariadne," she said earnestly. "I want the war to end, Joss," she continued with a sigh and slouched in her chair.

"Oh, 'Sethi," he said. "Don't you understand how many other officers before you have probably already tried that? You're not the first person to have such ideals," he softly replied.

Brisethi matched her tone to his. "For every new general who earns rank in the Dominion, five emperors and generals of the Pahl'Kiar have come and gone. It's all about persistence and convincing the right one. I want the Resarians to co-exist with the Kiarans once more on our continent."

Joss had always admired his friend's innocence and naivety. He didn't always agree with her ambitions, but tried his best not to interfere with them. "I hope you succeed, 'Sethi, I really do. While you're up in the palace with the emperor coordinating tactics and all that, I'll be trying to keep your economy up, selling the carriages I make," he laughed, and she smiled easily.

Silence followed for a moment until Joss summoned the courage to ask her one last question. "'Sethi, do you think we can ever pick up where we left off? From before?"

"No," Brisethi abruptly replied, knowing they hardly had a thing in common. After spending four years with men like Vorsen and Crommik; and women like Korteni and Ibrienne, her standards had changed in the kind of partner she would like. She sighed, remembering how long it had been since she was with Joss, let alone anyone. Her steely gray eyes met his soft brown ones. "I'd rather start *over* with you. We're different than we were six years ago." *And slightly desperate*, she admitted to herself.

He reached his hand over to hold hers. "Then let's start over, 'Sethi."

She held onto his warm hand, flaring up emotions she thought she'd destroyed years ago. She looked up at the stars and the red planet, Renegade. She was always bemused that the two planets, one red and one blue, were named Renegade and Paragon, whereas Falajen, was the ancient Kiaran word for "neutral". A memory struck her when she looked at a familiar winged beast of a constellation. "Joss, do you believe in dragons?"

"How many blows to the head did you take the past four years?" Joss teased.

"A few, but that's not the point. Do you think dragons still exist?"

"They don't even teach children that our spirits descended from them anymore. Did dragons ever exist? Where are their skeletons? Why do we not have dragon claws and skulls to prove they ever existed?" He debated, his logical reasoning ever present.

"Because they die in volcanoes," she mumbled.

<u>Spirits of Falajen</u>
Part II - Sacrifice of Souls

Chapter I

Despite doing nothing but relax for an entire month and rekindle a forgotten love with Joss, the leave went by quicker than Second Lieutenant Brisethi Sen Asel expected. She was early to her first day of officer training, sitting alone in the classroom and staring at the vaulted ceiling of one of the many Citadel schoolhouses. She let her mind go as her eyes drifted around the empty room, watching motes of light floating. Though her mind often wandered into voids of darkness, she told curious colleagues that she was meditating. The morning physical training she had started with the other ensigns and second lieutenants had left her exhausted after a month without the rigorous routine.

Second Lieutenant Etyne Vorsen materialized in the seat next to her. "Where is everyone?"

"Geez, Etyne!" she exclaimed, startled by his sneaky entrance, albeit excited to see him since they hadn't had much opportunity to catch up during the early morning workout. "I don't know, are we in the right class?" Other officers in training from that morning started to enter the room as if to answer her question. The two kept glancing at each person to see if they knew anyone else from their division. No one was recognizable and most of the junior officers were from prior divisions. Due to the incidents of both Division Thirty-Nine and Division Forty-One, this class was the smallest the Citadel had seen in centuries, containing only sixteen students - half of the usual attendance. Officer training was only held once every two years, offered only to those divisions that had graduated in that time. Brisethi and Etyne's Division barely made the cutoff for the class.

After the class stated the Dominion Creed, the instructor wasted little time on introductions and almost immediately launched into a lecture on the syntactic structure differences between Resarian and other worldwide languages. Brisethi struggled to stay awake, stifling several yawns. Twice, Etyne had to knock her arm out from supporting her head so she wouldn't fall asleep. Mentally telling herself she'd beg Etyne for his notes later, she began to zone out again, ensuring she'd stay awake but not expending any more energy than she had to.

Each morning was spent partaking in arduous physical training, including long distance runs and calisthenics. Three days were spent in class learning more languages of the world, other countries' histories, cultures, politics and economy. They learned how to break apart the military structure of each nation to initiate ingenuity among their own people by debating the merits of each organization. The engineering of the rest of the world was far more advanced than the Resarians, but, as Etyne had pointed out, the rest of the world didn't have spirit mystics to make some things in life more convenient or destructive. Brisethi was particularly fascinated to learn that the Aspion Empire had invented a steam-powered engine that ran on rails, the Kiarans invented the steam-powered warships made of metal, and the Lantheuns had started experimenting with airships all within the last decade.

"So what the shit are we inventing?" Brisethi mumbled to Etyne. He stifled a laugh, wanting to prevent a reprimand from the naval commander instructor. Brisethi was already notorious for her terrible luck with naval superiors.

"Sen Asel," Commander Olsine's voice echoed.

"Yes, Ma'am," she nervously stood at attention.

"Can you imagine a world where your father, Admiral Sen Asel, stationed upon a ship, could simultaneously communicate with General Satnir here in Res'Baveth in a matter of seconds? No telegraphs; waiting days for the messenger will be unheard of. Written letters replaced by instantaneous chatter with one another across hundreds of miles of sea?" The female commander kept her glare on the young Second Lieutenant.

"That would be spectacular, Ma'am," Brisethi replied, waiting anxiously for the command that would send her into intensive training.

"Take your seat," she ordered her. "Four years ago, I became separated from my division and met up with a squadron of Dominion soldiers patrolling the northern coast. They were escorting me to the northern post when we came upon a group of thirteen Kiaran marines. With only six of us versus thirteen of them, it would have been nice to have a device that could summon backup from the post. Instead, we risked the six of us to ensure the Kiarans were taken care of." She lowered her collar to reveal the scar of a shot that grazed her during the event. "But at the cost of painful memories and the life of one of our own men."

Brisethi sighed in relief, thankful to not receive reprimands for her inability to keep her mouth shut. Simultaneously, was unnerved by the commander's story. She remembered hearing about the event on the first night of Expedition Training, anxious to receive weapons and defend her country. But within months, her mindset had reverted to wanting to reunite Sariadne's natives instead of fending them off.

"Naval Captain Maerc Nessel is experimenting with such a device," the Commander continued. "Using his precise mystic, he may have developed a way to send communications from one station to another wherever the mystically enhanced devices are installed. Within a few years, we will have the power to speak to one another across great distances as if we were conversing in the same room."

Etyne and Brisethi were enthralled with the idea of their people finally creating something useful to the world. Several others in the class shared their enthusiasm and continued to spend breaks discussing the possibilities of such technology.

"We'd be able to talk to our families while we're out in the field," one of the other students said during one break. Brisethi scoffed, shooting a look at Etyne that clearly stated the soldier didn't have his priorities straight. "What, Sen Asel?" the soldier said, "Just because everyone will be relieved when you leave doesn't mean we all have that problem."

Brisethi started to rise, but Etyne put a hand out to stop her, saying, "Why would the Dominion spend valuable resources on family communication when they could be used to alert others of an attack?" The question sparked a discussion on the potential distance covered and if the device could be intercepted.

Brisethi heard Etyne let out his breath quietly and looked at him questioningly. "You and your temper," he muttered to her.

She pouted but said nothing, realizing he'd probably just saved her from a major misstep.

When the officers in training weren't in class, they spent three days a week in the field to retrain their skills in weapons and combat by learning even more techniques in mystics and hand-to-hand combatives. They were instructed in ways to devise their own strategies against every possible tactic thrown against them. Brisethi had thought she and Etyne had been good before, but the skills they were instructed in during field training made their Expedition skills look clumsy and childish. Brisethi thoroughly enjoyed the field training, especially when they trained combat techniques on horseback, but she often struggled with her studies. She felt fortunate that Etyne had chosen to take up the commissioning schooling with her and offered to be her study partner. In addition, he suggested they continue to be combat partners as well.

"Aww, you can't get enough of me," she jested.

"I just want to make you cry," he replied with his usual smirk.

"Good luck with that. I haven't cried from physical pain since the first day I ever felt my yearly menstrual cramps," she retorted.

"That's gross," he quipped, walking away from her in an effort to preserve some semblance of manly dignity.

"Hey are you going to join the command *chel'kan* team?" she asked, following after him.

"Yeah, are you?"

"Ha, no, I'm terrible at catching and throwing balls." Brisethi kicked at a rock in the path that led to the citadel quarters. "But thanks to the years of training with you and Sergeant Vilkinsen, learning to deflect oncoming projectiles with my sword, I'm going to try out for command *hak'ii*, as the goalie," she grinned.

Etyne tried to stifle an abrupt laugh, "I didn't even know you could ice skate."

-:- -:- -:-

"You seem out of it, Etyne. You haven't even insulted me yet. What's wrong with you?" Brisethi pestered him after their routine condition training spent in the gymnasium.

Etyne sighed, wondering if he even wanted to tell her of his personal life. Though they were nearing the end of their first month of officer training, spending a great quantity of time with one another, he rarely revealed personal matters to her. He glanced at Brisethi when she nagged him again before arriving at their respective quarters. "If you must know, my trust has been betrayed by Marinelle. She is four months with child."

"You're going to be a father? Already?" Brisethi grinned, disregarding the first part of his explanation.

"No, 'Sethi, the child isn't mine. We've only been back from Expedition for two months," he restated for her, a slightly pained tone in his voice.

Brisethi covered her mouth with her hands as if to erase her former utterance. "Ohhh, Etyne, I'm so sorry," she awkwardly patted him on the shoulder with her fingertips. "She couldn't wait two more months for you to come home after waiting four years?"

"I kind of felt this coming from the vague, far and few between letters she had sent. I can't be that upset with her for no longer wanting to wait, if she even waited at all" he muttered.

"But...you could have moved on ages ago instead of wasting so much time," her voice trailed off. "Nevermind, though. Do you want to take it out on the ice? I don't have practice until tomorrow night," she grinned, wanting any excuse to test her skills in the only sport she was decent in. The aggressiveness of the ice sport motivated her to excel in the game.

"'Sethi, you're never getting me out on the ice, it's just not in my blood to ice skate with a stick, chasing after a puck," Etyne yawned from exhaustion.

"It's in half your blood," she shrugged, somewhat discouraged he wouldn't join her in such an intensive sport for the command team.

When they parted ways for the evening to freshen up from training, Brisethi ran across the street to the general store, often frequented by the Dominion military personnel. She purchased a type of rum that was in a black-colored glass in the shape of a teardrop labeled, *Siren's Tears*. "Well this is suitable," she muttered to herself.

Etyne opened his door after the fifth round of obnoxious never-ending knocking from the other side. "What?"

Brisethi stared briefly at the unfamiliar sight of his shirtless chest, shoulders and arms before quickly looking up at his face, partly covered with dark wet hair. "Get your clothes on and follow me!" she excitedly ordered, holding up her prized bottle of rum.

"How did you know how to get up here?" Etyne asked when they reached the top of the highest tower of the Citadel overlooking the harbor.

Brisethi shrugged. "I sometimes explore when you're out having dinner with - I mean, when you're not here," she corrected herself. She took a swig of the rum and handed it to him.

He consumed a fair amount before giving it back. "I suppose you and I were due for a night of drinking," he exhaled sharply from the sting of the alcohol.

She smiled at him before taking another swig of the alcohol. Using her mystics, she started to create lines of red fire in the air, forming them into shapes of animals, flowers and even ships. It was a skill she could only show off while intoxicated. Soon, she was firing off her own mystic fireworks to amuse Etyne.

"You're definitely better at lifting my spirit than Antuni ever was," he said, watching in awe at the swirls of hundreds of tiny stars she was summoning.

"Oh yeah? Why is that?" she asked with amusement leaning over the ramparts.

"For one, he's not a fire mystic," he replied as another set of star-shaped tiny blasts went off over their heads. "For two, he usually only wants to hang out in taverns in search of single girls to take home if either of us are having a terrible day."

"You don't find that fun?" She tried to force her concentration on the dancing lights but let them fall after a moment.

"Not in the slightest. I prefer intelligent women found in libraries and colleges - I admire insight and learning from others," he replied and finished their bottle off. "Though, I do miss Antuni, I feel I should thank you, Brisethi, for being a great friend."

Brisethi remained silent at his words. She had never felt like she was the insightful type, nor did she admire reading non-fiction textbooks such as the intelligent women that Etyne spoke of. "I suppose I'm more of Joss' type who would find someone like me in the taverns, laughing and dancing, attempting to carry a tune," she nervously chuckled.

The sound of approaching guards startled them both from their quiet chatter. Brisethi led Etyne onto the roof of the tower in an attempt to remain stealthy but the guards were quick to spot them.

Laughing, she climbed and jumped to another rampart, sprinting in the dead of night to another tower. Etyne kept up with her, trying to not to lose his composure as well at the excitement of running from the guards.

"'Sethi, where the fuck are we?" Etyne chuckled. Each time he looked up at the sky, or the ceiling when they were finally indoors, he had to hold on to Brisethi to keep from losing his balance. Both inebriated junior officers were completely lost, trying to regain their sense of balance and direction.

"Dammit, Etyne, you're distracting me. Come on, I think - I think this corridor leads to our barracks," she took his hand to urge him to stay close. They dodged another roving watch a few more corridors down until they finally found the floor and hall of their rooms.

"'Sethi your room is over there," Etyne attempted to guide her four doors down.

She searched every pocket then looked up at him with glossy eyes. "I lost my key!" She giggled.

"Of course you did," he chuckled and brought her back to his room. He threw a small blanket over her on the chair she curled up in.

-:- -:- -:-

By their second year in officer training, Etyne and Brisethi had not only learned new combative stances from their trainers, but also taught each other several new fighting techniques. They would spend two evenings a week in the library researching the martial arts of the world, learning that only one other nation on the other side of the world outskilled the Resarians in hand-to-hand combatives. Considering the Dominion was the only empire who consistently defended for over three-thousand years, they weren't surprised to learn such global facts. They disciplined themselves to learn the foreign tactics from the diagrams in the classified books. Because the two friends held nothing back from one another when they fought, they were often used as examples for training during class and were commended on the new moves they improvised from what they learned.

"Roz!" shouted Etyne during one session when Brisethi was knocked unconscious from a blow she had brought upon herself. He caught her mid-fall and laid her gently on the grass.

"You two have my work cut out for me," Acolyte Roz replied when he ran up for what seemed like the tenth time that week.

"I told her not to head-butt me, that she'd regret it," Etyne replied, placing a hand over his own forehead feeling for the bump caused by Brisethi's bony skull. His other hand held Brisethi's wrist to ensure her pulse was steady.

"She has yet to knock you out, though," Roz pointed out as he directed his spirit's healing mystic on the unconscious Resarian.

"No, but she *has* dislocated my shoulder once, fractured my shin, a rib or two, my forearm, and stabbed me with a dagger down to the muscle in my back," Etyne listed off. "If anything, we're far from even." He watched Roz mend the cut in her forehead before he moved on to tend to Etyne's bloody forehead.

"And how many of her bones have you broken?" Roz asked.

Etyne didn't answer right away. "She may have broken her ankle once or twice trying to crack my skull. She also might have broken her knuckles a few times trying to crack my skull. I'm pretty sure that's it," he finally replied.

"Spirits bless you two. One day I won't be here, and you're going to leave each other suffering in pain for an entire day," Roz threatened lightheartedly.

Hours later Brisethi woke in her quarters with no memory of crawling into bed. She stretched her sore muscles, grasping at her chest and shoulders that were sculpted from her strength-training routines. She lit a lantern and placed a hand on her sore skull. A note waited for her on the desk with her favorite sweet pastry sitting on a small plate.

I'm sorry I let you knock yourself out again, 'Sethi. I warned you, though. Enjoy your sympathy snack.

~Etyne

She scowled momentarily then took the pastry and snuck over to his quarters four doors down. She tapped the door lightly, suddenly aware that she had no idea what time it was.

"Ugh, what do you want?" Etyne asked as he opened the door. He yawned and shielded his eyes from her lantern.

"To thank you for the pastry," she said, walking past him into his assigned room.

He sat back down on his bed, rubbing one eye while watching her with the other. She set down her lantern on his desk and crawled on the bed to sit next to him. Etyne grabbed his pocket watch to look at the time. "It's hour one; did you just wake up from the temporary coma you put yourself in?"

"And you say *I'm* cranky when I don't sleep," she said with a raised eyebrow. "Yes, I did just wake up. Here have some," she gave him half of her pastry.

He reluctantly took it and shoved it in his mouth if only to take away the taste of sleep. "You were out for ten hours," he spoke while chewing.

"I thought it was still evening, I didn't mean to wake you. Consider it payback for putting me out for so long," she smiled good-naturedly. She took a bite of her half of the pastry then turned to the window above his bed, sitting on her knees. Every time she visited him, she took advantage of the view of the grand palace since her own room's view was of the Citadel's tree-filled courtyard.

"You're very fortunate I don't hate you as much as I used to or I'd knock you back out so I can get my last three hours of sleep," he whined, stifling another yawn.

She glared at him chewing the last bit of her pastry. "Next time don't try to fatten me up with sweets." She pried herself away from the window and forcefully fit herself between him and the wall.

He playfully poked at her waist. "You're right, you don't need anymore sweets."

"Don't be rude, jerk," she swatted at his hand, trying incredibly hard not to laugh from the slight tickle. She used her mystic to extinguish the lantern flame to spend the remainder of her night in his bed.

"One day they're going to randomly inspect my room when you're sleeping here and get us both in a world of trouble," he lectured, lying down with his back against hers.

"You can hide me with your mystic," she mumbled, struggling to take over his pillow. She yawned and closed her eyes.

"And Joss?" Etyne persisted. "Is he fine with the fact you barge in here every now and then and pass out next to me? I can't exactly mention this type of routine to Kara without her following up with an interrogation of you." He wasn't as tired now that she took up half of his cramped bed. He had only been seeing Kara for a month, but wasn't willing to discuss with her the companionship he had with Brisethi.

"I haven't even spoken with him in months," she casually replied. Though tired and comfortable as she was, she sat back up and crawled off of his bed to walk to the door. "I suppose if I were Kara, I wouldn't appreciate my presence here, either."

The officers in training were allowed one day off per week to visit their family and loved ones or to just relax in their quarters in the Citadel. While Etyne spent his days with his mother or Kara, or Antuni when he wasn't out to sea, Brisethi took the chance to visit her parents or Korteni. When she was on good terms with Joss every other few months, she would visit him in his house by the shoreline. Though, a lot of their time was spent arguing, she still enjoyed taking his boat out to sea with him to go fishing or taking a carriage into the city for a fancy dinner at renowned restaurants. Sometimes, they would spend the evening playing with his muscular dogs in the middle of grassy fields, watching the stars.

"Quick, make a wish!" Brisethi shouted when they watched a star pierce the night sky at an incredible rate.

"My wish already came true," Joss smiled to her, planting a kiss to her lips. "What is your wish?"

She didn't want to ruin the moment by telling him she wished for world domination, but she wasn't about to lie to him, either. "Ah, you know, the same thing I've always wished for." She smiled and returned the kiss, leaving him recollecting her past wishes.

-:- -:- -:-

Etyne rarely visited any of Res'Baveth's fine bookstores. When there was a book he needed to read for class, the Citadel library provided it, free of charge. But he wasn't in need of a book for class this time. Brisethi's birthday was only a week away and learned that her favorite fantasy author had just printed his newest novel.

He heard the abrupt chuckle of a woman when he picked up the book. He arched a brow in her direction when he realized she was chuckling at him.

"My apologies, it's just that, most fans of his work wear very large spectacles and are extremely overweight," the woman told him, gleaming at his fit build.

He half smiled at the thought of the complete opposite description of this author's particular fan. "It's not for me," he declared when his eyes met hers.

"You're Kiaran?" the woman took a few steps toward him to have a closer look at his eyes.

He was used to the unwanted attention and simply stared blankly out of the window behind her until she was ready to leave him be.

"My apologies, I don't mean to be rude," she softly spoke and broke eye contact. "My name is Serythe."

"I'm Etyne," he muttered. He wasn't in the business of making new friends at the moment, especially since Kara had decided to end their relationship two weeks ago to pursue someone else. Brisethi's usual rum and fireworks to cheer him up had left him in bed his entire day off. A week later, when he spent his last day off in bed the entire day again, he couldn't blame it on rum and fireworks that time. He needed to stop with his self-pity and found himself at the bookstore if only to be outside away from his room at the Citadel.

"If you're not into fantasy books, then what *are* you interested in?" Serythe pressed on, following him to the register.

Etyne slightly sighed then glanced at the woman who he couldn't deny was very attractive. Her mahogany hair curled at the ends in layers from her shoulder down to the middle of her back the same as Brisethi's hairstyle. He paused in his thoughts when he realized he was comparing her to his dearest friend. *Forgive me, 'Sethi, you've suddenly given me different standards as of late*, he thought to himself. Since Antuni wasn't around as much while he was on sea duty, he had unintentionally replaced him with Brisethi. Unknowingly, he sought out his favorite traits of her in other women instead of having Antuni around for his opinion.

"I don't actually read that often," Etyne finally admitted after paying for the book. "I'm in school at the moment and my hobbies include mostly studying and mentoring."

"Oh, what college are you attending?" Serythe asked.

Etyne cleared his throat but still mumbled, "Dominion Citadel."

"I beg your pardon?" She wasn't quite sure she heard him correctly.

"I am not in college. I am attending officer training at the Dominion Citadel," he reiterated rather brashly.

Serythe smiled despite his annoyed demeanor. "There's nothing shameful about the military life. It's not as if you had moved back in with your mother to read these fantasy books created for the simple-minded in hopes of writing your own-"

"It was nice meeting you," he interrupted and proceeded to the exit. Though fantasy novels were not his interest, the term, "simple-minded" was not a term he would use to define Brisethi.

"Oh, I didn't mean to offend," Serythe called after. "Please, let me buy you a coffee, or a tea?" She gestured to the cozy cafe at the entrance of the bookstore. Various plush chairs and wooden tables were low to the ground while barstools neatly lined the counter much like the taverns.

"That's generous of you, but-"

"I have a paper due in two weeks about anything that has changed my perspective of anything, really. I have a feeling you could help me with such a task," she persuaded, slowly walking to the bistro table for two at the window.

Etyne reconsidered his evening plans. Ordinarily, he would be helping Brisethi with her studies but today was their day off from school and training - she was out with Joss this day and he told himself he wouldn't sleep away the afternoon from boredom and self-pity again of losing Kara. The sprinkles of rain quickly became heavy which only encouraged him to stay in the library until it cleared. "I suppose a cup of tea wouldn't delay too much of my studying."

Despite her first undelightful impression, Serythe turned out to be enjoyable company to Etyne. She allowed him to discuss his experiences in officer training while she attempted to compare them to her own experience at the college. Only their Resarian History and Language Arts classes were vaguely similar to one another. She wasn't anywhere near to taking the physics and advanced mathematics classes the Dominion had forced their officers to enroll in.

"Wow, so not only was Resarian your first language, but you're fluent in Kiaran *and* the common language of Trycinea continent?" Serythe asked with wide eyes.

Etyne nodded after a sip of his spiced tea. "The Dominion dedicates a certain amount of hours per week to learning Kiaran during our enlisted expedition for all four years. It isn't hard to learn considering Kiaran and Resarian derived from ancient Sariadnese. However, common Trycinean is a tad harder. Everything we learned in grade school is basically forgotten. Our first three years in officer training were spent learning the Trycinean language two days a week with one more year to go."

Serythe slowly spoke to him in broken common Trycinean, hoping to impress him. "I mostly have forget what was learned to us - no, *kigat*, teached to us in grade school. But my tutor is, ah, is teaching me again."

Etyne raised his brow to her broken attempt and heavy Resarian accent. "Ah, you'll get there one day," he retorted in fluent common tongue with a condescending smirk.

Returning to their native language she stammered, "Hey, I really want to continue this. You've changed my perspective about Dominion Officers - I honestly thought you were all just a bunch of know-nothing brutes that just want to keep a war going for all of eternity," she chuckled nervously when Etyne remained expressionless. "Would you want to meet again?"

He ran his finger along the handle of his teacup while staring into the emptiness. Marinelle had betrayed his trust, followed by Kara breaking his heart after an entire year with her. He was emotionally drained at the moment from the past two women, feeling as empty as his cup. With spirit's fortune, he would soon graduate from officer training and move on before anyone else could have the chance to abandon him again. Since Brisethi was always gone on their one day off per week, he decided he could use Serythe's company every so often after all.

"Same time, same place one week from today?" He suggested to her.

She nodded with a smile and stood. "Until next time, Etyne."

When she gave him a loose hug, he lightly hugged her back. Her frame was small and yet again, caught himself comparing her to the strong, friendly hugs of Brisethi's dense, muscular frame.

-:- -:- -:-

It was the one day a week the junior officers were allowed to sleep in past hour four. The abrupt knocking, however, had Brisethi startled from her deep sleep at seventh hour. "By the damned dragon spirits, what?!" She shouted when she answered the door to her quarters.

Etyne was standing before her with a wide grin on his face. "Happy Birthday!" He covered her revealing, low-cut nightwear by pressing his gift to her upon her chest. "Get your clothes on, I'm taking you out for birthday breakfast."

"What is going on right now? It isn't a holiday!" Brisethi groggily replied while stumbling toward her shared bathroom. Her achy body struggled to wake and her pounding headache made her cranky.

"Wow, 'Sethi, I'm hurt. Have you already forgotten the past three years of our Citadel gatherings?"

"No," she continued from the washroom. "Our game ran late last night into overtime, then my team took me out for drinks for my birthday. I'm certain I've only been asleep two hours." She groaned from the hot water she splashed to her face, careful to not press too hard on her newest injuries.

Brisethi threw on appropriate clothes while remembering that no one enjoyed holidays during the expedition. However, at recollecting the past three years at the Citadel with Etyne, he had a terrible habit of waking her up earlier on any holiday for breakfast before they would part ways for the afternoon. Her favorite holiday to wake up for was winter solstice when they would take a carriage to his mother's house where Drienna would make breakfast for them both. Summer Solstice breakfast was cooked and eaten at her parents house followed by a splash in the sea before parting ways for the evening to their lovers.

She was more awake by the time they sat at their usual booth in their usual breakfast cafe. "Ooh, what is it, a book?" she excitedly asked at testing the weight of her wrapped gift. She watched Etyne nod with a smile and began unwrapping it. "Terenth Gon Ikan wrote a sixth novel? How did you know? How did I *not* know?"

Etyne beamed at her excited face as she studied the newest novel, *Souls of the Forgotten*, from her favorite author. He finally stopped averting his eyes to ask about her darkened eye and cut on her cheek. "I don't recall leaving marks on your face this week, 'Sethi. Who did that?" He tried not to appear too concerned while cutting at his flatcakes.

Brisethi tenderly touched at her new wounds on her face. "Ah, the command doesn't allow healers on site for *hak'ii* games," she casually replied. "It would only encourage more fights."

Etyne laughed in relief. "For a moment there, I was worried you'd found a new sparring partner in Joss."

"Spirits no, I would destroy him," she attempted to smirk despite the cut on her cheek.

Their holiday breakfast continued with their usual banter and reminiscence of past holidays until they parted ways to their own afternoons.

Serythe and Etyne didn't spend much time at the coffee shop until he was invited over to her parents' manor. He was actually intimidated by such grandeur of the mansion and her incredibly wealthy parents. Butlers and maids tended to their meal and by the end of the evening, the two were walking under the stars in her own garden. She used her mystic to create water for the flowers then turned the remaining water into mist and fog. She kept the fog at ground level to create a mysterious environment throughout the pathways of the garden. The favored flower of most Resarians, the Nightsparks, glistened in cerulean luminescence, piercing the fog where they lined the cobblestone paths. "What is your mystic?" she asked. "Or, do you even have one since you're only half-Resarian? How old are you? How old will you live?"

"I have one, yes, thanks to my Resarian mother and I will live at least another eight hundred years. My spirit is a protective mystic wielder. I can shield others from projectiles, distort the air around us to appear nearly invisible. But mainly, I can turn into my corporeal form to quickly escape or traverse across great distances in the fraction of the time it takes on horseback," he explained.

"Mystical traverse, wow," she whispered. Spellbound by his physique, his mystics, and his mind, Serythe entangled her fingers into his. "I want to see you again, Etyne," she blatantly stated. She had become inured to demanding what she wanted and acquiring it.

So long as she didn't interfere with his own studies or demand too much of his free time, he obliged to her request. "I'm only available one day a week," he warned her from beneath his brow.

"That's fair," she softly told him, losing herself in his eyes.

"And I graduate next year which means I most likely won't be stationed in the city anymore," he added his hint that this would be temporary.

Serythe pressed herself into Etyne, running her hands along his sculpted arms and shoulders. "I would wait for you to return."

Heard that before, he thought to himself. He was empty of sentiment and wanted only to take Serythe for the night. Whatever she

Canvas

wanted, emotionally, she would not acquire from him. He was only a shell. He kissed her on the lips as they gave in to their shortly awaited desires of one another.

-:- -:- -:-

During the winter months when it was too cold to venture out, Brisethi taught Joss some of the card games she'd learned from other military members or she would drag him out to ice skate with her and help her practice for her command *ha'kii* games.

Every now and then they took the time to travel to Korteni's village of Worgale when she wasn't out at sea. Brisethi and Joss set out in a carriage one morning when the sun had finally peaked out after days of snow. The rays sparkled on the powdery white snow, and the faintest hint of spring was in the air.

Joss directed the carriage out onto the road, the runners making fresh tracks. He happily breathed in the cool air, bundled up in the blankets with the woman he loved by his side.

"Ohh," Brisethi said excitedly and pointing, "look at the blossoms!" Spiny trees with pale pink flowers lined the lane. "That's my favorite part of this season." She leaned up against Joss, staring all around, eagerly taking in the pretty scenery around her as they traveled. She wished she had her paints.

"Mine too," Joss said quietly.

Korteni welcomed them brightly when they arrived, hugging Brisethi and smiling kindly at Joss. "How was the journey? I hope it wasn't too cold. Come in, there's so much food to be eaten!" she said, not giving them a chance to respond.

They spent a happy day eating smoked salmon with sweet potato fries, drinking wine and ale, and catching up. Korteni always had plenty of sea stories to share now that she was already a First Class Petty Officer. "We were sitting in the mess deck when all of a sudden the alarm sounded. We didn't even have a chance to react before we hit something so hard that the stew flew all over the place!"

"No way!" Brisethi said, "what happened?"

"Apparently," Korteni continued conspiratorially, "the Nav on watch fell asleep." She started laughing, "Oh, you should have seen it! The CO standing there screaming at Nav, his uniform covered in the stew. He was so mad, he actually took a piece of the potato stuck to his shirt and threw it in the Nav's face!"

Brisethi's jaw dropped for a second before she burst out laughing with Korteni. "What does 'Nav' mean?" Joss asked, feeling a little out of place.

"Navigation officer," Brisethi answered quickly before continuing her conversation. "Sometimes I wish I would have gone Navy but then I remember the angry Chiefs and Officers I've had the pleasure of 'meeting' and I'm suddenly thankful I chose Army."

"Ah, you get used to constantly being chewed out for every little thing," Korteni replied. "Besides, the kinship of navy comrades after the reprimands unite us all as family. It's something that I noticed parts of your army doesn't have. The females of the army we've taken on board are not the friendliest, especially to other females."

Brisethi sighed, "I know what you mean, I've had the hardest time befriending them when they introduce themselves stating irrelevant quips such as, 'I don't get along with other females'." She swallowed a large gulp of wine in annoyance of those types of people. "Wanna know what I said to the third female to say that during her promotion board? *Promotion* board!"

"What did you say?" Korteni eagerly asked.

"I told that female sergeant, 'Neither I, nor the Dominion, give bull manure that you have issues being civil among those you consider to be your competition. As long as you're in the Dominion, we're sisters in arms and you're going to treat them a such'." Brisethi was intolerant of the narrow-minded.

"She must have *hated* being chewed out by a junior officer still in school," Korteni chuckled at the expense of her friend. "You should have walked out of her board and given four rings to the bell, 'ding-ding, ding-ding', 'First Lieutenant Sen Asel departing!' ding-ding, ding-ding," she shouted in an inner city dialect through her cupped hand to imitate shipboard announcements.

Brisethi buried her face in her hands and muttered through a chuckle, "Stupid navy jokes."

It was well into the evening when Joss and Brisethi made the return trip. Brisethi was finally happy that Joss had given up on trying to influence his lifestyle on hers and instead supported her ambitions. His change in priorities kept her from straying away from him as easily.

In his bed that night, Brisethi crawled on top of Joss, kissing his neck and chest until he started removing her shirt.

"Who did this to you?" He asked when he laid eyes on Brisethi's bruised ribs.

"Oh this," she gently touched her abdomen after returning a kiss on his lips. "Just some roughing from the last *hak'ii* game," she lied.

"I don't believe that. You're just an overly padded goalie, nobody roughs up the goalie-"

"Excuse you-I'm only the reason our team is undefeated! And that's why other teams try to take me down!" she shouted rather defensively.

"This isn't from roughing, this is a serious injury-" he was cut off.

"Acolyte Roz is in the south for mystic instructor duty and Acolyte Krain had the day off so I didn't get a chance to get this healed right away. This is nothing compared to the marks I usually get during the week that you never see," she admitted.

"Who did this, 'Sethi? I'll kill him!" Joss was outraged. He stood up, no longer in the mood for intimacy.

"Could you, uh, calm the fuck down, Joss? It's just a bruise!" Brisethi said quickly. "Like I said, the healer wasn't in yesterday or else you would have never known. We go through bouts like this every other day," she replied. "I slipped up, is all, and I ate his foot – with my stomach." She chuckled nervously.

"This isn't funny. How many times does this happen?" He interrogated her. "And why would you lie to me about this? What are you hiding?"

"By the spirits, Joss, I do more damage to him than he does to me if it makes you feel any better!" She was exaggerating about her strength as she threw her clothes back on. "And I lied because I wanted to avoid *this* discussion."

"So it's the same person every time?" He towered over her when she sat up on his bed. "Is it your Kiaran friend?"

"What if it is?" she hissed.

"I will fucking destroy him!" his temper flared as he searched for his clothes.

"I would *love* to see you try," she taunted, wondering why she couldn't simmer her temper. "Thanks for fucking ruining my one day I get to spend with you this week," she muttered darkly before she stormed out of the bedroom and into the dining room.

"How often does he do this?" Joss followed her, refusing to drop the topic. He was protective of his lover and loathed the fact that people intentionally beat her for "training" purposes.

"Joss! It's called combatives - I went all training expedition doing this and it's what we do every other day. It's what I will be doing every other day until I retire!"

"How can anyone stand to just strike you? How heartless does a man have to be to bring pain to you?" He was genuinely worried about her health but the jealousy in the tone of his voice told her otherwise.

"Oh, so am *I* heartless for succumbing others to just as much pain?"

"You can't possibly deal as much damage to a man that he can to you-"

"Don't tempt me," she deeply stated, cutting him off. She hadn't realized that her hands had become fists in an attempt to lure him to fight her. Her aggressive temper was taking charge of her rationality. "I may not have the physical strength of a well-trained man, but I can destroy the soul of anyone who dares cross me."

It was a dark side of her that Joss had never seen. He was used to her over-confidence while growing up with her, but he had never seen her ferocity thrown back at him with threatened hate. She was no longer the cheery, loving girl he had loved over a decade ago. "You should leave, 'Sethi," he reluctantly muttered.

"You're right," she sulked, petting his happy dog before gathering her things. She didn't dare look back as she opened the door, but barely forced a whisper, "I'm sorry."

The cool air soothed her temper, and she briefly wrestled with the idea of returning and giving Joss a real apology, but remembering his words just made her angry all over again. She took one last look over her shoulder at the house and set off for the long journey back to the Citadel.

Chapter II

Livian was overjoyed when Acolyte Elion Hadson returned from his six months of training an expedition on how to summon their mystics. She ran to him before he could place his packs down and leaped into his welcoming arms.

"I've missed you so much," Livian mumbled into his neck.

"I missed you, too, my dear sweet Livian. I read each your letters at least ten times a night!" Elion replied and kissed her forehead.

Livian found her footing and stared into his bright green eyes. She couldn't just remind him that her birthday was two months ago without sounding awkward. Instead, she reached up to him, and brought his face to hers. She felt his lips kiss hers.

Elion held her close once more, needing no reminder of what they had been waiting for. "Let me get settled in and cleaned up. I smell like an army," he chuckled. "Then we can go downtown for a belated birthday dinner."

Livian grinned and reluctantly broke from the embrace. "Alright!" She followed him to his living quarters two floors above the officer candidates rooms. Since her last birthday, she was relocated to the more spacious quarters of the top floor as well, complete with a kitchenette for permanent acolytes and citadel workers.

She sat at his dining table while he readied himself for the evening. Her heart skipped a beat when the door to his room opened. She stood and stared at him longingly. "Elion," she quietly spoke. "I don't want to go downtown."

"Oh? What would you rather do instead?" Elion asked.

"I thought you'd never ask!" Livian replied and playfully ran to him once more, pushing him back into his bedroom. They fell onto his bed and traded kisses. "Elion," she continued. "Will it hurt?"

He smiled while they began taking each other's clothes off. "No, my love. Two spirits who genuinely love one another will not experience discomfort."

-:- -:- -:-

A frosty breeze blew the ocean spray up onto the docks, nearly drenching Livian where she stood trying to read the sign that kept swaying in the wind. Her hand drifted to the pocket of her overcoat where two letters lay safely out of reach of the salty water. One was a list of supplies Acolyte Roz needed her to fetch for his trip to help the next group of Dominion trainees with their mystic training. The other was what had brought her to the docks.

Her ears began stinging from the cold air. She decided not to put it off any longer and opened the door. The light was dim inside, but a roaring fire in the center of the room cast a glow all around. Several faces looked up as Livian walked inside, but only one mattered to her.

"Liv!" a woman squealed, rushing toward her and enveloping her in her arms.

"Hello, Bri," Livian responded cautiously.

Ibrienne's excited expression fell only slightly, but she smiled at the younger girl and pulled her to a table at the other side of the room from where she had greeted Livian. "I was so afraid you might not come, and we leave in a couple of days, so I was worried I might not get to see you." Ibrienne's words fell out of her mouth in a rush.

Livian regarded her old friend with the slightest trace of a smile on her lips. Some things would never change. In the glow from the fire, Livian was still able to observe the changes in Ibrienne's physical appearance. She had lost more weight, but not in a necessarily good way. Her face did not look as full, and there were dark rings under her eyes, like she hadn't been sleeping well. Suddenly, all the bitterness Livian had felt at being left alone evaporated in concern. "Bri, are you alright?"

With a smile, Ibrienne waved a hand as if to dismiss it all. "Oh, I'm fine. We had a rough journey back, that's all. Ship life is not what I thought it would be. Nin isn't a bad captain by any means," she hurriedly amended with a furtive glance at the other side of the room. She shook her head and changed the subject, beginning to drill Livian on what she had been up to.

Livian obliged willingly, happy to share with someone her triumphs and all she had learned while earning her keep at the Citadel. "They wanted to send me back to the orphanage when it reopened, but Acolyte Roz said I had exceeded expectations beyond even what his apprentices did, so he vouched to keep me on until I am able to enlist."

Ibrienne beamed with pride. "You're still planning on enlisting?"

"I don't know," Livian said, shrugging but happy to see Ibrienne look more like her old self. "I've become involved with one of the acolytes."

"What do you mean, 'involved'?" Ibrienne asked.

Livian grinned widely. "We're in love, Bri. I can't imagine going four years without him. I have never been so happy," she didn't mean to boast. "I would love for you two to meet."

A group stood up and walked to the door near where Livian and Ibrienne sat. Livian saw Ibrienne give them an almost imperceptible nod. Then she turned back to Livian and reached across the table, tenderly brushing a strand of Livian's golden hair away from her face. Closing her eyes, Livian took several deep breaths.

"I'm so happy for you, my dear little Livi." Ibrienne's voice was so quiet that the younger woman had to strain to hear her. When she spoke again, her voice took on a hushed resonance. "You are so strong, so brave. No matter what, your resilience will always see you through." Suddenly, her tone was more forceful as she glanced at the door," Promise me that you'll never forget yourself. Never compromise your beliefs."

Livian's eyebrows furrowed, but she agreed. "I promise."

Ibrienne's intense expression relaxed a little. "I have to get going. But you be careful, okay?" They stood, and this time Livian fully returned the embrace. She whispered in Livian's ear then hurried out the door.

Livian stood stunned, then turned and ran out the door, pushing her hood up over her head as she went. It was too late. The docks were crowded with the crew of a ship that was preparing to depart. She scanned the crowd, but she couldn't find the brown furs that Ibrienne had been wearing. After several long minutes, Livian turned and began walking away from the piers. She pulled out the other envelope and started to plot the route back to the Citadel that would enable her to pick up as many of the supplies as she could.

As she headed up the stone stairs, her eyes began to sting, and not just from the cold air.

-:- -:- -:-

"Antuni, his new girlfriend, and Brisethi?" Drienna asked her son about his invited guests, gesturing for him to give over the handful of herbs he held.

"Ah, not 'Sethi this time, I couldn't find her this morning. I invited Serythe," Etyne replied.

Drienna tried not to scowl and turned to concentrate on the pasta. "Serythe isn't the most sociable girl you've brought over," she commented, trying to make her voice light. "Kara was sweet, however."

"Why would you bring up Kara?" Etyne whined and leaned against the doorframe of the small kitchen to get out of his mother's way. "I know that Serythe is on the quiet side. Her sense of humor isn't exactly the same as ours, but she's incredibly smart - smarter than me."

"She has more knowledge than you about uninteresting facts, Etyne. That doesn't make her smarter than you," she stated matter-of-factly. "I'm sorry I couldn't afford to put you through a nice college like the ones she has attended," she added. She waved one hand at the cabinets, keeping her eyes on the sauce, and Etyne obediently began withdrawing the dishes.

"Please don't ever apologize for my decision to enlist and commission into the Dominion," Etyne retorted sharply. "I can very well pay for higher education now, and I probably will once I rank up more. I've met some remarkable people in the military. I wouldn't trade that experience for anything else," he replied in a final tone as he laid the silver on the table.

Before his mother could reply, there was a quick knock on the door followed by the click of it opening as Antuni let himself and his companion in. Etyne rushed to greet his old friend.

"Hey, man, how is officer life treating you?" Antuni asked as he embraced his childhood friend. "You've been hitting the gymnasium a bit hard, haven't you? Just when I thought your ego couldn't get any bigger."

"Ah, you know I always enjoy a groping from a sailor," Etyne joked back, swatting Petty Officer First Class Antuni Crommick's hands from his shoulders and chest.

Antuni shrugged, "Someday you'll be as big as me, but today is not that day." He held out his arm with a flourish to introduce his partner, Alise, to both Etyne and Ms. Vorsen. Alise colored with embarrassment but smiled sweetly and thanked the Vorsens for allowing her to join them for solstice.

"Is 'Sethi on her way? She was here early last year," Antuni asked, pulling out a chair for Alise.

"*Serythe* is on her way," Etyne corrected.

Antuni dropped his head in disappointment. "Rest in peace your failed existence. I wanted Alise and 'Sethi to meet, to help share our expedition stories! Your boring teacher friend doesn't even laugh at any of my jokes. I could trade insults all night with 'Sethi!"

Etyne arched his brow, "First off, she's not a teacher-"

"It's alright, Antuni, I was just as disappointed in his choice of guest as you were, even Kara would have been a more delightful guest," Drienna interjected then retreated to the kitchen once more.

"You both are being pretty harsh-" Etyne started to say before being interrupted by Antuni laughing abruptly.

"Nah, we'll give her another chance, right Ms. Vorsen?" Antuni called out.

Etyne understood why they were both hoping for Brisethi, or even his last lover, Kara, who could make anyone smile by entering a room. He had wished Brisethi could be there as well to share winter solstice dinner but in a desperate act, agreed to continue a relationship with Serythe.

Etyne watched as Alise was quick to offer help to his mother bring the food out to the table, the way Brisethi usually did. Alise had quickly adapted to their family the same as Antuni, the same as Brisethi.

After a light knock at the door, Etyne opened it to greet Serythe. As he had expected, she was dressed in the latest fashion of long coat over her wool dress. Her hat and scarf were trimmed in white fur with gray ringlets; that of a young Mira Cat. He took her coat to hang with the others as she rolled her eyes at Antuni's greeting of "meow".

Etyne shot Antuni a glance. "Thanks for coming down, Serythe," Etyne quietly said, knowing she wasn't fond of his mother's neighborhood so close to the inner city. Res'Baveth didn't have slums, but there were parts where the families of lower income resided, where the crime rate was higher such as Antuni and Etyne's homes.

She gave him a kiss on his cheek. "Next year, we dine at my folks' manor," she quietly chimed. He hoped to the spirits he would have his own division to take on an expedition by then. She awkwardly stood by, wondering what she could offer even if she lacked skills of cooking and setting the table.

Dinner went on not quite as awkwardly as Etyne thought it would. Antuni spent the evening making Alise and Drienna laugh at his jabs at Etyne, who smiled genially but continued to try to include Serythe. Antuni kept making a point to bring up their memories at expedition training, particularly the ones that involved Brisethi. "She was trying to tackle you so hard and instead she tickled you until you released the ball and fell to the ground," Antuni laughed as he reminisced one of their games of *Chel'kan*.

"She's pretty terrible at *Chel'kan*, heh, but she's a fierce goalie for the command *hak'ii* team," Etyne added.

"Of course she is! All she has to do is scream at anyone skating near her with the puck and they drop from fright," Antuni chuckled.

Antuni and Alise insisted that Drienna enjoy a drink with Etyne and Serythe and let them clear up the dishes. "Really, Mrs. V, it's the least we can do after that incredible meal!" He was rewarded with a warm smile and a heartfelt thanks.

She sat quietly in the worn but still comfortable chair and listened as her son and Serythe debated the merits of Toliesto's *A History of Sariadne*. The conversation itself did not intrigue her, but she loved watching the intensity behind her son's convictions and dimly wondered if she had been wrong about this young woman who sparked a side of Etyne she had not seen for a long while.

-:- -:- -:-

"Stay with me tonight, why do you want to be alone in your quarters?" Serythe asked when the carriage parked at the Citadel's gate.

"I haven't seen my best friend all day and I still need to give her her gift," Etyne replied, saddened that they skipped winter solstice breakfast this year.

Serythe crossed her arms. "When do I get to meet this best friend of yours?"

"Uh, she has a game next week if you'd like to join me in watching how absolutely terrifying she is?" He suggested, unsure he wanted the two to interact. The two women were complete opposites in ways of personality and interests and feared they would clash just as Serythe and Antuni had.

Serythe sighed at the thought of watching a sporting event, compounded with her annoyance that he was rejecting her for the night. "Fine."

Etyne was unsure of her sudden irritability and exited the carriage.

"Antuni wanted me to tell you he says 'hey' and to stop being a stranger," Etyne told Brisethi when she opened her door.

"Well whenever he stops going out to sea he can come visit me," Brisethi shut her door behind him after he let himself in. She shivered slightly from the burst of cold air that had followed him in from the hall. "Did you just get in? It's an hour past curfew, how did the guards not turn you in?" she asked.

Etyne sat on her bed and placed her gift on her pillow. "It's the weirdest thing, 'Sethi, I possess this anomaly that allows me to turn incorporeal and quickly travel great distances in a manner of seconds."

Brisethi glared at his sarcasm.

"I can't help it Serythe was reluctant to let me leave the carriage," he jested with a grin.

"I'm never riding in a carriage again, thanks for that," she snidely remarked and handed him his festively wrapped gift, complete with curled ribbons.

"Not at all what you think happened," Etyne's grin vanished. "How was your day? I came by this morning to wake you for holiday breakfast but you were already gone."

"Oh, I never came back to my room from last night and then as usual, got into an argument with Joss this afternoon and came home early this evening," she somberly replied. She left out the details about Joss forgetting to put any effort in for her for Winter Solstice, so much as cook her breakfast as a gift. He figured that the amazing copulation they had the night before should have been a thoughtful enough gift.

"Why didn't you just come to my mother's? Everyone wanted to see you, 'Sethi."

She shrugged and rubbed at her teary eyes not wanting to discuss her rotten Winter Solstice.

"I really wish you two would just put this out of its misery," Etyne sighed at her distress of a broken relationship.

"I really wish you would stay out of it," she muttered, instantly regretting snapping at him.

"Should I leave you be?" he stood to make his way to the door.

"No," she quickly replied in a cracked voice. "I'm sorry, I'm irritable. Please, open your gift," she smiled to him.

He sat back down on her bed and unraveled the neatly wrapped gift. Three ancient coins fell into his lap along with the protective cloth that surrounded them. He stared in wonder, speechless. "'Sethi, you didn't," he finally managed to say. He picked up one of the coins and examined it closely. It was worn, but he could still recognize the cog shape imprinted in the coin. He held the ancient Kiaran coins gingerly, as though they might crumble in his hand. They were the Kiaran coins from the time they still lived on Sariadne with the Resarians. Dated over three thousand years ago he was barely able to translate the ancient text. He cautiously re-wrapped the cloth around his precious gift and stared at Brisethi. "These are replicas, right?"

Brisethi shook her head. "Why would I ever buy you fake crap? They're real. I bought them from the antique st-"

"I know where you got them," he cut her off, "and I wish you hadn't spent this much on them - for me," he said, pulling the cloth aside again to examine them.

"Trust me, I spent more on Joss," she muttered. "I don't really spend much on myself so I saved up frakshins for the people I care about."

Etyne looked up at her longingly and brought her in to hug her tightly. "I love them, 'Sethi. Thank you."

"That's right you do!" she grinned happily, her previous annoyance disappearing as she broke from their friendly embrace. She then started to open her gift from him. The smile on her face widened even larger at seeing the fragile book in her lap. "Etyne!" she gasped. "Where did you even find this?" In her hands, she held an original print of a surviving Resarian tome on dragons, also dated from thousands of years ago. Their original ink paintings still visible thanks to the protective mystics of bookkeepers.

"The bookstore, where else?" he smiled as she wrapped her arms around him once more.

Brisethi looked at her pocketwatch. "Eh, I have to get going. My father's on leave for the holidays which means he's downtown drinking his sorrows away at the tavern. Someone has to ensure he gets home since my mother will most likely get lost."

"What sorrows? He has a wonderful family," Etyne questioned her.

Brisethi shrugged a bit. "My mother is sometimes a bit off, very jealous and paranoid, often times drives him to drink. I might have helped fuel his drinking as a rebel teenage child. Or he's just your typical drunken sailor. Would you like to sneak out with me to hoist him into a carriage?"

"Sure," Etyne replied and reached for his coat.

-:- -:- -:-

"This sport is barbaric, I can't believe I let you talk me into this," Serythe whined among the loud and drunken crowd at the city's outdoor ice arena.

Etyne nudged her. "Nah, it's fun and takes a tremendous amount of skill."

"They start fighting every fifteen minutes, how is that skillful?" she asked just as a fourth fight of the game broke out on the ice.

The crowd was on their feet when one of the Citadel's rival team members pushed their goalie, Sen Asel, into the divider wall as she was retrieving the puck.

Etyne cheered her on when she began landing fists on the opponent. Her masked helmet was ripped from her head while the rival member was pushed down to the ice until the referees finally parted them. Only one more fight occurred in the remaining period.

The referee blew the whistle to end the final period. The Citadel Storm had defeated the Brigade Bears two to zero.

Most of the teams left the ice while others stayed out to greet their family or fans. Brisethi heard her name shouted and skated, with *ha'kii* stick in her gloved hand, toward the voice.

Etyne could barely make out Brisethi's facial features through the thick wires of her goalie mask until she finally removed her helmet. Her face was flush while her burgundy hair fell in sweaty, messy waves on her shoulders and chest. She smiled at approaching her classmate.

"Etyne! I thought you were going out tonight," she excitedly greeted him. Her ice skates had her standing as tall as him while her padded gear made her seem thicker than him.

"I *am* out, with Serythe. I wanted you to finally meet her," he beamed, leaning against the short wall that divided the audience from the ice.

Serythe peeked out from behind Etyne and stood beside him. Hesitantly, he began the introduction he'd been putting off for months. "Sethi, this is Serythe."

Brisethi wiped a drop of blood from her nose with her sleeve, removed her gloves, then held a clammy hand out to Serythe. "I've heard so much about you!"

Serythe's face was one of disgust at the bloody, sweaty, woman before her. Reluctantly, she allowed her fingertips to take Brisethi's hand in greeting. "I...so have I," was all she could muster.

Etyne stared blankly at both women until speaking once more. "Well that went as awkward as I knew it would - Hey, 'Sethi, want to get drinks with us at Mammoth Tavern?"

"Shit yes! Let me go wash up, I'll meet you there," Brisethi excitedly skated away.

At the tavern, Serythe sat across from Etyne in a cozy booth, sipping at her fruity beverage.

"Does this mean I won't be expecting you to watch my *chel'kan* games?" Etyne asked before gulping down his first ale.

Serythe shook her head. "Sorry, no. I find competitive sports to be mundane. However, if you pick up a musical instrument, I will watch you perform in a symphony."

"Oh, I love symphonies!" Brisethi chimed in and took a seat next to Etyne. She no longer lingered of sweat, but a hint of blossoms scented the air at her presence. "I went to see the university band perform at the amphitheatre just a month ago with a classmate of mine."

"Really? Which university was it?" Serythe asked.

"Which classmate?" Etyne curiously asked.

Brisethi placed her order of ale to the waitress before answering. "Oh, I don't remember the university name, but the composer was Mr. Valinsen-"

"Yes! He's our music professor at Malvikai University," Serythe excitedly replied.

"Who did you see this with?" Etyne continued to quietly interrogate.

"What songs did they play, do you remember?" Serythe asked, disregarding Etyne.

"I only remember the one, it was so beautiful, the piano melodies with the violin in the background," she closed her eyes at recalling the lovely tune. "*A Divine Ascension* was the name."

"Ah, yes, that is a very complex masterpiece," Serythe replied, finding an unexpected gratification in the conversation with Etyne's acquaintance.

"Do you play an instrument?" Brisethi asked, rather than answering Etyne.

Serythe nodded while taking a sip of her sweet beverage. She glanced up to study Brisethi now that she was cleaned up with her hair brushed. When she noticed the woman was as fit as Etyne, she wondered when she had time to read the fantasy novels she loved so much. "I play the violin, the flute, and the piano," she replied. "What do you play?"

"Oh, I don't play anything, sadly. Someday I'd like to learn the piano, though!" Brisethi replied, stretching her arms above her head to relieve her sore muscles from the intense sport. "Hey, what do you get when you drop a piano on an army base?"

"Um," Serythe pursed her lips in thought. "I've heard this one!"

"Oh, no," Etyne placed his forehead in his hands.

Brisethi paid the waitress and took a gulp of her ale before answering. "A flat major."

Serythe's laugh was infectious while Etyne sighed loudly.

Brisethi took another drink of her ale before turning to Etyne. "I'm sorry, you were asking me something?"

Etyne met Brisethi's eyes for a moment. "I, it's just, you never go out with the other classmates," he stammered. "I was wondering who you went to the performance with."

"Brisethi, what do you get when you drop a piano down a mine shaft?" Serythe asked.

"A flat minor!" she shouted to Serythe then returned her glance to Etyne. "Avacyn, the ensign. She's also the captain of my team."

Serythe's high-pitched laugh drowned out Brisethi's giggle.

"Ensign Avacyn Spire? She hates everyone, I'm surprised she tolerates even you," Etyne chuckled lightly.

"Uh, when you're the reason your team is undefeated, of course she opened up to me. A little more than I expected if you know what I mean," she said with a wink then finished her ale.

"Spirits, 'Sethi, you know better!" Etyne lectured.

Chapter III

"I understand that this is short notice but the Veteran's Assisted Living Home is looking for a volunteer or two for tomorrow; specifically a destructive spirit," announced Lt. Commander Olsine to the class before dismissing them. She let her eyes fall on Second Lieutenant Brisethi Sen Asel until she met the gaze.

"Oh, um, hunting down rodents, Ma'am?" Brisethi asked in return. The rest of the students tried to stifle their laughter.

Lt. Commander Olsine dismissed the class and asked Brisethi to meet her at the podium to discuss what she had been tasked with. She had already planned her day off to reunite with Joss but didn't dream of ever telling her instructor superior. Joss would just have to understand. "Sen Asel, have you ever been to the Home or know what it even is?" Brisethi was reminded of her mother when she was trying to get Brisethi to do anything remotely domestic that didn't involve fire.

"I haven't been there, but I do know it's where our military veterans who have no family are placed when they reach age eight hundred," she replied.

"And you understand why they are placed there at that age?" Olsine asked again.

"So that they don't lose control of their mystics and destroy the city."

"Correct." Olsine's voice softened as she continued, "Mystisomnia will happen to all of us, but most of us have family that can, *take care* of us. The caretakers of the VAL Home aren't commissioned to actually sever their spirit, only to alleviate their mystics. Under Resarian law, it is the Dominion personnel that shall be tasked to send a waning spirit to the Sea of Renewal."

She stood a little straighter, "And it must always be someone different, someone in officer training so as to prepare them for difficult decisions in the future or for your own loved ones. It is also the respectable tradition to the veteran that the newest generation sends them on their way so wear your full dress uniform with decorative rapier," she said pointedly.

"But why me, Ma'am? Spire, Chartes, they're both fire mystics as well-"

"They can't deflect projectiles the way you can, Sen Asel. I've seen you block pucks for your team. The VAL Home is depending on you to deflect the ice shards that this particular veteran can summon,"

Olsine continued. "Here is the map to the Home. The caretakers would appreciate it if you were there before fourteenth hour; they can't shield themselves from the spirit any longer than that," Olsine concluded, handing the map to Brisethi.

Brisethi shivered and watched her instructor exit the class. She hunched over the podium when light-headedness suddenly washed over her. She had heard stories in grade school about returning spirits to the Sea of Renewal but had never witnessed such an act, let alone performed it. The elder, more powerful family members were always the ones to sever the spirits. *I don't want to do this,* she thought as her hands trembled, creating creases in the map. *I can't do it.*

"What was that about?"

Etyne's voice startled Brisethi when she walked out of class. "Geez! I didn't think you would wait for me," she said, shading her eyes with her hand from the sun.

"Get changed, time for physical training, 'Sethi," he replied, energetic to go a few bouts with her.

Fighting Etyne would relieve some of her anxiety, temporarily.

The clock in her room tolled the eighth hour, waking Brisethi from her restless sleep. Anxiety had kept her up for most of the night. Ordinarily, she would have asked Etyne to come along, but his was not a destructive spirit, and she didn't want him to witness her carrying out that particular task.

The carriage ride took almost an hour to the foothills where those close to Mysticism were kept a safe distance away from the main population. *It just had to be a cold, snowy day,* she thought to herself as she eyed the dreary stone mansion. She paid the rider and straightened her uniform beneath her wool coat, making sure her few medals were still in order. Halfway up the cobblestone path, one of the caretakers greeted her.

"Thank the spirits you've arrived," she told Brisethi. The relief was apparent on the middling aged woman's face. "Did they tell you how to do this?"

Brisethi shook her head. "I'm sorry, but I was only told what I would be doing, not how to," she replied.

"That's because there isn't an actual instruction; the spirit usually knows what to do," replied the caretaker as she helped Brisethi to remove her coat. "In all six hundred and eighty years of my life, I've witnessed twenty spirits become severed from a young person such as yourself, who had no idea what they were doing. You'll be fine."

Another caretaker greeted her and guided her through the corridors to the room that the longing spirit resided in. If possible, the walls were even thicker than those of the Citadel, and all of the rooms were brightly lit.

Brisethi couldn't resist the urge to stop and mingle with those aging Resarians who smiled and waved at her. They wanted to share war stories with her, thank her for taking up arms to protect her millennia, and ask if she knew the commanding officers they once served. The Resarian elders were rarely visited, and they all knew why she was there. She listened as they whispered among themselves that they had said their goodbyes to the woman whose spirit was ready to leave its vessel. The few dozen men and women of this home had lived over eight-hundred years on Falajen and knew that they were nearing their end when submitting themselves. It pained Brisethi's heart to know that she, too, would find her fate here if she failed to achieve her life's ambition. Sariadne emperors had a similar fate, of a different place.

Brisethi was finally encouraged to carry out her task lest the caretakers lose their hold on the support shields containing the spirit's uncontrollable mystics. She felt the slight pressure of a shield cast upon her, the same as Etyne's, from the caretaker beside her.

"Spirits guide you, Lieutenant," said the caretaker as he left a folded Dominion flag on the nearby chair and closed the door behind her.

Brisethi inhaled deeply, taking a step into the cold room. She hadn't seen a Resarian in their latest age since she was a child; the last she had seen of her father's grandmother. She slowly approached the aged Dominion Veteran in her rocking chair, staring out the window at the falling snow.

"The Dominion should know better than to send a fire mystic to sever an ice mystic," the old woman told her.

Brisethi cleared her throat. "It wasn't entirely my decision-"

"I know, my dear, I know. I was once standing where you are at your age, eight-hundred and seventy-two years ago, wondering why we have such a cruel way to end our time on Falajen," she replied. "And then I had to send my husband to the Sea over a century ago." She stood from her chair and turned to face her. She was wearing her Dominion Navy uniform that hung loosely on what was once a sinewy and curvy body. Brisethi noticed that the highest rank she had achieved was Master Chief. Her dark hair had only begun to gray recently and thin lines covered her face. If she wasn't Resarian, any other human would guess her to be a woman in her fifties.

Tears welled in the woman's eyes at seeing the young officer. "What cruel irony that the spirits would send the mirror image of my daughter; hair of blood, eyes of storms - taken from me only forty years ago...I'm on my way to the Sea, my loves."

"I-" her words were cut off as shards of ice flew toward her. She unsheathed her sword quickly and deflected only a fraction of them. The ringing of steel cutting at ice pierced the air the rest shattered against the caretaker's shield upon her eerily resonating throughout the building. The shattered ice pieces falling to the ground echoed like chimes in a sweet melody. "Ma'am...tell me what to do," she softly spoke, wondering why she sounded so calm when she would usually lose her temper at being attacked. Though her body reacted fiercely, her mind was at peace as if she could feel her very soul take over the event forthcoming.

The woman's spirit wanted only to provoke her as ice formed at her feet. It melted instantly when Brisethi summoned flames around herself. She took a step forward through the slush.

"How?" she asked again while igniting her sword to assist in defending against her onslaught of sharp ice.

"It cannot be explained, just end it quickly!" the Master Chief shouted as she reluctantly allowed more spears of ice to form before her hurling toward the fire woman.

Brisethi continued igniting the rapier, flaming outwards to block the ice. Her quick movement of her sword deflected each life-threatening icicle. Tears of sadness stung her eyes and blurred her vision. She didn't want to do this. She could tell that the woman was in pain, however, causing her to falter. "Master Chief, please! Guide me!"

A shard of ice didn't melt in time as it cut through the cartilage of the tip of Brisethi's ear, causing her to nearly scream from the pain; the shields of the caretakers had diminished. She felt the warmth of her blood drip down her neck as panic started to settle within her.

"Do it, Lieutenant!" the Master Chief pleaded before sending more shards of ice at her.

Brisethi filled the room with lightning, shattering the only window in the room as she leapt forward. She pinned the woman against the bars of the window that was now letting gusts of snow inside. She felt her spirit take over and guide her, pulling the Master Chief's spirit from her vessel. Through the eyes of her spirit, she saw the corporeal link of soul and vessel. With one hand behind the Master Chief's neck and the other holding the rapier's hilt to her chest, she reached out to the spiritual bond and with a thought, used her lightning spell to sever the link. The Master Chief let out a final agonizing shout as her body became limp. She watched in bittersweet sorrow as her spirit ascended to the Sea of Renewal.

She dropped her rapier and instinctively unfolded the flag behind her to drape over the Master Chief's soulless vessel. The caretakers were quick to retrieve the Veteran's body to ready her for a proper, ceremonial burial. Brisethi could only numbly stare at the events taking place, deaf to the sounds around her.

"Lieutenant," the male caretaker brought her out of her catatonic shock, handing her the rapier and a wet cloth for her ear injury.

Brisethi took her rapier he was handing to her and sheathed it at her hip. She thanked him for the damp cloth, holding it to her ear as he left her alone in the room once more. Her heart-wrenching task had been complete.

Admiral Tirinnis Sen Asel stood outside the carriage he'd taken to retrieve his daughter. He was dressed in his full dress Dominion Navy uniform to attend the funeral of the Master Chief his daughter had put to rest. Other carriages full of sailors arrived shortly after. Anyone who had served in the Navy over eighty years ago had known the Master Chief in some way or another.

"Dadi," Brisethi spoke in almost a whisper.

The Admiral hugged his daughter to console her in sending her first spirit to the Sea of Renewal. "They told me you did well, 'Sethi-tree," he quietly told her with a hint of alcohol already on his breath.

"If this place is only for Dominion elders, where do civilians go when they lose control of their mystics and have no one to sever the link?" she asked upon breaking away from the embrace.

"Local law enforcement is usually called upon. And it isn't always as humanely as severing the link by a destructive spirit - sometimes they are physically killed in self defense from a sword or pistol," Tirinnis replied.

She was thankful to not have been witness to any such act during her short life.

Chapter IV

In order to gain an extra day of relaxation, the officers in training were given one day a week to volunteer at any various charity in need of assistance. Brisethi specifically avoided the VAL and found herself with Etyne twice a month either helping out in the stables or taking the short trip downtown at the local animal shelter. Every time they were downtown, they invited their significant others to join them in volunteering, Brisethi finally having resolved things with Joss, though she never returned to his home.

Since their first meeting, Joss had a hard time getting along with Etyne, seeing as how Etyne was the one leaving marks on his loved one. Similarly, Etyne disagreed with Brisethi's decision to give Joss yet a third, perhaps a fourth chance. Whereas, Brisethi had little to talk about with Serythe other than music, since she was of the intelligent sort, only stating facts or political nonsense that Brisethi was quick to tune out.

Joss and Brisethi tended to the bigger, messier animals since Serythe wasn't fond of getting dirty. Every now and then, Brisethi stared at each kitten and cat in their little cages, saddened that she couldn't take one to her quarters at the Citadel.

"Soulless creatures," Joss stated as he passed the cages.

"Did *I* ask, what you thought of them?" she quipped and took a senior cat out of his cage to cuddle with.

"All these animals are pretty vile and diseased-ridden," Serythe added, then lectured Etyne about how animals could never comprehend the wasted compassion that humans give them.

He ignored her and instead stroked behind the ears of the old cat that Brisethi was holding. She whispered to him, "What bothers her so? What kind of human doesn't like animals?"

He was about to reply when Joss walked up to regain Brisethi's attention in an effort to disregard Etyne. "What happened to your ear?" Joss asked when Brisethi habitually pulled her hair back. He was quick to glare at Etyne who had also not yet seen her new injury.

She quickly brought her hair forward again at his interrogation. "Oh, this happened a few weeks ago," she casually replied, having not disclosed to anyone what had occurred at the VAL.

"A piece of your ear is gone and you're casually shrugging it off? Etyne, you're done!" Joss started to remove his coat in a threatening manner.

"Joss! He didn't do it!" Brisethi shouted, shoving him to get his attention in the only way she knew how.

"If you want to take it out on me, by all means let's do this - outside," Etyne sternly remarked to Brisethi's pesky lover.

Serythe only glared at Brisethi, wondering why Etyne had suddenly become as savage as Joss.

Brisethi resisted using her mystics in the shelter so as not to startle the animals. She followed Etyne outside with Joss on her heels. Once outside, she released her flames between them both.

"A shard of ice cut the tip of my ear off!" she shouted when they both became silent. "I had to sever a soul and hers was of ice mystics."

Etyne finally understood why Brisethi's usually chipper mood had been so sullen since her solo volunteer event. And when asked, she hadn't been ready to talk about it. "'Sethi, I had no idea you were burdened with such a solemn task," he quietly said.

"You *what*?! Did I hear that right? You canceled our plans so you could go kill someone?" Joss's temper was not subsiding.

It was Serythe's turn to speak. "She released a spirit into the Sea of Renewal - an incredibly noble act - most officers are called upon to do so just as you someday may have to for a family member."

"Exactly," Brisethi nodded to Serythe, finding sudden respect for her amid her surprise at the other woman's defense of her actions.

"It's almost as if I don't know who you are anymore, 'Sethi. You've become so empowered by your own mystics, your training, and this fantasy dream of yours where you believe that our adversaries," Joss gestured to the only half-Kiaran in the group, "want our friendship-"

"I am terminating this discussion," Brisethi interrupted. She was intolerant of anyone who demeaned her best friend, even if at one time, it was Joss who was her best friend. "We are no longer the children you seem to keep thinking we are, Joss. We've grown apart with our own ideals of the world and the people that live in it."

"You're right, 'Sethi, your allegiance has changed," Joss replied before walking off.

Despite the brutal words, Brisethi's soul was crushed to see she had brought pain to Joss yet again.

-:- -:- -:-

The end of their fourth year in officer training finally arrived.

The class had just finished the sit-ups portion of their physical test and were about to commence the pushups portion. Just as was the case during the past seven exams in their four years of school, Etyne was her partner as usual as he readied to begin his count of her pushups.

"You have two minutes to complete as many proper pushups as you can. Everyone at the ready position - begin!" shouted the physical test proctor, Chief Bruer. "Ten seconds has elapsed!" he jokingly shouted.

At the one minute mark, Brisethi arms started to grow weary. She had already passed the medium standard grade but wanted to achieve the maximum score just as she had with her sit-ups.

"'Sethi you're at eighty," Etyne muttered to her.

She took a deep breath through her nose before pushing out ten more. She wanted to give a final ten to make it an even one hundred, but she only had ten seconds left.

"Fuck!" she grunted when time was called and was at ninety-seven.

The class was given ten minutes to rest and hydrate before the three-mile run. Brisethi dreaded running. She preferred ice skating, but that wasn't an option for the physical test. No matter how often she and Etyne ran together or with their class in formation, she always felt like her lungs wouldn't take in enough air. Her mouth would often taste of copper and could never drink enough water beforehand. She'd never failed a run, but couldn't push herself hard enough to achieve the best run time.

Her face flushed and struggling to inhale, Brisethi finished her run as the second to last person. She hunched over and signed her record, satisfied with her results. The class was given liberty for the rest of the day to have time to study.

"How can you not remember this?" Etyne tried not to show his frustration with Brisethi. He took a breath then spelled out the acronym that helped her match the requisite dates to events to nations, and she finally blurted out to him the answer.

She placed her head in her hands and leaned against the desk. The Citadel's library was empty but for the two of them staying up later than usual, preparing for their final exam in the morning. She was confident that she would pass the physical exam, weapons exam, and strategic combat exam with ease, but she could not remember anything for the written test. She'd always had a hard time remembering uninteresting facts from a textbook and resented how easy everything came to Etyne. "Why can't I be as smart as you?"

Etyne leaned back. "Because you're not half-Kiaran," he smirked.

"Get out of here with your engineered Kiaran brain," she teased.

"We're not *engineered*, we are *engineers*. And you *are* smart; you just have other things on your mind when you pretend to study. I know this text is boring, but someday you'll benefit from it when you're off making treaties with these nations."

"Let's move on to languages again, I'm good at that," she grinned.

"No, you've perfected Kiaran and the Trycinean common tongue; we don't need to waste time studying what you're already fluent in." He opened her science book instead and arched a brow.

Brisethi groaned. She realized that if she hadn't gone through officer training with Etyne, she wouldn't have had a proper study partner. She would have been alone every other night in the library trying to remember things by herself and failing miserably due to boredom. Suddenly she noticed that the past few months had involved so much studying that she never stopped to ask him about his personal life. He had never asked about hers, either.

"How's your mum? How's Serythe?"

"Great spirits, 'Sethi, why are you digressing?" Etyne asked.

"I just want to know, Etyne. We never talk anymore, not even during combatives. We just meet and study and go to our separate stuffy rooms then back here to study more. You haven't even visited me in weeks."

Etyne sighed in frustration, unable to tell her why he stopped spending time in her room. "My mother is fine. I haven't talked to Serythe in months. Honestly, I've been more worried about you, 'Sethi."

"Me?" she said incredulously, "what did I do?"

"You struggle on every written exam we take. You can't *fail* this one. I need you to focus, stop with the jokes and personal questions and just pass because I won't be here to help you next time if you fail and remain here another year." His voice genuinely sounded concerned if not a tad strained.

For once in her four years at the Citadel, she was speechless. She found herself unable to respond to the man who was so clearly passionate about her passing the final officer's exam. She didn't know how she could ever repay him for the amount of time he had invested in helping her study. He had sacrificed so much of his free time to her instead of building relationships with his past lovers. Her throat swelled and she swallowed hard to keep from crying. Instead, she turned a page in the book in front of her and stared at equations that she vaguely remembered learning about. She wiped a single frustrating tear from her eye and finally found her voice.

"Are you fucking happy now? You finally made me cry."

Etyne rubbed his face in regret for his sudden insensitivity. "I didn't mean to-"

"Just stop talking," she snapped. "I can study on my own. Go have a life, please. Leave me be."

"Stop being dramatic," he ordered and took the book from her. He wasn't accustomed to treating her as harshly as he had, but it was needed in order for her to find her motivation and to focus. He had her write down the formulas for simple equations to break down the sample problems in the physics textbook. In her sloppiest handwriting she finally reached the solution, exhaling in relief and earning an encouraging word from Etyne.

-:- -:- -:-

Each officer was allowed to choose their own mount out of the dozens of unnamed horses awaiting owners at the stables of the Citadel before their first expedition as a commander, or when handed orders to an outpost. The horse they chose would remain with them until the end of their service. Just as Resarians lived ten times the length of other humans, the beasts of Sariadne also had extended lives due to the nature of their spirits. The difference between the Resarians and other creatures was that Resarians had learned to summon the Mystics from their spirits whereas animals had not.

Most commanders chose white pristine horses or uniquely spotted ones of all breeds to stand out from the plain brown and tabby work horses. But Brisethi had wanted the all-black warhorse the moment she laid eyes on him the last time they volunteered in the stables. Desperately, she prayed to the spirits he would still be there when it came her time to choose one.

"By the spirits, you're more indecisive than a Lantheun woman at a parlour, Etyne," she said.

"This horse is going to be with me forever, 'Sethi. Don't lie to me and say you won't take as long when it's your turn," he replied.

"I already picked one," she snapped back. "That is, if he's still here," she amended.

"Which one? I'm going to pick him," Etyne jested.

"The gorgeous black one over there." She gestured to a tall gelding with a broad chest and powerful legs.

They walked over to view him again. "He's one of my top three so far," Etyne replied, stroking the silky black mane. "If someone else chooses him before you, I'm going to be pretty upset that neither of us got him."

Both had passed their final officer exams with ease the day before. Etyne excelled at the written exam, the weapons exam and physical fitness test, but had nearly faltered during the strategic simulation. Had Brisethi not been his partner, making the quick, life-threatening decisions and sacrifices of so many sailors and soldiers, he would have lost the simulated battles, and the war. Their team was the only team to pass the simulation. Unfortunately for Brisethi, her score on the written exam was so low, she wasn't meritoriously promoted to Captain with Etyne. She would remain at the Citadel in administration duties until she earned her next rank.

"My second choice is that dark gray one. I think you should have a look," she tugged on his arm to follow her four stalls down from the gelding.

Etyne carefully examined the rather large mount that almost competed in size with the black one. The horse immediately nuzzled him when he stroked his snout. "It's as if he's picking me and not the other way around," he quietly told Brisethi.

"You should take him so that we kind of match," she grinned.

"How would we match? There's only one gray horse and one black horse. The rest are brown, white or spotty-calico-colored," Etyne replied. Then he lowered his head shamefully. "Great, now I'm using adjectives that only *you* could make up. I can't wait to get away from you."

"Exactly! We'd be the only two with darker horses. I already named mine Abyss in my head. What are you naming him?" She stroked the gray horse's mane, ignoring the sarcastic jab at her.

"Abyss is a suitable name for yours," he stated. He peered into Brisethi's gray eyes for a moment, remembering that her eyes always reminded him of an approaching storm and her mind was chaotic like a maelstrom. "Tempest."

"That's…actually original," Brisethi said slowly. "I had no idea you had a single bone of creativity in you," she teased him.

"Which further proves my previous statement that we've spent way too much time with one another that I'm picking up your bad habits," he replied sarcastically. But they weren't bad habits at all.

When he recalled the last time he had been with Serythe, she scolded him for using the redundant word, 'snack-treat', that Brisethi had embedded in his head, criticising his intelligence. She went so far as to ask him to spend less time with his friend and more time with her on his days off, to include birthday and holiday breakfasts. It was at that moment he realized his time with Brisethi had become priority over Serythe.

"After spending nearly every day for the past eight years with you, this is going to be a rough goodbye," Brisethi quietly told him.

"It's only four years...or more whenever you get your own division to take on the expedition," he somberly replied. He held back admitting to her that he'd rather not be without her for four years, either.

"At least *you'll* be busy the next four years! I don't want a desk job at the Citadel," she pouted.

"Ah, it shouldn't take too long 'til you're Captain and given your own division. In the meantime, have fun on recruiter duty," he jested to lighten their mood.

Chapter V

Elion and Livian halted their violin practice when Constable Otoe and two other local officers stepped into the sanctuary.

"Good evening, gentlemen. Is there anything we can assist you with?" Elion asked, placing his instrument in his case.

Livian smiled at the familiar police officer. "Constable Otoe! Do you remember me?"

Otoe smiled and nodded. "Of course I do, Livian, how have you been?"

Livian replied shortly about how happy she was but noticed the distraction in his face. "But you're not here for idle chit chat, are you?" She stood slowly, already bracing herself for the notice that she was being removed from the Citadel.

Otoe shook his head. "Acolyte Hadson, may we step outside for a moment?"

Elion slowly approached the officers. "What is the problem?"

"Come outside, please," the second officer sternly suggested.

"What's going on?" Livian asked in earnest.

"Please stay here, Livian," Otoe told her as the officers led Elion out of the sanctuary.

"Elion Hadson," the female officer began. "You were in southern Sariadne four years ago training an expedition, correct?

Elion cleared his throat and clasped his hands. "Yes, roughly four and half years ago, it's my duty as an acolyte to train-"

"And is it your duty to train known suppressors how to summon their mystics without the consent of the Prelate, the Chief of Police, and the General of the Dominion?" Otoe interrupted.

Livian remained still inside the sanctuary, listening to every word outside the grand doors. She held a hand to her mouth in shock.

"Is this about Sergeant Xaviel? He promised me he was going to apply to the Res'Baveth Police Department-" Elion was cut off again.

"Did you suddenly forget the order of things, Hadson?" the stern female asked. "There are dozens of rules and guidelines of suppression mystics! The kid wasn't even half a century old!"

Constable Otoe attempted to calm the situation. "Acolyte Hadson, the man you taught to summon his suppression mystics, did not complete his Dominion Expedition training. He went absent without leave just before they boarded the *DSV Reliant*. The military commanders searched for him and after a year, deemed him as a lost cause. Little did they know what you had taught him, however."

The third police officer finally chimed in. "Last week, both of his parents and his grandparents were murdered. All four of them had their mystics rendered useless, suppressed. A witness claimed she saw her childhood friend, Xaviel, escape the house and she ran after him. When she caught up to him, he confessed to her his power, and his intention to flee to Pahl'Kiar."

Elion raked his hands through his hair. "Four people were murdered..." he whispered to himself.

"And many more to come now that he has defected to our adversary's nation," the female added.

Livian could hold back no more as she stormed out of the sanctuary to face Elion. "Is it true?"

Elion stared into her tear-filled eyes. He could never lie to her. "Sometimes people make terrible decisions for the promise of wealth."

Her eyes widened at the implication. The officers began cuffing his hands behind his back. The Constable tried to tell Livian to go back, but her distress deafened her to the Constable's plea. "Elion why?" Livian asked when her tears poured out. "You broke your divine oath, destroyed the promise to me. Was this life just a lie? Did you not even think of the consequences, of how this would affect us? Is wealth that much more important to you than me?"

"Under the Resarian penalty of law, you are hereby under arrest for the unlawful act of suppression instruction. If you choose to speak, it can be held against you during trial," Constable Otoe told him.

As they led him away, Elion recalled that he had taught a second Resarian to summon her suppression mystics and panic threatened to overtake him. The thought that the second suppressor could just as well murder innocent people had him contemplating his own purpose in life. He didn't know which officer was suppressing his own mystics. But now that he was bound, Elion was helpless. He could never outrun the officers to escape his mortal vessel instead of spending his remaining centuries in the Resarian prison.

Livian fled.

"I'm sorry, Liv!" Elion shouted after her as the officers led him to the carriage. "I'm so sorry, my dear sweet Livian," he whispered, his eyes stinging with shame and despair.

Livian was alone once again. All of the dreams she had shared with Elion shattered before her. She halted before the Dominion ships at the pier. Never again would she trust so many years of her life to anyone. She needed to learn how to be invulnerable and strong minded. She glanced back at the Citadel again. Instead of walking toward the sanctuary, however, she stormed toward the military administration office.

First Lieutenant Sen Asel shortly greeted the small, blonde woman at the entrance to her office. She was just about to leave for the night, staying later than usual to finish filling out paperwork of new recruits for the upcoming expedition.

"Is there room for me in the next expedition?" Livian asked the intimidating Dominion officer. Working a third of her life in the sanctuary connected to the Dominion citadel, she had seen uniformed personnel often. But she had never stood before a female officer as tall and strong as the one before her. She nearly lost her nerve.

Sen Asel sat back down at her desk. She opened a folder containing the roster for the next division readying for the expedition. "You're in luck. Division sixty-four just had someone back out yesterday before taking the oath. Have a seat, miss...?"

"Livian Reej," she replied.

Sen Asel asked the usual recruitment questions to the girl, starting with her age and any criminal activity in her past. She performed a short psychological evaluation and handed her a fountain pen and a form to fill out. After a few more questions and reading through the completed form, the First Lieutenant stood once more.

"Before we continue," she said, "I am obligated to ask if you are absolutely sure that you want to do this." Judging from the intent expression on the younger girl's face, Sen Asel guessed correctly that she was determined to follow through.

"Hold your right hand up like this and repeat after me," she then ordered. "I, state your name..."

"I, Livian Reej," she began.

"Vow to support and defend Sariadne against all adversaries..." Sen Asel continued. When Livian repeated the words she spoke again. "I will obey the lawful orders of those appointed over me."

After Livian spoke the words, she repeated the first lieutenant's final sentence. "According to the Uniform Code of Dominion Regulation."

Sen Asel spent another hour with the new recruit, explaining what to expect and warning her of the terrain and hardships to come. She handed her a booklet of various Dominion instructions. "Division

Sixty-Four will leave in two days. Meet here with the other recruits at sixth hour," First Lieutenant Sen Asel ordered her. "Spirits guide you a safe journey, Private Reej."

Livian thanked the officer and slowly walked out of the citadel. She didn't want to return to the sanctuary, where Elion had left his violin next to hers on the floor. She no longer desired to play the violin or any musical instrument. She bitterly regretted ever having let herself engage so closely with him.

She watched as Acolyte Roz and Prelate Li'Li somberly departed a carriage parked in front of the sanctuary. They slowly ascended the few wide steps to the doors and turned their heads when Livian approached.

"Prelate, Acolyte, I took the oath just now. I leave for the expedition in two days," Livian notified them, revealing her booklet.

Prelate Li'Li thanked Livian for the information and for her service to the acolytes for the past seven years. Roz mournfully placed a hand on Livian's shoulder. "I'm very sorry for what Elion did. None of us could have ever suspected him of such treachery."

She steeled herself against the threatening tears and nodded curtly. Taking a moment to find her voice, she said stiffly, "I am sorry for the Acolytes' loss." Livian desperately wanted to escape their pitying gazes, but forced herself to wait until properly dismissed.

Acolyte Roz watched as the girl's form disappeared towards her room. "How much damage can one man cause?" he asked, surprising himself with the anger evident in his voice.

-:- -:- -:-

Corporal Livian Reej scowled at the other two girls she had been assigned to share a tent with for the past two years. She was fed up with their constant bickering with one another, crying about boys they missed and their families. They were lazy and tried every way they could think of to get sent home, but her training commanders wouldn't let them leave as easily as others had.

"I need to talk to the captain," Livian demanded.

"Is that how we talk to our superiors, Corporal?" The female chief replied in a mild voice, but she stepped closer to her to get the point across.

"Chief, respectfully request to talk to the captain-"

"Denied. You can talk to me and I'll relay your message to him when he's not busy with paperwork," the chief replied in the same even tone.

Livian gritted her teeth. "Chief, for the past two years I've been the only female able to pass the physical tests, the archery and firearms tests, and I've passed every inspection."

"That's why you're the corporal and they're still privates. What's your point?" the Chief sighed.

"They both want to go home! I'm sick of carrying their burdens and picking up the slack. But if they go home, I would have to go, too, won't I?" Livian waited patiently for a response.

"They *are* going home, what paperwork do you think the captain's filling out as we speak?" the chief asked.

"That means you're going home, too, Reej," Sergeant First Class Tevor interjected. "Can't be the only female in a training division. Looks like you'll have to start over with a whole new division."

Livian Reej hated Sergeant Tevor for his chauvinistic, egotistical opinions and dominant personality. She risked physical reprimands each time she expressed her opinion of him. "I was talking with Chief, not you, Sergeant."

"Are you disrespecting me right now, female?" Sergeant First Class Tevor snapped, spitting out the last word like a curse. He began shouting in her face a volley of insults and ordered her to hit the ground for physical training.

The Chief sighed but had to allow the reprimand as per protocol when a recruit was disrespectful. Master Chief Denil approached the young corporal and knelt down next to her to shout words of encouragement instead of insults.

Livian's thighs, shoulders and hands burned from the half hour of intensive training she had brought upon herself. When the sergeant and master chief finally left her alone, she collapsed on her side in the dirt to watch the clouds close in on evening.

The captain of Division Sixty-Four stepped out of the command tent and looked down at the weary recruit below. "On your feet, Corporal," he ordered.

Livian's heart pounded. She wanted to get up to salute the captain and talk to him, but her weakened body would not oblige. Dirt clung to the sweat on her face and body. Her recruit cut hair was partly frizzy and partly matted.

"Corporal, on your feet. Now," he repeated, stern but not harsh.

Struggling, she finally brought herself to stand at attention and saluted him. She didn't want to withstand the captain's intensive reprimands that were always more fearsome than the sergeant's.

He returned her salute. "Chief Pyraz told me you don't intend on going home with the other two females in your tent." He crossed his arms and glared at her in the glow of lantern light.

Livian glanced around, realizing the Chief had disappeared long ago. She avoided eye contact with the officer, not only because he was her superior, but because of his strange, almost glowing blue eyes that seemed to have no pupils. Having never met a Kiaran before, let alone a half-Kiaran such as her captain, she was still uneasy when in his presence. "Sir, I don't have a home to go to. I'm too old to remain working and living in the citadel for the acolytes – my room has already been occupied. I'm homeless if you send me back. I don't want to sleep in an alley ever again, please don't make me start the expedition over with a new division-"

"Enough! I've had it with the incessant whining from half of this division!" Captain Etyne Vorsen's voice echoed through the camp, halting each of the other recruits at their evening meal and sending Livian into an anxious wreck. "If one more recruit comes up to me or your other training commanders complaining about the order of things, I will cancel the next three language training sessions and replace them with intensive training sessions, am I understood?"

"Yes, sir!" The division shouted back.

Disappointed, Livian turned and started walking back toward her tent.

"I don't recall dismissing you, Corporal," the captain sternly called after her.

She halted, took a breath, spun on her heel, and walked back to him.

"Inside," he ordered as he held the tent flap open.

He sat on a wooden chair at the desk that had been made to easily take apart for expeditions. He placed a large book in front of the corporal standing at attention. Without even looking, he flipped it open to a page and spoke, "At ease, Corporal. Read this instruction then tell me in your own words what it means." He leaned back in his chair to await her response.

She skimmed over the page reading what she already knew. "It says there can be no fewer than two females in an expedition training division."

"Your two tent-mates are going home for failure to adapt. How many females will that leave in the division?" he asked. His steady voice betrayed nothing, but Livian could have sworn she saw the hint of a smile.

She hesitated, unsure if it was a trick question. "Only me?"

Captain Vorsen put his hand to his head in exasperation. "Reej, what gender is Chief Korteni Pyraz?"

Her eyes lit up. "I didn't realize the instruction also included the division commanders."

Vorsen glared up at her through his hand. "I'm not kicking you out of the expedition, even if you did fail at keeping the morale up for your fellow recruits. You will share Chief Pyraz's tent starting tomorrow when the guards arrive to escort the other two females back to Res'Baveth. Now you are dismissed."

Livian couldn't hold back her smile when she departed, "Thank you, sir." She nearly skipped back to the tent to collect her things.

"You're getting too soft, Sir," Chief Korteni Pyraz stepped into the tent after the young recruit departed. Korteni smiled warmly at her old friend.

Etyne leaned his elbows onto the desk. "I don't enjoy being mean, but I don't want to train soft soldiers, either. Corporal Reej is strong, stubborn. I can't let her go home – to nothing."

"Speaking of strong and stubborn women, Captain Sen Asel's division should be here tomorrow night," she reminded him.

Etyne stared blankly. "Has it been over two years already? Time flew by in the mountains. *Captain* Sen Asel, you said? They finally promoted her? *And* gave her a training division?"

Korteni chuckled. "Why are you surprised? She's a great leader!"

Etyne agreed, "That doesn't mean I won't tease her first chance I get." He suddenly grew anxious knowing it was *her* division that was meeting up with his.

Korteni smiled widely at his sudden change of demeanor. It was only last year during their winter mountain training that Etyne unexpectedly admitted to Korteni the unlikely thoughts he'd had about Brisethi. "Oh, Captain, you still think about her? Did you ever think maybe to tell her?" Korteni laughed heartily.

"You promised me you'd never bring that up. I'm not ready to give up my career nor would I ask her to do the same if she shared the feeling." He sincerely hoped she couldn't see his face flush in the dim glow of the lantern. Etyne silently cursed that silly drinking game he'd played a year ago with the rest of his enlisted commanders, revealing the inner thoughts he believed had dissipated since the last he'd seen his former combat partner.

The next evening, a familiar Dominion cadence could be heard echoing through the grasslands with footsteps marching in time coming up the path. Captain Vorsen summoned his commanders and recruits to stand in formation on the outskirts of the camp, ready to greet the young division approaching.

A stout master chief halted the division just before Captain Vorsen's formation. The captains saluted one another. Etyne almost didn't recognize the woman in front of him. Captain Sen Asel's uniform was pristine, if a little dusty from the trail. Her dark burgundy hair was styled to fall to one side in waves, but pinned back for the march. There was not even a hint of recognition in her eyes, and her expression was solemn.

When the formal greeting was over, Captain Vorsen turned to address his division. "They are our guests for the time that they will be training with us. I expect there to be no incidents of misconduct between the two divisions, is that clear?" His eyes fell on a few of the more troublesome recruits.

"Yes, sir!" came the response. The two groups were dismissed among orders from the senior enlisted commanders for setting up the new division's camp alongside the other.

Captain Vorsen led the other captain to his command tent to delegate administrative roles, strategic plans and combat training lessons for their integrated divisions.

"General Satnir must be suffering from Mysticsomnia to have signed you off with your own training division," Etyne said, the first to tease.

"Nice to see you too, Captain, your division looks small," she snapped back, having heard his division had already sent quite a few recruits home during a rough winter in the mountains.

"Whoa now, it's not the size that matters, but the effectiveness and quality of their flawless training," he replied, smirking at her. "Speaking of small, did you lose more of your ear?"

"Is the size of my cut-off ear intimidating you? Ah, I've missed this!" Captain Brisethi Sen Asel finally smiled back at her friend. "My senior enlisted can't compare to your crappy humor."

Two years had passed since he last saw her captivating smile, heard her infectious laugh, smelled her blossom scent, and hugged her goodbye. He didn't remember her having such a spellbinding smile. *I must be lonely is all*, he thought, *the smile of every woman is spellbinding if you've been away from them for this long.* He hoped the time and distance between them hadn't changed either of them too much and they were very much still best friends.

"Fortunately for me, I have Pyraz to keep my humor going," he finally said.

"Don't you mean *unfortunately for her* that she has to put up with *you* for another two years?" Sen Asel had waited a year to use that one, ever since Korteni had first written to her.

"You're not going to make these two weeks very pleasant, are you, Sen Asel?" He conceded.

"I believe you brought this on first, Vorsen." Now that it had started, she couldn't keep from smiling in his presence. She wondered if the next two weeks would continue to be as if they had never been apart. She looked up at the small painting hanging on the side of his desk. "You brought it with you?" she said incredulously.

He glanced at the dark painting of clouds and lightning over an erupting volcano in the middle of a restless sea. "Of course I did. You painted it for me – what good would it be stored away in my quarters back at the Citadel?"

Her grin broadened even more. "Where the shit is the one I made for Korteni?"

"She didn't want to risk damaging or losing it like I probably will with mine," he replied.

"You better not!" she grimaced. Her voice seemed a little reluctant as she said, "I should go help my camp lest they set up the command tent inside out."

"I'll be out there shortly, just locking up all of this classified paperwork Korteni left out," he replied, still leaning against his desk and wondering where his sudden anxiety flared from.

Brisethi used her spirit's mystic to enhance the lantern lights to burn brighter as evening approached. She snapped at two of her recruits who had stopped setting up to chat and then attended to helping her enlisted commanders to set up the various weapons racks, supply and artillery tents.

"Captain!" Korteni surprised her when it came time to set up her own tent.

"Chief!" she shouted back, returning the salute then embracing her.

"What in the bony collar bone?" Brisethi asked when poked in her sternum by something protruding from Korteni's chest.

Korteni revealed the gift that Brisethi had given to her two years prior of a rather large pendant of a rat's skull, plated in silver. "I don't go anywhere without this!"

"Gosh, that could be used as a flail," she joked.

They took some time to chat about their last two years, comparing their best recruits with one another, commenting how uneventful the divisions had been since their own training expedition. Finally, Korteni asked Brisethi how Joss had been, eager for the mindless gossip.

Brisethi didn't reply right away and shrugged. "He's great," she sighed.

"That's very convincing," Korteni said pointedly and pried more.

"He's great for anyone else other than me," she reiterated.

"Well that only took a couple of decades to determine. Are you actually done torturing him?" Korteni pressed, her concern obvious in her soft expression.

"By the spirits, you sound like Etyne," Brisethi chided. "I know, I'm a horrible person for always going back and giving him hope," she continued quickly, "But it's not as if *I'm* the one pressuring *him* into these bouts of mindless correlation. I feel guilty for not living up to his expectation, for leaving him before and make it up to him with quick fixes. I'm not even certain if we've ever been in love; it was just a matter of convenience that we kept going back to one another."

Korteni made as if to attempt to strangle her dear friend. "Can you just - you're both very good people, but in different ways. He needs a stay-at-home wife, and you need an adventurous warrior."

Brisethi sighed. "Most 'adventurous warriors' tend to join the Dominion and end up in the same command as me, so, that's a no."

"Are you meaning that you and Etyne, can't...?" Korteni winked.

Brisethi paused while her face flushed. "Who the fuck is Etyne?" she jested, hiding behind her water flask.

Korteni bursted out in laughter. "I still don't understand how you kept forgetting his name."

Brisethi shrugged. "Lack of attention to detail, I suppose, which is why I didn't join the Navy or I would have sunk an entire fleet by now."

Korteni chuckled once more. "Stop deviating the conversation. How are things between you two?"

"Korteni, I don't really crave intimacy the way some of you girls do. I crave mouth-watering consumables more than intense copulation with an intriguing human," she replied when her stomach growled.

"Well when you word it that way," Korteni griped with an arched brow. "Are you saying, if you had to choose between dinner at my house or an intense hot night with, 'he who shall not be named', you would choose dinner?" she teased.

Brisethi thought for a moment. "If you're making that delicious salmon, yes, I would choose your dinner over hot sex with your captain," she grinned, wondering why she was even humoring Korteni with such adolescent talk. "Honestly, Korteni, I love my job too much to throw it away for a fling with my best friend," she replied in an attempt to deny having any feelings for him.

"I thought *I* was your best friend," she pouted when they finished Brisethi's tent.

"I'm certain I have a new best friend every four years," Brisethi laughed. They both moved on to assist with the final steps of setting up the command tent and furniture with the other enlisted commanders and Captain Vorsen.

"I'm sorry I didn't go to commission school with you, 'Sethi. I mean, Ma'am." Korteni often had trouble maintaining proper decorum, especially with her two good friends as officers. "I just didn't want to train another four years at the Citadel and wanted to go straight to the sea!"

"If I was beyond an expert swimmer such as yourself, making the waves able to increase my swim speed, I might have gone Navy with you," Brisethi concluded and looked down at her pocket watch. It was well into the second hour of morning by the time the camp was finished being set up. The recruits were sent to their tents as she crawled into her own tent, exhausted from the day's trek and fell asleep as soon as she found her bedroll.

At dawn, the Master Chiefs of both Division Sixty-Four and Sixty-Six sounded reveille on the horns for both camps. The notes echoed throughout the lines of tents, bringing sleepy recruits out of their sleep to set about the morning routines. Both divisions were soon formed up on the grassy plains in their combat armor listening to the briefings of the sergeants.

Captain Vorsen and Captain Sen Asel casually walked up to the formations, side by side with stern faces. Their black and scarlet leather uniform coats swayed in the wind behind them revealing their ornate swords and pistols at each hip. Their demeanor alone demanded authority without saying a word. They came to a halt next to their respective Master Chiefs.

The two Captains glared silently at the recruits until Vorsen shouted his order to both divisions, "Attention to the Dominion Creed!"

The spirit of our land resides in us

through the breath of dragons.

Our fire from the sky scarred the nations.

From the scars of Sariadne, the Dominion was born.

I will defend her from her enemy.

I will die before I commit treason.

I represent the antecedents

who have passed their spirits unto us

And I will use such spirits to honor our nation,
never against my brethren.

Master Chief Denil's voice bellowed, "Division Sixty-Four are you ready to teach the baby division how to fight like warriors?"

Vorsen's division shouted back wildly.

Captain Sen Asel nodded to Master Chief Riquez, a small smile playing at her lips. He complied with his own chant, "Division Sixty-Six, are you ready to embarrass the senior division?"

Although the division didn't reply wildly, they had replied as one loud voice that echoed throughout the grassy plains sending chills up the Master Chief's spine.

"Your captains will demonstrate how you could be fighting by the time you get to your fourth year of not only the enlisted expedition, but at the end of officer training as well," Chief Pyraz announced, addressing both divisions as one. "We will teach you each of their beginning moves one at a time throughout the next few years, starting today." She motioned for the recruits to break formation and group up. "Watch and retain, children!" she called out with a laugh.

Corporal Livian Reej gasped at the sight of her enlistment officer. She was eager to watch her captain face off against the recruiter captain. She had come to admire the half-Kiaran, unexpectedly, when he spoke to her one on one, while fearing him during drills and reprimands to the division as a whole. She had yet to witness anyone use their mystics during combat and was craving an impressive show.

The two captains faced one another, saluted, then each wordlessly leapt back, breaking into a fighting stance with swords instantly drawn. With a wink from Sen Asel, seen only by Vorsen, they suddenly lunged at each other and clashed their swords. The grassy plains soon rang with the continued strikes and parries as the two swung furiously. They had deflected each other's swings with swiftness and precision as though it were a choreographed dance. In fact, they did know what move the other would make because of the length of time they had spent as combat partners. The two years apart did not negate the seven years of time dedicated to learning each defensive and offensive move and even inventing new skills together.

Livian had to keep closing her mouth each time her jaw dropped from the remarkable bouts. Her eyes widened watching the two experienced captains fight one another. To her, they weren't just simply fighting, but dancing exotically with swords flying dangerously close to their flesh. She gasped when Captain Sen Asel's sword had been thrown behind her and quickly drew her pistol. Shots fired at Captain Vorsen but he deflected each shot with his sword until she ran out of ammunition. He closed in on her but she squatted to dodge his sword, rolled back onto her elbows and brought her foot up to his hand, knocking his sword free.

It was now his turn to fire his pistol at her but she evaded each attack with a roll to the left, or falling on her back only to bring herself up with the leverage of her legs. When he had finally emptied his own chamber, she sprinted toward him and leapt into the air, landing a foot to his chest to knock him to the ground. He held onto her leg and brought her down with him as they commenced into hand-to-hand combat.

Neither of them spoke a word to one another; they were able to communicate with their eyes each rehearsed move they would make and when. Vorsen threw a fist toward her face but she caught it, pulling him toward her and leapt onto his back to attempt a choke-hold. He somersaulted to lay her flat on her back and was now the one holding her in a choke-hold.

Livian knew her captain would win, it seemed too easy. She grinned with anticipation to listen for th   e other captain to yield.

Instead, however, she witnessed her enlistment officer use her powerful legs to untangle herself from his grasp as they rolled with each other, more kicks flying out and punches deflected as the mock battle went on. Livian caught herself cheering on Captain Sen Asel, infatuated with her martial prowess.

They were far from tired when Brisethi finally signaled to Etyne that she would be summoning her mystics. An avalanche of red flames hurled toward him but he summoned his shield to absorb her mystics. The recruits cheered as he turned himself invisible and instantly re-materialized behind her, kicking her forward. He lunged on top of her but she summoned a layer of fire around her, causing him to roll off and extinguish the flames of his uniform. He didn't want to admit how clever she was for that trick and thanked the spirits he had kept his gloves on. They both stood once more to face one another. She let loose sparks of purple and blue lightning straight for him but he was too quick to summon another shield that, instead of absorbing her mystic, reflected it back to its source. Brisethi unexpectedly felt the power of her own lightning and was sent flying into the taller grass.

The recruits applauded wildly. The enlisted commanders rushed to their captains.

"Ugh," she finally exhaled, struggling to stand. She'd never been struck by her own lightning before. "When did you learn to reflect?"

He shrugged, walking toward her, "It's harder to do with just your flames; did that hurt?"

"You could have killed me!" she shouted dramatically even though she knew that she couldn't possibly take fatal damage from her own mystic. She braided her long hair that had fallen out of her bun while strands of lightning still passed along her vessel's surface.

"So you were trying to kill me?" Etyne mocked, a shocked look on his face as he crossed his arms, captivated by the strands of lightning flickering throughout her uniform and skin.

"I figured you'd absorb it in your shield not deflect it back at me," she shook the remaining sparks of light off of her. "Besides I can resuscitate lightning victims if I *choose* to get to them in time," she smirked.

Livian was spellbound by the fiery captain, wishing she could approach her and ask if she remembered her. She was the female warrior she only ever dreamed to become. Her new ambition in life was suddenly to become as strong and agile as Captain Sen Asel. The

Captains collected their weapons, holstered their pistols and sheathed their swords. They relinquished command to their senior enlisted amid cheers and shouts from the recruits and returned to their respective command tents.

Brisethi stared at her log book, listening to the divisions in the distance learning advanced combat tactics. She realized she didn't want to spend her two weeks of integration alone if she could work side-by-side with Etyne. She gathered her log book, pens and various other forms and found her way to Division Sixty-Four's command tent.

Etyne was instantly distracted by Brisethi's entrance of his tent, making himself vulnerable to the ball of twine being thrown by Master Chief Denil. Etyne groaned and leaned over, cursing to himself when the ball had found its target between his legs. Sergeant First Class Tevor cheered the Master Chief on for his shot.

"Are you really playing this game right now, gentlemen?" Brisethi chastised them. "Are we back in grade school?"

Etyne recovered from his temporary pain, aiming the ball at her. Her glare dared him to throw it. When he found his voice, he relayed to her, "If I recall correctly, Ma'am, it was you who once told me, 'if we're always serious and never stop to live life, then what's the point in fighting to live?' or something like that," he imitated her voice horribly while folding the tip of his left ear over to also look like her. He instead threw the ball at Sergeant Tevor, causing him to double over this time.

"That's a terrible impersonation of me," Brisethi said and finally picked up the ball before any of the men could.

"Out of the tent, you two. The captain and I have work to do. Stop leaving Chief Pyraz to do all the training," Etyne ordered. He then moved his chair back to behind his desk, innocently looking at Brisethi as if he had just been scolded by his mother. He took one of his letters on the desk in hand to summarize what he had read earlier.

"They finally identified the squadron that attacked us a decade ago that you melted," Etyne explained.

"Let me read," she attempted to grab the letter but he held her back with an arm, leaning back in his chair.

"This report says that the ship that was sunk by Master Chief Synsun had the same design and banners as the Lantheun ships."

"The Lantheuns? What do they want with us? We've never had any quarrel with them. Sergeant Vilkinsen was right all along when he told us it wasn't Kiarans," Brisethi added.

"It took them this long to dive deep enough to investigate. I wonder if someone just needed the right mystic to withstand the water pressure," Etyne continued. "Did you not read the memorandum from about a month ago about the Kiaran and Lantheun alliance?"

"I skimmed through it..." Brisethi leaned against his desk. "I wonder if General Satnir and Emperor Arquistas are declaring war on them, too, now. Recruitment will be through the roof, I suspect. Sending multiple training divisions out in a year, doubling their sizes, decreasing the training time from four years down to two, I can't wait to start another."

"You thrive on chaos and destruction, don't you?" Etyne looked up at his friend.

She shrugged. "Considering I summon destruction, yes. I'm comfortable when things are awry. When life is calm, bad things happen." She played with the twine ball, tossing it in the air and catching it.

"Bad things are happening now, 'Sethi," he retorted and quickly caught the ball in mid-throw.

"War isn't always bad. It makes us stronger, more resilient. If we weren't at war, we'd be growing soft and lazy knowing that no one hates us and wants our land. Instead, we're always evolving with our mystics and combat techniques, finding ways to stay alive and keep our defenses up," Brisethi went on catching the ball Etyne tossed in the air.

"But war brings death-"

"Death to the enemy. Death to those that mean to harm us. More people die in war, yes, but not much of our people, everyone else's." Brisethi put the ball back on the desk and pulled out her pistol, taking it apart for cleaning.

"I suppose you have a point," Etyne put his pistol next to hers and handed her his cleaning kit. "Today was the first time I actually used this in a couple years and it was to fire it at you," he said.

"Sariadne needs to make new allies," she stated, ignoring his banter.

"There are hardly any nations left in Falajen that haven't already sided with Lantheus or the Kiarans. We were too pompous and certain that we could never be defeated. And now, no one would dare break away from them to join us. Everyone wants to destroy us. They want to rid us of our spirits," Etyne told her.

"Do you understand why I must change the world, Etyne?" Her voice took on a sense of quiet urgency he rarely heard from her. "Our past generals and emperors have been sitting idly by behind our mystical defenses waiting for someone to ask *us* to ally instead of going out there and demanding treaties. We need to demand negotiations of peace or rain fire upon any nation who denies us. We've lost the influence that Emperor Sentiar Asellunas once created. I've come to conjure it once more." Without even moving, the blue lantern flames of the tent changed to red by her command.

Etyne remained silent, not wanting to falsely give her hope, nor did he want to crush her ambitions. He didn't doubt that she would rank up into a diplomatic position, but he doubted her influence among stubborn leaders of the world's nations. She would never actually destroy whole nations to prove a point. *Or would she?* He thought.

"You don't believe in me, do you?" she interrupted his train of grave thought.

He had hoped she wouldn't ask him something of this nature. He breathed in deeply and stood to emphasize his next words. Etyne leaned against his desk next to her and took the pieces of weapon out of her hands that she had been cleaning. He set them down and looked her in the eyes. "'Sethi, since the first day I saw you in expedition training setting yourself apart from the others, I knew there was a serious storm brewing in that maelstrom of a mind of yours, just like your chaotic paintings. Little did I know just how far your ambitions were reaching until the end of our officer training when you reminded me how passionate you were to change the world.

"You always admired the heroes in those fantasy books you read because of how they came to power by accident," he left out explaining to her that he had read the first book of a fantasy series by her favorite author. "You're not one of those heroes, 'Sethi. You're not going to 'accidently' come to power because a sword and a wizard 'chooses you'-"

Brisethi giggled, "Did you just reference-"

"Don't interrupt me. You're going to work for it, *demand* it. I have faith that you will achieve this, but I've yet to experience your diplomacy and influence among world leaders. And that's the only reason I've held back thus far. The men leading other nations aren't the smartest people, but they won't be easily swayed; not even by a beautiful, powerful woman such as yourself."

Brisethi looked away as she blushed. She was unnerved by both his sound logic and the fact that he had never called her beautiful before. His usual sarcastic, bickering tone was absent. Finally, she was able to return his gaze. "I won't be able to do do it alone, Etyne.

I'll need help and encouragement. I'll need the support of people like my father, like Korteni, Acolyte Roz and you. I need *you*, Etyne. But I'll understand if you think I'm irrational. We've only known each other over a decade-a third of our lives already-and I won't expect you to remain a good friend if my decisions cause a rift." She gave him a wry smile.

"The moment you demanded me to be your combat partner ten years ago, you've had my support, albeit reluctantly at first. And I want to be there with you when you finally do what others could not." He smiled, hoping she could one day truly influence more than just him.

She took his hand in hers momentarily. "Thanks, Etyne. I appreciate the companion you've been to me this past decade." She hesitated to go on but summoned just enough courage to speak again. "When they gave you a training command and stuck me in administrative duty at the citadel for a year, I thought I was going to lose my sanity without you." She let go of his hand and busied herself with the weapon again, lest he see her face redden.

"Why didn't you write?" He asked in a low voice, taking his seat back and wiping down the pieces of his own weapon.

"I did write! Twice, actually. I just never sent them out. I didn't want to sound like a desperate, lonely child without you. And by the time I had sat down to write a third letter, I was told that I would be leading the next expedition to leave so I wrote to Korteni instead in hopes I'd get the chance to surprise you." She stopped talking the moment she sounded fraught.

"'Sethi we're friends. You can tell me anything you want whenever you want. I won't think differently of you no matter how crazy it initially sounds." He gave her arm a nudge before returning to his task.

If only you knew how much I continue to hold things back from you, Etyne, she thought as she fidgeted with her ear.

Chapter VI

Livian grew frustrated at herself. Her combat partner for the day was someone from the newer division who seemed to deflect every one of her swings.

"You've been in training a year longer than me. How are you this bad? You shouldn't even be allowed to finish your expedition. Do the Dominion a favor and go home," her partner from Division Sixty-Six told her. He seemed bored with her attempts to land a hit.

"Fuck off, moron," she angrily replied.

"You should have more respect for me, you little twit," he swung his sword furiously, causing her to lose her grip on her sword and laughed at her.

"What is your problem? Is your whole division trained to be assholes?" Livian then took the first chance she had and kicked him between the legs.

He dropped to his knees, swearing at her.

Sergeant First Class Tevor was the nearest to them and ran over as soon as he heard the yelp. "Corporal Reej, report to the command tent, now!" he shouted. "Captain Vorsen's gonna send you home for sure!"

Sergeant First Class Kile of Division Sixty-Six was next to run up. He laughed when he saw who had been downed. "I knew that mouth of yours would get your balls pushed in. Get to your tent! I don't want to see your ugly face for the rest of the day." Sergeant Kile declined sending in their divisional healer, Master Chief Riquez, to tend to the delinquent recruit.

The recruit staggered when trying to stand up. "Please don't tell the captain, she'll rip me a new one!" he whined in a pathetic whimper.

"I'm pretty sure she'll find out from everyone else before I get the chance to report," Kile chuckled again.

"What is it now, Corporal?" Captain Vorsen sighed, still leaning against his desk next to Captain Sen Asel.

"Sir, Sergeant Tevor ordered me to report to you," Reej replied, standing at attention. She tried to avert her eyes from staring at Captain Sen Asel's gaze.

"At ease, Reej. Report," Vorsen crossed his arms.

"Reej!" Sen Asel interjected. "I recruited her," she digressed to Etyne.

"You probably recruited half of my division-"

Brisethi interrupted Etyne to speak to Livian. "Are you doing alright, Corporal? I hope you're stressing out your commanders as much as I did-"

"Sen Asel, do you mind?" Etyne stood to get his point across to her.

"Carry on," Brisethi lightheartedly replied.

Livian nervously licked her dry lips then cleared her throat. "Sir, I kicked my partner in his groin area."

Captain Sen Asel stifled a laugh which ended up sounding like a snort. Vorsen glared at Sen Asel for her lack of professionalism then asked the recruit, "Was your partner our division or hers?"

"He was from Sixty-Six," Livian replied, wanting to giggle at Sen Asel's unprofessionalism but too terrified of Captain Vorsen to do so. *At least*, she thought, *she remembers me.*

"Was his name Jiken? Bigger guy with dark brown hair?" Sen Asel asked.

Livian nodded, "Yes, Ma'am."

"Spirits bless you, Reej, for doing what I've been wanting to for months," Sen Asel said softly. She then stormed out of the tent with a sense of urgency.

Vorsen considered his corporal for a moment. "You're very fortunate that Captain Sen Asel has suddenly taken a liking to you. This day would not have ended well for you had she been upset. Report back to Sergeant First Class and tell him you require a new combat partner," Vorsen ordered.

Captain Sen Asel was on the prowl, knocking over weapons racks, kicking supply over in her search of Corporal Jiken's tent. She was letting her rage and frustration take over on inanimate objects lest she accidently murder her recruit for embarrassing her in front of the other division, in front of Etyne. When she located his tent, she stormed into it, flaring her hands of fire for dramatic effect. "I'm not even going to ask you what you said to the female corporal of Division Sixty-Four. I have a vivid enough imagination and have heard for myself every word of filth that has left your shit-stained mouth."

Corporal Jiken shuffled to his feet in an attempt to stand at attention in her presence but was still sore where he had been kicked so that it looked more like a half-bow. "Ma'am, she was so terrible at fighting-"

"I didn't ask you to speak, recruit!" she shouted. "We're not here to demean and belittle the senior division!"

"Yes Ma'am-"

"If I hear another word out of your fucking mouth today, I will sear your fucking tongue off!" She extinguished the flames from her right hand to grab his collar. With a swift tug, she ripped his corporal rank insignia off. "Rest well for the remainder of your evening, Private First Class; you're standing watch the next three nights."

-:- -:- -:-

Both divisions were ordered to their tents for the night with the exception of three watch-standers from each division. The night was warm, perfect sleeping weather. Private First Class Jiken yawned and leaned against a cottonwood tree when he was suddenly approached by two of Division Sixty-Four's watch-standers.

"We saw what she did to you, man," said one of them.

"And I care why?" Jiken quipped, adjusting his rifle strap.

"We know which tent is hers," said the other, "and she happens to be alone right now since the chief and the rest of our commanders are having 'tea time' at your division's command tent." Private First Class Uland spoke again with a sinister smile, "For a fair price, I'm willing to take you to her."

Jiken considered the offer and took a few frakshins out of his pocket. "Show me."

Livian Reej finished sewing on a replacement button to her uniform then she snuffed out the lantern light. She hadn't known a peaceful evening since joining the expedition. When she had to spend every night listening to other girls bicker and whine, she suddenly took comfort knowing she would hear them no longer. The stationary she was issued was still untouched, having nobody to send a letter to. Her thoughts of Elion never subsided and wondered if she should write to him in prison. *Maybe another time*, she thought as her eyes grew heavy. She curled up into her bedroll, closing her eyes and listening to the footsteps approaching her tent. She assumed Chief Pyraz was coming to retire for the night.

"Chief, I'm sorry for the trouble I caused today," Livian muttered when she thought Chief Pyraz had entered the tent.

"You will be," whispered Jiken as he covered her mouth and stripped her blanket off of her.

Her muffled screams went unheard as the recruit she recognized from her own division, Uland, helped to hold her down and rip her under-uniform layer. She tried to kick and punch, even head-butt the man on top of her but the other man held her down with all of his strength. Still struggling against their combined force, she could hear Jiken on top of her unbuckling his belt and felt forceful hands grabbing at her exposed chest. Her legs were then forced open but before he could thrust, she released her spirit's mystic, sending both men flying through the canvas tent, carried by the shockwave. The third who had been standing guard outside was also tossed. She immediately screamed as loud as she could and scrambled for her blanket.

Chief Pyraz was the first of the commanders to arrive at her obliterated tent, nearly out of breath from sprinting the moment she heard the piercing scream. A quick survey of the two male recruits on the ground, groaning in pain, told her everything. She knelt down beside Corporal Reej who was hunched over on her bedroll wearing only her uniform coat. Livian instinctively jerked away from the Chief's touch on her shoulder.

Both captains along with their enlisted commanders arrived on the scene moments later. They quickly assessed the situation and dispatched Sergeant Kile to gather the rest of the watch-standers.

Sen Asel immediately ignited her flames when she made eye contact with Private Jiken. "The fuck did you do now?" she roared unforgivingly.

The shock of Reej's blast had left him sluggish as he clumsily buckled his belt and tried to stand. His eyes widened when the fiery captain reached over to him and threw him back to the ground.

"Do I need to sear off your dick along with your tongue? What the fuck are you thinking? What is your fucking problem, recruit?" Sen Asel's temper flared dangerously. Even Korteni and Etyne backed away lest they feel the heat of her flames.

Jiken was too startled to respond and remained on the ground as the other commanders joined in screaming at the three recruits who all lowered their heads as though hoping that would earn them some pity. Jiken suddenly felt hot hands grab his neck, forcing him to stand. Captain Sen Asel was unbelievably powerful, tossing him around like a bag of hay.

Private First Class Uland was thrown by Captain Vorsen who was also enraged. "We're in a constant fucking war with Pahl'Kiar and you want to cause harm to your own people?"

"No, Sir," he weakly replied.

"You're fucking pathetic - you have no right to wear that uniform!" Vorsen continued shouting, taking turns with his enlisted commanders to push the recruit, along with the third culprit around. Instead of forcing him to his face to commence in push-ups, which would only benefit his strength, Vorsen had the recruit initiate mountain climbers, a routine Uland was quick to tire in. His lack of endurance would hastily fuel the rage of each commander.

Captain Sen Asel's flames kept igniting with each statement she shouted, lunging forward and resembling a mythical fiery phoenix. "As if having your balls kicked in wasn't enough of a reminder to not fuck with your fellow recruits, you had to give me a better reason to have you permanently taken out of the Dominion! Was she worth it, recruit? Was she fucking worth losing your rank, your pay, your freedom on Sariadne? You'll be in prison for decades!"

She left the other commanders to take over reprimanding the watchstanders and marched over to her division camp. "Division Sixty-Six, form the fuck up!" she screeched. Within minutes, her entire division was in formation outside of her command tent, terrified of what was to come. Some had dressed so quickly that their uniform overcoats were not buttoned all the way. Sen Asel's eyes lingered on those who had failed to finish dressing before she spoke. "I did not spend the past year training you to be assholes! Everyone on your faces, now!" Her voice echoed throughout both camps. She sounded off the count in an annoying tune that every recruit loathed. It was the same tune Chief Renast counted off when reprimanding her. They knew it was her way of telling them how much pain and for how long she would put them through intensive training.

"One, two-a, three!" Sen Asel's voice soon grew hoarse from the constant yelling at top volume. She allowed Master Chief Riquez to take over for her and stormed back over to the other division's camp to tend to Pyraz and Reej.

They were in Vorsen's tent, with Reej sitting on the cot and Pyraz in a chair at her side. She squat down beside the Chief and asked Reej the usual formal questions, which Livian answered in a dull tone. When she was done, she gathered Reej's bedroll and uniforms, telling Pyraz to carry Reej's recruit rucksack, all of which had been retrieved from the scene. Sen Asel then softly told both of them, "Come on you two, we can all fit in my tent tonight."

"I'll start the paperwork," Sen Asel muttered to Vorsen as the trio passed where he was supervising the senior enlisted placing the three delinquent recruits in binds. A message would be sent out that night to request the nearest Dominion base guards to take charge of their criminals.

Captain Sen Asel led the others to her division's camp, walking behind the group of recruits still carrying out their punishment under Master Chief's commands. They arrived at her tent located just behind the command tent. She removed her mountain cat fur blanket from her bedroll to place Reej's bedroll on top of hers for extra cushion. She assumed she wouldn't be sleeping that night to deal with administrative separation papers and figured Reej could use the extra comfort if it would help her to sleep.

"Do you need anything, Reej? Hot tea to calm your nerves? Rum to help you sleep?" Sen Asel asked.

Livian shook her head, not wanting to bother the prestigious captain with serving her anything. *I should have you reported for letting your soldier get out of control,* she thought in anger. Her former admiration of the Captain was depleting.

"Oh, I'll take some tea," Pyraz chimed.

Sen Asel glared at her mockingly. "I'll have someone check on you two in a little bit. Do not leave her side, Chief."

"Yes, Ma'am," Pyraz replied.

Brisethi walked past her division still on their faces, steam rising from their sweat dissipating into the crisp night air. She tapped the shoulder of one of her more obedient female recruits, ordering her to fall out. "I need you to brew a pot of tea for the two members in my tent. Afterward, return to your tent for the night, Talmin."

"Yes, Ma'am," Corporal Talmin panted, thankful to have been chosen to abandon the Master Chief's vicious reprimand.

Brisethi sat at her desk in the command tent filling out forms for the three aberrant recruits. Master Chief Riquez finally sent the beaten division back to their tents, but she could still hear Chief Baderstoff and Sergeant First Class Kile lecturing the other three outside.

"Would you like some help?" Etyne let himself into her divisional command tent.

Brisethi threw her fountain pen down and stretched her arms and chest. "I finished the letter to the guards at post three for the request to take our convicts. I'm nearly done with the memorandum to the command. If you could help fill out the separation papers, I'll log the event in both of our log books."

He walked over to her desk to examine the pile of papers. "Your handwriting hasn't improved much," he teased.

"That's why I left the extensive writing for you," she grinned. She then reached into a drawer and pulled out a rolled up scroll. "Here, add this to your collection," she handed him the paper not looking at him.

He broke the seal and unraveled the heavy cloth-like paper. He was instantly infatuated with the painting of two moons and hundreds of tiny stars over a calm sea shining brightly on an ancient Dominion ship. "Why is it so calm? I'm used to your dismal paintings of destruction," he jested. "I wish I had made something for you, but you know I have no skills in fine arts."

"Consider it my belated thank-you gift for helping me make it to where I am today," she told him.

He smiled genuinely. "Not needed, but I do appreciate it. Thanks, 'Sethi."

Her smile diminished when she looked down at her writing. "I'm slightly upset that we didn't see this coming. You should have told me she was your only female recruit left."

Etyne rolled up his precious new painting and peered down at her. "I didn't think to tell you. She's stronger than some of the males in my division and very vocal, much like yourself."

"Do you think she'll want to return home after this? If so, I can take Korteni and trade you one of my other enlisted commanders since you'll have gotten rid of all your females somehow," she slightly berated.

Etyne shook his head. "Reej fought me to stay in regardless of her option to leave if she wanted to. I will ask her in the morning, but I'd hate it if I had to carry out my remaining two years out here without her and especially Korteni." He leaned against her desk and glanced around briefly, noticing the blanket she had placed on the other end. "Is that the same one I gave you?"

"Of course. You really think I'm going to hunt down a mammal and deal with the blood when I can just bring that one?" she replied.

"How is it that you can kill dozens of human bandits without a second thought but flinch at the thought of killing a beast?"

"Easy; the humans are trying to kill me. I'd kill a beast if it were hunting me, too. I just don't want to dismantle it. "

Etyne laughed. "In that case, I'm glad the blanket went to you instead of what's her name."

"How have you forgotten her name? It's only been six years," she stood up to stretch her legs.

"And in those six years I can't even remember the names of the girls that came after her," he shrugged.

"You hardly talked about them which is why I don't remember their names, even if you only told me of about two of them," she glared at him with a slight hint of jealousy that she couldn't hide, control, or subside. Why am I envious at all? She thought.

"You kept count?" He asked, winked at her then walked out of the tent. Moments later he returned with his divisional logbook and his bedroll. "Korteni told me you gave up your sleeping place for her and Reej. I hope you didn't give her Ten-Tickles the octopus, too?" he teased.

"Aww, Ten-Tickles, I contemplated bringing him for cuddles, but it's a tad unprofessional. I'd be somewhat embarrassed if a recruit stumbled upon him," she faked a gasp, "I'd be devastated if I lost him!"

Etyne chuckled. "I'll fill out both logs and the separation papers. Come sleep. You're a horrible person when you don't sleep six hours or more," he joked.

Even in the middle of the lackluster command tent across a decorative rug beneath the lantern light, the setup was all too inviting. She stood and removed her uniform coat and hung it on her chair. "You're the greatest," she wearily told him and walked over and crawled under her favored blanket.

"I know," he murmured to her, taking her seat at her desk to continue the paperwork where she had left off.

Chapter VII

More than a year passed uneventfully since the divisions went their separate ways; Captain Etyne Vorsen's to the south through the desert and mystic training, Captain Brisethi Sen Asel's to the north and west Mira'Shan Mountains. A year later, her division finished mountain training and started second integration with a new division to meet. In two weeks, they would be on their way to the desert while Vorsen's would be finishing up their mystic training in the tropics before moving on to commence naval training.

Brisethi clenched her teeth and pounded her desk with a fist after reading the message.

"Something the matter?" Sergeant First Class Kile asked.

She crumpled the letter in her other hand. "My father's been captured, and his captors are asking for ransom," she blatantly replied in a terse voice.

"Who? How much are they asking for? The Dominion will pay it and then we'll take it back," Master Chief Riquez fired rapidly, quickly moving into problem-solving mode.

"The letter doesn't say who it's from. And they don't want money, they want me," she coldly told them both.

"*You*? That means it's someone you know. But what could anyone possibly want from a Dominion captain if they have an Admiral?" Sergeant Kile asked.

She shrugged and sighed. "I don't know! Just send for my replacement right away, I have to leave as soon as I can."

"Yes, Ma'am," Sergeant Kile began writing the memorandum for request of a new officer. "We're not too far from Third Outpost; they'll receive this letter by tonight and have our replacements here the next morning-"

"*Our*?" She interrupted. "Neither of you are coming with me, Sergeant, Master Chief. This is a hostage situation. I can't risk my father's life by showing up with anyone. Nor can I risk getting any of you harmed. I'm going alone." The letter ignited in the palm of her hand so no one else would see the location.

"With all due respect, Ma'am, it's our duty to-"

"Ensure these recruits eventually put us all out of jobs," she interrupted again.

Defeated, Sergeant Kile turned to the Master Chief.

"Ma'am, will you at least send word of your destination when you're close? In the unfortunate possibility that neither you nor your father return; it would help us to know of your last whereabouts for the search and rescue," Riquez pleaded. Normally all business, he had actually grown quite fond of the fiery-tempered officer.

Brisethi crossed her arms. "We'll both be returning," she sternly replied. She then softened her tone of voice. "But…if it will help you to sleep at night, I suppose I can send you a letter of my destination the day before I get there."

"Thank you, Ma'am," they both exhaled.

As Sergeant First Class Kile had stated, the replacement officer for the recruit training division arrived the next morning from Third Outpost.

Navy Lieutenant Gatrian Vazeley reported to the Army Captain, relieving her of her command. A two-hour long brief of her recruits was given to him along with the status on their combat training and the lesson they had left off for Kiaran Language training and various Dominion military sessions.

She packed lightly, expecting to return in five days with her father who would then be escorted back to Res'Baveth from Third Outpost. She instructed her Master Chief, Chief, and Sergeant First Class to wait for her for up to seven days. If she didn't return by then, they were to continue on with the recruit training without her.

Brisethi armed herself with a pistol and a rifle, sword and shield, and various hidden daggers in her belt, boots and gloves. She had a feeling that if her father had been captured, it meant he was unable to use his mystics to defend himself. Rumors were abundant stating that the Kiarans were devising an elixir that temporarily disabled Resarian Spirits. Once the Resarian was disabled, they needed only to keep him or her unconscious if not killed.

Lieutenant Vazeley gave Captain Sen Asel a short lecture, ordering her to stay alive. "I don't want to be the one taking credit for your division at their ceremony, Ma'am," he lightheartedly told her. "But I'll make sure they surpass your standards by the time you return to them in the few days they'll have been in my care."

"I couldn't ask for more, Sir, thank you," she saluted him. "Don't let Master Chief Riquez, Sergeant First Class Kile and Chief Baderstoff lie to you about my 'lenient' ways – I have none!"

"She's lying," Navy Chief Baderstoff smirked. "She lets us drink every night."

The rest of them saluted her, watching her climb atop her black warhorse. She had decided that she needed only her armored beast of a charger in the event she would need to fight off an enemy battalion.

Brisethi trusted Abyss to stand his ground over a smaller, quicker horse.

It took her two days and nights to reach the eastern shore, allowing only the minimum amount of rest for both her and Abyss. She even took a minor detour to send the letter back to her division of her destination. Her journey was uneventful, only marred by the nearly overwhelming sense of urgency.

The overcast morning matched her mood when she came upon the specified shore as she watched the ship anchored in the distance. She remained seated on Abyss and summoned a series of red flames that shot in the air, bursting loudly and signaling the strangers on the ship. They did not keep her waiting long. She kept her eyes on the three rowboats approaching her. A familiar man stood fearlessly on the lead boat until it hit the shore. She aimed her rifle at him, briefly enhancing it with her mystic for accuracy and force.

"Well if it isn't my old comrade, Sen Asel. The Dominion must truly be desperate if you're the one training their recruits," taunted former Sergeant Kanilas Trenn. The last she had seen him, he had been dressed in the Dominion dress uniform for graduation. He had exchanged his uniform for mismatched clothes in varying shades of grey and blue. His dark hair had grown out long enough to be pulled back into a short, messy ponytail. Otherwise, he seemed unchanged.

"*Captain* Sen Asel," she corrected tersely. "Bring out my father. I'm not here to discuss military movements," she said, still aiming the rifle at his head. Abyss snorted, growing restless and uneasy at the tone of their voices.

Kanilas glared at her. "Get off the horse, leave your weapons, and get on the boat. Your father is still on the ship, and that is where the trade will take place."

Her blood boiled at being ordered what to do by him. He was smart to have not brought her father along or she would have shot each member of his crew with or without her mystics. After a moment spent considering doing that anyway, she finally abided by his command and boarded the boat, leaving her horse prancing nervously on the shore.

"Nice pirate garb, I had that same outfit when I was five" she muttered to him when she passed.

"I'm a mercenary, not a pirate. I've already made three times more frakshins this year than I have the entire ten years that you've been a Dominion slave," he gloated. "Did you ever imagine ten years ago we'd be together again, embarking on a new journey?" Trenn's grin made her sick.

Before he could blink, Brisethi's elbow slammed into his face followed by her fist. She was able to get in a kick to his knee before two of his guards were able to take hold of her and forced her to the seat of the rowboat. "*That's* the scene I imagined ten years ago," she said snidely.

"Stupid move, bitch," he retorted. "No matter, your time will come." He wiped blood from his nose. "You're very fortunate she wants you unharmed and presentable for our customers." Brisethi sat in silence for the remainder of the ride.

When they climbed onto the deck of the ship, she was immediately apprehended by four guards, all of whom wore misshapen and mismatched clothes in random shades. She watched two more guards arrive on deck dragging Admiral Sen Asel behind them. At the sight of her beaten and bloodied father, she found herself unable to keep her emotions in check. "Dadi," her voice cracked.

He looked up at her with the one eye that wasn't swollen shut. "'Sethi," he rasped, "why are you here? I brought you up smarter than this – to never risk your life for mine." His voice was barely audible.

"Throw him overboard," a female voice ordered brusquely.

The figure of a woman with cornsilk hair came into view. Unlike the crew, her clothes were cut to fit and styled to accentuate her figure. As soon as the woman turned to face Brisethi, recognition hit her once more. "Sulica," she hissed.

The guards dragged the older man to the railing and pushed him overboard. At the same moment, Brisethi released her mystics. As she expected, her mystics were not responding. Before the guards could bind her she crouched down in a spin, grabbing one of the guards' pistols and aimed it at Sulica. She fired at her, but one of the guards had quickly shielded Sulica, taking the shot for her. Brisethi continued to fire at every guard near her, dodging every hand that tried to grasp at her.

When the pistol's chamber was empty, Brisethi rolled from more guards and pulled her two daggers from her boots, leaping in a spin to deflect nets attempting to catch her. She suddenly realized they weren't trying to kill her, only restrain her and used that to her advantage, showing no mercy. She cut the throat of one of the guards nearest her and elbowed another as more of Sulica's bandits continued to close in on her. She jumped onto ballasts and swung from one boom to another, throwing her daggers and piercing the chests of her would-be captors. Crouching low to unsheathe the two daggers from the inside of her sleeves, she began taunting the remaining guards holding their nets. They flung the net on her but she cut through them viciously and leapt back toward them, kicking them to the ground.

Brisethi finally understood the true importance of Dominion combat training without mystics. She had never imagined needing to fight without them when she was outnumbered. She silently thanked the spirits for having Etyne as a combat partner all those years to teach her the martial fighting that they had learned from ancient textbooks during their officer training. These bandits had nothing on her, and not even former Dominion Sergeant Trenn could keep up with her keenly honed agility and endurance.

She ran along the railing of the ship, ready to dive and meet up with her father when the sound of a rifle blasted, and a sharp pain pierced her back. She fell to the water, shocked from excruciating pain then sudden paralysis.

"I said not to harm her!" Sulica shouted. "Quickly, send for my healer!"

Kanilas Trenn dived in after Brisethi to save her, as he had the first time she fell into the ocean. "Just like old times, eh Sen Asel?" he told her, swimming with her in tow to the ladder. He slung her over his shoulder when they reached the rope ladder and carried her up it.

There was no response from the barely conscious Dominion Captain.

"You fucking morons! She's worth thousands, and you just killed her! Fuck!" Sulica knelt down next to her prize captive, checking for a pulse.

"I'm here," replied their healer. She knelt down next to the fallen captain to examine her. The healer rolled her onto her stomach and concentrated immediately on pulling the shot out of her back. She allowed her mystic to flow through the woman's veins, enhancing her cellular structure to repair the damage to her spine.

"She's lost a lot of blood and her lungs still have water in them," the healer said. Brisethi was rolled onto her back again so the healer could perform chest compressions. "Resuscitate her, Kanilas, while I work on inducing her neural system."

Kanilas happily obliged to place his mouth upon hers and moments later, the Dominion captain was coughing up blood and water and weakly moving her limbs.

"Bind her now!" Sulica ordered. "How did this crew ever function without me?" she questioned aloud to no one in particular.

Kanilas restrained Sen Asel while another guard tied her hands and feet, removing the remaining knife hidden in her belt.

"You morons let her kill half of you off! How the fuck was she that hard to control?" Sulica shouted when the prisoner was fully contained. She paced back and forth, running a hand through her disheveled hair.

"Shut up, Sulica!" Kanilas finally replied. "Her father had just as much fight, we were just lucky to knock him out quickly."

She glared at Kanilas mercilessly. "Should have captured her *before* she became an officer," Sulica muttered to herself.

"The fuck do you want with me?" Brisethi asked when she was finally done coughing. She prayed that her father had enough strength to survive the return to shore.

Sulica smirked gleefully down at the beaten captain. "How the Dominion's *finest* have fallen." She placed a hand on Brisethi's damp, burgundy hair. "You're going to make me so much money, little 'Sethi." The nickname sounded like a curse when Sulica said it. "I hope you enjoy your new home in Pahl'Kiar. Take her away."

"Bitch! I'm going to kill you!" Brisethi screeched. Her mind was empty of any other comebacks in her panicked state of mind. She struggled against the binds to no avail.

Kanilas and two of the crew dragged her below decks to the brig. "Now that you have no powers, I can finally do to you what someone should have done in training," he told her in a menacing tone. He proceeded to begin removing her uniform, but she wriggled away and fell to the ground.

"Get off me!" she shouted, desperately trying to flare her mystics.

He crawled on top of her. She waited until he was in the right spot then head butted him in his nose. Kanilas fell back, yelling in pain and clutching his nose for the second time that day. He kicked her in the ribs, hard. "Finish removing her uniform. Sulica wants it in pristine condition for the trade and needs to repair the hole in it," he ordered the two men.

"I wouldn't leave only two guards alone with me," Brisethi shouted at his retreating back.

The bigger guard held Brisethi tightly and rammed her head into the deck to shut her up, knocking her unconscious once more in order to remove her binds and her uniform.

"Not so strong after all," he muttered.

Chapter VIII

Brisethi woke from what felt like the longest sleep she'd ever had. Her lower back slightly ached from where the shot once penetrated. Her ribs were tender and bruised where Kanilas had kicked her. The rest of her body ached from lying on the hard deck for so many hours. Her hand, no longer bound, rubbed at her bruised head, feeling for blood, dried or otherwise. She'd taken blows to the head before, from Etyne and various rival teams during hak'ii, that put her out for hours, but none left her aching so badly as this one had. But there was a healer nearby to soothe the pain each time the officers in training knocked one another out during combative training.

Her body sat up slowly, struggling against the painful dizziness that threatened to put her to sleep again. Her eyes wandered around, taking in the relatively clean space around her. A porthole far above let in the moonlight, lighting a tray of food just inside the barred door. Her stomach rumbled at the sight.

She examined the burnt meat and stale bread and sipped at the cup of water. Shivering without her uniform, she proceeded to eat the old meal before the rats could. As she chewed on the crunchy bread, she looked around the rest of the small cell. Only a bucket in the corner meant for human waste shared the space with her. Not even a mattress or a blanket had been provided. *What century was this ship made in?* She asked herself upon observing the primitive, barren brig. The wooden boards beneath her were soiled and warped. The creaky bulkhead behind her had her worried for the structural integrity of the old galleon.

She couldn't remember the last time she had shivered from being cold. Her fire mystic had always been available to keep her body warm, but something was keeping her from summoning it. The rumors of mystic suppressing elixirs had proven true and somehow affected her without even physically being in contact with it. The thought of an entire Kiaran force using this potion against the Resarians frightened her terribly. With the elixir, it would have been easy for Sulica's crew to capture her father, and she prayed to the spirits for his safe return to help.

Dressed in only her black undershirt and undershorts, she shivered again, feeling more vulnerable than ever before. Taking a deep breath, she cleared her mind of her powerlessness to concentrate on a way to free herself. She scanned the cell bars of the brig, each one perfectly intact. She pulled at the lock to inspect its design and rattled the door. She stared up at the ceiling and found no vulnerability. She would have to devise a plan of attack for when the guards came down to hand her over to the Kiarans.

Brisethi lost track of how many days and nights passed, guessing from the four meals given to her, that it had been four days, but it was probably longer. She heard the light steps of someone walking down to the brig. She watched a hooded woman place a bucket of warm, soapy water in front of the cell along with a wash rag and a drying cloth.

"Hey," Brisethi attempted to say, her voice dry from lack of use, but the woman ran off quickly, uninterested in making friends.

Brisethi knelt down in front of the bucket and dipped her hands in the warm, soapy water. It was scented with the familiar sweet smell of the pink blossoms that bloomed in Res'Baveth every winter. The destination was apparently near if they expected her to clean up. She contemplated refusing on principle, but the warm water was too inviting. Her underclothes were quickly removed, and she used the rag to scrub down her body with the hot water. She rinsed her hair and clothes as well, wishing she had her mystics to dry herself.

Some time later, Kanilas Trenn and four guards visited her cell. He shoved her repaired uniform through the bars and ordered, "Get dressed. The more presentable you look, the more gold we'll receive."

She complied, insisting that she wasn't dressing to impress the Kiaran merchants for them; but to appear imposing, glorious. She would not be beaten by pirates and bandits. Dominion personnel retained their dignity and honor even while captive.

"Your hands," Kanilas stated, holding out the manacles.

"Come in here and I'll let you have my hands," she taunted, knowing he couldn't draw blood from her just before the trade.

He scowled. "Get in there and drag her ass out!" he ordered the four guards.

"Don't hurt me," she warned. "I'm sure the Kiarans aren't looking to buy 'damaged goods'," she sarcastically replied and backed into the wall on the opposite side.

The cell door opened and all four guards hastily made their way in, charging at her. She faked that she was going to roll toward them and instead leapt upon their shoulders and darted behind them – a trick that Etyne had spent weeks teaching her to master. She pounced on Kanilas, giving him no time to react and beating at him with her fists.

"Get this fucking animal off of me!" he shouted, finally pushing her off of him. Her wet hair covered part of her face, giving her the appearance of a savage woman.

The four guards finally restrained her, placing the manacles on her hands behind her back.

"You're so terrible at fighting, Trenn. You should have stayed with the division instead of playing scout for two years and missing out on combatives training," she spat, fire dancing in her eyes.

Brisethi was escorted to the main deck where an entourage of Kiaran officers and merchants were gathered, turning their heads to look at their prize. Sulica argued with the lead merchant who wanted proof that the Resarian girl was as powerful as the claim stated.

"Sir, you do realize that if I relieve my suppression mystic on her, she will summon devastation upon us all," Sulica said. She looked pale, and her eyes seemed more sunken in than the last time Brisethi had seen her.

Suppresion? She's a suppressor! Brisethi thought, stunned. *She's the reason my mystics won't work, not because of some elixir.* Young suppressors were not allowed training in their mystics because of the dangers of disabling entire Dominion squadrons if they chose to defect. Only the most dedicated law enforcement officials and high ranking officers of the Dominion were allowed such training. Once a suppressor was trained, they were never revealed to the public for their own safety. Brisethi wondered where someone like Sulica had learned to summon such an impairing mystic.

"If she's as powerful as you say she is, then my anti-mystic will do no good to me and I'll have to keep her unconscious until I get her to my customer," the Kiaran replied in his best Resarian translation. He was a gruff-looking man, a full head taller than Sulica. He had dark brown hair and a full beard, a trait not often seen on Sariadne. "But I don't even know what she's capable of because as you say, you have 'control' over her. No deal, ma'am."

"If I release her of my mystic, she'll set both of our ships on fire!" Sulica repeated frantically.

"How do I know you're not selling me a useless, weak Resarian! You've wasted my time, ma'am. Sink this ship," he ordered his men as he turned to leave.

"No, wait!" Sulica pleaded. "I'll do it. But I have to be out of her line of sight so that she doesn't incinerate me. I'd move out of her way, too, if I were you," she warned.

Brisethi smiled cynically at the event unfolding. She would have only one chance to summon the quickest but most devastating spell on only one of the ships. She still needed a way to get back – and a crew. She decided she'd rather take her chances with the more advanced Kiaran ship and its merchants in forcing them to take her back to Sariadne.

Sulica hid behind the helm on the bridge, peeking over at Brisethi and reluctantly stopped her suppression spell, anxiously waiting for the devastation she was sure would come.

"Well, what are you waiting for, Dominion *soldier*, summon a volcano from the sea," the Kiaran merchant ordered. His brown eyes had no pupils, much like Etyne's, though absent of any of his warmth.

Brisethi suppressed a smile. She shrugged and replied to him in Kiaran tongue. "I'm just a healer. She lied to you."

She dodged his hand when he attempted to strike her. He then ordered his guard to pull out his pistol and aim it at her head. "Show me your fucking magic or heal this shot that's about to puncture your head," he ordered.

In an instant, lightning flashed all around them, striking the masts of the Resarian ship, setting fire to its sails and masts. She had aimed a lightning strike at the Kiaran leader, but something about him saying he had anti-mystic on him had actually proven true and deflected her lightning strike, hitting one of his unfortunate guards instead. She felt her spirit crush in on her once more as Sulica's suppression mystic overpowered her.

The Kiaran merchant's attitude changed immediately as he stared in awe from the clear sky above to the Dominion military officer who summoned lightning from the sky. "I'll take you both!" he shouted to Sulica.

"*She* costs ten thousand frakshins – that was the deal," Sulica reminded him.

The Kiaran shook his head. "I don't think you understand, young lady. I can't bring this powerful Resarian on my ship without someone to control her. I am paying your second in-command ten-thousand frakshins but I'm taking you with me as well. Guards, seize them both!"

Brisethi laughed maniacally at the outcome of the deal. Chaos ensued as both ship's crews fired upon one another in the catastrophic turn of events.

Chapter IX

Master Chief Riquez and Lieutenant Vazeley anxiously waited for Sergeant First Class Kile and his scouts to return from the location that Captain Sen Asel had given them in her letter. The recruits milling around the camp started chattering loudly when Sergeant Kile finally returned, leading a black armored horse through the camp carrying a weary admiral. Captain Sen Asel was nowhere to be seen.

Lieutenant Vazeley and Master Chief Riquez rushed out of the command tent to meet the returning group.

"Sir," Vazeley greeted the admiral, saluting him out of respect and helped him to dismount his daughter's warhorse.

"Lieutenant, they have her. They took my little girl to Pahl'Kiar," Admiral Sen Asel stammered, wasting no time with formalities.

Riquez unleashed his healing mystic on the battered admiral, easing his pain and healing his wounds. "Who did this? You're certain that's where she's headed?" he asked as he worked.

Admiral Sen Asel nodded. "Yes, a group of Resarian bandits are selling her to Kiaran merchants." He briefed the commanders of everything he had learned of the ex-Dominion soldiers, including the suppressor, and the merchant ship they resided in.

"Sir, I can make it to Res'Baveth in eight days – faster than any messengers, to relay the news to Dominion command," Sergeant Kile said to the Lieutenant. His endurance mystics proved useful during the few days of tireless running to the southeast and then back to the north. His mystic was capable of enhancing both he and his mount to run faster and longer with only a quick rest once a day.

Lieutenant Vazeley agreed. "Leave as soon as you're rested. I'll have Chief Baderstoff and a handful of recruits escort the admiral to the nearest outpost to take him to Res'Baveth."

"Aye, Sir," Kile replied.

"A suppressor," Chief Baderstoff muttered. "When's the last time one of those were around?"

"Not in our lifetime, that we know of," Riquez replied.

"It's hard to imagine the poor captain without her mystics. Hopefully she put up a good fight," Baderstoff added.

"After the show she and Captain Vorsen put on a year ago, I'd say she did," Riquez said. "Can't wait till she tells us the story when she returns to us."

"In about two weeks, eh?" Baderstoff hoped.

-:- -:- -:-

Sulica stared at the sky that could barely be seen through the porthole. Hearing a noise, she turned and watched as Brisethi woke up. "How can you sleep so long on this hard deck?"

Brisethi rubbed at her eyes, sitting up in her rack and stretching. "How long was I out?" She unraveled her uniform coat which she had used as a pillow to refold it and keep it stowed away.

"I don't know, you sleep a rather long amount every night," was Sulica's reply. Her golden hair looked bedraggled and there were shadows under her hazel eyes.

"Well, one of us has to get beauty sleep," Brisethi retorted. The two women were being held in separate cells in the slightly nicer Kiaran brig per Sulica's request. She had pleaded with the Kiarans, claiming that, if Brisethi had the chance, she would kill Sulica with her bare hands and the suppression would be lost. She wasn't wrong.

"How long does your suppression last on a mystic, anyway? You need to regenerate sometime, don't you?" Brisethi crawled out of her rack to the deck. She laid on her stomach and placed her hands on the deck, shoulder-width apart. Though drowsy, she felt the need to retain her strength and proceeded to do push-ups, forty at a time.

Sulica shrugged, staring at the odd Resarian through the iron bars, containing her and protecting her simultaneously. "You're the tenth or so person I've used it on and never for more than a few days at time." She rested her head on the side of the cell not covered by bars. "I can feel the strain of it though, you're trying to overpower me."

Brisethi halted mid push-up to smirk up at Sulica. "I wouldn't want you to slip up, even for a second." She attempted to flare her mystic and watched Sulica flinch.

"Brisethi, I'm sorry! I realize the terrible mistake that I've made!" Sulica pleaded, already tired of having enemies all around her. "You're a very rational person, will you ever forgive me?"

"No!" Brisethi swiftly stood up and stormed over to the bars that divided them. "*You* suppressed my father, abducted him, beat him, threw him overboard – I don't even know if he's *alive*! If he managed to survive and swim to shore while still in binds, he's now mentally suffering knowing that his only daughter has been handed over to the Kiarans, betrayed by his own people. He has to tell my mother that he lost track of me and send her into a worried frenzy. And you're *sorry*? Fuck your apologies, Sulica. You're fucking dead."

Sulica sighed, realizing that trying to converse with Brisethi was pointless. "You always were the dramatic one with all your shouting."

Brisethi didn't deign to answer. She went back to her push-ups until her arms and chest were too weary to do more. Her focus would be on retaining the strength in her legs the next day. She sat down on the deck and leaned against the wooden bulkhead behind her. The swaying of the ship listing back and forth on the sea relaxed her, though she'd prefer it if she were in the open berthing instead of in the brig. She could hear the sound of rain and thunder outside, reminding her of the last storm she'd weathered. She yearned to return to the plains of Sariadne to finish training her recruits.

Her last memory of the stormy plains was when her division had integrated with Etyne's for two weeks. They had spent their last full day sparring from the crack of dawn until the evening when the two captains sat in Etyne's command tent, filling out logs and final memorandums to Dominion command, reporting the success of the integration. Massive cell clouds had rolled in from the sea that afternoon to cool off the arid plains, bringing a cool breeze through the tall grasslands around them. The cottonwood trees applauded the camp with their audible leaves. The two captains had remained oddly quiet, listening only to the drip-drops of rain as it poured down on the tent. At one point, they ceased all their paperwork momentarily to enjoy the small comfort of one another's friendship. They had walked out of the tent to stand under the covered entryway to watch the storm clouds casting lightning and thunder all around.

"I can't tell if that's natural lightning or if you're the one doing it," Etyne softly spoke.

"It's natural," she replied. "However, I *am* keeping it in the sky or far away so as not to strike our camp."

"Your mystics never cease to amaze me." He peered sideways at her, watching her eyes light up each time lightning struck. He felt her small hand inconspicuously take hold of his. He glanced around to ensure none of the recruits were in sight as he held her hand tighter momentarily.

She never forgot the look in his eyes each time their gazes met during those two weeks. There was a different aura that surrounded them both each time they were together. It was an inexplicable sense of calm, comfort, security, and an incomprehensible feeling of desire. She felt as though her very soul was craving him. She only hoped he had felt that as well. She wondered, if they hadn't been in uniform that day, surrounded by nearly two hundred recruits and senior enlisted commanders, if that night would have ended differently between them knowing it would be three years until they met again.

"I've missed you so much," she whispered. Eight years was a decent amount of time that they had spent with one another since meeting in the expedition. Though they didn't consider each other as friends for the first two years, they had shared enough memories during that time to reminisce about with one another. Since then, there was only one month of leave just after their expedition that they had been without the other. At the time, their friendship was completely platonic and he had barely crossed her mind when she was with Joss.

When Etyne was promoted to Captain at the end of their officer training, he was sent away to lead his own training division. For an entire year, Brisethi was left in Res'Baveth to lead the recruiting division which took little to no effort for her to charm the hearts of willing Resarians to join the Dominion Armed Forces. While surpassing her monthly quotas, she passed her time with the command hak'ii games, always picked up for goalie.

Brisethi reluctantly forced herself to stop reminiscing, to stop wondering. She was a Dominion captain and had a task to carry out. Her first task was to return home, her second task was to finish training her recruits. From there she could work on ranking up and carrying out her ambitions of diplomacy around the world. She had no time for flings or relationships. That much had been proven after Joss. She especially couldn't make her closest companion a temporary lover – she would lose him forever when things didn't work out. Things never worked out personally for people like them. The military lifestyle carried so much stress with it that it took a special kind of person to accept it.

"I can't believe I'm a prisoner of war," Sulica whined, interrupting Brisethi's thoughts.

"You're not a prisoner of war, *I* am," Brisethi corrected her. "You gave up your Dominion reservist status the moment you turned on your people, betraying the creed. Your family can plead all they want to Dominion command to have you rescued, but the Dominion has already exiled you. When I escape, and I will, I'll at least do your family the honor of returning your corpse back to them."

"Stop with the threats already, they no longer scare me," she replied, not caring to reveal that she no longer had a family.

"Is that why you're still suppressing my mystics?"

When she didn't answer, Brisethi reached into the pocket of her pants and pulled out a folded piece of paper. It was the one letter she'd received from Etyne since their integration. She read it for what must have been the tenth time.

'Sethi,

I finally had some time to sit down and write to both my mother and to you. I figured I'd spent enough time staring at the two paintings you gave me to actually let you know that I'm staring at them. I don't write much, as you can tell – my mind is always on work, sadly. As of late, however, not so much. I seem to have become distracted since our integration. Did things seem different between us during that time? Or was it just me? I tend to rarely let my mind wander about 'what could have been' and 'what could be' about anyone or anything. But you keep barging into my mind and having me wonder about such things. I miss you from the depth of my soul, 'Sethi.

~Etyne

Brisethi sighed and folded the letter to place it back in her pocket.

Neither she nor Sulica kept count of how many more days they spent at sea with minimal gruel and water fed to them every few hours. Sulica was given slightly more if only to keep up the strength needed to continue suppressing Brisethi's mystic. The women were not allowed to wash up unless they sacrificed their drinking water to do it. As the days passed, the dirt greased up their hair and sullied their clothes and skin.

"You could end this, you know," Brisethi said quietly one evening, wondering why the journey to Pahl'Kiar lasted days longer than it should have. She had become so weary on the little rations given that she was unable to even continue trying to keep up her physical routine.

"And let you kill me? Not a chance." Sulica's voice was even lower, exhausted from the continuous effort of suppression. She had no idea how much longer she could keep it up without some reprieve for regeneration. Her body could barely even move from exhaustion. She just leaned up against the bars so the food and water their captors pushed in was easily reachable with minimum effort. More and more, she found herself falling asleep, awakening with a start the moment she felt Sen Asel push against the suppression.

The following day, the two women could hear a rush of activity above them as the crew went through the motions of pulling into port and mooring the ship. The whole process took several hours to complete. Brisethi was just beginning to wonder if the Kiaran crew was completely incompetent when two of them came down the stairwell to retrieve the prisoners.

The two Resarians were escorted to the dock of the busy harbor when the sun was at its highest point in the sky. Brisethi was astonished at the view of tall buildings, carriages that weren't pulled by horses but powered on a rail system, and, most fascinating of all, the hot air balloon ships floating in the sky. When she glanced at the nearby banners and the language on the signs, it dawned on her that they were not in Pahl'Kiar.

"Why are we in Lantheus?" Brisethi asked aloud to no one in particular.

The Kiaran merchant chuckled. "Because they'll pay me far more for the two of you than our own emperor would. Besides, I can't risk someone as powerful as you running around in Pahl'Kiar." He patted the Resarian on the head, like he would to a child. "No, no, my dear it's best we hand you over to the Lantheun scientists to pull your mystics out of you and sell those back to my people to use against your people."

Brisethi was too weary and sickened to lecture the merchant about a potential future of uniting Kiarans and Resarians. She assumed it would fall on deaf ears of the greedy man.

A gathering of Kiaran and Lantheun shipyard workers started to follow the entourage when one of them noticed the Dominion uniform. "Great maker! What's that you got there? She another one of those witchcraft recruits?"

The Kiaran merchant chuckled again. "Oh, my no. She's a captain, and a damn powerful sorceress at that. Her mystics will bring glory to the Kiaran Empire, you'll see."

"Dominion scum! Not so tough outside your magical walls are you?" One of the workers shouted. Brisethi didn't even bother trying to see where the voice had come from.

"And that's why I no longer wear the uniform," Sulica muttered as they were led along the street.

"Because you're ashamed?" Brisethi sniped.

"No. But the whole world does hate us, you have to admit. We'll always be hated," she replied.

"Good. Let them fear us," Brisethi muttered.

The women were thrown into a rickety carriage, forced to sit across from one another, with two guards still assigned to them.

Brisethi examined Sulica's face. She had dark, nearly purple, circles under her eyes. She was suffering from having to keep her suppression mystic activated on Brisethi. She decided to push back with her own mystics and watched Sulica physically flinch from the pain of Brisethi's slowly overpowering mystics. *Soon, you'll fall, too,* she thought. *But I don't want to kill you with mystics. No, that's too unfair. Maybe you'll kill yourself trying to keep me from killing you.* She smiled menacingly at the thought.

After what seemed like an hour of a blind ride through the large city, the carriage came to a halt. A large building stood before them, one of the largest ones to be seen. It was slate gray in color, with few windows scattered sporadically along its facade. The two women were led through a black double door at the front. With the Kiaran escorts, they walked through massive corridors and climbed stairs to the third floor.

Lantheun scientists greeted the Kiaran merchant and his guards. They were slightly smaller in stature than the Kiarans but still taller than the Resarian women. The scientists were dressed in gray lab coats with masks covering everything but their eyes, making them look like giant bugs. They were holding an apparatus with a gauge that tested their mystic strength, they had explained to the Kiaran after noticing his wary look.

The three scientists appeared satisfied with their product and sent for their financial advisor to bring in the payment. He placed a large stack of paper frakshins into the hand of the Kiaran merchant. The Kiaran swiftly counted each printed bill representing various numbers of gold coins. When he reached the fiftieth frakshin marked with the number one-thousand, he smiled widely.

"Pleasure doing business with you," the Kiaran spoke in common Lantheun tongue.

"Likewise, sir," the Lantheun replied. "We will keep in contact with you should something unfortunate happen to these two and find ourselves in need of a replacement." His clipped tone was devoid of any emotion.

"Just remember to keep them apart. And if the short blonde dies, kill the tall fire one as soon as possible or she'll obliterate you all," the Kiaran warned with a chuckle, thankful to be rid of his charges.

"I'm sure that won't be an issue soon enough."

Lantheun armored guards took the two Resarians by their arms and escorted them down the remainder of the corridor. The chamber they entered was dark, lit only by the sunlight peeking through small windows high above. It reeked of death, the stench worsening the deeper they went. Both women peered into every cell they passed, seeing a few dead bodies, but mostly other humans of indeterminate nationality wearing only white gowns stained with blood and filth. The living humans shouted at the Resarians incoherently, tossing out unknown words in languages neither recognized. Some simply stared out of their cells with a catatonic gaze. Many had been picking at scabs or pulling at what was left of their hair. While others still, had no fingers or hands to pick or pull at anything. Only one other female resided among the others, and she stood in the center of her cell, pulling at her teeth and mumbling.

The women were shoved forcefully into their own cells across from one another. Their clothes were quickly torn from them, even their underclothes, and they were each given one of the white gowns to wear instead, clean for the moment.

"This is sick. I'm ready to leave already. Just give in, Sulica, let me end this!" Brisethi struggled against the panic that was threatening to envelop her mind.

"I'm not going to die from your fire," she replied stubbornly.

"Then fucking die in here like the rest of these people! Their minds are dead. And soon ours will be, too." Brisethi fought the hyperventilation but quickly lost control, screaming curse words in every language she knew.

Chapter X

Side by side they walked along the cobblestone lane lined with iron street lamps illuminating amber hues in the early morning. The fog was thick, giving them visibility of only a few blocks. The smell of woodfire from nearby homes mixed in with the dampness of the air leaving its evidence of a night rain. They avoided small puddles of water where the wet street and sidewalks were uneven.

It was a day off for most hard-working Resarians as the streets were quiet of carriages and horses. Large, ancient trees lined the medians of the roads, shedding their golden leaves to the stonework below. Neither of them were in a rush that day since both had been without their usual partner to see that afternoon.

Their favorite breakfast cafe, The Speckled Egg, awaited the two friends with their regular booth. Etyne had ordered his typical spiced tea while Brisethi sipped at her sweetened coffee. A stack of fluffy, buttery flatcakes were placed in front of each of them. They smiled at one another as they smothered their warm flatcakes with sweet syrup before giving in to their morning hunger.

"This is probably the first day that neither of us has anyone to see this evening," Etyne spoke while chewing.

"I don't suppose you want to go to the zoo with me?" she asked. "The animals will be more inclined to show face on such a cool, cloudy day."

Etyne nodded with a smile. "What animal do you want to see the most?"

"If the aquarium is finished, I want to see the giant octopus! Otherwise, the great cats have always been my favorite," she replied, unable to keep the childlike excitement from her voice.

"You've not been to it recently?" he asked.

She shook her head. "We tend to usually run errands if we're not at our parents' or relaxing at his house," she muttered in reference to Joss.

"'Sethi, I will gladly take you to see the great cats and the giant octopus," he smiled once more to her, his eyes bright and playful.

Brisethi woke from the memory, strapped down to a table, pieces of leather tethering her wrists, ankles and head so that she could not move. The throbbing sensation in the back of her skull reminded her of the fight that had ensued when two armored guards retrieved her from her cell. She had cried for Sulica to release the hold of her mystic but she still refused. Instead, she'd felt a sharp pain hit the back of her head as her world faded to black. The cruel reality of her situation was coming back to her, threatening to erase any pleasant memories she'd ever had. At feeling crisp air tingle the sides of her head, she realized half of her head had been shaved to allow an apparatus to cleanly attach to the skin above her ears.

An incision in her arm startled her. "What-" she tried to say, but the words died in her throat as the pain hit her. Her skin was neatly sliced to her veins to allow her blood to be collected in the containers below her. A piercing scream ripped from her mouth at the pain and shock of seeing the amount of blood pour from her arm.

The Lantheun scientist placed a rolled up rag into her mouth, stifling the sound. "Can't have you turning me deaf with your constant shrieking," he told her. His tone gave the impression that she was no more than a buzzing mosquito to him, mildly distracting, but not a real issue. He then proceeded to activate the machine connected to the apparatus around her head. Seconds later, flashes of blue lights struck the metal band on her head, binding her mystics to her blood. She frantically tried to escape like a rat caught in a vicious trap, sending her into tears as she continued screaming into the rag.

They're fucking with my mind, she thought in terror. She screamed again when she felt her blood burn in every artery of her body as her spirit tried to tear away from its vessel. Every drop of blood was a piece of her spirit separating from itself. She prayed to the spirits to let it end, to take her away to the Sea of Renewal.

Sulica watched the guard and the scientist drag Brisethi's limp body back to her cell. She heard the other woman's screams just moments ago that made her tremble in fear. She wondered dimly why they had shaved the sides of her head then noticed the burn marks left in perfect circles where Brisethi's head had been shaved that sent shivers up her own spine.

"You may release your suppression spell of her for now, to allow yours to regenerate. She won't wake from her coma until I say so," the scientist told Sulica. Reluctantly, she released her hold on Brisethi and immediately felt the relief washing over her as her mystic began regenerating.

After seeing the fight Brisethi had put up with the guard earlier that morning, Sulica quickly abided by the guard's orders when he opened her cell door in hopes they would be more lenient with her. She allowed herself to be led off without a struggle. "What do you want with us?" she asked the scientists strapping her to the table.

"The same as everyone wants with a Resarian: to capture the anomalies you conjure and use it as our own," the lead scientist replied with a sigh. He made it obvious that he'd had to answer the question multiple times and wasn't in the mood to discuss it again.

"Our mystics? But they're given to us through our spirits. You can't just take away our spirits and expect to use them. They are returned to the Sea of Renewal. Spirits are incorporeal souls of ancient beings – not physical entities to be contained," Sulica explained, bemused by their lack of research.

The sides of her head were shaved by a second scientist, giving her the same deplorable look as Brisethi. That scientist then said, "Someday you'll realize that there's no such thing as spirits and your heathen, fabricated sea of renewal. Our Maker would never bless one race of beings with such power. There's a scientific method for your ability to manipulate the elements. We just need to find the right equation to clone it so we don't have to keep paying Kiarans to abduct you."

"Your *Maker?*" she hissed and recollected her basic world history classes and their various religions. "You believe in some deity you've never seen before yet think that our 'spirits' are just anomalies?" She groaned through gritted teeth when the third scientist sliced at her arms, allowing the blood to flow to the new containers below. The scientist repeated the torture on her other forearm while the metal band was placed upon her head. She, too, felt the painful shock of mystic blood binding and screamed into the rolled up rag. The containers below captured the fused, mystical blood.

"She's only a suppressor," one of the scientists stated. "We'll make more gold selling her back to the Kiarans. We should keep only what we need to keep the other one under control." Moments later, Sulica's world went dark.

-:- -:- -:-

A distant owl's hooting that night startled Sulica and Brisethi from their already restless sleep on the cold stone floor. The scientists didn't have the decency to replace the filthy mattresses causing both women to huddle in a random corner of their cells when they required sleep. Their lack of sleep, combined with the advanced apparatus that "bonded" their mystics to their blood was fuel to their throbbing headaches.

"Why is that owl so damn loud?" Brisethi asked in the dark of their cells.

"It isn't any louder than the owls back home. It's just incessantly quiet in here," Sulica retorted. After spending more than five years on ships surrounded by her crew, she wasn't used to the silence either. She hardly had social interaction since becoming a captive and yearned to talk to anyone. "Do you think anyone's out there looking for us?"

Brisethi remained on her sore back staring up at the mildew-infested ceiling as her eyes adjusted to the darkness. Her neck, shoulders and hips ached from lying on her side on solid stone for the past hour. "The Dominion is looking for me, yes. I doubt if the crew you treated so terribly is on their way for you, however."

Sulica realized now why Brisethi ignored her so often in expedition training. The way Brisethi spoke to her now must have been how Sulica sounded to her back then. "How long do you think they'll keep us in here?"

"Until we die if we don't escape," Brisethi assumed. "Look at those others, the ones who have lost their minds. How long do you think they've been here?"

As if attempting to answer, one of the other females in the cell further down mumbled incoherently. Sulica picked at a thread from her still decently clean gown. Her legs and feet were cold from the stone floor as she brought her knees to her chest under her gown. Neither of them were given shoes or socks. She wondered if they would be allowed to bathe as she stared at the small toilet in the opposite corner of her cell. She was already missing the small necessities of her daily routines such as a toothbrush, a hairbrush, soap and washrags. It was only their second night in the laboratory but the hours seemed to last days. She heard heavy breathing coming from Brisethi's cell. "Did you already fall back to sleep?"

"No, my nose is stuffed, I'm about to use my gown to blow into it, gosh I'm already disgusting. Are they ever going to give us more wipes? I used the last of mine earlier to 'bathe'."

Sulica furrowed her brow at Brisethi. "With what water? The toilet?"

"Yeah," Brisethi replied with a short laugh. "I'm not trying to impress anyone, I just wanted to wash the dirt off my feet." She held a foot toward Sulica and wiggled her toes.

"Are you already going mad?" Sulica asked and reached over to her pile of unused cloth wipes. She wadded a few of them up and started throwing them across the corridor to Brisethi's cell.

"Probably," Brisethi replied as she reached for the pieces of cloth given to her by Sulica. Some of them didn't quite make it to her cell as she reached her arm through the bars. Her fingers barely reached them to pull them in. "Thanks."

Brisethi had already spent over two weeks as a prisoner, combining the two ships and the current laboratory. She felt as though her sanity was already slipping away and found a sort of calm in scrubbing dirt off of her body. For a moment, she almost forgot how much she hated Sulica for putting her through this madness.

Both girls turned their heads toward the main door at the end of the corridor when they heard the lock release.

"I hope that's the cleaning crew," Sulica chimed, attempting to find any small amount of content in a visitor.

"Oh, it's just the guards. They're here early, even earlier than the scientists," Brisethi muttered.

They became silent when Dasni, the smaller Lantheun guard, unlocked Sulica's cell. He placed a small lantern outside her cell and let himself in.

Brisethi curiously watched, wondering if he was the one replacing their cloth wipes, perhaps preparing them for a bath.

"What are you doing?" Sulica asked the guard when he began forcefully removing her gown. She threw fists at the guard but he casually grasped both of her hands and cuffed them. "Get off of me!" she shrieked with cringe and terror when he grabbed at her breasts. He began to unbuckle his belt and remove his trousers.

"Hey!" Brisethi instinctively called out. The woman was her adversary, but even she didn't want to be in the presence of what was about to happen to her.

"Oh, you want to join in, fire girl?" Dasni asked her.

If it would allow her out of her cell for a chance to escape, she replied in a voice of desire, "Yes, actually."

"Ha, I'm not that stupid!" he replied while holding his hand on Sulica's mouth to quiet her screams. Sulica was already stripped of her underclothes as she kicked at the man. He threw her onto her face and held her legs down, spread apart.

Brisethi covered her ears and closed her eyes at what happened next. Sulica's screams of pain echoed through her covered ears. For a moment, she wanted to help her by trying to distract the guard. But deep down inside her vengeful thoughts, Brisethi realized it was Sulica who got them both in this situation. As far as she was concerned, she had it coming. She glanced over one last time, certain it would be her turn if she didn't strategize a plan of attack.

Chent, the bigger Lantheun guard startled Brisethi when he arrived at her cell.

"Why are you both here so early?" Brisethi courageously asked, rising to her feet.

Chent grinned widely. "The scientists won't be here for another hour. Guess what we get to do in the meantime?"

"Sulica! Release your suppression of me!" Brisethi shrieked. She would not be able to overpower such a brawny man.

But Sulica was already disconnected from herself, retreating mentally to avoid further injury. She went limp, trying to shut out any and all of her senses, squeezing her eyes closed, tuning out Dasni's grunts and Bresethi's shouts.

Weakened from lack of nutrition and minimal water, Brisethi faced her perpetrator. Chent grinned at her, reaching for his belt. Brisethi waited until he was away from the cell door as she sprung into action. She sprinted to the cell door, knowing it was unlocked. She pulled it toward herself, awaiting her freedom.

The cell had automatically locked.

Chent laughed. "You're going to need this key," he held up the same key to the outside of her cell door.

Infuriated and disheartened, she lunged at the man. Her fists landed to his face, her kicks found his ribs, but he was careful to guard his most vulnerable area, accustomed to fighting off weakened prisoners.

Chent continued laughing, enjoying the fight. He was surprised at how skilled she was at dodging all of his attacks. Growing frustrated he finally unsheathed a small knife from his boot. "You're going to tire me out before I've even had you," he heavily breathed.

"You would stab me? Property of the laboratory?" Brisethi taunted, knowing her blood was needed by the scientists and shouldn't be wasted.

Chent wiped at his bloody nose his prisoner had given him with his sleeve then spit more blood and saliva out onto the floor. He advanced toward her, knife in hand but she dodged yet again. She was quickly tiring from lack of proper meals for the past two weeks. She couldn't keep running, dodging and fighting someone stronger than her, weak as she was and without the aide of her mystics. She kicked toward his groin area but wasn't quick enough to retract in her weary state. Chent was quick to plunge the knife into her foot, causing her to yelp.

Brisethi couldn't ignore the tear of a tendon in her foot and fell to the ground. She applied pressure to her open wound but was quickly grasped by Chent.

He used all of his might to bring her hands behind her back and cuffed them. "Hey Dasni, I don't think you'll be able to handle this one, she's most likely stronger than you," Chent chuckled.

Brisethi looked over to Sulica who had finally been left alone as Dasni locked her cell. She was still in a catatonic state, naked and lying on her stomach. She shuddered to think that she too, would be left in that position.

Panic crept into Brisethi when Chent pulled her legs toward him and pushed up her gown. Her underclothes were ripped from her body. She strained to keep her legs together, crossing them and kicking at him despite her foot injury. Blood from her foot and reopened wounds caused by the scientists seeped onto the ground. Chent, healthy and energetic, overpowered her and began to strangle her.

Brisethi couldn't believe this was about to happen to her.

She had been through the training, multiple times. Her mother lectured her more times than she could remember, to not get raped, as if it were the victim's fault for not taking every precaution to avoid predators. She had fought off multiple bandits, pirates and sparred with fellow Dominion soldiers. She could defeat almost anyone, even her own best friend who had trained her to become as skilled as him. But she had never fought any of them after two weeks of little to no food, weakened muscles, and without the use of her mystics.

It could never happen to me, she used to think. *I'm stronger than a lot of men*, so she thought.

She inhaled deeply when Chent released his grip on her throat and shrieked when she felt his fingers shoved into her. She shouted once more to wake Sulica but to no avail. Her body was succumbing to defeat as he finally pried her legs open and forcefully let himself in.

Sulica, with eyes full of tears and unable to process what just happened, looked on with remorse.

When the Lantheun guard was finally finished with her, Brisethi crawled to the toilet. Her foot was throbbing, her thighs ached, her tender skin burned. She hunched over the toilet and proceeded to vomit. She suddenly regretted her earlier thought that

Sulica had this coming to her. No one, woman or man, deserved to be violated like that.

After spitting out the rest of the bile from her mouth she sat on the toilet. Her body was defiled; ripped and torn in places not meant for such acts. She needed her body to flush out everything the Lantheun had left in her. At feeling completely broken and helpless, she planted her face into her hands and sobbed.

What kind of monster takes pleasure in destroying another human's life in such a way?

-:- -:- -:-

The air was crisp with the leftovers of night fading away. Dew still clung onto the grass, waiting for the morning sun to warm the field where the horses had been turned out to graze. There were four of them, two strong quarter horses, a prancing paint, and a beautiful, grand Bediaran stallion.

Sulica and her sister Ganasi stepped up onto the bottom rail of the fence, watching raptly as their mother entered the pasture. Marisil Nin was beautiful - the kind that seemed effortless and captivating, even when cleaning out the stalls. Today, she had tied back her bright golden hair to keep it out of her face as she worked. Her thin frame approached the group of horses, but she kept her face down and hand outstretched.

The paint and one of the quarters turned on a dime and dashed away. Gasani gasped while Sulica gripped the fence harder, silently. Their mother did not even flinch. She kept moving towards the two who remained, slowing her steps. The other quarter, chocolate brown in color, didn't move. He'd been through this before, knew that the lady was kind and rewarding. Marisi focused her attention on the white Bediaran, who had looked up and snorted, alternating lifting his forelegs. Marisil slowed more, but still moved forward, never lifting her head.

The two girls on the fence held their breath as Marisil inched closer to the powerful stallion. Finally, after what seemed like an eternity, the woman's fingers felt the soft hair on the horse's nose. She glanced up, and he was staring intently at her, quivering, but his hooves had stopped. Marisil grinned, continuing to rub the horse and reaching up with the rope she'd concealed, wrapping it around his ears to fashion a halter. Still patting him, she led the horse back to the fence where her daughters were waiting.

"Be gentle," she warned the girls quietly, looping the halter around the fence to secure the horse.

Ganasi moved slowly, imitating her mother, to rub the horse's nose and sculpted neck. Sulica stepped off the fence, too frightened by the power in the chest and legs to even try. She preferred the demure quarter horse that Marisil had gone to retrieve next for their ride through the woods.

-:- -:- -:-

Chief Pyraz had just finished handing out everyone's mail to the recruits when she handed Captain Vorsen his stack; mostly from Dominion command.

"Ugh, that's more than usual," he sighed. He was in the middle of responding to the letter he received from Brisethi over two weeks ago. Some of the things she'd written in it disturbed him, a dampened mood evident in her words. It almost sounded final, as if they'd never see each other again. He read it over for a third time:

> *Etyne!*
>
> *I imagine by now that you're wallowing in your sorrows of how much you miss me. I'm sorry that I took nearly five months to write back to you, although I was surprised you had finally written to me. Two more years to go until we get to spar again, I can't wait to knock you to the ground once more- if that time ever comes. I will defeat you in a strangle one day!*
>
> *To answer your question from your last letter, yes, Etyne, things were different between us – more personal and calming. I only wish I would have given you a proper goodbye, though – had I known. You know, more than just a handshake and a salute. That's way too formal for how good of friends we are, don't you think? Anything could happen to us out here in the expedition, and I don't want my last memory of us to be a handshake. There are things I should have told you, Etyne. Things that I'd rather you heard from my voice instead of read in my horrible handwriting. But I lacked the nerve and now it's too late. Maybe I'll get a second chance to find my courage if we meet again.*
>
> *Spirits be with you,*
>
> *'Sethi*

Etyne folded the letter and placed it in his pocket to finish penning the one for her. Her letter had nearly driven him insane for unspoken words of two different subjects; what she was feeling for him, and what she was feeling in general. Her cryptic words alluded to something going on that she either would not or could not speak of. He finished his letter and placed it in an envelope, finalizing it with his Dominion seal on it.

He hoped he hadn't been too forward but couldn't help but recall their last sparring bout on the grassy plains. They had tired one another out from fighting from sunrise until the thunder clouds started appearing that evening on the horizon.

Lying on his back, she was on top of him and had him in a fairly weak and playful chokehold; but all he could do was stare at her face, holding her hands that were still on his neck. Her burgundy hair had come loose from her bun, scenting the air around them with the blossom oils she used in it. The gray sky enhanced her gray eyes and for a second, he swore he'd seen lightning flashes in them. She gave up on trying to choke him and instead stared almost longingly at his face, at his eyes almost smiling.

"I never knew I could miss someone as much as I missed you," Etyne had softly told her. He was feeling his very soul longing to be near Brisethi's spirit, as if they had somehow bonded without their vessels knowing.

She smiled widely at such innocent, meaningful words. "It's only been two years. And I know how busy you've been, I'm going through all of the same bull manure as you are leading an expedition. Time is flying by!"

"I'm uncertain if I can go three more years without your silly antics, your laughter, this bond we somehow forged with one another," he courageously stated, lightly caressing one of her hands she had still not removed from his neck.

Etyne especially remembered the touch of her fingers along the side of his cheek after that statement. He never wanted to forget when she began to lean in just as Master Chief Riquez had called for her attention. Startled and terrified of being caught about to break the Uniform Code of Dominion Regulations, they quickly separated to tend to her division's needs.

Korteni finished reading the first letter from command and quickly got to her feet. The sudden movement caused Etyne to look up at his Chief who was staring at him with worry all over her face. "Sir," she handed him the letter. "'Sethi's gone."

His thoughts scattered at the haunting sound in her voice the way she spoke of Brisethi sending chills up his spine. "What do you mean?" He tore the letter from her hand and read it quickly.

"She's gone, Etyne!" Tears began to blur Korteni's eyes, all thought of military bearing dashed in her grief. "She could be dead for all we know - this happened over a month ago!"

Etyne's heart sank lower with each line he read. "No, they're out there looking for her. She's probably already been rescued."

"Since when has the Dominion ever successfully rescued a Resarian from the Kiarans?" She immediately covered her mouth with her hands, not intending to shout.

Etyne ignored her outburst. After he finished reading about Brisethi's father and the suppressor who captured them both he slammed the letter into his desk. "That's what she fucking meant in her letter." Angered, he took it back out and brandished it. "She wrote this the day before her capture-she knew she was risking her life for her father. She was so cryptic and I didn't see it!" Etyne grew frustrated and sat down to rub at his face. "I have to find her."

"How? How can we infiltrate Pahl'Kiar and find her?" Korteni wiped the tears from her cheeks.

Master Chief Denil stormed in the command tent with a civilian man and a hooded woman behind him. "Sir, apologies for the intrusion, these two say they have information regarding Captain Sen Asel? Did I miss something?"

"Trenn?" Etyne recognized the egotistical man from their initial training expedition. He stood up once more to approach the reservist, his eyes narrowed. "What do you know about her?"

"Please, Sir, you have to help. They've taken Sulica to the Lantheun capital. I need your help rescuing her, yours was the closest division to the harbor," Kanilas Trenn pleaded, displaying a courtesy Etyne had never before seen from him.

"What about Sen Asel?" Etyne crossed his arms.

"Yes, they have her, too! They took them both! Please, Captain," The desperation in the man's voice was evident.

"The Dominion sent their rescue efforts to Pahl'Kiar. They have no idea she's in the Lantheun capital. What are they doing there? How do you know that's where they are?" Etyne interrogated.

"I'll fill you in on all the details on our way there, Sir," Kanilas told him.

"How can we be certain this isn't a trap?" Master Chief Denil asked.

"Because you know I could never lie to you," the hooded woman said, dropping the hood to reveal her face.

"Ibrienne?" Korteni and Etyne said together, shocked.

Ibrienne instantly lost her composure. "I've done terrible things. Please let me redeem myself by going with you to save our friends." She took Korteni's hands in her own. "Please," she repeated.

Etyne raked his black hair with his hands, contemplating his dilemma. He desperately wanted to believe his former comrades and go to Lantheus to save Brisethi, but it very well could have been a trap conjured by the Lantheuns.

"We have to risk it, Captain," Korteni encouraged his decision. "It could take another month once word gets to the Dominion command to have them redirect to Lantheus!"

Etyne nodded. "You're right. Better to have died trying to find her than waiting around for the Dominion to do something while she suffers."

"We *are* the Dominion, Sir. Let's go save her," Master Chief Denil replied.

The training division had just completed their six months of mystic training, leaving them only a day away from Ancient Kiar and the Dominion Naval harbor where the *DSV Reliant* awaited them. Etyne needed only to convince the training commanders onboard and assumed they'd oblige in helping to rescue the daughter of one of their admirals.

Chapter XI

"Why won't you end it for us already?" Sulica pleaded to Brisethi when the guards arrived for what felt like the fiftieth time that month. Though it had become a daily routine to bleed just enough mystics out to remain alive, each new cut to their skin was more painful than the last. Their arms and legs were covered in scabs, causing the scientists to move on to cutting at their backs for new blood.

"Release your suppression of me!" Brisethi shouted back to her, fending off the two guards in her cell. Both of their voices had become hoarse from their screams.

"I stopped suppressing you weeks ago! I would rather you killed me than live out the rest of my days in this atrocity!" Sulica cried out right before the single Lantheun guard in her own cell forced her onto her front. Sulica had been fortunate enough to have only been taken to the lab twice a week after the first week since her suppression mystic wasn't in demand of the Lantheuns. But her counterpart was still undergoing the painful task of removing her spirit every afternoon.

"Then why can't I cast anything?" Brisethi's voice broke when one of the guards held her by her throat. She had already forgone her torture in the lab that afternoon and couldn't understand why the guards returned for them.

"Shut up, both of you!" The third guard shouted then pointed to Sulica's cell. "Dasni, don't touch that one, she's being sold today. You'll have to share the red-head with Chent."

"The fuck he will!" Chent shouted, still holding his prize by her throat.

"Come on, Chent, you've had her this whole time-" Dasni was cut off.

"No! She's coming home with me when the scientists are through with her," Chent shouted back. He grinned down at Brisethi. "You'd like that, wouldn't you?" he said in what he must have thought was an arousing voice to her.

Brisethi kicked at the guard as she usually did every other day, but he was bigger than the average man, nearly twice the size of the scientists, and he easily held her down. She lost the fight every time he had her, but not without leaving dozens of bruises, bite-marks and scratches on him. Each time she put up an even weaker offense, though that didn't stop her from trying.

Dasni watched the vicious fight and instantly walked off. "Never mind, Chent, she's all yours. Too much trouble, that one is."

Chent chuckled. "The Dominion doesn't joke around when it comes to training their little officers." He encouraged her fight, thoroughly enjoying the victory each time. It was easier to plant her face to the cold stone floor and bind her from behind when she was worn down.

Sulica turned to face the stone wall and cover her ears. Brisethi's screams pierced through what was left of her soul every time the guards had their way with her. The sight of watching the same acts performed on her had her quivering, knowing it would soon be her turn again.

The first time the guards had taken advantage of Sulica, Brisethi glanced momentarily at the atrocious act. In Brisethi's mind, Sulica was the reason they were undergoing the torture at all. She wanted only to verify that her adversary was enduring the same heinous treatment as herself as recompense for their capture. But by her second, third, and each time after that, Brisethi did the same as Sulica and turned to face the wall, covering her ears from the screaming.

Brisethi weakened faster than usual. She was running on adrenaline alone, unable to recall the last time she ate solid food. Blood dripped from every inch of flesh that had been cut in the laboratory as each wound re-opened during the battle. Her white gown was stained with her blood and the black inky substances the scientists had put in the water she was forced to drink. The substance was Sulica's suppression mystic in liquid form.

She kept her ferocity up with the guard but didn't scream this time. She knew that men like him liked making their victims scream and beg for them to stop. She also knew that this one in particular loved the fight. She was running low on options in preventing the inevitable.

It was the worst feeling both women had ever experienced every time the men visited them. Each time they were rendered powerless, her body was in control of the malevolent guards; the possibility of extensive, horrifying physical injury or death was very real to her. Each was truly frightened each time they grabbed at her, humiliated her. Every bit of sovereignty was stripped from her with every painful thrust into her body. The only option seemed to be disassociation each time they had their way with her, feeling her spirit abandon her body.

Sudden realization set in that he would probably leave Brisethi alone if she were unconscious, or at least, she wouldn't have to consciously endure the despicable acts. She stopped resisting, feigning that she was tired. The guard finally had the chance to dominate her. When he leaned in close enough, before having the chance to turn her onto her stomach, she slammed her forehead into his, knocking them both unconscious.

Sulica glanced back at the sudden silence, horrified at the sight of blood pouring from both of them. The two remaining guards laughed at their idiot comrade and dragged him out of Brisethi's cell, locking her door.

"Sen Asel," she whispered. "Wake up, *please.*" She peeked down the corridor through the iron bars of her cell to make sure the guards were gone. She thanked the spirits they did not take their turn on her this day. "Brisethi," her voice echoed. "Don't you fucking leave me!"

Sulica's vision darkened. She was dehydrated. What was left of her nails scratched at the scabs on her arms. She tried to remain conscious, but her hunger pangs overwhelmed her, forcing her to fall into blackness.

-:- -:- -:-

"Oh gosh, he's beautiful!" she gleefully exclaimed, walking toward the giant octopus. The finished aquarium at the Res'Baveth Zoo was the main attraction that year. The crisp, foggy overcast had kept most of the citizens at home that day, leaving the zoo fairly empty of crowds.

Etyne was more focused on the overwhelmingly large hammerhead shark swimming in and out of the live, vibrant coral. Both were astonished as soon as the majestic stingray floated by, unbothered by anything not as big as himself. The two friends proceeded to walk through the rest of the park, stopping at every area where an animal was present. The giant snow bears swam in their makeshift icy river, the ancient elephants pushed around wooden spools with their trunks, while colossal giraffes chewed on leaves from the towering trees.

Brisethi stared in awe at the sleek black panther strolling along the low tree branches. His huge paws revealed predatory claws while his lengthy tail helped him to keep his balance. It's deep yellow eyes looked up at her from beneath his brows. "So majestic," Brisethi murmured.

They spent more than three hours viewing most of the animals at the city zoo and found their way to the gift shop. She wanted to get something for Korteni and picked out a pendant in the shape of rat's skull plated in silver to appease her friend's fascination with dead things. Brisethi couldn't pass up picking out a plush octopus for herself to adorn her lonely bed in her quarters. Etyne insisted on buying it for her, as sort of an early winter solstice gift and she happily obliged.

Brisethi stirred from one of her more cherished memories and opened her inky eyes. Her head was pounding, her stomach was empty, every muscle in her body ached and her open wounds, including her tender skin between her legs burned from infection. She couldn't possibly fight anyone off in her ailing state.

"I await for madness," she softly spoke.

She stared up at the ceiling trying not to think about how filthy she was, the amount of diseases flowing through her veins. She pulled at matted hair that hadn't been shaved off of her head and began grinding her teeth. When her teeth and gums began to hurt she attempted to pull at them until her fingertips hurt. She then pulled at her fingernails until they bled. She grew frustrated that she could no longer scratch at her itchy scabs and began to bite at them. It was a vicious cycle her mind had created to pass the time. Every little annoyance drove her to lose another piece of her sanity.

She slowly rolled onto her side to look at Sulica's debilitated form either asleep or unconsciousness across the corridor. In the dim lighting she was able to see that Sulica had been dressed in a new, white laboratory gown. She peered through the bars and watched half a dozen men walk toward them. Two Lantheun scientists, one Lantheun guard, two military men, and what looked to be a tall nobleman dressed in an ornate coat stopped between her and Sulica's cells.

"This subject is the suppressor we mentioned. The one behind you is but a mere firebringer," the scientist said to the well-dressed man.

"She's so frail; don't you feed your prisoners?" The noble asked. His slight accent told Brisethi that he was not a native Lantheun.

The scientist dry washed his hands. "Just enough to keep them alive. They are rewarded with food every now and then-"

"She looks sickly. Will she even make it back?" The noble interrupted the Lantheun.

He nodded. "She will live her expected nine-hundred year lifespan, I assure you."

"I'm not paying full price for her, she's not even conscious. I'll pay you half of what you asked," the nobleman said off-handedly.

"If you pay full price for her, I will give you that one for free," the scientist haggled, pointing at the other ill Resarian.

The noble man walked over to Brisethi's cell. She glared up at him, too weak to stand and instead, clung to the iron bars to sit on her knees. She found an inexplicable inner calm at the prominent features of his turquoise eyes without pupils, his long ebony hair that was tied behind his head, and his bronzed skin, reminding her of someone she knew.

The foreign man leaned over to examine her. Unbothered by her repulsive appearance and potential disease, he gently grasped her jaw in one hand, and raked her messy hair with the other. It was a tender touch she hadn't felt from anyone in years, experiencing only violence and suffering for the past weeks. "If I had use of you, I would end your torture and take you with me as well," he softly told her in her native language. His voice struck a chord of familiarity in her.

Her voice was barely audible. "I, I promise that I won't-"

"Unfortunately, I cannot sustain two Resarians at once," he cut her off to spare anymore emotions in such a morbid building. "I hope the spirits allow you to rest in peace soon."

His rejection of her was torment to her emotions.

She tried to reach for his hand, but he turned away to walk back to the other cell and knelt down beside Sulica. "I only want this one, for half the price you're asking," he demanded. His military men grew restless and cracked their knuckles before the scientist.

"But, she can keep me suppressed," Brisethi's plea went unheard, her voice scratchy and hoarse.

"Fine, fifty-thousand frakshins," the scientist ceded, slightly pleased that he'd made all his money back from the sale of the one Resarian.

One of the foreign man's military guards handled the currency trades while his other guard gently picked up Sulica from her cell. Brisethi's heart ached as she watched every member of the entourage exit the dark corridor.

"Please come get me!" Brisethi cried aloud. She longed to hear that Kiaran man's soothing voice again, feel his gentle touch, and stare into his comforting eyes. She was falling apart inside at watching the woman who brought them both to torture, find freedom in the arms of a savior. When everyone had exited the floor, she screamed in mental agony. "What about me!" she shrieked over and over, followed by tormenting screams until her voice gave out. Profoundly deranged she searched for her voice and crawled back and forth along the bars of her cell.

Her insides churned from the despair as she crawled to the toilet in the corner of her cell. She tried to vomit, but only the smallest amount of clear liquid oozed out. She wiped her mouth with her filthy gown. She was disgusted at herself and what had befallen her. She was infuriated that Sulica had found freedom without her. Her minor consolation through the whole ordeal was that at least her original captor was suffering with her, but now she would suffer alone.

-:- -:- -:-

The sunlight broke through the branches of the trees along the path, but the air remained cool as the two girls and their mother rode through the forest. Sulica eased back into the saddle of the calm chocolate quarter horse, comforted by his easy pace. Her sister Ganasi had the brown and white paint, as spirited as the girl was, while Marisil rode the majestic Bediaran, not trusting him to be calm enough yet for her daughters.

"Will Dadi be waiting for us when we get there?" Ganasi asked.

"If we've timed it right," Marisil answered with a smile.

Sulica heard a crack, like a branch breaking, and urged the horse to catch up to the others. Ganasi pulled further ahead, the paint breaking into a trot.

"Careful," Marisil cautioned. "There are creatures in this forest which will spook the horses."

Ganasi tossed her hair and laughed. "Pin won't let anything happen." She leaned over to rub the horse's neck.

Sulica wished she could share in her older sister's confidence. She felt a prickling at her senses that made her uneasy. Her mother seemed to catch on to it as well, trying to be subtle as she looked around while they rode. Ganasi had continued ahead, carefree, around a bend in the path. Suddenly, they heard a piercing shriek, and Marisil told Sulica to stay while she spurred the Bediaran forward.

Not wanting to be alone, she defied her mother and pushed her horse onwards as well. As she turned the corner, she heard the shouts then felt hands grab at her and force her off the quarter horse, but they couldn't keep a hold of her slight frame. She scrambled to her feet and ran, shouting for her mother and sister.

"Sulica!" her mother yelled back, trying to fight off her attackers. Ganasi was lying still on the side of the path, red spots on her blouse. Her horse, Pin, was being wrangled by one of the bandits. Marisil dodged around two of the men, hitting a third and dashed towards Sulica, summoning her mystic. She whistled shrilly, and the Bediaran appeared from between the trees. The horse and Marisil reached Sulica simultaneously. She grabbed her daughter, putting her on top of the Bediaran then slapped his hindquarters to send him off.

Sulica twisted around in the saddle, yelling for her mother who had turned around to face the remaining bandits, determined to save her other daughter.

She stirred slightly, feeling a touch, but she was unable to open her eyes. The guard adjusted her weight in his arms to carry her out, away from tortuous prison. He moved quickly but carefully so as not to jostle her too much, feeling sick from the stench and sight of the laboratory. *Whatever is in store for you,* he thought as he glanced at the young woman in his arms, *it has to be better than this.*

-:- -:- -:-

Brisethi awoke from a restless, short nap on the cold, hard floor. Her recent dream had replayed once again the memories of the same day she had spent with her now distant friend. She longed to relive that day. She wanted desperately to return to that evening where Etyne sat in her room all evening playing cards with her and helping her to pick out a name for her cherished new plush. She remembered lying on her bed and cuddling with the soft octopus looking across at Etyne putting the cards away.

"What should I name him?" she asked Etyne, tossing the plush at him.

He shrugged. "I haven't named a stuffed toy since I was eight. He was a little puppy my mom got me from the consignment store. I named him Sir Wuffruff."

Brisethi busted out laughing at such an adorable little kid Etyne story. "Hey, how many tickles does it take to make an octopus laugh?"

"Eight?"

"Ten tickles..." she bit her lower lip to keep from prematurely laughing.

"Tentacles, yes. You're a child," he slightly chuckled anyway at the joke. "I think you found his name, then."

She caught Ten-Tickles when Etyne launched him back at her. The roving watch was hovering in their hall and since it was past curfew, he would have to summon his mystic to sneak to his room.

"Or you could just hide out in here until the morning," she had suggested and moved over to allow him room on her bed. Though they were never intimate with one another, she enjoyed his company and he found comfort in her warmth each time they fell asleep next to one another.

She heard birds chirping when the sun began to rise. She lay still, awaiting the guards to take their turn on her, now that Sulica was gone, then drag her to the laboratory. If they weren't in the mood to feed her watered down oats, she hoped they would at least give her water, with or without the inky suppression that prevented her from calling upon her mystics.

Hours had passed while she sat in the middle of her murky cell, listening for any sign of activity from anyone. Her stomach perpetually ached from hunger while her mouth and throat longed for any sort of liquid relief. She had never been so hungry before and hadn't realized how painful it was to have nothing in her system.

"Does anyone hear me?" she raspily cried out. The other inmates in the prison chamber had passed on days ago, leaving only Brisethi left alive. The Lantheuns had not removed the bodies, so she had to live with the scent of death hovering in the room. Her senses were more or less used to it except for the overwhelming amount of excrement that was also still in the cells.

She wondered if she was even needed anymore or if the Lantheuns had abandoned her to die like the others. For all she knew, her mystics were completely exhausted from their inhumane experiments. With her mystics gone, she was left to waste away until new Resarians were captured so they could continue their crimes on them. She picked at a scab with her teeth letting out a sudden, shrill shriek from the pain. She covered her finger in the dripping blood and began to paint symbols and designs on the wall of her cell.

"*Summon the stars from the skies, Asellunas,*" a voice echoed through her head.

"I can't," she replied and instead painted bloody stars falling from the maelstrom in the sky she had created. She was convinced that her spirit had left her. She should be dead without it. "Our doctrines are lies," she whispered, frantically biting at more scabs for more blood. "Our spirits really are nothing but scientific anomalies." There was no such thing as the Sea of Renewal. The spirits condemned her, abandoned her to rot in a foreign land. *The Dominion never even tried to find me*, she thought with final resignation of life. "Worthless fucking spirits," she stifled a sob as tears formed. She attempted to wipe the tears from her cheeks only to have smeared her bloody arms across her face.

She felt her hopeful ambitions in the Dominion, on Sariadne, in the world of Falajen, escape just as Sulica had, just as her spirit had. Her recruits probably already forgot who she was. She felt forgotten by her commanders, given up by her friends, including Etyne and Korteni. She could only imagine the anguish her mother had gone through at hearing what befell her husband and daughter. Her father probably infiltrated the wrong continent, misled into believing she was in Pahl'Kiar and drinking himself into unconsciousness. She was going to die of infection, starvation, dehydration. She wasn't even going down as a hero, or a warrior. She was dying of helplessness as a slave in a foreign land, in clothes that were not her own, bleeding out if only to finish painting walls with her own blood like a madwoman.

"The spirit of our land resides in us through the breath of dragons," she muttered, mixing her tears into her blood. "Our fire from the sky scarred the nations." Her voice cracked at repeating such sacred words. In a parched whisper, she continued, "From the scars of Sariadne, the Dominion was born. I will defend her from her enemy. I will die..." she paused at those words. "I will die before I commit treason."

Black tears stained her cheeks as she crawled from the walls to the gate of her prison, rattling it with the last of her strength. "I refuse to die here," she gritted her teeth. "I represent the antecedents who have passed their spirits unto us! And I will use such spirits to honor our nation, never against my brethren."

She searched her vessel for any sign of mystics, summoning the smallest spark of the hottest fire to melt the iron bars. But nothing happened. What remained of her energy disappeared, and she lost consciousness at last, her body collapsing to the floor.

Chapter XII

Korteni used her mystic to snuff out the lights of the street lanterns all around their vicinity with a slight hiss as the water met fire. Even though Etyne's distortion shield protected them from any onlookers in the middle of the night, she did not want to take unnecessary risks. Both of them stood before the locked doors of the large building, translating the words above it. "Anomaly Diligences" it had read in common Lantheun language. They nodded to one another and gestured for Sergeant Livian Reej to make her way out of the bushes to them.

Korteni applied mystical ice to the windows on the doors. Etyne gestured a countdown to Livian. He kicked the glass at the same time as she summoned a wind with her mystic to buffer the sound of the breaking glass. They hurried in with Ibrienne and Kanilas following after.

"Search every floor," Etyne whispered. "I'll start at the top." He raced up the stairs three at a time, disappearing into his vapor form to travel faster. He wasn't even sure this was the right building, that Kanilas Trenn could have very well sent them into a trap to fill his own pockets again. It all seemed too convenient that he happened to know a Kiaran who knew a Lantheun who knew where Resarians were being smuggled in for mystic testings.

Etyne arrived at the large chamber containing multiple barred rooms. The smell of death nearly sent him retching. He hooked his coat over his nose to breathe better. Using the small lantern he carried, he stormed through the unsettling corridors. Each cell he peered into housed a rotting corpse wearing a blood-stained gown. He felt disturbed at the thought of finding Brisethi in such a place and hoped with every ounce of faith in the spirits that she wasn't among the dead.

Near the end of the chamber, he found the only completely empty cell he'd seen so far then hurried across to see one occupied by a person he couldn't tell was dead or just unconscious. The blood-red paintings of destruction on the wall flared recognition in confirming her identity. He placed his lantern down then turned to mist to easily traverse through the bars, rematerializing on the other side in the cell. He knelt down beside her and brushed away strands of hair from the woman's face. His heart pounded at the sight of the tortured vessel of Brisethi's spirit. "What have they done to you?" his voice cracked as he wiped the blood from her face.

He whistled loudly to alert the others of his location, the sound echoing in the long chamber. Then he searched for Brisethi's pulse. Her skin was warm at her neck, and he felt the faintest pulse slowly beating.

"'Sethi, come to me," he whispered, cradling her head and allowing his mystic to flow through her vessel in search of her spirit. It was all he could do to keep from panicking that he was about to lose her. He felt that his life would never be the same if he no longer had someone to look forward to seeing alongside him. *Not just someone, you, 'Sethi, don't leave me alone, please,* he mentally pleaded as though his soul was speaking for him.

He heard the footsteps of the other Resarians who accompanied him running in their direction.

"Cursed spirits," Korteni whispered when she reached the cell, applying ice to the gate's hinges and kicking it in with the help of Reej. Korteni instantly dropped to her knees to begin hydrating Brisethi with her mystic by conjuring drops of water from the air and slowly trickling it into her friend's mouth, lest she choke on it. She allowed warmer water to flow along Brisethi's skin, wiping the blood and dirt with her own hands in an attempt to clean her.

Ibrienne spared no time healing the open wounds and curing the myriad infections running through her veins. "I'm trying to regenerate the missing pieces of her skin," she told them earnestly. Brisethi's skin began to stretch and form over the open wounds on her arms and back, leaving it bright red where Ibrienne's mystic touched her. "Dear spirits, she was filled with diseases," she muttered woefully as she purified her blood.

"Where are you, Sulica?" Kanilas angrily called, searching the remaining cells.

Etyne, meanwhile, struggled to find his companion's spirit. His mind raced back to expedition training, when the acolytes had taught the strongest of the spirits the ultimate remedy, were it ever needed. He hesitated momentarily, not because of the sacrifice he was about to make, but to assure he was in the correct stance and state of mind lest he accidentally release both of their spirits, killing them both. It was at that moment that he was certain he'd rather die to let her live so that he didn't have to live without her.

He gently dragged her frail body toward him to set themselves in the proper position. Holding her from behind, he placed one hand in the middle of her sunken chest and the other on her forehead. He summoned the deepest part of his spirit to partition a small portion of it, separating it from his own vessel. What followed next was an inner painful shock he never imagined could hurt so much that for a second, he thought he had died. He flinched visibly at feeling the smallest tear of his incorporeal aura separate from his spirit and flow into Brisethi's vessel.

"What is he doing?" Livian asked Korteni, staring in shock at the illuminating blue aura surrounding Etyne and Brisethi.

"Dear spirits, he's performing Soul Reclamation," Korteni replied. The acolytes hadn't taught her the mystic, saying that she might be eligible in another century because her spirit was still too young. A spirit that was not strong enough to endure the tear risked prematurely sending it to the Sea of Renewal, ending the lives of both parties in an instantaneous, painful death.

Ibrienne knew the sacred act he was performing. She, too, was one of the few to be taught how to partition her spirit in order to revive another's. Chills crept up her spine at hearing Etyne yell from physical agony.

Livian and Korteni looked on with fear and reverence. Seconds later, the ambient aqua glow dissipated from Etyne and Brisethi, leaving him breathing rapidly in exhaustion and incomprehensible pain. Brisethi inhaled deeply, opening her eyes and blinking away inky tears.

Her breathing intensified when she sat up, staring in disbelief at each Resarian looking back at her. "Korteni," she whispered, her voice still weak. "What are you all doing here?" Her eyes filled with tears of overwhelming emotions.

Korteni wrapped her arms around her, despite the disgusting mess of water, filth and blood on her friend. "We're getting you out of here, silly!"

"Sen Asel!" shouted Kanilas, seeing her rise. "Where is Sulica?"

Brisethi leaned against Korteni for support. "She was rescued some time ago – maybe yesterday or the day before?"

"Rescued? By who?" he demanded.

"I think he was Kiaran," she mumbled, still drowsy and weak. "He bought her freedom."

Korteni gave her standard issue rations to help replenish her nutrients, which Brisethi tore into. Korteni turned to look at the wall and stared in horror and awe at the dreadful bloody paintings. Ibrienne, still hooded to conceal her identity, pulled the half-finished rations from Brisethi's hand, admonishing Korteni for overloading Brisethi's malnourished body.

"Freedom? Do you know what Kiarans do to lone Resarians?" Kanilas was outraged as he stormed into the cell. "How could you let this happen to her?"

"Do *not* blame me for the fuckery she caused us both to endure!" Brisethi screeched. She cast a longing gaze at the food in the hooded woman's grasp.

Though still slightly disoriented from the Soul Reclamation, Etyne's anger caused him to reach over to Kanilas, and pin him against the wall. "You will stop talking to Sen Asel! If you have something to ask, I will ask her for you!" His training commander persona flared up.

"I just wanna know where she is," Kanilas whimpered under the force of Etyne's forearm against his throat.

"Sulica is the reason for both their suffering! Go find your precious Sulica before I do," his voice bellowed dangerously. The only thing holding Etyne back from murdering the man before him with his bare hands was the presence of his fellow service members.

Kanilas pulled himself away from Etyne and glared at Ibrienne, "Let's get out of here, Ibrienne."

"Ibrienne," Brisethi whispered, her eyes moving from the rations to her former friend beneath a hood. "You aided them? What have you done?"

"'Sethi you don't understand – I had no choice!" She couldn't bring herself to meet Brisethi's eyes. Dropping the rations, she ran out of the cell to catch up with Kanilas.

"You're letting them go?" Korteni questioned Etyne's decision. "After what they put her through, you're just letting them go?"

"As you were, Chief," he ordered.

"Belay my last, Sir," she muttered through gritted teeth.

Through blurred vision of teary eyes, Brisethi watched the uncanny conversation, washing down her rations with Korteni's flask of water. She wondered about Etyne's choice as well but did not feel the need to question him. She wanted Ibrienne to return, and her own dignity to return. She wanted it all to return to how things were at the end of their expedition training.

"Sir, with my help, we could have apprehended them-"

"The decision's been made!" he shouted, cutting Reej off. "We're not going to stand around debating the two criminals. Chief, go find her uniform or anything other than this filthy gown," Etyne's spirit had darkened quickly. He glanced at Brisethi, "Are you capable of walking?"

"Yes," Brisethi immediately replied, unsure if she could walk for long, but too unsettled by his tone of voice to tell him.

Etyne felt mentally exhausted from retrieving Brisethi's spirit. His patience was too short to safely bind Kanilas and drag him along with them to their rally point miles away. Furthermore, the sight of Brisethi's abominable appearance had him discreetly losing his composure. All he wanted was to hold her close, to protect her from anyone ever harming her again. Her very soul was tormented, and he had felt all of it at once in the second he had seized her spirit. So many emotions poured into his grieving spirit, overwhelming his decision-making functions. Wanting to place the blame on someone for everything that had just happened, there was a high chance that Kanilas would suffer mortal injury by Etyne if left in his presence.

Sergeant Livian Reej glanced at the indisposed officer that she had once considered powerful, intimidating and beautiful when she enlisted her three years ago. Before her now stood a broken, defeated weakling. She was even more concerned about the haunting images on the wall the captain had painted with her own blood. *What kind of troubled mind does that?* Reej wondered. As far as she was concerned, the Dominion captain had failed in escaping and was giving up on life when they found her. Had Captain Vorsen not given her a second chance, the woman would be dead by the morning.

Brisethi turned her palm up. She stared into it, feeling a sense of renewal wash over her. Something anomalous yet at the same time familiar inhabited her vessel. Somehow, her spirit had returned, but with more vigor and enhanced mystical virtue. Scarlet flames ignited in the palm of her hand, flowing outward to the iron bars of the chamber. The mystic leapt to her command, like an old friend she hadn't seen in a long time.

Once the four Resarians were outside, Brisethi spread her flames throughout the entire building, crumbling it to ash.

Spirits of Falajen

Part III - Fallen Paradigm

Chapter I

When did it all go so wrong? Ibrienne asked herself. She glared at Kanilas Trenn sitting across from her in the cargo hold of the train. "What was she thinking, going after Dominion officers?" Ibrienne asked aloud. "We're enemies of our own empire, now. We can never return to Sariadne."

"It's a good thing we're going to Pahl'Kiar, then, isn't it?" Kanilas replied flippantly.

"And then what are we going to do? Ask our adversaries if we can live in their land despite the fact they're not allowed to live in ours? We don't exactly look like Kiarans-"

"But we *do* look like every other race they get along with," he interrupted. "When we get to Beccilia we'll change our clothing and work on our accents. I need to message one of my Kiaran contacts for word of Sulica as soon as we're there." Kanilas busied himself with a few documents he'd pulled out of his travel bag.

Ibrienne sighed heavily. When she agreed to work for Sulica's father, the youngest son of a very prominent family in Res'Baveth who had fallen from grace, in his shipping business, she never imagined they would end up as adversaries of their own people.

She recalled the day that their lives took a tragic turn. Four months ago in the winter of 4th millennia, 3rd century, 28th year, the sea-faring lives of Sulica, Ibrienne and Kanilas were changed forever. What started as a routine international waters inspection from Lantheun authorities escalated into catastrophe when contraband was found on their ship. Sulica's father, Hantir, had acquired schematics of Kiaran weapon systems and fortifications when his crew, posed as Lantheun allies, burglarized a Kiaran frigate in port. Upon discovery, Hantir's crew opened fire on the Lantheun officials, causing an outbreak of violence on his ship.

Ibrienne and Sulica both suffered minor injuries during their escape to the berthing compartment. When the ship fell silent, the two emerged from below deck to search the bodies of dozens of men. Most were from their own crew, including Sulica's father.

Sulica had told Ibrienne that her mother died giving birth to her. Losing her only living parent at such a young age for a Resarian traumatized her. Ibrienne remembered how Sulica spent the remainder of that evening grieving for her father, forgoing any attempt to give her food. She stayed in her father's cabin, refusing to speak to anyone, even Ibrienne.

Sulica emerged the following morning, her hazel eyes red from tears, and began issuing orders. Sulica took command of the surviving crew, a diverse group of Resarians, Beccilians, and various other neutral nations. After sinking the vessels of her company along with the bodies of her father and fallen comrades in a ceremonial funeral, the crew seized the Lantheun ship. She had it refitted by removing any sign of Resarian and replacing all banners and emblems with her own family crest of the Nin's. The ship was dubbed the *Hantira*, in honor of Sulica's father.

As the months passed, Ibrienne grew increasingly uneasy with the new clientele. At first, the profits were high. Since their trading business no longer took place on a Resarian ship, Sulica had fewer restraints with whom to do business. Then they began catering to customers who were less noble and more unprincipled. Sulica had learned much from her father, but not enough on economic skills. The amount of coin coming soon began to decrease, and her crew became desperate for money.

One day, a half-Kiaran, half-Beccilian man tipped Sulica off about a lucrative opportunity. The Pahl'Kiar was paying outrageous sums of gold to anyone turning in Resarians with powerful mystics. Sulica, having reached a dark path in her mind among the gods and monsters of thieving guilds, jumped at the chance to regain lost coin and the loyalty of her crew.

The *Hantira* pulled into port at a harbor town south of Res'Baveth where Sulica could gather information on any Resarian who acquired the skill of summoning mystics. It was a humble town, mostly made up of fishermen who could barely heal one another with mystics, let alone summon any type of destruction. Sulica directed Ibrienne to make daily visits to the town, trading healing techniques for information on the more prominent mystic-wielders. When she saw the Dominion warship pull in for replenishment, however, her plans became bigger. She knew that at least half of the Dominion sailors would have some type of destructive mystic that she could suppress until the trade could be arranged.

Sulica spent hours observing the men who disembarked the warship, trying to feel for any specific type of mystic that would be worthwhile to the Kiarans. Ibrienne had feared the look she saw in Sulica's eyes when she spotted the rear admiral. They both knew exactly who his daughter was and the power she possessed. "In fact," Sulica had reasoned, "why not make double the gold for two Resarians?"

Sulica selected three skilled assassins to sneak onto the warship with her under the cover of darkness. While she suppressed four sailors at a time – the limit of her mystics as long as they were in her line of sight - the assassins crept along the deck. She had ordered her men not to kill any of them, but two of the sailors still died in the process of her men overpowering them. When they finally reached Admiral Sen Asel's cabin, the rest of his crew was incapacitated.

Even inebriated, Admiral Sen Asel put up a nasty fight with the three men, but, without the unusual use of his mystics, he was outnumbered and eventually knocked unconscious. One of the assassins had nearly killed the drunken admiral out of frustration once they finally brought him down. Sulica was furious when she and the others reboarded the *Hantira* with their charge. Immediately, Ibrienne was summoned to ensure the admiral would live. She felt she should have known then what Sulica had in mind when she was ordered to not fully heal the broken man. They left the harbor that very night.

The following morning, Sulica inquired as to the location of their former comrade. Foolishly, Ibrienne believed Sulica had a change of heart and assumed she would return the admiral to his daughter. She had no idea that the information of Brisethi's whereabouts given to her through the letters she exchanged with Korteni and Livian would be used to abduct the young captain. Sulica suggested that they meet up with her when her division would be near a harbor. Eventually, Sulica found out Brisethi's division number and sent her message as soon as she was able to.

When Ibrienne discovered the content of Sulica's letter and the wrongdoing she'd inadvertently contributed to, she pleaded with her friend to at least abide by the words in her letter and set Brisethi's father free. Ibrienne hoped that, by attempting to abduct Brisethi, her fire would easily overpower their crew, thereby setting Ibrienne free from the purgatory she found herself in.

Once Brisethi was on their ship, Ibrienne had to suppress the urge to talk to her, to beg her for forgiveness and help her get back on the right path. Leaving the thieving guild they had joined wasn't an

easy procedure, but if anyone could help her, Ibrienne believed
Brisethi could. Unfortunately, Sulica's power was stronger than
Ibrienne had imagined, and Brisethi was unable to best it. When
Sulica was forced to escort Brisethi to the Lantheun capital, Ibrienne
desperately hoped that Brisethi could overpower Sulica's mystic and
escape.

Due to the damage Brisethi and the Kiarans had brought upon
their ship, Ibrienne and Kanilas spent two weeks repairing the *Hantira*
before sailing to another port. Then they spent another week or so
tracking down any division with a competent commander to help them
find and rescue the two women.

They hoped to find a patrol division with experienced soldiers
but instead found a recruit training division. Kanilas nearly
overlooked the division to search for another one when Ibrienne
convinced him to at least talk to the commanders if only for the remote
chance they would tell them where to find a patrol division. Ibrienne
instinctively kept her hood over her face, partly in shame, when they
realized the commander of the division was someone they knew. But
when Captain Vorsen was reluctant to believe Kanilas, and for good
reason, she had to show her face to prove they were acting in good
faith. And that they were desperate for help.

While on the *DSV Reliant* on their way to Lantheus, Captain
Vorsen and Chief Pyraz had an overwhelming amount of questions for
her and Kanilas. Their instinct was to lie to protect their own
reputation, but eventually Ibrienne crushed under the pressure and
confessed all. She told them of Sulica's father's contraband, how they
were initiated into a thieves' guild, and the abduction of both Sen Asel
officers. Kanilas understood why she folded and forgave her. Unlike
Sulica, Kanilas still held the Dominion in high regard and would beg
them for mercy when it came time for his trial.

Ibrienne stared through the partly open cargo door, refusing to
let her memory take her any further. The Lantheun laboratory still
haunted her dreams. Outside, the countryside of Trycinea continent
was flat as far as she could see. Tall grass swayed in the wind among
the plains where few cottonwood trees scattered the land. The plains
reminded her of eastern Sariadne, and she felt a pang of homesickness.
She yearned to return home, though realistically she had no home to
return to.

"While in Beccilia we'll find work on a Kiaran transport ship,"
Kanilas spoke, startling her out of her reverie. He was studying a map.
"I hope you're still fluent in Kiaran."

"Re bava'khan mikar," she reassured him in Kiaran with a sigh.

"That's more than I remember. You're doing all the talking," he ordered.

-:- -:- -:-

Sulica awoke in confusion. She lay still for a few moments, trying to make sense of her surroundings. Suspicion set in as she realized she'd been sleeping in a soft, clean bed. The gentle familiar swaying of a ship put her at ease, but it was louder than any ship she had ever been on before.

She struggled to recall her last memory. She remembered sitting on a cold floor, screaming at Brisethi to end their torture, watching her former adversary turned fellow prisoner fighting a brute of a Lantheun guard. Brisethi then lay unconscious in a pool of her blood. She dimly wondered if Brisethi had died or was on this ship with her.

Sulica sat up, wincing in pain. Taking a breath, she looked down at her aching body to assess the damage. Bandages covered the open wounds where her pieces of her skin had been stripped away. Where it was intact looked blotchy but clean, and her hair smelled of scented oils. She no longer wore the disgusting white gown from Lantheus, but simple, clean undergarments. Pushing the plush covers off, she placed her sore, bare feet on the carpeted deck. She tried to stand but felt weak and lightheaded, forcing her to sit back down on the bed.

The small table next to the bed held a silver tray displaying various fruits and pastries. Her stomach grumbled at the sight, so she reached over and placed the tray on her lap. She hadn't eaten anything solid in weeks. She bit into the sweet, juicy apple with no regard to where it came from. Tears welled her eyes as Sulica realized she was no longer suffering behind bars, starving and dying of infections and torture. When the scent reached her, her stomach flopped, feeling nauseated despite the swollenness of her belly.

Forcing herself to forgo the tempting fruit and pastries, she moved on to the pitcher of cool water, drinking straight from it. Her stomach still ached as she drained the water, but she felt satiated for the first time in weeks. She leaned back on her arms to stretch, wanting to regain energy enough to walk freely around the room and the ship without feeling like she was going to pass out. Her eyes wandered around the cabin, taking in the plush furniture and unique carvings.

Using her mystic, Sulica scanned the ship for Brisethi's unique power and sensed no mystics at all. There were no other Resarians on board the ship. She glanced behind her, then did a double take as she saw the dark blue banner on the wall displaying the gold clockwork emblem of Pahl'Kiar.

She froze momentarily while her thoughts raced. *What am I doing here?* she asked herself. *Now what are they going to do with me?* The idea of looking for a place to hide was useless on a ship full of people who already knew she was there. Someone had brought her here, rescued her from one nightmare only to be placed in another one. *The food and water were probably drugged,* she thought, furious with herself for her thoughtlessness.

A soft tapping on her cabin door startled her. She didn't know how to respond or what to do. The tapping sounded again and the door finally cracked open. She remained seated on the bed, too weak to move, but her eyes were riveted to the door.

"My apologies, Miss, I didn't realize you had awoken. I only meant to check on you," the man in the doorway spoke in fluent Resarian. He walked over to the dim lantern to brighten it. "How are you feeling?" He was tall and fair-skinned, with dark hair, few age lines and bright blue eyes that were pupil-less, giving her the distinct feeling she had met him before.

"I drank all the water," she replied. She didn't know why that was the only thing she could think to say.

The man in ornate clothing smiled. "That's a good sign, Miss. Would you mind telling me your name? The Lantheuns only had you listed as a number."

She briefly considered giving him a false name. "Sulica," she said quietly.

"You may call me Ekani," he replied with a slight bow. "I imagine you must have dozens of questions. So let me explain. As the Kiaran ambassador to Lantheus, I was ordered to buy your freedom and escort you to Pahl'Kiar. Emperor Vimbultinir is interested in hiring you for your unique abilities." He paused, considering her for a moment. "Once he has spoken with you, he will offer you two choices; either accept the position he's offering you, or he will have you returned to the Dominion."

"He would allow me to return home with no consequences?" she asked skeptically. She wondered why even waste time speaking with the emperor if she could just go home.

Ekani cleared his throat. Still smiling, he rocked back on his heels and said, "Would you mind refreshing my memory on what the Dominion does to ex-military members who abduct their officers and abandon them to their death? They consider that an act of treason, yes?"

How could she have forgotten the crimes she would pay for? She momentarily looked away from Ekani's timeless eyes. "They are beheaded," she hesitantly replied.

"Ah, yes, such is the savage culture of your people." He gave her a sympathetic look. "I would hate to be the one allowing them to abolish such a valuable paragon like yourself. As of now, you are under the protection of the Pahl'Kiar. Deny service to the emperor, and your people would gladly take you off of our hands."

"I understand," she weakly told him. She didn't realize how tightly she had been holding the blanket in her hands.

"Do feel free to roam the ship, Sulica. When you are up to it, of course. You are our guest. There are suitable clothes in the dresser. The galley is the deck below if you're still hungry. We'll be in Pahl'Kiar in twelve days."

She watched him leave her room, sighing out loud as she thought about her new unfortunate circumstance. She had no compulsion to align her loyalties to the Kiarans. But she also had no desire to return to Sariadne where the Dominion would convict her of her crimes and likely sentence her to death.

Chapter II

After Livian took the short hike toward the stream, Korteni finally approached her distraught commander. She hesitated since Captain Vorsen had snapped at everyone after rescuing Brisethi that morning. Since their arrival at the rally point, he had distanced himself from the three women to sit alone on a rock.

"Captain, are you well?" She softly asked.

"I'm fine. What do you need?" Etyne quickly replied.

"Do you think we should wake her? It's been over ten hours since she went to sleep," Korteni fretted.

"She likely hasn't had proper rest since she was captured. Her body needs to continue healing." Etyne replied, finally rising from his perch to stretch his achy muscles.

They stared at the shack the small group shared that morning and afternoon since freeing Brisethi from the Lantheun capital. Their setup was a small abandoned tool shed nestled among a dead garden north of the city. They were close to the shore, awaiting pick-up from the *DSV Reliant* which had to stay out of sight of the Lantheun patrol ships. With any luck, they would be on the way home soon.

Livian Reej sat upon a tree that had fallen across a stream, turning it into a small bridge. Wearing only her undershirt and undershorts, she basked in the late afternoon sun, drying from her bath in the stream. As she watched the shallow water bubbling and tumbling over the rocks and sand, her mind began to wander.

Her spirit had been troubled since the previous night when she witnessed Ibrienne Sestas running away from them. Korteni filled her in on Ibrienne's entire confession when they finally felt relatively secure. It nearly broke Livian's heart to hear that her childhood friend had defected. Ibrienne had been like her older sister in the orphanage until she left for the expedition. When the orphanage burned down, she had lost contact with Ibrienne until the day they reunited at Ibrienne's graduation ceremony. Livian didn't know much about the other woman, Sulica, except that Ibrienne was working for her and her father. That man who traveled with her, Kanilas, seemed to have thought the world of Sulica, however.

"Elion, are you responsible for that suppressor?" She asked toward the sky. Her heart still ached at remembering her seven years spent at the citadel with him. Her eyes watered at remembering the day he was arrested for his crimes against Sariadne, driving her to seek out the Dominion recruiter. She recalled the first night she met Sen Asel and how easily persuasive she was to Livian. The way she advertised the Dominion military could have convinced the most belligerent, stubborn child to enlist. Livian thought about Sen Asel's impressive powerful demeanor and ability to command authority from anyone during their two-week division integration. But whatever had happened to the woman had left her a shell of her former self.

When Livian was initially asked to assist Vorsen and Pyraz on their mission, she was inclined to respectfully tell them no. She didn't join the Dominion Armed Forces to rescue Resarians who had gotten themselves captured. She joined to protect her continent and *prevent* said cases of abduction. However, if she declined Captain Vorsen's request, she would have been transferred to the division that was eight months behind them, extending her expedition by that much longer. Her choices were to either go where Chief Pyraz went, or get set back, repeating desert training again.

She wasn't at all interested in sailing to Lantheus to rescue some nobody that Ibrienne and her male friend knew. All she wanted was to finish her enlisted expedition training so she could attend officer training and finally take charge of fortifying Sariadne's defenses.

Upon seeing the fallen captain last night, barely alive, Livian lost what little pride she'd had in achieving their goal. Her respect for the officer had also diminished greatly. Livian's recruiter, her enlistment officer, had allowed her mystics, her strength and her dignity to be taken away from her by petty Lantheuns. For all Livian cared, the woman could have been left to die in the puddle of blood they found her in instead of allowing the Dominion to risk the lives of the *DSV Reliant* to rescue her. In spite of her convictions, she still felt queasy recalling the conditions of that laboratory and felt a pang of pity for her Captain and Chief finding their friend in such a condition.

It took them over six hours to reach their small refuge outside of Lantheus City. They had left their packs and provisions in the abandoned shack the day before. Captain Vorsen arranged for the ship to pick them up from the shore nearby after a couple of days in case the group needed more time to find Captain Sen Asel. The *DSV Reliant* would return to them by tomorrow night to take them back to Ancient Kiar to finish the expedition training. Livian splashed her bare feet in the stream, sighing loudly and impatiently.

Brisethi jerked upright, clutching the thin blanket as the cold water hit her face. She wiped her eyes to see Etyne squatting down next to her holding an empty cup.

"Oh, you're awake," he said, giving her a strained smile. No matter how happy he was to have her back, he found it difficult to show it knowing what had happened to her.

Brisethi kicked him playfully to knock him over out of habit and quickly winced from the stab wound in her foot. "I was just dreaming about drowning in water, you jerk," she mumbled, pushing her wet hair behind her ears.

He forced a chuckle and sat on his knees next to her. "Probably from the sprinkles of water I initially started with. How do you feel?" His tone was light, but the concern was evident in his face.

She turned away from his sympathetic gaze, wishing he'd stop looking at her. "I feel disgusting," she said, "but rested for the first time in weeks," she continued gratefully. Though she wasn't home, she felt safe with her friends.

Brisethi wondered if the foul taste in her mouth was similar to what feces and death tasted like. She kept her head down when speaking. "What time of day is it?"

Etyne reached for his pocket watch. "It's half past hour seventeen. You've been asleep since six."

Brisethi's eyes fell on the pile of provisions in the corner opposite her. After the need to itch her scabbed arms and legs, mostly healed from the night before she felt a sudden pang in her heart for Ibrienne, further dampening her mood. She glanced back up at Etyne, but he shifted uncomfortably, avoiding looking at her. She wished he would leave, fearing she still smelled of the wretched cell of the laboratory.

"I'll have Korteni take you to the stream to wash up," he said, standing up, as though he'd read her mind.

Korteni walked into the shack at her name. She grinned and waved excitedly to Brisethi, grabbing the pack that contained her friend's uniform and a set of military issued hygiene supplies. Etyne and Korteni both leaned down to help Brisethi stand. She waved them off, rolling to her knees, but she found herself unable to move any further. Humiliated, she allowed her friends to help her wordlessly to her feet.

Brisethi reached over to grab a pouch of rations to munch on while she and Korteni walked to the stream, grateful for the bland taste. She doubted her stomach could handle anything richer. Still using Korteni to support a good portion of her weight, she asked, "Was there any word on my father?"

Korteni nodded. "The official memorandum from Dominion Command stated that Sergeant First Class Kile found him and took him to your division, actually. They made sure that he was taken back to Res'Baveth."

Brisethi thanked the spirits for the good news, nearly forgetting she had cursed them the night before. They spent the rest of the walk in silence. Brisethi focused all her energy on putting one foot in front of the other. She was thankful that her foot was mostly healed from Ibrienne's mystic touch, leaving only pressure pain left to heal on its own.

Livian had just finished putting her recruit uniform on when the two superiors arrived at the stream. She walked past them but not before asking Korteni, "Chief, do you think we'll have time to hunt for real food?"

"I think Captain was readying his bow when we left. See if you can catch him," Korteni replied.

"Aye, Chief," Livian replied, avoiding any and all eye contact with the monstrous Captain Sen Asel.

"How has she been since that night?" Brisethi asked when Livian ran off.

"She's been well, actually. She wasn't too thrilled at the idea of leaving the expedition to come here, but she didn't want to get set back by half a year or so either. Besides, she won't admit it, but I know she enjoys the face time with Etyne," Korteni rambled, sitting upon the log-bridge Livian had abandoned.

"That's more than I needed to know," Brisethi replied with a small smile. She carefully removed her boots and waded into the cold stream. She used her mystic to warm her skin against the rushing waters, feeling the familiar warmth come over her like a long-lost friend. She removed the horrid white gown and threw it high into the air, igniting it with mystics to watch as it incinerated into ash. *Never again will I take my mystic for granted,* she swore to herself.

Korteni gasped at the sight of Brisethi's bare, skeletal back scabbed in diagonal, symmetrical lines on either side of her spine where flesh had been sliced. She couldn't dare wonder what it looked like before Ibrienne closed the open wounds. "Oh, 'Sethi," she sadly whispered.

Brisethi heard her and quickly submerged her whole body in the shallow water, using the soap to scrub away weeks of crusted blood and Lantheun filth. "It doesn't hurt as much anymore," she said in answer to Korteni's unspoken question. "It's more of a stinging nuisance, really. Would you mind scrubbing off my back?" Korteni jumped off her post, stripped off her own boots and rolled up her pants before taking Brisethi's soap from her outstretched hand. She carefully scrubbed the dried blood and filth off of her back, avoiding re-opening any of the cuts and not saying a word.

Brisethi rinsed the soap and oils from her body and hair, feeling instantly refreshed. Although the lower half of her head was shaven, she was thankful the rest of her hair was still thick and long, easily able to hide her horrid sides. When she was done, she waded back to the shore and dried off using her mystic to evaporate the water droplets before pulling each article of clothing from the leather bag Korteni had packed for her. "I'm surprised the Lantheuns didn't destroy my uniform."

"Just be glad Etyne reminded me to grab it. I nearly forgot over the excitement of finding you," Korteni grinned. It was slightly easier to look at her friend once she appeared slightly more like her normal self.

After dressing, Brisethi took the toothbrush from the hygiene pack along with the cleaning solution. "Do you know how disgusting your mouth gets after a month of not brushing your teeth?" she asked, thankful for Ibrienne's healing of her canker sores.

"I hope to never know," Korteni sadly replied.

Ignoring Korteni, she continued, "I'm convinced I was trying to remove a cavity or two before Ibrienne healed them." When she finished thoroughly cleaning her teeth and mouth, she climbed onto the log to sit next to Korteni and watch the sun set through the trees. Her bottom was still slightly sore from what the guards did to her. The sky turned from light blue to hues of pink and orange as night slowly approached. "All the baths and showers in the world will never make me feel clean," she muttered. "I'm worried I may never desire intimacy ever again." She then decided to confide in Korteni with some of the more atrocious acts the Lantheun guards performed on her.

Korteni moaned in pity for her friend, wishing there was something she could do for her. Despite her hatred of Sulica and Kanilas, nobody deserved the treatment the women went through, not even their adversaries. She held back the tears, sick of crying at every terrible event that others were suffering. Korteni had always hated that specific trait about herself, how empathic she became at anyone's expense. She wished she could harden her heart to feel nothing for no one. Finally, she found her voice to speak to Brisethi. "I'm certain that in time, that feeling will return. Our minds have a way of letting horrible memories fade away to allow the good ones to remain. When a good enough person comes along, you will slowly crave affection once more," she reassured her, leaving out Etyne's name now that she knew what he once felt for Brisethi.

Livian remained quiet as she trailed Captain Vorsen while he hunted. He favored his silent, accurate bow and arrow over the rifle for hunting. They soon came upon a flock of pheasants, and the captain easily took one out for their small group.

"Something on your mind, Reej?" he asked his quiet subordinate as they began retracing their steps to the shack, bird in tow.

"Not really, Sir," she mumbled.

Even if he wasn't in the mood to talk, he felt obligated to include the young Sergeant in their discussions. "Thanks again for helping us out last night. I know you didn't have the best options to choose from, but I wanted to let you know how much I appreciated your help. I'm sure Sen Asel will express her gratitude as well, when she's feeling better."

Livian forced herself to remain respectful to her commanding officer by not expressing her feelings about the situation. "You're welcome, Sir," she said with the little sincerity she could muster.

He gave her the task of gathering firewood and kindling while he prepared the pheasant. He raised his eyes from the task after a little while to see the other two women return from the stream.

"What's with the darkness?" Korteni asked as she watched Etyne and Livian struggling to see in the smallest amount of daylight left.

"I may or may not have misplaced our fire-starters," Etyne admitted in a quiet mumble.

"Good thing I *am* a fire-starter," Brisethi said, igniting both the nearby lantern and the campfire with dramatic flare like the sorceresses of her favored fantasy books. "I'll keep it at a red flame so that it's not attracting unwanted far-off attention."

He forced a smile up at her, thankful she was back in her uniform. It did a poor job of disguising her thin form, appearing like the clothes were secondhand from a male compared to her malnourished frame, but it was much better than the hideous, stained gown he'd found her in.

"I'll speed this up." Casually she flicked her hand again and heated the pheasant from the inside out until it reached the desired temperature within seconds. "Alright, let's eat!"

"You finally got your heating temperature under control?" Etyne asked.

Brisethi nodded without a word and ripped off an entire pheasant leg for herself.

-:- -:- -:-

"How much longer until the *Reliant* gets here?" Brisethi asked later that evening, staring into the calm sea under the light of one of the moons.

"Commander Fevan told us if he doesn't return by tomorrow night, then chances are they were captured or destroyed," Korteni explained.

Etyne walked up to the three women standing along the shore line of the Dralenian Ocean. He'd finally had his turn to bathe and wash his clothes in the stream and carried his drenched outer layer of his uniform coat and pants, walking toward Brisethi. He was wearing only the issued black undershirt and black knee-length underpants that were also wet. "Hey, would you mind applying your mystics to my clothes?"

Brisethi smiled widely at him, waiting until the other two turned to see the half-drowned man, enjoying the show. "Do what now?" she asked light-heartedly.

Livian blushed while Korteni giggled.

"Can you help me out?" Etyne asked, shivering. He then muttered thanks to her when he felt his clothes become warm and dry, quickly putting them on. Ordinarily, he would have played along with her antics, but he had lost his cheerful mood the past few weeks.

"If the ship doesn't come back for us, what do we do?" Livian asked, after brushing her teeth and rinsing with treated, minty cleaning water, courtesy of Korteni.

"The neutral Aspion Empire will be our destination. Beccilia has a major port where our transport ships stop. It's about a seven day travel, including rests," Etyne explained. "But I have faith that Commander Fevan hid the *Reliant* well enough and will be here as promised."

-:- -:- -:-

"Incoming!" Shouted Chief Crommik.

Commander Fevan summoned his mystic barrier once again around the entire ship to absorb the projectiles from the Lantheun airship fleet. The fleet had chased the *DSV Reliant* since the same night they had dropped off Captain Vorsen's team. Fevan knew that his ship didn't stand a chance against seven speedy, well-armed airships and pushed the *Reliant's* crew to increase the ship's speed back toward Sariadne.

They had long ago left Lantheun waters, even international waters, finally reaching Dominion territory, but the Lantheuns still pressed on.

"They're firing another round, Sir," Crommik told him while looking through the scope.

Commander Fevan readied his mystic, concentrating on each projectile heading toward his ship. He raised his hands as soon as he could track every missile and summoned his own spheres of light for each one. The spheres attached themselves to the projectiles, redirecting each one back to its source.

The two airships that had fired the ammunition took heavy damage from the returned missiles, setting them both fully ablaze in seconds. "Two down, six to go," Fevan told Crommik. He was growing weary from the constant use of his powerful mystic.

The *DSV Reliant* was a retrofitted training warship with only thirty-two guns. Although it was no longer meant for naval warfare, it was fortified with iron-plated hulls and reinforced masts, sails and lines to be able to withstand modern weaponry. Because it was generally only used for the naval training portion of the expedition, the skeleton crew of ten experienced sailors plus Master Chief Denil had to quickly train Captain Vorsen's division on as many shipboard procedures as possible.

"They're still on our tail," Crommik said. "We'll be in sight of Northwest harbor any minute. Master Chief Denil and three recruits are at the fore, ready to sound the horns and light the distress signal. They'll hear us and see us coming soon and should respond with firepower to the enemy."

The ship's booming horn sounded as bright mystic light flashed rapidly in a cryptic sequence beaming toward the continent before them. What should have taken six days to travel to Sariadne from the Lantheun shore had only taken three thanks to the experienced sailors who had wind and water mystics to increase the ship's speed, aided by the recruits with the same. The ship was nearly levitating from the unbelievable velocity it had reached.

Both Chief Crommik and Commander Fevan watched as the remaining airships readied their weapons. Commander Fevan breathed heavily. His powerful mystic was exhausted from the three consecutive days of use. The mystics were no longer replenishing, completely drained. He shuddered to think what would happen if they didn't get relief soon.

Master Chief Denil peered through his scope at the response from the Northwest Dominion harbor's mystic beams of light. He then scoped the port, watching lanterns light up and sailors quickly board the three ships that were docked. A smile stretched across his face at seeing the anchors pull up, the sails drop, and the cannons manned.

"Slow her down!" Denil shouted when he suddenly realized how quickly the *Reliant* was approaching the bay.

The sailors assigned to accelerating the sails immediately reversed their winds while turning the sails in an attempt to halt the ship. The helmsman turned the ship's mighty wheel to prevent crashing into the docks. The *DSV Reliant* drifted dangerously close to the harbor, just missing a fellow warship pulling out, sounding its own horn at them.

Commander Fevan somberly watched the final volley of ammunition on its way to his ship. He could command his mystics no longer. Sergeant First Class Tevor quickly took stock of the situation and, dropping to the deck, he pushed upon the air surrounding their ship, ceasing all projectiles in mid-flight. They fell harmlessly into the water below. Those who witnessed his actions cheered his quick thinking.

The ship finally came to a halt as the more fortified warships sailed forward, firing their mystically enhanced cannons at the airships above. The manned turrets on base began firing their dual-projectile missiles as well. Sariadne's defenses were determined to keep the enemy out.

Commander Fevan watched as flaming projectiles hit their targets far above, sending each airship crashing to the sea below, one by one. A single airship turned away in time, escaping with only a small fire in its side. He doubted the airship would make it back to Lantheus.

Fevan ordered his helmsman to dock the ship for and ready the damage control teams to evaluate necessary repairs and maintenance, but, most importantly, the crew needed rest. They had already missed the deadline by a day to pick up Vorsen's crew. He hoped they had escaped and were well on the way to Beccilia.

The commander was the first to disembark the ship to meet with the other commanders as soon as their ships were back in port. He briefed the naval captains what he knew of the whereabouts of Admiral Sen Asel's daughter, along with Captain Vorsen, Chief Pyraz and the recruit Sergeant Reej. He told them of their plan to meet in Beccilia if for any reason he was unable to return to them.

Captain Maerc Nessel nodded, listening to every word. "Now that you're back, Commander, I'd rather you continued with Captain Vorsen's scheduled training division. Your crew did well, but I can't risk the *DSV Reliant* crossing international waters again. She's not the best equipped for battle, though after the ordeal you've been through, she sure could hold her own. I'll take a warship along with two frigates to Beccilia to retrieve Vorsen's team and Sen Asel."

"Aye, sir," Commander Fevan replied.

"*DSV Sovereign* crew; we leave in three hours!" Captain Nessel shouted. The docks flurried with activity as the three vessels prepared to deploy.

Chapter III

The shrill train whistle forced Ibrienne awake. Kanilas was curled up in the corner of the box car, still sound asleep. Ibrienne regarded him for a moment. His shaggy dark hair fell into his eyes. With his calculating eyes closed, he seemed calm, almost vulnerable.

The car rattled on the track, jostling them both. Kanilas immediately woke and jumped into a crouch, staring all around. Ibrienne giggled a little, earning her a glare in return. Once Kanilas had verified there was no immediate danger, he slowly sat down on the floor and stretched.

"Do you know where we are?" he asked.

She shrugged her shoulders. "You know as much as I do," she replied.

Kanilas stood and opened the door to the train car just enough to peer out. He turned to face Ibrienne. "We're getting close to our stop." He pulled the door open farther for her to see.

The peaceful countryside had given way to farmland. Soon they would be in the first major city inside of the Beccilia border. After more than twenty hours on the train, Ibrienne would be glad to be on solid ground again. "Ready when you are," she said, joining Kanilas at the door.

They waited until the car slowed to a safe enough speed for them to jump before they made their exit. Quickly, the two dashed across the tracks, avoiding any with moving trains. Finally, they reached the station and joined the throng of people heading out onto the cobblestone street.

Beccilia was a large, industrious city. The buildings were several stories tall, mostly made of brick, crammed tightly together on the walkway. Timed oil lamps lined the streets, there for lighting the way for the ornate carriages passing by after sunset. The men and women surrounding them were dressed in dapper suits, complete with tailcoats, and beautiful ruffled gowns, tight at the hips to show off their lovely forms.

Ibrienne immediately felt conspicuous in her worn traveling cloak and dusty pants. "Everyone's staring," she hissed to Kanilas.

He rolled his eyes and started down the street, leaving her no choice but to follow. They walked for some time, until the well-kept buildings gradually became older and more worn down. The few people they saw seemed tired and shifty, always in a hurry, unlike the regally slow pace of the uptown streets.

Kanilas halted in front of a particularly unremarkable building and examined it for a moment. Ibrienne was about to ask what Kanlias was looking for when he suddenly turned to her. "When we go in there," he said, voice low, "you can't say a word. This isn't like home. Just keep quiet and stick close to me."

She nervously bit her lip and nodded.

He took a breath and led her through the door.

-:- -:- -:-

Sulica built up her strength slowly by exploring the ship. Each day she'd venture a little further, eager to mingle with people after her months spent in captivity. The Kiaran crew was surprisingly friendly towards her, probably obeying Ekani's orders, but she still appreciated it. At first, she took her meals in her cabin, but by day three, she was dining on the mess deck with everyone else.

She easily readjusted to ship life, and not as a commander. Sulica spent hours in the galley helping prepare food, dedicated time to assisting the helmsman, and holed up in a cabin with the mapmaker for a while, studying navigation charts. She learned more in one week aboard the Kiarian ship than she had in the years she'd spent on her father's.

One evening, Ekani knocked on the door to Sulica's cabin. He opened it to find her curled up on the bed, deeply enthralled by the book in her hands. Her silvery blonde hair masked her face. In the short time since he'd rescued her, Sulica had made a fairly swift recovery. Her hair was shiny and thickening, the shaved spot less and less noticeable, and the clothes seemed to fit a little tighter.

Ekani cleared his throat to alert her to his presence. She looked up, her hazel eyes bright. "I apologize for interrupting you," he said, entering the room.

Sulica smiled, "Quite alright. What can I do for you, Ekani?"

He did not answer her straight away but came further into the cabin, letting the door shut behind him. Sulica's smile faded instantly. Her instincts screamed at her to get out, wanting to never end up trapped again.

Ekani stopped moving, apparently noticing her discomfort. His smooth voice slightly reassured her. "We will be passing alongside some Kiaran vessels shortly. I think it would be best if you remained below decks for the next day or so." Seeing her confused expression, he clarified, "Women do not often come aboard Kiaran military vessels, diplomatic or otherwise, and it would be sure to stir up some rumors, ones we don't want getting around until we are ready."

Sulica nodded slowly, realizing the Kiarans had taken a cultural practice from some of the other nations rather than continuing with the Resarian tradition of equality in all matters.

"That being said, I would very much enjoy your company in the interim." Ekani gave her a charming smile which she gratefully returned, visibly relaxing.

He led her to his own cabin. It was a stately room, elegant but practical. In the corner was a small bed adorned with blue sheets that were most likely satin. Three large trunks were strapped to the bulkhead. On the far side stood a grand mahogany desk, firmly secured to the deck. Sulica followed Ekani over to the desk where a book lay open. She sat at one of the plush chairs he indicated for her and picked up a frame that sat on his desk, the only thing not bolted or strapped down.

Expecting to find some beautiful Kiaran woman, she was surprised to see a painting of Ekani himself with a man who looked very much like him but much more aged around the eyes. His hair was jet-black, streaked with white, but his eyes were strikingly blue and pupil-less.

"That's my father," Ekani said, looking fondly at the image.

"Are you close with him?" Sulica asked, surprising herself.

Ekani studied her for a moment before answering. "Yes, he's the only family I've ever known."

"I know the feeling," she muttered sadly, thinking of her own father.

"Tell me, what is it that makes you so upset?"

The gentleness in his voice unlocked something inside of her, and all the unshed tears from the past few months fell freely. She found herself confessing all to the Kiaran. They spent the following several hours talking in Ekani's cabin, telling each other stories of everything from their childhood to their careers.

"Our training is a bit intense," she admitted. "I was in the Dominion military training for the entire four years. It consists of training in every type of weapon, hand-to-hand combat, endurance and strength training, even naval warfare. It was pretty miserable; I was nearly sent home. But someone helped me halfway through, lied for me, and encouraged me. I had nearly forgotten that she spent six months doing this for me and another girl, Ibrienne. And then I betrayed her, Ekani. I fucking sold her!" She hung her head in shame.

Ekani took her hand in both of his. "Sulica, we've all made bad decisions; we've all hurt someone to better ourselves without fully thinking things through. Sometimes it's best to forget those people and move on. It's not as if you'll ever see her again."

Sulica inhaled deeply. "You're right. I won't see her again. We were both dying, and suddenly I woke up in your ship. Unless you saved her and she's on her way here as well, I imagine she's dead by now."

Ekani arched a brow. "The other girl in that Lantheun horror house with you was her?"

Sulica nodded.

"Then yes, she is dead by now. I couldn't save her. We needed only your mystics, and I wouldn't have been able to risk bringing aboard a destructive spirit. Starvation and infection certainly took her."

Chapter IV

Brisethi hadn't yet fully recovered when the small group needed to start their journey. The *DSV Reliant* did not return for them, so they would have to travel south to the Aspion empire, resting after every few hours of brisk walking. She was slowing her companions down, and the heat of the late afternoon sun wasn't making her feel any stronger or friendlier.

"Come on, 'Sethi, this isn't the best place to rest – we're out in the open," Etyne told her. He glanced around at the grassy plains in search of trees for shade then back at her. When she fell to her knees and scratched at her scabbed arms and legs, Etyne dropped down beside her. "Don't do this, not now, please. Fight it!" he urged.

"We're losing her," Korteni said, watching her dilated pupils reflect lightning that wasn't there.

"Spirits, not again!" whined Livian as she crossed her arms and watched the evolution unfold for the second time in two days. "I really wish Ibrienne had finished healing her before running away." she muttered. She was dripping with sweat in the heat, her mood soured by irritation with her former friend and the female captain's illness.

"We don't have hours to wait for it to pass. Give me your coat, Korteni," Etyne ordered.

He removed Brisethi's coat first as she screamed at him and incessantly beat at his chest. He was easily able to overpower her in her weakened state and tied her coat around her arms and waist. He tied Korteni's coat around her legs so that she would stop kicking at him.

"Get off of me you fucking piece of Lantheun shit!" Brisethi screamed, biting at Etyne, not realizing who he was. Her hallucinations brought her back into the sick time she had been living not so long ago.

Finally, Etyne removed his own coat and started to tie the sleeves around the back of her neck and place part of his coat in her mouth to silence her screaming and cease her biting. It broke his heart to be the one to demean her in such a humiliating way. He hated the teary-eyed look she gave him as if he was the enemy trying to hurt her, begging him for her freedom. It tore Etyne's spirit apart that he was treating her like a rabid dog. He gently lifted her off the ground and carried her over his shoulder until she gave up trying to wriggle her way out of his grasp. She fell into a restless sleep, exhausted from the physical exertions.

With the exception of the pain his soul had felt from hers, he had no idea what exactly Brisethi went through in the Lantheun building. For all he knew her agony might have started on the transport ships. He didn't want to ask her, he never wanted to find out for fear the anger would propel him to do something rash. But he would listen to her should she ever decide to voluntarily tell him.

They took one last break after an hour of walking to allow Etyne to rest his arms and back from carrying the restrained captain. Unsure if she was herself again, he knelt down in front of her to remove the coat tied to her mouth.

"Etyne…" she exhaled his name. "Why? Did it happen again?" The forlorn look in her eyes destroyed him.

He removed the coat from her arms and then the coat from her legs. He nodded in response to her question. "I'm so sorry that I had to do this," he quietly told her, wiping the tears from her face with his thumbs.

"Did I hurt anyone?" she solemnly asked.

He shook his head. "Fortunately for us, you seem to think your mystics don't work when fending me off," he assured her.

"Oh spirits," she gasped. "I can't even imagine what I'd do if I awoke to learn I had incinerated any of you," she buried her face in her hands at the thought.

He thought to pull her in close to hold her; something he had been wanting to do since the night he found her. Instead, he reluctantly placed his hand on the side of her arm, feeling held back from showing her physical affection. "It's a good thing I can shield myself from you," he replied with a half smile. He wasn't only comforting her, but comforting himself as well. He was genuinely scared for her, and *of* her.

He helped her to stand when Livian and Korteni returned from scouting ahead.

"Not a single person in sight," Korteni reported. "Are you able to go on, 'Sethi?" She couldn't keep the concern from her voice.

Brisethi nodded, smiling to her. She gave Korteni her Dominion Navy coat back. She examined Etyne's before handing it back to him, saddened that she had left teeth-marks in his sleeve. "I'll replace your coat as soon we get back," she told him.

He donned his coat and half-smiled at her small bite-mark. "Nah, it adds character," he told her. "I'm more concerned about getting you back to Dominion standards so you can keep up with us." He handed her his bow and arrows. "It's your turn to hunt as soon as we get to that hill up ahead."

-:- -:- -:-

She drew back the bowstring to her cheek, aiming for the boar's heart. Without a second thought, she released the arrow, watching it swiftly pierce her target. She ran up to her kill, realizing it was bigger than it looked from far. She placed two fingers to her lips and whistled loudly.

Moments later, Etyne emerged in the tall grass, eyeing the wild boar. "I see you haven't lost your bear appetite," he teased her for such a mighty kill.

She smiled sadly at the memory of the name he had once given her almost a decade ago, when life was simpler. "You haven't called me that..." she didn't finish her sentence.

"I thought it irritated you so I stopped," Etyne admitted when meeting her eyes. He unraveled the rope and tarp he had in his pack to wrap the boar and hoisted it over his shoulder.

"It didn't irritate me," she continued. She squatted down instantly at seeing a tarantula just smaller than her hand. "Hey look!" she excitedly called Etyne over.

He placed the boar down and knelt beside her. "Since when have you been infatuated with spiders?"

"I'm not. Tarantulas on the other hand, well I'm fascinated by them," she smiled and allowed the fuzzy eight-legged arachnid to slowly crawl onto the palm of her hand.

They both stared at the docile tarantula until Brisethi set it back down. "I wish I could take you with me."

Halfway through their hike Etyne made Brisethi carry the carcass to begin her strength training.

Livian and Korteni's eyes lit up at the sight of dinner. "You really are still hungry," Korteni jabbed at Brisethi.

"And weak," Brisethi replied, picking up Etyne's sword. "I'm going to whack at that tree to work on rebuilding my strength till the food's ready."

"I'll go with you," Korteni said.

"Before you go, could you, uh…" Etyne nodded toward the fire pit Livian and Korteni had assembled.

"Spirits forbid we make a fire the way we were taught in expedition training!" Brisethi retorted then set the twigs and branches ablaze.

"Appreciate it," Etyne replied with an unusual monotone.

-:- -:- -:-

Livian removed her recruit coat. "Do you want help, Sir?"

Etyne looked up from cutting at the boar. "I can take care of it."

"Unlike Captain Sen Asel, I'm not afraid of getting my hands dirty. Remember the bear I took down when it was chasing after Sommin?" she reminded him.

"Yes, that's why I allowed Chief to promote you to Sergeant for your bravery," he ignored her jab at his friend and politely smiled at her when she knelt down beside him to assist in removing entrails.

"Do you think she'll be crazy for the rest of her life?" Livian bluntly asked.

"Who, the captain?"

Livian nodded.

Etyne cleared his throat. "She isn't crazy. She's just not fully recovered."

"She'll probably be discharged from the military. I don't feel safe at night, sleeping while she's near, Sir," Livian expressed, glaring into the scarlet fire.

"As long as you're not touching her when she's having a flashback, she won't have reason to harm you. And it would behoove you to give her the same respect as you give me, regardless of her mental state," he sternly replied.

Livian was chagrined from his sudden outburst toward her. He was treating her as if she was an undisciplined private once more. She acknowledged the chastisement and went back to work.

-:- -:- -:-

"Etyne hasn't quite been himself since..." Korteni's voice trailed off as she let her sword hit the ground.

"I've noticed," Brisethi sighed. "I've seen him in every emotion, even heartbroken. But, when I look at him, his mind is wandering elsewhere. The way he looked at me last, it's the way a father would look at his dying child. I've never seen him with watered eyes until yesterday when I first awoke from that relapse."

"When you were out for ten hours the first day, he didn't talk to any of us for the first six or so hours. He walked over to a boulder to sit on and just stared into the forest. He was almost catatonic, 'Sethi," Korteni relayed to her.

Brisethi frowned. "I haven't really had the chance to speak with him, alone, anyway. I'm kind of afraid to."

"How so? You two spent nearly every day together during officer training, not to mention however many years during expedition training," Korteni added. "I thought by now you two held nothing back from one another."

"It's hard to explain, but it's almost as if I can feel his spirit - and it seems a bit off," Brisethi continued.

Korteni assumed the Spirit Reclamation had something to do with it but wasn't sure if Etyne had revealed to her yet what he had done. "Off, how?"

"Well, as I said, after spending so long with someone I can tell what mood he's in. This is more severe than a broken heart - his soul is in some kind of pain," Brisethi concluded.

"I don't know what's worse than a broken heart. You should really go talk to him, though. Of all the spirits here, yours is the one to best mend his," Korteni confidently told her. "Maybe he just needs time to cope with almost losing his best friend. I was more fretful while on our way to finding you. I was overjoyed and all of my fears washed away at finding you alive."

"Maybe you're right. He's barely teased me or laughed at anything I've said. I miss the way he used to smile at me," she whined.

"Hey, what's that?" Korteni ceased their spar and peered over Brisethi's shoulder.

Brisethi turned to view the road in the distance where a procession of eight mounted horses could be seen. Two trained dogs were leading the men off the road and toward the direction of their camp. "Korteni, just when and where exactly did Etyne lose that fire-starter? Did he lose anything else while you were on your way to rescue me? Because I have a feeling those dogs have our scent."

They shared a split-second look of concern and darted off toward Etyne and Livian.

"Put this fire out!" Brisethi whispered loudly, extinguishing her own flames with her mystics to prevent the smoke that would have risen if it had been doused by water and dirt instead. She grabbed her pack and took out a smaller pack to help gather both the cooked and uncooked meat.

Etyne needed no explanation when he heard the sense of urgency in her voice and helped to gather their belongings. He followed after her and Korteni with Livian at his side to disappear into the grasslands. They paused when they heard the dogs bark and watched as the men on horseback started charging in their direction.

"Fucking run!" Brisethi hissed, breaking into a full sprint. She had no desire to attack men that were simply carrying out an order. Moreso, she was uncertain she would have the energy to put up a fight.

Etyne summoned his mystic on each of them to distort their appearances. He realized Brisethi was leading them to the plateau that rose nearly forty feet above them and spanned for miles north to south. Sprinting through the waist-high grass proved to be risky as each of them tried to avoid tangling their legs in the grass, stumbling over unseen rocks, and nearly crippling their ankles in rodent holes.

"The rope I packed isn't long enough so you'll each need to climb at least ten feet," Etyne told them. He then dematerialized himself into his spirit form and rushed up the cliffs until he reached the top. He became corporeal again, unpacked his rope to tether it to himself and let the rest of it fall below. "Come on, Reej! Reach for the rope!"

"I'll distract the dogs!" Brisethi shouted and retraced her steps back into the grasslands. She wanted only to throw off the scent to keep the patrol men from seeing the slight distortion in the cliffs of her comrades. Since she was still under Etyne's mystic protection, she kicked at rocks to spur up dust and even whistled to grab the attention of the dogs.

Livian quickly reached the rope and wrapped it around her arm. She grabbed it with her other hand when Etyne swiftly pulled her up. When he helped her onto the ledge he tossed the rope down again for Korteni who had already climbed halfway up in the time he attended to Livian. She took a hold of it and used her feet to help climb when he pulled her up.

"That climb was way easier than the one near Mt. Bavala," Korteni exhaled.

"Just a tad," Livian panted.

"Get out of sight, run over there," Etyne pointed to the small outcrop of boulders in the distance. "I'll go help 'Sethi."

Brisethi had initiated her climb by the time Etyne spotted her. The two dogs were barking wildly beneath her while the men on horseback fired their rifles at the cliff walls, unsure of their target. Debris from the bullets hitting the rock around her caused her to flinch. She saw the rope just above her and swiftly climbed toward it, adreneline and muscle memory taking over until she grabbed it in both hands. She kicked at the cliff with her legs while Etyne brought her up.

"That was odd," she told him, nearly out of breath when he helped her to stand.

"What was? You didn't think they'd chase after us?" Etyne asked, packing the rope away.

"No, not that. My mystics – they were, trying to summon something other than destruction," she told him, following after him toward the other two.

"Your spirit is probably just trying to get used to defending you again now that it's returned to your vessel," he explained.

She gave Etyne a confused look and was urged to ask. "What do you mean 'returned to your vessel'?"

Etyne cursed to himself, not meaning reveal to her what he had done. "I'll tell you as soon as we get to those boulders," he told her, squinting in the faintest light left of the evening.

They waited until long after the sun set, to start a small fire, when they could be sure the hunting party had moved on. The circle of boulders where the Resarians hid portrayed evidence of past visitors from the carefully placed rocks around a fire pit. After cleaning the meat rack, Brisethi placed the remaining uncooked boar meat on it to let it cook naturally in the fire instead of her instant cooking.

Etyne was perched on one of the boulders, trying to study a map of Trycinea in the dim firelight. He listened to the soft footsteps approaching and guessed correctly that Brisethi had come to pay him a visit.

"What do you have to tell me?" she asked, sitting down next to him.

"There's a town nearby - Essenar, along a massive lake. We can make it there in two days if we leave just before dawn," he explained to her, straightening the map folds on his lap. "I think we deserve to stay at an inn for once, with a proper bath, replenish our supplies…"

"Tell me, Etyne," Brisethi replied. She glared at him until he could no longer take her scornful gaze.

He folded the map and placed it in his coat pocket. "Let's go for a walk." He helped her stand and climb down the boulder. He signaled to Korteni and Livian that they would return soon.

Awkward silence initiated their slow walk under the starry, indigo sky. Brisethi took out a few pieces of cooked boar meat wrapped in food cloth and shared some with her companion.

"I'm waiting on you. The sooner you tell me what happened, the sooner we can get sleep before our watches," she yawned.

He swallowed the mouthful of food before beginning his confession. When he did speak, his voice was soft. "When I found you in that laboratory cell, I couldn't sense your spirit. Not even a trace of it. I thought for sure it had returned to the Sea of Renewal."

"There's no such thing as a Sea of Renewal," she muttered. "We simply embody paranormal anomalies. Sariadne is nothing more than a land of unexplained scientific singularities."

"'Sethi, what the fuck are you talking about?" He halted their walk to turn and face her. "Is this what the Lantheuns told you?"

"You of all people with your logical, Kiaran mind should know this fact!" She wasn't sure why her voice had risen in volume.

Etyne suddenly lost all interest in letting her know what he did after her blasphemous words had cut through him like a dagger through his soul. He looked over when she had fallen to her knees. The illuminating white flashes in her eyes told him she was having another flashback. He silently cursed the Lantheuns again for the effect they had on Brisethi, the effect his soul was starting to feel from her. Since there was no chance of harming the others, he let her carry out the fit, watching her, listening to her.

"Sulica!" she shouted hoarsely. "Then why can't I?" Her words drifted in and out of his hearing as if she was somehow talking through a warped time plane. After a long minute, she stood and started to fight her own phantom, punching, kicking, and leaping at nothing.

In the distance to the west, Etyne watched lightning illuminate the cell clouds, too far to hear the thunder. His eyes returned to Brisethi who still fought her demon, a demon she hadn't conquered and still lived somewhere in Lantheus. He watched her fall to the ground and kick at nothing in front of her. Moments later she fell unconscious as the light in her eyes dimmed with her closed eyelids.

He knelt down and lifted her, noticing she had regained some of her weight. They returned to camp, and Etyne set Brisethi down on the opposite side of the fire, away from Korteni and Livian's bedrolls.

"Did you two fight?" Korteni teased at seeing her unconscious friend.

"She fought someone, yes," he replied, untying his sleeping mat from his pack for his friend to rest on. Since someone would always stand watch, they had only brought three mats with them.

Korteni did not need more of an explanation as she handed him her mat since she would stand the first watch of the night. She doused the fire with her water mystic and equipped her sword and pistol. She climbed the highest boulder near them and took a seat upon it.

-:- -:- -:-

"Sen Asel," the voice bellowed in her head. "Daughter of Sentiar Asellunas."

"No, Tirinnus Sen Asel is my father. His grandfather's father was Sentiar Asellunas," she corrected the obsidian dragon, taking in the view of the stars above in the crater. "How did you know my name? I don't recall telling you."

"I'm in your mind, in your dreams, '*Sethi*,'" he replied using her nickname lightly. "I read your thoughts, your desires, your ambitions. Would you like me to enact vengeance upon Sulica for your torture?"

"You would do that for me?"

"Spirits, no, I would never leave my volcano for fear of ending up like my unfortunate mother," he sadly reminded her. His giant scaled form walked around the Resarian girl, examining the wounds she tried to hide under her uniform. He saw what she had seen, though, and knew they were still there. "I was unable to disturb your dreams while you were away from Sariadne," he continued. "Though, you are still not returned to our homeland. Your adversary must have prevented my spirit's infiltration of your mind."

Brisethi realized the dragon hadn't haunted her during her entire stay in Lantheus. She wondered if Roz had been visited by him more during her absence but asked about something that had piqued her curiosity more. "Did you know Sentiar Asellunas? Just how old are you?"

"I have watched the rise and fall of both your people and the Kiarans. I witnessed your warlord ancestor rise from the ashes of

Res'Baveth to avenge his people. Do you have any more questions?" the dragon impatiently growled.

"Yes," she quickly said, still standing in the crater of the once again dormant volcano. "Why is Sariadne the only continent with anomalies that embody the creatures who inhabit this place?" she asked, echoing the words of the Lantheun.

He growled again, letting flames flare from his nostrils at her description of his sacred spirit. "Sit down!" He shouted at her.

She slowly sank to the ground and perched on a lava rock, abiding by the dragon's frightening command.

The dragon walked up to Brisethi and lowered his rear haunches, resisting the urge to eat her. He would have had she not embodied such a powerful spirit for fear he would upset those in the Sea of Renewal. "Before humans existed," he began, "dragons ruled the world of Falajen. When the millennia of ice overtook the surface of the world, we fled to Sariadne, the last continent to fall to the devastating winter of eons."

Brisethi sighed impatiently, "Yes, I know, we're taught that we have dragon spirits-"

"Do not interrupt me." His claws raked the ground with his words. "We fought one another for the heat of the two volcanoes in a constant struggle. In the end, only forty-eight of us survived; forty-eight out of hundreds of thousands of us. As each immortal dragon froze to death, their spirit was returned to what you call the 'Sea of Renewal', near the northern volcano. When the ice melted, and creatures emerged throughout Sariadne once more, the dragon spirits who wished to leave their incorporeal state began to reside in these creatures. When the first Resarians and Kiarans left the caves to initiate civilization, we embodied them, too.

"Unfortunately, the Kiarans were keen on destroying the dragons who gave their vessels extended life and mystic spirits. We stopped choosing their vessels to inhabit and remained loyal to the Resarians who feared us enough to leave us alone. That is," the dragon growled, "until a group of your people decided to hunt down my mother." He flared his fire and clawed at the ground beneath him to calm his anger. "Because of this, I have asked the spirits to never inhabit any human again. But my mother's spirit is too forgiving and wanted to experience this 'human' life of yours.

"Your immortal spirit is a gift, Sen Asel. Treat it as such. Or we will take them back suddenly, ending the life of any Resarian older than the average human and leaving you all vulnerable to your adversaries." He spread his wings wide and roared.

Brisethi inhaled deeply at the sight. She felt a pang of guilt in her heart for her temporary loss of faith. The urge came over her to kneel down on one knee before the majestic dragon. "I'm sorry that I ever doubted your spirits," she told him, hoping her words conveyed the appropriate amount of shame.

"Save your apology for your companion. He's the one who prevented your rare dragon spirit from returning to the Sea of Renewal before his time," he flapped his wings and leapt into the sky.

"What?"

Brisethi opened her eyes and stared up at the immense amount of stars in the endless sky above. She sat up, waiting for her eyes to adjust to see Livian and Korteni asleep on the opposite side of their camp. Etyne's silhouette could barely be seen sitting atop the boulders facing the northwest.

She climbed the massive rock and sat down next to him and watched as he put his pocket watch away. Removing a pack of sweetened hard cinnamon candies, she popped one in her mouth and offered one to him as well.

"You're about an hour early to watch," he quietly told her, taking a candy from her hand and unwrapping it.

"He told me what you did," she vaguely stated, rolling her tongue around the cinnamon-flavored chew in her mouth.

"Who told you what?" Etyne slowly asked after yawning.

"Oh, spirits, I never told you," she nearly whispered. She scratched at the back of her neck then raked at her uneven hair.

"We have a bad habit of keeping certain things from one another," Etyne admitted, biting down on his candy.

Brisethi nodded and looked down at her hands. "Since you already think I've lost my mind, I might as well tell you." She inhaled slowly. "Acolyte Roz and I met a dragon during expedition training."

Etyne remained silent. A confrontation would risk destroying their suddenly fragile friendship, especially given the recent event. Doubting her was the last thing on his mind, so he carefully listened to her instead.

"I know you don't believe me," she continued after a pause. "You're probably thinking that the Lantheuns completely fucked up my mind more than I'm willing to admit. But he exists, and he haunts my dreams every now and then. I'll even take you to him when we return to the harbor outside Ancient Kiar – he's wanted to eat a human lately and I think you'd satisfy him quite well." She half-smiled.

Etyne leaned back on his hands to look at her easier. "You met him over eight years ago? How could you have not told me after all this time? Especially during the four years in officer training where we spent nearly every day with one another. Why didn't you trust me then to tell me about this unique encounter?" His words were calm, but he seemed hurt by her mistrust.

Brisethi looked away again, glancing up to the endless sky for courage. "I wanted to tell you the very next day, but there was a time that I had a reputation to uphold to you. I didn't want you to think I was mental or making things up to impress you. Despite my somewhat arrogant persona, I *do* care what some people think of me – what those I care about think of me."

Etyne leaned forward again and placed his elbows on his knees. "You have no idea how highly I think of you, 'Sethi. I will always admire the person you are, no matter how difficult it is for me to believe some of the things you tell me. But I will never call you a liar, and I will never call you crazy. I hope you believe me."

She brought her knees up to her chest and held them. "I do believe you," she sighed.

"Tell me from the beginning. I want to know how the two of you avoided this dragon's teeth," Etyne asked, giving her his genuine smile. It was the first genuine smile he was able to show her since their two-week integration.

She bit her lower lip to keep from grinning childishly. She eagerly recounted to him the entire event from the moment she inadvertently summoned the dragon, fended his flames from them, and the dreams he had inhabited.

Even in the dim light of the stars, Etyne could see the passion in her face from the way her eyes lit up while telling him her story. He could hear the excitement in her voice of every detailed action. But what surprised him more than her story, was how he had actually believed her. He was envious of her that she was blessed by this dragon and was particularly intrigued to learn that she was a descendent of Sentiar Asellunas.

"And just what did this dragon say I did to you?" He asked carefully when she paused.

"He said that my spirit was on his way to the Sea of Renewal. Etyne, please tell me you didn't perform Soul Reclamation on me." Brisethi repositioned herself to sit on her knees, almost as though begging him to say he hadn't.

Etyne nodded slowly, staring into her eyes. "I had to," he softly replied.

Tears distorted her vision for the ultimate sacrifice he made to prevent her life from ending. *That explains your recent demeanor*, she thought. "Etyne, why? Why would you shorten your own life to extend mine? I had given up, I was practically dead."

He shrugged. "I'm a bit selfish, actually. I'd rather you suffer in sorrows when I die before you, instead of the other way around," He chuckled dryly, but was only holding back his own tears from the recollection of his partner's broken vessel. He had been mere minutes away from losing her forever.

Brisethi reached over and brought his head to her chest, holding his neck and shoulders tightly against her while leaning her head on his. "You foolish, insane man. I'm not worth sacrificing half your life for. Your dragon's spirit is probably plotting its revenge as we speak," she tried to tease him but stifled a sob instead, holding him even tighter when she felt his arms wrap around her. "You once made a wish with me, in the desert, to live forever. Oh spirits, why?"

He buried his face into her uniform, not wanting to let go of her from his embrace. He couldn't allow her to see the tears he'd been holding in since the night he found her. "'Sethi, don't," he replied, not wanting to be reminded of simpler times. When he was confident that most of his tears were wiped from his face he looked up at her. "You have a bigger goal in life that I need you to carry out for both our peoples. You've told me of all of your ambitions. How could you expect me to allow you to die if I didn't have to? It's not like I won't still be here another four hundred years or so."

She reluctantly let go of him as Etyne gently pulled away. "Looks like I have less than four hundred years to reach that goal so you can see me succeed," she smiled at him. "You should go get rest, Etyne. Leave me your sword and pistol."

He looked at his pocket watch again to see that she had taken nearly the entire hour to explain her dragon encounters to him. He obliged, standing to stretch and relinquishing his weapons to her.

Tired though he was, Etyne laid awake for some time on the bedroll, considering all that Brisethi had told him. His spirit still remained restless from experiencing a fraction of what she had gone through. When sleep finally took him, his dreams consisted of crimson fire, flight and an inexplicable pain.

Chapter V

The inside of the tavern was dimly lit, and the lanterns that had light were so covered in dirt that they cast shadows all over the room. Tables and bars were scattered haphazardly around. At the back of the room was a long bar with only one person behind it. There were only a couple of other patrons, sitting half-hidden in a corner. The very air seemed to scream at Ibrienne to turn away.

As Ibrienne followed Kanilas to the bar, she examined the bottles behind the counter. None of them had labels, and more than a couple looked as if they'd never been wiped down. Nervously, she pulled her hood up to cover her face.

The shifty bartender greeted them in Beccilian. Kanilas leaned in and spoke an unrecognizable language in an undertone. Ibrienne shot a surprised look at him. She was fluent in Beccilian, Kiaran, and could pick up most of what a Lantheun would say, but she had no idea what words Kanilas was speaking.

The bartender narrowed his eyes suspiciously. After a moment, he squeezed out from behind the narrow bar and gestured for the two Resarians to follow him. He opened a door at the back that had been completely obscured by shadows then led them down a dingy hallway. Ibrienne stayed close to Kanilas, not even sure if she trusted him anymore. The bartender stopped at a door and peeked his head inside. Ibrienne could barely make out more of the unfamiliar language. Suddenly, the man stepped aside, opening the door wider for Ibrienne and Kanilas to pass. It slammed behind them.

Ibrienne was completely taken aback by the scene before them. Rather than more shadows and dirt, the room in which they stood was nearly sparkling in comparison. A single lantern hung from the center of the ceiling, directly above a large table. Seated all around it were several men. The one at the head of the table was unmistakably Kiaran. His black eyes were without pupils, just as every other Kiaran she had ever met. The dark pools met her gaze, despite the hood she wore.

He smiled and spoke quietly, immediately ceasing the chatter from the other men around him. "Trenn," he said in perfect, though slow, Resarian, "what is it that brings you back here?" His eyes moved to Ibrienne's companion.

Kanilas lifted his head higher. "I need information again. She wasn't there."

The Kiaran tilted his head, still smiling. "That is not how this works, you know that. You do not come into my place of..." he trailed off as though struggling to find the words, "business and demand my knowledge." The men around him chortled.

"She wasn't where you said she'd be!" Kanilas said again, stepping forward.

The laughter died quickly. "I gave you the location where she was when you asked," the Kiaran said. "It is not my fault you took so long in Sariadne." His grin returned on Kanilas's surprise. "You do not think you were my only informant? You were very useful for a time, giving shipping routes, manifestos, even crew details."

Ibrienne turned to Kanilas, her jaw dropping. "You did *what*?" she asked incredulously. At her reaction, the malicious laughter began again.

Kanilas kept his eyes on the Kiaran. "We know she's in Pahl'Kiar," he said in a low voice. "You had something to do with this, didn't you?"

The Kiaran openly grinned. "You expect honor among those who deal in darkness?" He grew somber once more. "Do not seek to blame anyone else for what guilt you feel."

Kanilas's face reddened angrily. but he said nothing.

"If you can come up with some valuable information, then we can talk. Until then..." The Kiaran did not bother continuing.

Kanilas turned on his heel and stormed out. The Kiaran motioned for Ibrienne to stay. She took a step backwards but did not move any farther. The man nodded to the others, and they filed out, leaving the two alone.

"Miss Sestas," he began. "Yes, I know your identity," he said in answer to her unasked question. "But that is not important." There was no hint of the humor or condescension she'd seen him use with Kanilas. He regarded her for a moment before continuing. "I can not say much, but you have a very important role in the events that will come to pass. You have a kind spirit, my dear, be careful that the troubles you will find yourself surrounded by do not corrupt it."

He leaned back in his chair and closed his eyes, clearly indicating that he was done speaking.

She didn't say a word but turned and fled the tavern, completely unnerved.

She found Kanilas waiting for her outside. "What did he want with you?" he asked, glaring at her.

She shook her head and changed the subject. "So all of this is your fault, isn't it? You told Sulica about the Kiarans buying Resarians for their mystics, and you told *that* Kiaran," she pointed back at the building, "what Sulica can do."

He couldn't meet her eyes. "Let's get out of here," was all he said.

-:- -:- -:-

The small town of Essenar spread out over the Culidan River at the edge of Lake Sankling. North of the river lay the Lantheun Empire, while the southern side belonged to the Aspion Empire. The riverside town was a welcome break from the seemingly endless grasslands.

The four Resarians removed their coats with Sariadne's Dominion insignia and packed them away before entering the town's limits. Since their undershirts and pants were still in uniform colors, they split into two groups to appear less conspicuous. Although Resarians were welcome in the neutral empire of Aspion, Dominion personnel could become targets for anyone looking to make a fortune if they could overpower their spirit.

Korteni and Brisethi casually strolled along the paths where small trade shops and cafés lined the walkways. They began searching for comfortable civilian attire so as to blend in with the rest of the nations of the Trycinea continent. The first shop they entered catered to noblewomen looking to purchase fancy evening gowns. After a quick exchange of looks, they hurriedly exited, holding back their laughter. The second shop they entered offered subtle, common clothes that wouldn't hinder them while traveling.

"Do women not wear pants out here?" Brisethi whispered to Korteni.

"It's kind of a warmer climate than Res'Baveth which means you're doomed to dress like an actual female," Korteni teased.

"It's all so revealing," Brisethi whined, hesitating as she held up a red backless dress. Her unspoken words reminded Korteni of the disgusting scars along her arms, chest and back.

Korteni picked out a dark blue sleeveless blouse and matching skirt along with a silver threaded corset. "We're supposed to blend," she said, plucking the dress from Bisethi's hand.

Brisethi finally found the only long sleeved blouse in a burgundy color, along with a matching long skirt and a wide black belt that was worn at the waist. It reminded her of their desert recruit uniforms. She had been drawn to the gold embroidery on the black belt designed with stars and pointed curves similar to the dominion insignia. It wasn't until they purchased their new garb and changed into them that Brisethi noticed her shirt had a hood attached to it. She thanked the spirits that she could hide her uneven hair.

After visiting a general store for extra rations and traveling supplies, including two small daggers for Brisethi who complained of being unarmed the entire time, they were on the way to meet the other two at a café. Brisethi suddenly stopped, distracted by a trinket shop. The window displayed various pocket watches, clocks and compasses.

"You still collect those?" Korteni asked as she followed her inside the shop.

Brisethi nodded, infatuated with the unique designs and engineering of the advanced mechanisms. "Those ones are pocket watches *and* compasses in one, I need it."

"How much did Etyne lend you?" Korteni asked with raised eyebrows when she saw the price of the stylish apparatus. Since Brisethi had been unexpectedly taken away from her continent, she barely had enough frakshins untouched in her coat to cover their clothing allowance. Etyne was smart enough to have withdrawn some of his earnings and exchanged it for Trycinean paper currency when he was at the Dominion's Southwest Naval Base before departing on the rescue. He had loaned her half of what he'd brought with him for the remainder of their journey.

"Not enough," she sighed. "It's not like he brought his whole salary with him like I would have. He actually has a bank account."

"Hello, ladies, welcome to Granith's Trinkets," an older, stout man approached them. He recognized them as foreigners from their accents. "Do you two travel often?"

Brisethi answered yes while Korteni answered no simultaneously.

"I don't quite recognize your accents; may I ask where you are from?" He kindly inquired.

"Vipurg," Brisethi replied when she remembered one of her favorite history lessons in officer training. "It's a small mountain town in Micinity."

"Ah, yes, that would explain it, then. I know nothing of Micinity except of the Kiarans. In any case, welcome to Trycinea," he humbly smiled. "Would you like to look at any of these pieces up close?"

As much as she wanted to admire the silver plated pocket watch and compass in one, accented in sapphire gemstones and engraved stars, she found the least appealing one which had the lowest price tag on it. After the shopkeeper allowed her to observe the pewter mechanism, she purchased it with some of Etyne's borrowed frakshins and the remainder of her own.

"Allied with the Dominion, are you?" The shopkeeper asked after counting the Resarian paper.

"Nobody allies with the Dominion," Brisethi replied in a serious tone of voice. "But we trade with them, just as they trade with Becillia and other coastal, non-aligned cities."

"Of course," he smiled under his bushy gray mustache, wrapping her compass pocket watch in a silky fabric and placing it in a wooden box for her. "Thank you for your patronage. Do return!" He bid them farewell.

Etyne and Livian were seated at a table for four outside a café overlooking the lake and the river. They had just finished their meal of trout and vegetables. They sat in continued silence since leaving the clothing shop where they purchased their civilian clothes.

The common clothes Etyne had settled on consisted of a dark brown long coat to cover his regular uniform blouse and black trousers. Livian, on the other hand, was more enthusiastic about wearing civilian clothes, having been restricted to the uniforms for a few years already. She took the opportunity to purchase a purple sleeveless dress that flowed like satin, accented with a gold embroidered corset enhancing her bountiful revealing chest. Etyne had kept pressuring her to buy a coat or shawl, even offering to pay for one but she refused. He had to constantly avert his eyes each time he looked in her direction.

He felt relieved when Korteni and Brisethi finally arrived at their table to break the awkward atmosphere. Korteni and Brisethi placed their order with the waitress and, when she left, Etyne couldn't resist commenting on Brisethi's choice of clothing.

"I'm almost certain that's our recruit desert uniform, 'Sethi," He said in a half-mocking tone. His spirit had lifted, feeling less irritable since his talk with Brisethi.

"I tried to tell her," Korteni sighed with a shrug.

"You're still wearing your uniform, just with a different coat!" she retorted.

"Shh, you're drawing attention," he whispered even though nobody even so much as glanced in their direction. "What's in the box?"

She slid the box to him. "For my collection."

He carefully removed the lid and unraveled the silky cloth. He took the mechanism out and examined the two-in-one apparatus. "I hope you didn't spend everything I loaned to you on this."

Brisethi glared at him, taking a bite of the food that had arrived.

"She didn't. She wanted to, but I talked her out of it," Korteni replied to him with a wink.

"It's really impressive; it suits you, 'Sethi," he finally told her, still testing the compass part of it, turning away from the group to examine it further.

"Did you find us an inn to stay at tonight?" Korteni directed the question at Etyne and Livian

When Etyne didn't answer due to his distraction with Brisethi's apparatus, Livian answered instead. "Yes, Chief, we did. I chose the Lakeside Inn a few blocks that way," she pointed south. "They have balconies overlooking the lake!"

Etyne turned his attention back to the three women, but specifically to Brisethi. "Hurry up and finish eating so you can take me to the shop you bought this from." He placed it back in its box.

"Why, what's wrong with it?" Brisethi asked through a mouthful of her flatbread filled with shredded meats.

"Nothing. I want my own, is all," he replied and stood from his seat. He stood behind Brisethi, "Let's go, the sun is setting, the shops are closing, eat and walk."

She shoved the last big bite of food into her mouth and stood, relieved that some of Etyne's chipper mood had returned. "It's not like the shop won't be there tomorrow." Her words were lost on him, mostly due to the flatbread that nearly spilled from her mouth.

"It'll be closed when we leave at the crack of dawn," he anxiously told her.

They parted ways with the other two women and walked hastily to Granith's Trinkets, hoping it was still open for the evening.

"Ah, welcome back my Vipurg friend," the shopkeeper greeted Brisethi. She received a questionable look for her title from Etyne. "Were you not satisfied with your purchase?"

"I am! My friend here wants one as well. He's always doing everything I do," she grinned.

Etyne studied the compass pocket watches, realizing that his companion had purchased the most ordinary of them all, he assumed due to its inexpensive price. He watched her for a moment, trying to see what it was she was so intently staring at. He took out his own pocket watch and showed it to the shopkeeper. "Do you trade at all, or take coin and frakshins only?"

The shopkeeper adjusted his monocle to view the device in Etyne's hand. He looked up, his eyes wide in amazement. "This is magnificent, how did you, as a Kiaran, get ahold of a Dominion-crested pocket watch?"

"I have a half-brother in the Dominion. He gives me his Dominion items all the time," Etyne lied.

"Intriguing," the shopkeeper replied.

"What is so fascinating over here?" Etyne nudged Brisethi.

"I'm eventually going to come back here for this one when I have my own money on me," she pointed to the silver-plated compass pocketwatch lined with sapphire gemstones in the shape of stars.

"Can we see that one?" Etyne asked the shopkeeper.

The gentleman opened the case and handed the ornate mechanism to Etyne. He examined it, testing out the compass and listening to the gears ticking inside. As he placed it in Brisethi's hand, he turned his attention to the shopkeeper again.

"If I gave you my Dominion pocket watch, how much would you take off of that compass for me?"

The shopkeeper stroked the side of his mustache thoughtfully. "I will deduct half of the price of that one for your pocket watch."

"Deal," Etyne told him.

"But, Etyne, I wanted this!" She gave him a pout and forced herself to hand the apparatus back to the shopkeeper so he could wrap it and box it.

The shopkeeper chuckled. "She doesn't understand, does she?"

"Sometimes one of her gears stops working," Etyne teased, taking his purchase and handing it to Brisethi. "Trade me for the one you bought earlier."

She arched a brow in confusion then looked down at her own box. Her eyes lit up when she finally realized what he had done. "Thank you," she grinned, exchanging compass watches. "I'll pay you back once we return home."

"Before you go," the shopkeeper said. "You two should really work on those Resarian accents of yours. It took me a moment to figure it out and I know why you had to feign, but you have nothing to fear from the people of Aspion." He dramatically lowered his voice. "We were recently threatened by the newly formed allegiance of

Lantheus and the Pahl'Kiar. Our Prime Minister is becoming desperate to seek out an alliance with anyone at the moment. If you two wouldn't mind helping to spread word to your leaders, I know I'd appreciate it."

Brisethi and Etyne shared a look. "We'll see what we can do," Etyne replied and escorted his companion out of the shop.

"It's good to know we might have friends," Brisethi quietly spoke, admiring her new compass watch. "If only we could get a message out to Major Paush."

"As soon as we get to one of our ships we'll be able to relay the message. If the major could relay the news to General Satnir and then to Emperor Arquistas the Dominion could ally with Aspion before Lantheus forces their own alliance on them," Etyne explained, leading them to their inn.

"I only hope Emperor Arquistas isn't as stubborn as he lets on," Brisethi sighed.

The sun slowly dropped in the sky, turning the sky from blue to orange to pink. Etyne and Brisethi walked into the lively inn, which was more of a fancy resort than a common inn. The walls were made to look like a tropical palace that reminded both of them of the resort near Ancient Kiar. The beautiful island music and tall torches made them forget they were inland by a lake and not on an exotic island.

"Due to the cost of the rooms," Etyne told Brisethi as they made their way through the lobby, "I only got two rooms instead of four. You three ladies could fit in one bed, right?" He feigned a serious tone.

"That isn't funny." Brisethi followed him up the stairs and down the tropically furnished hall. "Either Livian stays with you or I do. Pick one." She silently prayed to the spirits he wasn't foolish enough to pick his subordinate.

He stopped at his room before unlocking the door to think for a moment. "That's an obvious decision; I'll take Livian. She won't complain when I make her sleep on the floor."

"Fine, where's the other room?" she asked, trying desperately to hide the jealousy in her voice.

"I was only jesting, 'Sethi, you're with me - just like old times at the Citadel," he smirked. "Also, I'd rather you didn't accidently hurt Korteni if you fell into one of your fits," he said as an afterthought. He led her into his room and set his pack down at the foot of the bed. "You were really going to allow me to have Livian in here for the night?"

Brisethi placed her pack down as well and took her new compass pocket watch out of its box and satchel to place in her pocket. "You're a grown man, capable of making your own decisions. I wouldn't have told anyone," she finally said and walked out onto the balcony. The view of the massive lake might as well have been the ocean. The beach below had very few people enjoying the last rays of light from the setting sun as they played on the water's surface. "So if you'd rather have her company for the night, I would understand. She's definitely beautiful."

Etyne joined her on the balcony and leaned on the railing. He was nearly infuriated from Brisethi's sudden self-pity and her assumption that he would ever think to bed Livian. "You're kidding, right? Do you really think I need that kind of temptation right now? I'll admit, you three ladies have not been the easiest to cope with at the moment – what with your revealing civilian clothes."

Brisethi looked down at her very much covered skin.

"I meant *theirs*," he sighed. He never realized how much he could miss the camaraderie of his male acquaintances until spending a single week with three females every hour of every day.

"You can't blame them. I would be wearing something similar if not for my horrid scars and lack of weight," she let her voice trail off. She poked at her bony hip, feeling for any sign of fat and muscle. She inconspicuously placed her hand on her chest that thankfully did not feel as sunken in as it had a week ago.

"Well in that case, thank you for not being a third sight I have to divert my eyes from," he said, though it was her eyes he had secretly been infatuated with. "It's been way too long," he muttered and stared out at the twilight's reflections on the lake.

Brisethi understood what he meant, for she had also been without affection for two years while on expedition. Neither was the type to take advantage of the pretty girls looking to take in any of the soldiers at the towns they stopped in during the expedition. "Such is the sacrifice we make when leading expeditions," she finally stated.

Etyne forced his thoughts from the surface lest he surrender to his solitary feelings and allow regrettable actions. The romantic scenery of lanterns that lit the pier at the lakeshore where couples slowly walked hand-in-hand wasn't helping him and only encouraged him to be around loud people. "Let's wait for the other two down in the tavern. I think we both could use a drink," he suggested.

The two of them were fortunate to swipe up the corner booth which a vacationing family was just leaving. The busy tavern had one wall missing where the lake could be seen. Beautifully flowered vines draped from the ceiling, and a breeze traveled around the room, smelling of delicious food. A bronzed waitress with long, ebony hair dressed in island attire took their orders and quickly retrieved their choice of drinks.

"In addition to the compass watch, the two rooms you rented, and the rest of the currency you lent me, how much do I owe you? I'm bad at keeping track of numbers," Brisethi admitted. She took a sip of her fruity alcoholic beverage to test it then a gulp of it when the taste satisfied her. "Let me reimburse you for Korteni and Livian's room – they shouldn't have to use their own earnings for necessities on my behalf."

Etyne finished his first ale before replying to her. "I'll tally it all up when we get home," he lied. He had no intention of taking money from her, even if it was his own money she had been using. "Maybe we can get reimbursed," he chuckled.

Brisethi tried to fight the urge to ask him, hoping it wouldn't start a confrontation. But the thought nagged at the back of her mind just as it would any other woman with the slightest hint of jealousy. She finally ceded to her curiosity and the liquid courage and asked, "If she wasn't your subordinate, if she were just a civilian girl you met out in town..." She couldn't finish the question.

Etyne thanked the waitress for his second ale. "Were you going somewhere with that?" he asked, returning his attention to Brisethi.

"I think you know what I'm trying to ask." She glared at him from under her hood. She felt unusually self-conscious and finished her first drink quicker than she would have under normal circumstances.

"If you're still going on about Sergeant Reej, because you suddenly have this crazy notion that I'm into her, I can assure you I'm not. And even if I was, what's it to you? Why this sudden bizarre behaviour, 'Sethi?" He pushed back on the table to lean into the booth and stare at her.

Brisethi pressed on, staring back into his blue eyes. "How can you not? Even if she was a civilian?"

"She's too young." He finally gave in and humored her. "She was twelve years old when we were in our first year of expedition training."

"When you're two-hundred and forty, she'll be two-hundred and thirty-two," she pointed out with a blank stare.

"I thought you weren't good with numbers -we'll make you a physicist yet." He finished his second ale.

"My mother is eighty-four years older than my father," she added.

He shrugged, looking longingly at her when she turned her head to stare out at the lake again. Despite her uneven hair, her loss of weight and sudden bitter attitude, he still cared for who she was and who he hoped she would be once again. "If there's something you're trying to tell me, just say it."

If Etyne had told her those exact words a year ago during their two-week integration, she would have had the confidence to tell him. But the Lantheuns changed her appearance, scarred her skin, violated her, and mentally set her askew. She assumed Etyne could never have feelings for the abomination she had allowed herself to become. *I don't know if I could even find solace in your words anymore, or return the love anyone would want to give to me,* she dejectedly thought.

When Brisethi remained silent to his request, he became fully aware that he had completely misinterpreted the last letter he'd received from her. Whatever it was he thought she was feeling for him during integration, had dissipated over the last year. *And rightfully so,* he thought. *I was too cowardly to reveal anything to you then, and now you've either moved on, or the Lantheuns destroyed your emotions.* He was fortunate that his response, that he carried with him in his pack, had never been sent out.

Korteni and Livian finally joined their two captains after freshening up in their room. Etyne and Brisethi couldn't have been more grateful for their presence and interruption of the unusual awkward silence. "Did I show you this one?" Brisethi reached into her pocket and placed her silver watch compass on the table to display for Korteni.

Korteni sipped at her ale before picking up the prettier apparatus. "Did you spend the last of Etyne's money on this?"

"Uhh, we did a trade, but yes, I owe him at least twenty frakshins," she quickly replied, hiding her mouth in her third cup of ale.

Livian was incredulous at the frivolous captain. She barely spent three of her own frakshins on her clothes and supplies at the general store. She could hold back her opinions no longer. "You've spent twenty frakshins already? Money that isn't even yours?"

Brisethi's eyes fixed on Livian. "The rooms of this extravagant resort you chose aren't cheap, Sergeant," she replied, instantly regretting opening her mouth while slightly intoxicated.

Etyne was not about to deal with this again. When the three women remained silent, he sighed in relief that they reverted back to professionalism. To break the tension as he ordered another ale, he thought to have Korteni tell them the story of her dagger that hung at her hip. "Hey Korteni, let me see your dagger again; I bet Livian would want to hear about our epic ship battle," he awkwardly attempted to break the silence.

Korteni's eyes lit up when she recalled their heroic adventure of saving the crew of the *DSV Reliant* while Brisethi giggled into her drink at the situation. The tavern finally began to grow rowdier as the nightlife crowd arrived.

"And that was the first time I was shot," Brisethi added when Korteni had finished her elaborate and accurate recollection of their fourth year in the expedition together, much to Livian's amusement.

"You were shot a second time?" Korteni asked as Etyne leaned in with his own curiosity.

Livian looked away, admiring the crowd around the room in their various colors and styles of dress. She found it much more interesting than anything Captain Sen Asel would have to say.

"How do you think Sulica captured me? They had to shoot me down when I had my back turned!"

"SHH!" Etyne loudly hushed her. "Nobody's supposed to know you, remember?" he whispered. "Continue, quietly."

Brisethi leaned in to quietly recall her actions when trying to escape with her father. It didn't sound nearly as exciting as it did in her head due to how softly she had to explain the events unfolding. "Getting shot in the back is paralyzing," she closed.

"How many times does that make now? Is that three times of falling off of a ship?" Etyne couldn't resist.

Brisethi mouthed a curse word to him while the Korteni laughed.

"When was the other time she fell off a ship?" Livian innocently asked, suddenly interested again.

"Let me tell it!" Korteni excitedly shouted.

"No!" Brisethi hid her face further into her hood.

"I'm telling it!" Etyne finally stated. "His name was Master Chief Braul-"

"And he literally flung 'Sethi off of his ship on our second day of naval training!" Korteni blurted out.

"You're a horrible person," Etyne retorted at her spoiling his grand story.

"Wait, what? Why?" Livian grew excited as Brisethi leaned against the corner of the booth, staring up at the lantern light.

"Because she said out loud that she felt like a pirate just as he walked by!" Korteni told her.

Etyne continued, "He was so enraged that she had insulted the 'centuries of naval traditions' that you could see his face turn red, his single forehead vein about to burst. He stormed over to 'Sethi, grabbed her by her neckerchief, and dragged her to the railing. He dangled her over the sea like a sad child and shouted 'You want to be a pirate, shipmate? Go be a pirate somewhere else!' and threw her overboard. I can still hear her screaming until the splash," Etyne laughed.

Livian, who rarely showed emotion at all, lost all composure and nearly dissolved into tears from how hard she was laughing.

Brisethi finally chuckled lightly. "You're all awful friends. I'm going to sleep."

"Aww, so soon? But it's only," Korteni looked at Brisethi's compass watch, "well, it's the first hour of the morning already."

"Exactly, and it's the first real bed we'll all have slept in since we left Res'Baveth," she replied while grabbing her compass watch and stood to urge Korteni to let her out.

"We're leaving ninth hour, be ready," Etyne told everyone as they parted ways.

Waiting for the bathtub to fill, Brisethi brushed her teeth at the sink. As tired as she was, the thought of a hot bath in a real bathtub with real scented soaps and oils was much more tempting than sleep. She removed her clothes and slowly stepped into the tub, adding more heat with her mystic. She smiled at the piles of bubbles that generated from the new type of soap she purchased that day. She submerged her entire body, testing how long she could hold her breath under water. She was disappointed that she couldn't hold her breath nearly as long as she used to just a year ago.

Etyne sat in a plush, velvety chair, reading her letter to him, and the one he had meant to send to her. The thought of crumbling them up to set them ablaze in the sconce crossed his mind, but the smell and smoke of the aftermath would only raise questions from her. He begrudgingly shoved them back in his pack instead, deciding to wait until they were outside at a campfire to let them turn to ash, perhaps using them as kindling.

Recalling her terrible silence at the table only encouraged him to completely smother his continuous feelings for her. It wasn't worth jeopardizing their unique friendship just because he'd been lonely for three years. She deserved better than a desperate situation. He convinced himself that his feelings were only temporary due to Dominion Expeditions. That, if he were back in Res'Baveth among the soft, beautiful civilian women of the city, his feelings for her would diminish. He told himself that he was simply allowing his expedition solitude to take place over logical reasoning.

The door to the washroom slightly creaked open and the sound of running water refilling the tub could be heard. Dressed in her day clothes but without the wide belt, Brisethi stepped out. "I heated the tub so the water is as hot for you as it was for me," she shyly told him.

He tried not to stare at her kind eyes and replied with a smile, "Thanks."

"I also added this new soap stuff I found at the general store that creates bubbles – I thought you'd find it amusing," she added.

"Bubbles?" He arched a brow. The blossom scent of that new soap filled the air around him when she walked by. *I need off this continent*; he thought when her enticing scent threatened to surface his feelings once more. He grabbed his pack and entered the washroom, smiling at the inviting bubbly bath.

She crawled into bed, the first bed she had touched since the start of her command expedition two years ago. She removed her outer layer of clothes to comfortably sleep in her underclothes under the blankets. Her body spread out in the middle of the bed at first, to relax and rest her sore, healing muscles until Etyne was done with his bath. Before she knew what happened, a slight nudge woke her. She scooted over to allow Etyne to crawl in next to her. With his back to hers, she leaned against him for support and comfort.

"Rest well, Etyne," she mumbled.

"You too, 'Sethi," he whispered.

Chapter VI

When the Kiaran vessel was safely out of Sariadne's waters, Sulica was free to roam the ship again. At the first chance, she went topside. Despite finding that she thoroughly enjoyed Ekani's company, she hated being cooped up in the cabin.

Sulica rushed to the rail and breathed deeply, taking in the smell of briny water as the light breeze wafted around her. She leaned forward, resting her forearms on the railing. The crystal blue water shimmered in the morning sunlight, extending as far as she could see. The sky above was barely tinted with the pink hues from the sunrise. For the first time in what felt like an age, she allowed herself to relax. No longer did it seem like she was a prisoner on board, and she did not fear for her life.

She glanced down at her hands. The skin was tanning again, masking the translucent look it'd had in Lantheus. Her body was filling out again as well, so that she no longer felt weak after a few hours of moving around. Her hands clenched at the thought of the torture she'd been through. *One day*, she thought, *I will see that place burn.*

"Am I interrupting?" Sulica heard the smile in Ekani's voice even before she saw it. He leaned his back against the rail to look at her. The uninterrupted blueness of his eyes reminded her of the ocean.

"Just...thinking," she told him. After a beat, she asked, "Why do your people hate mine so much?"

"Not all Kiarans despise Resarians," he replied carefully. "Do all Resarians hate Kiarans?"

She paused to consider the question. "I don't think so. Sen Asel..." she began. The pang of guilt that hit her was nearly too strong to continue. "Sen Asel had this crazy goal to become Empress and bring the Kiarans back to Sariadne."

"Why is that so crazy?" His voice was quiet. When Sulica did not answer, he continued. "The war began long before our time. Still, we fight. Is it because one side truly was wrong? Or because it is the only thing our people know now? War is an excuse to argue over resources or further one nation's own goals and abilities. Because it is so successful, leaders continue to promote war-fighting capabilities. And the cycle repeats."

"I never really thought about that before." She nervously chewed on her lip as she debated how much to reveal to him.

Ekani waited patiently. His eyes roamed, seeing the crew go about their morning duties. The relief for the midwatch conducted turnover nearby. Minutes passed. He glanced at Sulica and noticed her eyes had a faraway look to them. Her hands began turning white from how tightly she was gripping the rail. He said her name and moved toward her when she didn't respond, but quickly stopped himself. If she was having a day-terror, he did not want to trigger a more violent response.

Sulica seemed frozen in place, reliving a painful memory. He continued to bide his time, keeping his eyes on her. Ekani had been the one to save her, but he never before felt so helpless.

Quite suddenly, Sulica gasped for air, tossing her head back as though breaking from water's surface. She leaned heavily against the railing, a bead of sweat trickling down her brow. "I-" she stammered, slowly sinking to the deck.

Ekani kneeled beside her and put his arm over her shoulders. "Hush, no one will harm you now," he consoled softly. When she was ready, he helped her to her feet.

Head hung low, Sulica meekly returned to her cabin to wash away the shame and guilt.

Ekani watched her depart after declining his offer of assistance. The Lantheuns had their uses, and, until he bore witness to their results, he hadn't much cared to think about how they got them. After meeting Sulcia and the burgundy-haired skeletal figure he'd left behind at the laboratory, his resolve at accomplishing Pahl'Kiar's goals using any means available no longer felt quite so noble.

-:- -:- -:-

The sweet sound of the chirping birds outside the window followed by the local bell tower striking eight times slowly brought Brisethi out of her sleep. The room was bright from the open window and balcony door. She blinked and yawned then shifted in the comfortable bed, wondering how long Etyne had been awake when she heard the sound of running water. She quickly threw on her day clothes to hide her skin before Etyne could finish with his morning routine.

He walked out of the washroom and awkwardly greeted Brisethi. She did not reply. When he glanced at his companion, he saw her sitting at the edge of the bed in an almost catatonic state and realized she was in her own world for the moment. Keeping her in sight using his peripherals, he packed his belongings into his bag. Then he walked over to stand in front of Brisethi, studying her for some time. The silent battle seemed to be a markable improvement from the fits she suffered from before. Etyne hoped that meant she was recovering.

At one point, Brisethi pushed her sleeve up and began to absently pick at a scab. He pushed her arm aside gently and placed his own under her hand instead, hoping she wouldn't actually draw blood from his flesh. Brisethi didn't even seem to notice it wasn't her arm and began scratching at his, still staring blankly in front of her. He held his breath when she went to bite his arm. She barely nibbled at it. After a few moments, her fingers glided across his shoulders and chest, outlining designs. Etyne realized that she was flashing back to the time when she must have used her blood to paint the designs on the wall. He thanked the spirits that she was in one of her more peaceful fits.

She blinked and suddenly met his eyes, quickly withdrawing her hand. "I didn't fall into unconsciousness this time," she told him, almost in disbelief.

He slightly shook his head with a smile, placing a hand on her cheek before walking away from her.

-:- -:- -:-

Ekani resisted the urge to check in on Sulica to see if she'd recovered from her episode earlier. Instead, he made his way to the navigation room. Knocking on the door, he poked his head inside before entering. The petty officer at the chart table jumped from his seat with a start.

"Ambassador Vorsen!" he exclaimed, quickly rendering honors. Nervously, he continued, "The Chief and NAVO aren't here right now, sorry, Sir."

Ekani smiled reassuringly at the young Kiaran sailor. "Quite alright. How much longer until we reach Vipurg?"

"Are you that tired of my ship already, Vorsen?" said a familiar voice behind him.

Ekani turned to see a tall, burly Kiaran with dark hair and eyes, grinning from ear to ear. He stepped into the space and embraced Ekani, which he heartily returned.

"Lieutenant Simtel," the ambassador said when they parted. "How have you been, stranger?"

Simtel guffawed and motioned for the young sailor to carry on. He walked over to the navigational equipment and charts for a moment then indicated for Ekani to follow him out of the space. Ekani could hear the sigh of relief from the petty officer as they left. "Good kid," Simtel said, nodding back at the room. "Nervous as a hound pissing peach pits, though." They continued walking to the aft side of the ship. "Apologies for not seeing you sooner," he added.

"I didn't even know you were on board still. Weren't you supposed to transfer?" Ekani said, ducking his head to avoid hitting it on a piece of gear roped to the bulkhead.

"I was, but the XO's old lady just had a baby. So skipper's got me running about all over creation." Simtel couldn't see the blank look on Ekani's face, but he knew it was there. "Sometimes I forget you're still a civilian. Executive Officer," he clarified with a chortle, "Second-in-command of your fancy transport vessel here. Speaking of, I got a good look at the cargo. She's a pretty-looking one." He gave Ekani a sidelong glance.

Ekani ignored it and asked, "Just where are you taking me?"

Simtel responded with a mischievous grin. "Remember when we were lads and climbed the tower in Pahl'Kiar? I found a sight darn near as incredible."

He led Ekani to a ladderwell at the far end of the ship and began climbing. They passed several landings, but Simtel continued on up. Ekani became grateful for his rigorous physical training, required of all Kiaran representatives. Minutes later, they reached the top landing. Simtel stepped off the ladderwell and reached above him to open a hatch. Without a word, Ekani crouched and cupped his hands for Simtel to use as a step. Simtel hoisted himself up and out of the hatch then reached down to grab Ekani's hands and pull him out.

They stood on top of the bridge, slightly higher than the mast, with nothing preventing them from falling off into the ocean. The view was breathtaking. The sun was high in the sky, illuminating the deep blue water all around. As the ship moved smoothly forward through the calm water, Ekani could see a land mass not so far in the distance.

"One step closer to home," Simtel said aloud what they were both thinking.

Ekani nodded. "I have a question, though. How do you get up here when you're alone?" he laughed.

Simtel grinned and playfully punched his arm.

-:- -:- -:-

Livian sipped at her hot coffee, sitting at a small table in the inn's cafe. She had a perfect view overlooking the massive lake which she was only too happy to take advantage of. Silently, she began bidding farewell to the little luxuries she'd been able to indulge in. A bittersweet feeling came over her as she thought about how she'd soon be back in uniform and on her way to resume the expedition training. Her fingers traced the amulet around her neck and the softness of her dress.

An image of her past flashed before her. The last time she had enjoyed coffee outside near a body of water, Elion was sitting across from her. She never meant to allow him to become such an important part of her life. She thought by now, more than halfway through the expedition, she would have forgotten about those feelings.

Korteni joined her with her own mug of hot coffee and a plate of four sweet pastries. She urged Livian to take one but the girl was suddenly in no mood to eat.

"Korteni, may I ask you something?" Livian began.

"Anything," she replied through a mouthful of pastry.

"How much longer will it hurt?" Livian asked, failing to hold back her tears.

Korteni leaned in immediately. She knew what pain she was referring to when Livian had vaguely told her the story of her young life just a few months ago. "I can't say that I know how you feel. A broken heart as the result of betrayal isn't an easy thing to overcome. You want answers from him, you want that happiness back that was stripped from you. We all fear that we may never find the happiness we once had that came with innocence."

Spare me your psycho-babble nonsense, she wanted to say, "Sorry I asked," Livian inhaled sharply. Her trust had been brutally betrayed once before, she would never make that mistake again.

Etyne and Brisethi walked up to Korteni and Livian at the patio table. They both grabbed a pastry, thanking them for the treats.

When neither of them replied, Livian found her voice. "It was Korteni who purchased them, Ma'am...I mean...Bri-sethi."

"Call her 'Sethi, it's a less repulsive name," Etyne teased, eating half of the pastry in one bite.

"At least my mother didn't name me after a type of butterfly," Brisethi countered. "Besides, I like the Sethi Pine trees of northern Res'Baveth," she added defensively.

"Oh, someone's been researching insects, I see. And it's not a butterfly. It's a moth," he retorted in attempt to regain his masculinity, slowly taking another bite of his pastry only to have a bit of cream fall from it, landing on his coat.

Korteni and Brisethi giggled, but Livian could only stare blankly at the table.

The foreigners finished their quick morning meal and followed Etyne to the central canal hub. Etyne bade the women to wait as he chatted quickly with a few boat owners and paid them in frakshins. Smiles broke out at the discovery that they would take a riverboat to Beccilia instead of walking for two more days.

"She ain't much, but she'll get ya where yas need to go," the owner said with a toothy grin as he welcomed his guests.

The small riverboat had only one deck. Its white and blue paint was faded, but the deck itself looked relatively clean. Half of it was given to a flat portion which presumably carried cargo or supplies. The other half comprised of two cabins. At the back of it was a wheel meant to churn the water and power the boat forward, helping fight the current when needed. The four travelers entered the cozy guest cabin complete with a table booth, a small bed, a plush lounge chair, and a washroom. The smallest stove they had ever seen was neatly tucked away in a corner with a chimney leading up through the roof.

Livian sunk into the plush chair, relaxing instantly. Her mood had lightened considerably since arriving in Essenar. She began to appreciate the environment of a foreign land and everything it had to offer, almost wishing they could delay longer. Her gratitude increased at the thought of how she wasn't enduring stressful ship life with the rest of her division, not that her own trip had been a particularly easy one. With the special mission and the close proximity with her superiors, she even had hopes of earning a special achievement medal for her part in saving the incredibly eccentric captain that she still couldn't quite adjust to. But for every small enjoyment she found, it was only a cruel reminder of the life she shared with Elion. *What's the point of even trying to be happy when my mind refuses to let him go; when my soul won't pry itself away from his,* she sighed heavily.

When the riverboat embarked on its two-day voyage, Korteni retrieved a small box from her bag. She sat next to Brisethi at the table and motioned for Livian to join them. Livian reluctantly climbed out of the soft chair and walked over to take the last seat next to Etyne.

"Liv and I found this game at a vendor. The artwork on the cards reminded me of yours, 'Sethi," Korteni excitedly explained, placing the cards and dice on top of the small table.

The cards were already grouped into specific genres of strategies and elements. Korteni gave each companion a deck and left the three dice of different numbered sides in the middle. She explained the card game titled, Fates of the Enchanted, to the best of her and Livian's knowledge then began her turn by placing down one of the five cards in her hands.

"'Sethi, stop cheating!" Korteni swiped at Brisethi's hand, which had been turning over every card in her deck.

"I'm looking at the artwork!" She snapped, admiring the incredibly designed mythical creatures before enchanted landscapes.

Meanwhile, Etyne consecutively picked up the three dice and dropped them rather loudly to calculate his odds of rolling high numbers.

"By the spirits, you two, can we start the damn game already?" Livian said in exasperation. She pushed her straw-colored hair behind her ears.

All three of the senior personnel looked at her in amazement. Livian, abashed, muttered, "I just want a distraction." Her three seniors laughed heartily. Both Etyne and Brisethi quickly stopped their unintentionally disruptive antics.

"I've found that the more you treat officers like children, the better they behave. I'm glad you're catching on so quickly, Liv," Korteni teased, earning her a feigned glare from both officers.

An hour quickly passed as the group played. Brisethi was the only one struggling to understand her deck of cards, constantly losing to everyone else. "This game's hard," she whined. "But fun, let's go again!"

The addicting game lasted them well into evening with short breaks to snack on the bread, fruits and cheeses they had acquired from the street vendors earlier that morning. Finally, Etyne called an end to the game so they could have a proper meal from the boat crew's catch of the day. Korteni prepared rainbow trout seasoned with lemon and herbs, a specialty dish she had made for Brisethi and Joss on more than one occasion in Sariadne. She extended a heartfelt invitation to the three crew-members to eat with them. The three men, all from the Aspion Empire, appeared as friendly as Granith had been, entertaining their guests with their lute, drums and vocals.

Brisethi was first to exit the cabin for fresh air. The sound of distant coyotes sang to the darkness while the calming splash of the Brennon River soothed her ears. The wide, man-made river was peaceful, flowing in the southward direction for three days at a time as a result of the people of Essenar releasing the gates of Lake Sankling. The next three days it would flow north back to Essenar when Beccilia released the dams of their reservoir to allow their boats to float effortlessly back.

She walked to the aft of the boat and leaned against the railing, taking in view of the celestial sight above. Neither of Falajen's two moons had yet shown nor her neighboring planets, leaving for an incredibly dark night. A familiar sight she hadn't seen in months met her gaze. The magnificent presence of their galaxy's spiral arms cut across the night sky in a billion twinkling lights, spread out in a long tubular shape with light from an unknown source surrounding it from either side. She stared in awe at the incredible expanse before her.

A horrific image of Sulica covered in blood and mounted by a Lantheun guard suddenly flashed across her vision. *No,* she thought, squeezing her eyes shut and gripping the railing tightly, *go away.* She focused her mind on anything other than a second image of the same guard coming after her. She stared at the sky again and imagined hundreds of falling stars streaking down from above. The flashes of her tragic experience in Lantheus attempted to cut her down but she only filled her mind with the chaos and destruction that her mystics empowered. She imagined those stars crashing into an abysmal sea, causing tidal waves that reached the skies above. In those skies she formed clouds lit by lightning, caressing the restless sea below. In an instant, a spiraling ring of scarlet luminescence escaped from her vessel like her own miniature galaxy, dissipating into twinkling cerulean sparks. The horrible images of Lantheus were destroyed by her own mystics.

Rushing footsteps approached her. "Was that you?" Korteni asked her friend who was hunched over the railing.

Brisethi nodded slowly, sighing in relief from her small victory over her fits. "Was it that bright?" Her face was flushed and sweat glistened on her brow as though she had just been sprinting.

"It was loud, too, are you summoning thunder?" Korteni asked. She walked over, glancing from Brisethi to the sky.

Brisethi wasn't entirely sure of what happened and merely shrugged. "I prevented myself from falling into a fit."

"Are you certain?" Korteni worriedly questioned.

"Of course I'm certain, it's how they always start. I get sucked into the dreadful images, forced to relive them. But I finally fought back the oncoming frenzy instead of the people *in* them. I don't know why I summoned the sound of thunder, though." She bit her lip and her brow furrowed.

Korteni pursed her lips. "I'm worried about you, 'Sethi. I don't want them to discharge you. Even though you're not in the Navy with me, I can't imagine you sitting at home alone with your thoughts instead of what you do best; training as a warrior."

Brisethi smiled at her companion's kind words. "I'll be fine, I've nearly got this under control," she told herself.

When Brisethi had cooled off from the night air, they returned to the cabin to discuss who would sleep and when in the bed that could barely fit two people comfortably. It was decided that Livian and Korteni would sleep first to allow the two captains to physically train on the deck outside.

"By physically train, I meant you need to help me figure this game out," Brisethi said, carrying a blanket and the Fates of the Enchanted game.

Etyne smiled and placed his sword back into its scabbard, thankful he wouldn't have to fear hurting her without a healer. He sat across from her on the blanket while she summoned a red flame into the lantern hanging nearby. "First off," he started, "the deck of cards you were given is a pretty terrible one. It's mostly spells and countering. No wonder you struggle, it takes too much thinking."

"I'm offended," she said shortly. "Go on." She examined the other decks she hadn't been able to see much of earlier.

He handed her the deck that was Korteni's. It consisted of simpler beasts requiring less dice throwing, and it would counter the deck he chose to use, which had previously been Livian's. Etyne felt a reminder of the days they had spent in officer training, when he was tutoring her in the late hours of night. Except this time, it was on a silly game they would probably never play again.

She grinned excitedly when she won her first round of the game after Etyne's careful instruction.

"Best two out of three," Etyne demanded and shuffled his cards.

Once they completed their fifth game, each using yet another set of cards, both of them refrained from playing any more, choosing instead to lay on their backs, staring at the stars above. Brisethi took away the light of the lantern, letting her heavy eyes close.

-:- -:- -:-

"What are we doing?" Ibrienne questioned Kanilas. He had left her alone for hours at a time the past two days, presumably scouting out anything that would be worth exchanging with the Kiaran spy for information on Sulica's whereabouts. Ibrienne hadn't minded. She was still disgusted with the whole arrangement.

When Kanilas had burst through the door of inn where they were staying and started blabbering about a brilliant idea he'd had, she was completely lost. He grabbed her hand and began leading her down the street. "I know what to do!" he said.

They turned a corner onto another road. Ibrienne recognized the tavern ahead and dug her heels in to stop Kanilas. "No way," she said, yanking her hand away. "I'm not going in there until you tell me what is going on."

Kanilas stared at her in disbelief momentarily. With a shake of his head, he said, "I can't explain here. We're too close."

She crossed her arms. "So let's go back then." Seeing the stubborn look on her face, he relented and followed her back to the inn.

It was located in what was known to the locals as mid-town. After months of ship life and running, Ibrienne had chosen a quaint townhouse converted into a small inn on a quiet street near the canal. They returned to the inn and walked around the building to the garden behind it. Ibrienne took a seat on a bench under the gazebo, but Kanilas chose to remain standing.

"What's the plan?" she asked tentatively.

Kanilas chewed on the inside of his cheek. He turned away from Ibrinne's gaze. "We tell him about Sen Asel," he mumbled.

"Tell him what, exactly?" Her eyes narrowed suspiciously.

He pretended to be engrossed in a flowering bush on the other side of the gazebo. "Everyone thinks she is dead. We can tell him what we saw when we were in Lantheus."

"Really?" Ibrienne said, stunned. "You haven't learned anything, have you? I am not betraying my friends because of you again!"

Reaching up to pull his dark hair in frustration, he turned to face her. His face was reddening. "Look, we're going to have to act fast, before he hears about it from someone else. I need you to just trust me."

"Trust you?" she screeched. "After everything you hid from me, everything you *did*, you want me to trust you?" She stood and made to leave.

Kanilas put himself between her and the exit. He put his hands together. "Please, Ibrienne," he begged. "I'm trying to make things right. I'd never forgive myself if something were to happen to Sulica."

"Something already did. Or did you forget how we found 'Sethi? Do you really think the same didn't happen to Sulica?" The frigid tone in her voice made Kanilas take a step back. Ibrienne suddenly noticed the darkness under his sunken eyes, how shaggy his hair had become. "When's the last time you slept?" she asked, softening the edge in her voice slightly.

He shook his head again and met her eyes. The pleading, desperate look he gave her seemed to be completely sincere, and Ibrienne's resolve began to melt.

She soon found herself standing with Kanilas outside the Kiaran's door once more. Her heartbeat quickened with every minute they waited for it to open. The plan Kanilas had come up with wasn't a bad one. She just hoped it would work.

Finally, the door swung open, granting them entrance. The room was just as clean as the last time they had been there. The Kiaran sat at the far end of the table, same as before, with his back towards them, but the cronies were nowhere in sight. The chair turned slowly around to face them, and Ibrienne could see a look of confusion cross the Kiaran's face.

His pale eyes narrowed at Kanilas. "She is not supposed to be here," he said in that same, slow speech as before.

"We have information," Kanilas said, stepping further into the room. His head was high, his face determined. He paused and glanced back at Ibrienne, who nodded her encouragement. "Brisethi Sen Asel, the Resarian taken with Sulica, was also in the laboratory."

"Yes," the Kiaran hissed, "she died in the explosion that destroyed that building."

Kanilas licked his lips, took a breath and said, "She did not die. Sen Asel still lives. She made it out of the building before it went down."

The Kiaran stood, his hands hit the table. "You lie!"

Ibrienne quickly stepped forward. "He does not lie." Her hands shook with her words, but her voice was steady. "She was near death when we found her. We were looking for Sulica and found her instead. I healed her wounds, not completely, for I didn't have time, but enough for her to move. She was the one who told us Sulica was taken to Pahl'Kiar."

As Ibrienne spoke, the Kiaran sat down again. He put his head in his hands. Speaking through them, he said, "Her powers? How do you say...mystics?"

She recalled the horrendous smell of that prison, Brisethi's blood on the walls, her limp body in the cell with her spirit already halfway gone. "The Lantheuns stripped her of all they could," she answered. Her voice choked from the memory.

The Kiaran met her eyes and knew she spoke the truth. He seemed truly apologetic as he said quietly, "I am sorry you are here."

She heard a thud, and the body of Kanilas fell beside her. "No!" she shrieked, dropping to her knees beside him. Barely conscious, he grabbed her hand. Ibrienne quickly called up her mystic and began reviving him.

The Kiaran had gotten to his feet once more and nodded. Ibrienne saw someone approach her from the shadows. She felt a sudden pinch in her neck, and the darkness closed in quickly. With her last strength, she willed Kanilas to wake up. She struggled against the darkness, but a copper taste on her tongue grew stronger the more she fought.

Before she completely lost consciousness, she heard his voice whisper, "I'm sorry, Ibrienne. Good-bye." Indiscernible yelling followed, and the scent of smoke reached her, but she could fight no more.

-:- -:- -:-

At approaching the massive dam, the river veered slightly to the east to remain on the only canal leading into Beccilia. The industrious city greeted the travelers with the bustle of evening shops coming to a close. The four curious Resarians remained on the deck of the river boat to take in the view of tall, brick buildings set closely together. As the boat approached the inner city, they once again looked like foreigners in their simple Essenarian traveling clothes. At least they didn't look like Dominion soldiers.

The boat came to a stop in the small city lake and moored at the pier. The Resarian travelers thanked and tipped the boat crew for their safe and quick passage, then disembarked to journey to the ocean's harbor at the other side of the city.

"Hey, look, you're famous, 'Sethi," Etyne casually remarked, tearing down a small poster from the advertisement wall. He held up the crude charcoal sketch next to her face. "Spot on - they even made sure to nip your ear off," he smirked.

Brisethi swiped the poster from his hand. "Ten thousand frakshins is all I'm worth now?" She felt insulted. "I was worth five times that to the Lantheun scientists."

"How do they even know you're alive?" Korteni mockingly questioned, bringing her fingers to her chin in pretend thought. She then shot a pointed glare at Etyne.

Etyne brought his hands up as though to block her scorn. "Don't blame me for the Dominion feeling the need to stamp their label on every single issued item, including fire-starters!"

Brisethi tossed the poster and pulled her hood up, nervously glancing around at the crowd who seemed to not notice the group at all.

The four of them continued to stroll along the orderly streets of the city, following the main road leading down toward the harbor. Other streets branched off in all directions, leading to neighborhoods and smaller shops. The lanterns that were evenly spaced out along the streets started to brighten the streets under the evening twilight.

Within an hour, the masts of dozens of ships came into view. Brisethi's heart skipped a beat when she saw it. The tallest mast among the five stood alone in its own pier, flaunting its well-lit red and black banners. They swayed in the wind, boasting its presence with the Dominion's gold insignia of three stars falling to Falajen. She had to suppress the sudden urge to sprint the remainder of the way and instead watched along with her three awe-struck companions as they moved closer to the majestic warship. She was so entranced that she didn't notice the group of mysterious guards suddenly standing before them.

"Sir, is this her?" One of the guards asked the other and nodded toward Brisethi.

"Run," Brisethi ordered through gritted teeth and shoved her friends the opposite direction. She knew that Etyne could easily hide them while she drew the guards further away from the harbor to give them time to get to the ship.

She sprinted along the sidewalks of the street, dodging the native Beccilians, and side-stepped into an alley. She looked back to see that the entire group of eight guards had followed. Although she could have simply fought with her friends against them, she didn't want to draw unwanted attention. She hadn't recognized the uniform of the guards and didn't want to risk fighting Beccilians in the event of creating another enemy of her people.

Ducking into the open entrance of a tall building, she ran up the stairs two at a time, unknowingly climbing a bell tower. She had to hold the sides of her dress up to make the running easier and wistfully thought of the pants folded in her bag. Her thighs ached and her lungs burned from the six stories of stairs she ascended. When she finally reached the top, her legs wobbled and she fell to one knee. The touch of a guard's hand on her ankle forced her to quickly twist her way out of his grip.

"I had a feeling you had survived," rang the voice of Chent, the Lantheun guard who on occasion, in her horrible past, had his way with her.

Brisethi breathed heavily and stood wearily against the corner of the open architecture of the bell-tower's roof. Her hand twitched with desire to incinerate the Lantheun and Beccilian guards, but she clenched it to keep control. She nodded her head and finally found her voice. "I don't know what you think is going to happen here." She stared each man in his eyes, one by one. Four of them were Beccilian guards. She didn't want to use her mystics against them, feeling the need to remain inconspicuous.

She exhaled loudly and knelt down to one knee, holding her hands out in front of her to allow them to bind her.

Chent was the first to hastily storm at her, but she quickly drew the daggers from her boots. She leaped suddenly, swinging both arms out to slice his throat with both blades, leaving an 'X' on his neck. Blood splattered in every direction onto her dress and face, as he fell back, gurgling until his death.

The remaining guards paused for a moment before attempting to chase after her, but she jumped once more onto the four foot wall and stared down behind her. She faced the men about to grab her and threw her daggers at the two closest, piercing them both in their necks.

Feeling like the heroes in the books she read, she felt inclined to speak a final phrase to the enemy. "I will never live behind bars again," she declared. With a quick breath, and a feeling that nagged and pulled at her, she then leapt backwards, falling freely from the top of the seventy foot tall tower.

She watched the ground below rapidly approaching. Instinctively, she summoned a mystic she shouldn't have known how to conjure. Just a few feet from the ground her body became a burst of scarlet flames. A second later, she re-materialized into herself once more, landing with a crouch and one hand on the ground, as if she had merely jumped from the four foot ledge.

She rose and stared at her hands incredulously. "By the spirits," she whispered, "I possess his mystics." She finally figured out what it was her spirit had been trying to summon the first night the guards had chased them to the cliffs. Her spirit wanted her to simply become flames, the way Etyne became mist, to quickly levitate up the cliff instead of climbing it.

Before the guards could catch up with her, she took off in a sprint back toward the harbor. She felt the urge to summon her new found mystic once again, but instead of becoming a flame, she transformed her vessel into a rushing bolt of lightning. She again rematerialized, this time at the harbor, traversing four miles in a single breath.

"There you are," a voice startled her.

"Etyne," she exhaled his name. "You're never going to believe what just happened."

He looked her up and down, not wanting to know why she was covered in blood. "Tell me when we're finally safe!" He grabbed her hand and hurried her along to the pier where the Dominion warship was moored.

The Dominion guardsman at the edge of the gangplank to the warship verified Etyne and Brisethi's Dominion identification cards and allowed them to board the *DSV Sovereign*. Korteni and Livian had already gone aboard. Although they weren't in uniform, they proudly saluted the Dominion flag and requested permission to board from the watch officer.

Chapter VII

Captain Maerc Nessel and Chief Petin Kayula walked onto the quarterdeck, welcoming Captain Vorsen's crew aboard. He assigned a crewmember to Sergeant Reej and Chief Pyraz to escort them to the enlisted berthing to set up their racks, freshen up and return to uniform. Chief Kayula escorted the officers to their separate berthing compartments to allow them time to clean up and change into their uniforms as well.

Staring at her side profile in the mirror of the head, Brisethi examined herself. Slowly, muscle and fat were filling in once again in the areas she cared most about. The chief returned in half an hour to escort the uniformed army officers to the wardroom for a proper debriefing by Captain Nessel. The captain handed both army personnel their own log books and pens, instructing them to record every event that occurred in their perspective.

Sitting at the head of the massive mahogany table in elegant matching chairs, the naval captain spoke once more. "Sen Asel," his voice was soft and consoling, "I know you may not be in the best mood to recount your past seven weeks, but the command needs to know every detail you can remember. General Satnir and Emperor Arquistas need to have substantial evidence backing their declaration of war upon the Lantheun Empire."

"They're declaring war because of me?" She gave him a confused look.

Captain Nessel slightly nodded. "Their initial attack on us in the fall of Forty-three Nineteen and their alliance with our adversary was already leading up to conflict. The irrational imprisonment of an admiral's daughter, who happened to be a Dominion service member as well, became the tipping point."

"I understand, Sir," she nodded. "Is my father well? Can I send a letter to him?"

"Of course you can, I'll have it sent as soon as we reach Southwest Harbor," Captain Nessel replied. He pulled a few sheets of paper from his drawer along with an envelope to leave beside her. "We go underway at hour twenty-two. If there's anything else you two need, Chief Kayula will be standing by on the quarterdeck to assist you. I can be reached in the main cabin," he explained. He stood from his seat at the head of the table and dismissed himself.

"I'll let the two of you talk among one another about your logs. You can find me on deck harassing my crew," Chief said with a slight chuckle to himself.

Sen Asel and Vorsen nodded to the odd chief as he exited the room. They were sitting across from each other at the large table trimmed in gold designs. The two shared a somber look, wondering what the other was thinking, and where to start on keeping a professional written record of the several weeks that their worlds collided.

"I don't even know what today's date is," Brisethi quietly stated.

"Sixth of Sessing, Forty-three twenty-eight," Etyne replied. He was first to begin writing in his logbook.

"I don't remember what day I left-"

"Fifteenth of Trewint," he answered shortly. His eyes met hers when he diverted from his writing. "That's the day that the command annotated your disappearance in their memorandum."

"Thanks," she mumbled and began to write in the most legible handwriting she could. At first, her hand struggled to form the Resarian letters, having been out of practice for so long. But soon the markings flowed easier. "I absolutely despise writing," Brisethi said after the first paragraph.

Etyne nodded. "I know you do. It isn't my favorite subject, either. I'd rather solve equations."

"I hate math, too. I fucking hate everything," she muttered while hastily writing her story.

Etyne paused to glance up at her. He knew she was angry at being forced to recollect her past month and half of torture. He was just as angry when he first felt her sorrows through the Soul Reclamation. He thought of an idea that might calm her anger as they sat in the room. "Will you draw me something?"

Brisethi finished another paragraph before meeting Etyne's eyes. "What do you want drawn?"

"Starfall over a desert. Just like the night you and I raced each other back to the garrison after making a wish. Take us back to that night, 'Sethi," he gently requested.

A smile formed that shone through her eyes at him. She stood to reach across the table to take one of his papers. Her spirit felt overwhelmed with relief and gratitude at the sense of normalcy when Etyne took hold of her small hand. She consigned to his warm touch and fell heavily across their papers. The side of her face cooled against the cold surface of the polished table as her breathing intensified. She was profoundly confused as to why her heart started to pound. "If I had the power to take us to any place and time, is that really where you would want to go?" she softly asked.

Etyne leaned forward to gently brush aside the loose hair out of her face while still holding her hand in the other. "Do you have a better time and place you would take us?"

She turned her head to glare up at him with a sinister smile. "The time, two hundred years from now. The place, Dominion palace. I am queen of the world, and you, I guess, can be the General of the Dominion."

Etyne released her hand with a chuckle. "Finish your log so we can get food."

Half an hour had passed when Etyne finished writing five detailed pages of his recollection from the past four weeks; starting from the day he had learned of her disappearance. He glanced up at Brisethi. She had placed her face into her hands. She wiped at her face with her sleeve, and, when her watery eyes met his, she turned in her chair to look completely away from him. Cautiously, Etyne stood and walked over to her side of the table. He stood before her and placed his hands on her shoulders but did not pull her in. He waited for her to initiate a response.

Brisethi collided into him with no regards to regulations. She smothered her face into his chest.

Wordlessly he held her close, feeling her shudder from the quiet sobs. He glanced down and smiled at a rough sketch of his request of the desert scene they shared with one another under the meteor shower. He then stared at her shaky handwritten log. A single word stood out and confirmed his fear, and quickly looked away from the papers. Rape had been the profoundly intimate trauma brought upon Brisethi's body. Her authority over her own physical experience was usurped, denying her capacity to prevent intrusion and violation.

She knew he had to have known as she broke from the embrace. She cleared her throat before quietly relaying a vague description to him. "The visceral terror and horror of every act upon me forced me into a state of dissociation of consciousness. When you found me, I was at a loss of connection to myself."

"You don't have to explain anything to me. If it's what you need to do to be able to cope, then I will listen," Etyne softly replied.

Through the dozens of military training lectures given to the soldiers and sailors, it was rape and sexual assault that had been almost overly discussed. It wasn't something that a person could overcome quickly nor did it require someone else to help them. Just because Resarians were inhabited by divine spirits, didn't mean they were incapable of committing crimes against one another.

She couldn't find her voice anymore, not to a man she considered her best friend. She handed him her papers instead. "Proof-read for me?"

Etyne reluctantly nodded, looking over what she had written. He overlooked her limited vocabulary and focused on her story at hand. She left no details out. It sickened him to know that his best friend had gone through such atrocious violations. There was nothing he could do for her or say.

They neatly stacked their completed reports, letters to home, and pens upon the table. Brisethi handed her sketch of starfall to Etyne. He smiled in appreciation of the gesture and folded it to place in his pocket. The two strangers to the warship allowed Chief Kayula to escort them to the galley where they met with Livian and Korteni.

"What are they serving? Is it any good?" Brisethi asked upon approaching the two uniformed women.

"It's your favorite, chicken dumpling pie," Korteni replied and shoved her last bite into her mouth. "Remember how excited you used to get when we were training on the *Reliant*? Every third day of the week you were pushing the other recruits out of the way and causing fights in the galley for fear they'd run out of pie and serve you leftover watery oats again."

"I didn't push just anyone, mostly Sulica and Kanilas for holding up the line-"

"That usually ended up in riots," Etyne concluded for Brisethi.

"Did you really, Ma'am?" Livian asked incredulously.

Brisethi smartly nodded and was off to the serving line with Etyne on her heels. They acquired their food and returned to Korteni's table, taking seats across from each other.

"I'm going to give Sergeant Reej a tour of the warship," Korteni told them as she left with a wave and Livian following.

Too excited to wait for her food to cool down, Brisethi shoved a spoonful of chicken pie into her mouth, instantly regretting the burning decision and letting it fall back onto her food. "Oh, that's fresh out of the oven."

"'Sethi what – you're the epitome of a lady, you know that?" Etyne sarcastically scolded his unmannered friend. "How is it even possible for you, as a fire mystic, to feel burns?" After recollecting the burn marks upon the sides of her head, he immediately regretted asking.

She blew on her spoon of food several times then successfully consumed it. "I can't explain it. My outer flesh is unaffected by fire and even sunburns, but I can't just pour lava into my mouth," she paused momentarily. "The burns on my head were caused from electricity through metal, not fire. Oh that reminds me, after this I need to show you what I can do."

Etyne finished chewing a chunk of chicken before speaking. "I thought I've seen you do everything there is that a fire mystic can do."

She shook her head, smiling suspiciously.

Upon finishing their meal, they returned their trays to their designated spot and walked out of the galley. The call for muster sounded on each deck as the sailors gathered in their designated spots. Once each member of the crew had been accounted for, they prepared the ship for underway operations.

Etyne and Brisethi found their way to the deck after a few dead ends and wrong ladder wells. "That's the last time I follow you," Etyne quipped to her. "I trusted you."

"I don't know why you would trust my navigation of this beastly warship," she replied. She observed the masts and sails lit by dozens of lantern lights and led him to the stern of the ship where it was practically deserted. She stood in front of Etyne, making sure all of his attention was on her alone. "For my first demonstration, I shall disappear."

In the blink of an eye he watched her vessel disintegrate into a small, red flame levitating before him. The shocked expression on his face was priceless to her when she rematerialized before him a second later.

"First of all," he began with a finger pointed at her, "You called me stupid when I asked if you could do exactly that way back when we were retaking the *Reliant* from pirates."

She grinned widely. "I don't remember saying that. But in my defense, I couldn't do it at the time!"

Etyne crossed his arms and narrowed his eyes.

"And now, for my final act," she continued and simply waved goodbye to him. Her vessel disintegrated once more but into a bolt of lightning spanning to the crow's nest. As quickly as it had flashed, it was gone, and so was she.

Temporarily blinded from the bright flash, Etyne suspiciously looked around and turned his eyes upward to where the bolt had struck. He summoned his own mystic to turn himself into an incorporeal form and instantly appeared next to her in the crow's nest. "When did you find out you could turn yourself into fire and lightning?" he excitedly asked, leaning against the railing.

"Just a few hours ago, before boarding the *Sovereign*," she replied. "I accidently ran up a bell tower, found myself trapped, and did what anyone with this capability would do – jumped off."

"You already knew you could become fire?" he asked, raking his fingers through his hair. She enjoyed the confused look on his face.

"Oh no, it was a hunch," she grinned.

He resisted the urge to strangle her for such recklessness with her life and instead, gave her a scornful glare. "Your spirit was returned to you, and you're fucking jumping from buildings on a hunch?" The sounds of the ship's horns and the flashing beams of mystical light announcing its departure only enhanced the apparent rage on his face.

"It's your fault, you know," she glared back, crossing her arms.

"How so?" he said and finally relaxed, unable to remain seriously upset at her. Etyne was still concerned about her, but he hid it from his face. He looked over the railing to watch the sailors ready the sails for departure. The anchor was brought in and seconds later, the *DSV Sovereign* was carried off by the wind across the dark, calm sea.

"It's your mystics that I'm summoning, Etyne. Just as you can become an incorporeal spirit, I can become my mystic's elements now. You gave me your mystics in addition, to your..." her voice trailed off. She turned away a little and leaned on the railing.

"Damn," he whispered. "You're practically invincible, 'Sethi. What have I created?" He diverted his eyes from her to examine her hands as if he had actually created her.

The corners of her mouth formed a smile. "You've created a power like no other. And I will be sure to put it to good use: In a future – where Sariadne opens up its borders to the Kiarans once again under the rule of the Dominion."

"But at what cost, 'Sethi?" he asked with concern on his face.

She felt a pang in her heart at remembering his shortened life. "As grateful as I am for your mystics, for saving me, I wish I could return your lifespan to you."

"That isn't what I meant. The cost of what you had to go through that enabled me to perform the act - was that worth it to learn my mystics? There are other ways..." his voice trailed off not wanting to give her the impression that he intended to intimately bond his soul with hers.

She shrugged. "It's over now, they can't harm me anymore. The damage is done and I will fully recover from it."

-:- -:- -:-

The crew of the Kiaran diplomatic vessel bustled about in anticipation of the port call ahead. When Sulica emerged from her cabin, preparations were already well underway for the task of mooring the ship in Vipurg. She soon found herself swept up in the excitement and spent the afternoon assisting the crew in clearing the topside deck of debris. That evening, the cooks took the opportunity to use all the potentially expiring ingredients, creating an unidentifiable combination of food, but it still tasted good.

The mooring process lasted several hours, well into the afternoon. When the call finally came for liberty, Sulica accompanied Ekani into the city of Vipurg. The pier stretched out along the bay for quite a distance. On the shore lay the walled city, with large wooden doors propped open to welcome the traders, merchants, and visitors. The frigid air pierced Sulica's thin clothing, and she bemoaned the loss of her thick leather jacket, presumably still on board the *Hantira*.

The city seemed to be divided into quadrants. Buildings made of wood and stone huddled close together in the trading sector. Shops, inns, and taverns with bright glass windows showed cheery scenes of revelry within. A particularly large building stood in the center of the square, topped with a carved head of what looked like a large deer. The antlers appeared to be bowled at the base rather than branched like a tree.

"It's called an elk," Ekani told her, noticing where she was looking. He led her to the building and walked inside. The majority of the people inside looked much like herself, except taller. It was noisy inside the lodge, filled with laughter and boisterous storytelling, not only from the sailors.

Ekani ordered a couple of drinks and directed Sulica to a corner where he introduced her to an apparent life-long friend of his. The two men took turns swapping embarrassing stories of one another as the drinks continued, causing Sulica to alternatively blush and laugh from the Kiaran words she was able to make out. Aderok Simtel seemed particularly interested in making Sulica blush, giving her a wink after a particularly raunchy recounting of a childhood adventure in Pahl'Kiar. "He came outta there grinning like a possum eating a sweet potato, eh, Vorsen?" Simtel said, laughing heartily. Ekani seemed like he couldn't decide whether to join or hide behind his drink.

"You must forgive him," Ekani said later when leaving the lodge. "He has not seen a woman in weeks."

"So what's your excuse?" Simtel chuckled, elbowing Ekani. He bid them good-night and took off, presumably in search of another drink.

Ekani and Sulica began the journey back to the ship. They stayed close to brace against the chill, despite the calm night. "Are women not allowed to serve?" Sulica asked, realizing she had not yet seen one on board the ship.

"Oh, they are," he replied. "Just in limited capacities such as medical and logistics, mostly. And never on a ship bound for Lantheus."

Given her own experience of Lantheun hospitality, she did not fault the Kiarans for their reasoning. "He called you 'Vorsen'," she stated after they crossed the gangplank.

"Yes." A look of confusion crossed his face. With sudden realization, he continued, "I never did give you my full name." He paused and extended his hand to her. "Ekani Vorsen, Kiaran ambassador to Lantheus," he said in half-mocking formality.

She smiled and took his hand. "Sulica Nin, commander of the *Hantira*."

Ekani returned the smile and half-bowed gracefully, still holding her hand. When he let go, they continued through the passageway in the direction of their cabins. Glancing at him, she asked, "Is Vorsen a very common name?"

He thought for a moment. "Not that I am aware of," he said. "It is a very old name, though. Anyone in Pahl'Kiar who bears it is of direct descent of an ancient Kiaran line. There are not many of us left. I believe my father and I are the only ones now." His voice had a hint of finality to it.

Biting her lip, Sulica remained silent until they reached her door. "Sleep well," she called to him as she quickly entered the cabin and shut it behind her.

As she lay in the bed that night, her mind pondered what Ekani had told her. *What if he's not the last one?* she thought. *Would he be happy? Should I even tell him?* She rolled on her side to face the wall. *What if he's wrong and it's just a coincidence?* She convinced herself that it was possible a Vorsen from Ancient Kiar managed to stay in Sariadne and that was how Etyne had come to have the name. *Except Etyne is truly half-Kiaran,* she reminded herself as she drifted off to sleep.

-:- -:- -:-

The next morning found Brisethi sitting upon the examination bed in the infirmary, shivering in only her underclothes. She flared her heating mystic to force her goose bumps to dissipate. She was already nervous at the thought of having someone examine her and worried that the Dominion would see her unfit for duty, sending her home with a small pension until she found other work. The fear that her ambitions to influence military leaders across the world could cease forever had her mind uneasy and stomach wrenching.

What could I possibly do if I was no longer in the Dominion? She thought, biting on her lower lip. She shuddered at the thought of no longer having any kind of authority and going back to wearing civilian clothes. Her bleak future probably included marrying Joss and living the life he and her own mother wanted her to have. *As long as those flashbacks never return, they should allow me to stay in,* she thought desperately.

"Captain Sen Asel," the blonde-haired female corpsmen entered the room. "I am Lieutenant Commander Jeksan. Are you feeling well, this morning?"

Brisethi wanted to vomit her anxiety. "I'm great, Ma'am," she nervously replied.

The corpsman looked over a few sheets of paper before continuing. "That's good to hear. I was given the report you wrote last night to have an understanding of what you went through," she gave her a worried look. "My deepest regrets that you had to endure such atrocities, Captain."

Brisethi shrugged, unsure of how to reply. Anything she tried to say would only cause her voice to crack and tears of self-pity to fall.

"Before I start the examination, is there anything you want to tell me that you might have left out in this record?" she kindly asked.

Brisethi considered the question for a moment, pursing her lips in thought. She shook her head and said, "I think I was as detailed as possible with everything."

The Lieutenant Commander eyed the papers once more before making eye contact with the captain. Her piercing, cerulean eyes reminded Brisethi of Livian. "I'm just going to ask a few questions while I poke and prod you for pressure points and out of place bones. When was the last time anyone applied healing mystics to you and by who?"

"The day I was rescued by Captain Vorsen's team, by Ibrienne Sestas – about seven or eight days ago." She replied.

"Are you currently pregnant, nursing or think you may be pregnant?"

"Nope."

"What was your last month and year of womb blood?"

Brisethi scrunched her brow in recollection of her last yearly Resarian cycle. "Sesswint, this year - it's usually around that month every year."

Jeksan wrote the information in her log. "Tell me about your eating habits."

Brisethi explained her eating habits to her, answered more questions about her physical endurance, her sleeping patterns, her dreams and various other personal questions regarding her mental health.

Jeksan applied her healing mystics upon Brisethi to finish what Ibrienne had started. She removed any trace of Lantheun infection or virus, cleansing her blood, her spirit, and her flesh. The tingling sensation of healer's mystics left Brisethi in a state of deep relaxation, almost a meditation. The corpsman spoke again after a moment's pause, "Ibrienne's healing was nearly flawless despite how rushed she had been. It really is too bad she has defected from us."

Brisethi nodded in dismal agreement of losing a talented and benevolent friend in a complicated mess of personal bad decisions. Depending on Ibrienne's circumstances, and once Brisethi was of higher rank, she would seek out her estranged companion and question her in hopes of justifying her return to Sariadne without repercussions.

The doctor's warm hands pressed upon Brisethi's forehead and chest to search her mind and spirit for deficiencies. "Does Captain Vorsen's mystics overpower yours at all or do you have control of it?" she asked.

"They do not overpower me. And yes, I have control over them, I can summon them as well," she replied, overcome by the officer's mystics flowing through her mind and soul. The feeling of another spirit flowing through hers felt very intimate, almost euphoric.

"No amount of medals and commendations from the Dominion could ever measure up to a person who willingly cuts his lifespan in half so that someone else can live," the corpsman said solemnly. "The ultimate sacrifice of life given to you can never be repaid by material objects," Jeksan sympathetically told her. "And for that, I will not have let his sacrifice be in vain by discharging you from the Dominion. Your dangerous flashbacks that you forgot to mention are enough to send you home."

Brisethi felt an inner panic attack rise once again. *She must have read Etyne's report, too*, she feared he may have revealed too much. Anyone who paints on a wall with their own blood was surely considered insane and mentally unfit for duty.

Lieutenant Commander Jeksan removed her hands from Captain Sen Asel and looked her squarely in the eyes. "But Captain Vorsen assures me that you have found a way to keep them under control. You will resume your training of Division Sixty-Six under the supervision of Lieutenant Vazeley until the graduation ceremony. If his reports to Major Paush show that your mental health is unchanged by these flashbacks, and that no one was hurt, you will no longer require supervision. However, if your health declines and the flashbacks prove uncontainable, then it will be up to the command's corpsman to make his or her decision of your career."

"Thank you, Ma'am," Brisethi gratefully exhaled her reply, observing the white lines left on her skin where the skin was healing over her scabs. Lieutenant Commander Jeksan's mystic had removed the disgusting sores, only leaving behind permanent diminutive scars.

"You do know what's causing those flashbacks, right?" Jeksan asked.

Brisethi shook her head.

"Your soul left its vessel to escape the trauma. Etyne's soul brought it back. The flashbacks are your spirit's post traumatic stress from everything it has encountered in the past few weeks. Etyne, no doubt, has suffered a bout of depression from his own spirit's experience of retrieving yours," she explained. "His soul now knows everything yours went through."

Brisethi remained silent upon the dire news.

"Both his spirit and yours are mourning, Captain, just as a spirit mourns when it's bonded mate returns to the Sea of Renewal. I wouldn't fret too much if he is distancing himself from you. Time will heal you both." The corpsman handed Brisethi her orders that were to be given to Lieutenant Vazeley upon return to her division and sent her on her way.

Chapter VIII

"How was your examination? They're letting you stay in, right?" Etyne asked, genuinely concerned for his companion.

They were seated alone in the captain's ready room once more for an afternoon brief of the plan of the week.

"I have to have a baby-sitter for two years but yeah, they're letting me keep my job," she grinned. "I guess I should have asked you not to mention my flashbacks in your logs," she mumbled.

"You didn't report them?" He was taken aback by her lack of integrity.

"Etyne, I'm trying to *not* get sent home, of course I didn't log it – but thank you, for somehow convincing the corpsman that I have them under control." She wasn't upset at him, but annoyed that she didn't think to talk to him first to compare their reports.

He leaned in after confirmation that no one was around. "If it's any consolation," he quietly told her, "I didn't report your paintings on the wall."

"I appreciate it," she quietly replied. "I'll never quite remember what drove me to use my own blood as paint." She absently rubbed her arm where the scabs had been.

"I can imagine why anyone would lose their sanity in a place like that. You needed a distraction and painting is your pastime. I would have been more concerned if you had painted with feces," he chuckled.

Brisethi laughed. "You're fucking gross," she lightly smacked his arm. "Did I ever tell you how two days after you gave me that Bearsethi name, Antuni asked me, 'does a Bearsethi shit in the woods?'"

Etyne laughed. "I actually told him to ask you that, I figured it was more his style of humor."

"I just figured you two shared a brain," she commented then changed the topic. "Are you looking forward to five more days of sea life on a warship just to go back to sea for another year with your division on the small *Reliant*?"

"I am just incredibly happy that I finally have my own space again, away from the three of you women," he said, half joking.

"Ah, come on, we're not that bad," she playfully kicked at his feet under the table to contradict her own words.

He withdrew his legs to cross them at the ankles beneath his chair. "*Not that bad?*" he repeated. He pitched his voice an octave higher, "'Hey, Etyne, let's stop at that stream so I can bathe for a third time today'; 'Hey Captain, did you happen to bring any spices or did you lose those, too?' 'Sir, respectfully request for you to take control of Captain Sen Asel's craziness'."

Brisethi laughed hysterically at his terrible impersonations of her, Korteni, and Livian.

"I hope to never have daughters," he concluded.

"I hope you have *ten* daughters, a set of twins every five years!" She teased in a hiss.

"Well it's a good thing I'm attracted to Resarians so that the most I'll have is two - ever," he smirked, knowing it was physically impossible for Resarian women to bear more than two children in a lifetime, but quite the opposite for Kiarans and the rest of the world.

A sudden realization at his words struck Brisethi when she recalled that her people embodied the spirits of dragons, a mythical faith recently revealed as fact to her. *No wonder we struggle to have multiple offspring, there aren't enough dragon spirits for all of us*, she thought to herself. *If I bring Kiarans back and their children are born with their returned spirits, will there be less of my people once more?*

Captain Maerc Nessel and Chief Kayula entered the ready room, taking their usual seats on either side of the table. The captain placed a small, smooth box and two devices in front of them. "The future of communications is nigh," the captain joyfully expressed.

Brisethi was inclined to touch it but the naval captain swatted her hand away. He then handed one of the small, oval devices to Etyne and ordered him to find a quiet area in the aft of the ship.

"Sir, may I go with him or do you need me?" Brisethi was curious of the event about to transpire.

Captain Nessel stared at her momentarily. "Yes, go do whatever it is you army type do just don't get in the way of my sailors."

"Aye, Sir," she replied and followed after Etyne.

Etyne leaned against the bulkhead on the lowest deck of the ship where supplies and ammunition securely scattered the cargo hold. Brisethi was sitting upon a large crate across from him, staring at the device he held in his hand. Neither spoke a word, waiting for whatever was supposed to happen.

Their silence was interrupted by the sound of Captain Nessel's voice transmitting through the oval apparatus which began radiating turquoise light. Both were startled by the sounds and lights, causing Brisethi to jump from the crate to listen more intently to the device.

"Captain Vorsen, if you can hear me, press the button on the front of the device and voice your response," the voice in the device said.

Both army captains were instantly impressed. Etyne pressed the button with his thumb and awkwardly replied into the inanimate object. "Captain, this is Vorsen, I hear you loud and clear." He kept his eyes on Brisethi if only to assure himself he was talking to a person and not an object.

She was grinning like a child and wanting to hold the device to have her turn at it. He handed it to her and she instantly pressed the button to speak. "Captain Nessel! This is Captain Sen Asel. I heard you, too, are you hearing us?" She handed the device back to Etyne.

A moment later, Captain Nessel's voice transmitted again. *"Yes, I heard both of you; keep chattering over the device while I tune the frequencies. State your names, rank, identification and chain of command if you can't think of a story to tell me."*

Etyne cleared his throat and pressed the button again. "This is Captain Etyne Vorsen, Dominion Army, identification number six-two-five-five-four-zero. Next to me is Captain Brisethi Sen Asel, Dominion Army, identification number," he held the device to her.

"Identification number six-two-five-five-nine-nine," she stated.

"Fifty-nine recruits after me, were you the last person added to the division?" Etyne asked, still holding the button.

"Yes, actually, I was, according to the recruiter. The division was waiting on one more person to start the expedition, and I was just waiting for my twentieth birthday to enlist," she grinned.

"Oh, I suppose that makes sense, considering you were born four months after me," he replied. When neither of them had anything else to say he continued with their chain of command. "Major Paush is our direct commander who reports directly to Colonel Pelinara. After him is Lieutenant General Zadden followed by commander of the Dominion, General Satnir."

"You forgot," she started to speak but Etyne had released the button. She grabbed his hand and forcefully squeezed his thumb to press it again, "And lest we never forget, the glorious Emperor Arquistas, ruler of all of Sariadne," she dramatically stated then released her grasp on Etyne's hand. She grinned at him when he rolled his eyes.

"*Outstanding, you two,*" the naval captain replied. "*You may return to the ready room with the communication device.*"

"On our way," Etyne replied into the device one last time.

Etyne entered the ready room alone, having walked Brisethi back to the main deck to go about her own business. He placed the device on the table, complementing Nessel on his spectacular work. "This is incredible, Sir, how did you invent this? Just a few years ago we were told in officer training that you were implementing the idea of ranged communication. What's the range of these?" Etyne could hardly contain his excitement.

Captain Nessel grinned with pride and handed the army captain a stack of papers with various schematics and equations scribbled upon them. "The glassy stone," he said, pointing to the box made of the material, "was harvested from the southern volcano which, when fused by our mystics, works as a sort of transmitter. It has to be powered by our mystics but can hold a charge for years before needing the Resarian touch again. I've engineered the stones and mystics to form wavelengths for our voices to carry over on a bandwidth across short distances. When our voices are impressed upon a signal it is demodulated and sent back out to any one device set on the correct frequency. The length of the *Sovereign* is the farthest I've been able to communicate thus far."

Etyne was enthralled by his lecture and casually studied the first few pages of the Captain's work before speaking, "Sir, would you mind briefly summarizing the physics of this? I'm completely intrigued by your invention and may have a theory on how to increase the strength of these 'signals' of yours."

Captain Nessel grinned widely. "I thought you'd never ask, Mr. Vorsen," he excitedly gestured for him to have a seat and began his first lesson of basic modulation.

-:- -:- -:-

"Mystic transmission captures our voice as a signal and instantly sends it to a transmitter. Our mystics supply energy to facilitate voice transmission across a communication channel. I'll be spending the next few days assisting the captain with formulating a solution to modulating our signals for longer distances," Etyne explained to the three women at the table in the galley that afternoon when they reconvened to share a meal and a game of Fates of the Enchanted.

Brisethi, Korteni, and Livian each stared at him, completely mystified by the words coming out of his mouth. Korteni had made the mistake of asking Etyne why he was so tired. The reply had been a drawn-out lecture to them about engineered communication mystics, and he even drew diagrams on the back of a piece of paper from his pocket.

Brisethi could tell he was passionate about this new system and tried her best to pay attention to him. "Etyne, this is very fascinating, it really is. But every time you say the words, 'mod-u-lation' or 'trans-mission', I'm that much closer to grabbing your pistol and shooting you in the throat," she blatantly stated before placing a card down for her turn and initializing an attack on his cards.

"That's the violent response I expected from you, Bear, are you sure you wouldn't want to just maul me?" he smirked, roughly patting her on the back. Since he had spent most of their game talking about the Captain's new development, he found himself losing the round. Meanwhile, Korteni had retained much of what he'd said and even asked questions about their scientific processes to further her knowledge. Livian was as lost as Brisethi but wasn't as ready to silence Etyne by way of threatening to end his life.

The following days at sea found the four friends tending to their own tasks. Korteni had befriended Chief Kayula and both introduced Livian to various shipboard procedures, readying her for the next year she would spend on board the *Reliant*. Most of their time was spent on the top deck tying knots and intricate lanyards out of twine while swapping sea stories. Livian found an unexpected calm when focusing on making ropes and lanyards with the two chiefs.

"Are you planning on staying in the Dominion or lifelong reserves?" Chief Kayula asked Livian. He shielded his eyes from the evening sun piercing the clear skies to better see the young girl when she replied.

Livian reluctantly diverted her concentration from her rope. "I'm definitely going officer. I don't like how weak our people have become lately. We need to fortify our defenses, build more ships, and recruit more soldiers and sailors. The Lantheuns are so advanced, how could we think to ever stand against such a powerful people?"

"Have you seen the new dreadnought-class, *Retribution*?" Korteni asked. She was leaning against the railing, staring down at the *Sovereign*'s edged bow piercing through the ocean waves.

Livian shook her head then stood up to stretch her legs, slightly annoyed that she couldn't be left alone. She joined Korteni at the railing, "I've never heard of it."

"That's because it hasn't been commissioned as a Dominion Service Vessel yet. It's the first engine ship made of steel to have been developed for the Dominion. It's three times bigger than this ship, made to withstand entire fleets and obliterate whole commands," Korteni explained. "They're almost done building it. Captain Nessel had a lot of input on it and will most certainly have his communication device installed upon it."

"I hate the thought of sea life but I would love to see this new destructive ship. Why don't we have airships like the Lantheuns?" Livian asked.

"Bah, airships are impractical," Kayuela scoffed. "They're easily taken out and are only as fast as our sailing ships. With the right mystic-powered Resarian sailors, the *Retribution* will be faster than any other ship in existence,"

"Don't the Kiarans already have steel ships powered by steam or coal?" Livian pressed.

"They're still new to them, working out the kinks and flaws and amount of steam power needed to propel one of them. If we hope to defend against their firepower, however, we need to keep up with their advances and do away with wooden ships for good," Kayula replied.

Korteni pouted her lips. "I'm going to miss wooden ships and their sails – they're so majestic. Steel ships are just – bland."

"It'll take at least five more years until the *Retribuion*'s commissioned and then another twenty years to mass produce them," Kayula told her with a smile. "You'll get a little more time out of your toy ships yet."

-:- -:- -:-

Brisethi had been given permission to borrow a few books from Captain Nessel's cabin. She took advantage of the wardroom where she requisitioned a desk for herself to study up on Aspion Empire history, politics and economy.

One of the other navy officers, Lieutenant Sieter, offered to help her study. She had learned more about him in six days than she knew about her own closest friends due to his overwhelming ability to talk incessantly. She could recount how old his wife was, how they met, the names of their two daughters, his past five commands and the ships he served on. They shared stories of each continent and port he visited compared to her one instance on Trycinea. Never before had she met another man who could ramble on about uninteresting things as much as he could. Her politeness had prevented her from turning him away, and, every time he brought up a story, she would counter it with one from her admiral father's past.

Brisethi quickly realized that the life of a sailor was a lonely one when out to sea with the same hundred people for months at a time. No wonder they were easy to talk to when a stranger was among their crew. If all navy officers and senior enlisted shared the ability to talk others to death, she nearly feared her next two years with Lieutenant Vazeley.

When she wasn't struggling to retain the knowledge of the Aspion Empire and their main capital, Beccilia, she was in the cargo hold with Korteni and Livian for strength training. They didn't risk using weapons in the small amount of space and focused only on hand-to-hand techniques. Korteni would spar with Brisethi to wear her down to allow Livian to train with her. Livian was apprehensive to strike the officer at first, but when Brisethi finally taunted her by way of a light smack to the cheek, she held nothing back. Livian longed to fight the way she had seen Brisethi and Etyne before. Unfortunately, Brisethi managed to block every throw at her.

"You'll learn most of those moves in officer training," Brisethi told her, reassuring the girl after a particularly rough bout. "Here, I'll teach you the first moves they showed us." She held her hands out to Livian. "First, you need to take me down."

Livian scrunched her forehead in confusion and grabbed Brisethi's hands. She pulled on them but Brisethi didn't move. She held them tighter and pulled harder, only slightly nudging her.

Brisethi scoffed. "Korteni, go find Etyne, she probably doesn't remember the move. Just tell him it will only be ten minutes," she ordered.

"On it," Korteni replied and scurried off.

Brisethi grabbed Livian's hands this time and pulled her forward off-balance, quickly knocking her down, with her back to the deck.

"How did you do that?" Livian stood suddenly, wanting to try again.

"I'll come at you and you need to focus on grabbing my hands and shoving me to the deck, using your body as a counterbalance to mine," Brisethi instructed. She took a few steps back and ran toward Livian.

Livian dismissed her basic expedition training of blocking and did as she was told. She stepped back and took hold of Brisethi's hands, pulling her to the ground with her instead of remaining standing. Brisethi fell on her and rolled to alleviate the impact.

"It's a start," she chuckled and helped Livian to her feet.

"What's so important that you needed me down here? I swear if it's a question about that damn card game," Etyne said as he arrived.

"Livian doesn't remember how to fight," Brisethi teased.

"I know how to fight!" Livian shouted back, breathing heavily.

"Ladies, I'm exhausted and won't be going to sleep until hour four at the earliest-"

"Good - defend yourself!" Brisethi interrupted and shoved him forcefully into a stack of crates.

Korteni and Livian cheered when he immediately retaliated with a backhand aimed at her face but she was quick to dodge.

"No mystics!" She shouted in a grunt when he kicked her. She wanted to establish the one rule before he could disappear into spirit form.

She held onto his foot and pulled him forward to meet her elbow but he deflected it and pulled free. Every move they had taught each other suddenly felt fresh in her memory. She moved as agile as a cat and pounced upon her prey. Etyne dodged her incoming fists and grabbed her hands, pulling her forward this time in an attempt to knock her to the deck. She rolled instead, followed by her swinging her legs to trip him. He fell hard to the deck and quickly blocked more of her punches and kicks. He leapt up and tackled Brisethi, but she used her feet to throw him behind her. When they both got to their feet, he waited for her to attack. As she leapt toward him, he grabbed her by the waist and flung her into the same crates he had met earlier. The crates broke on impact and she had to flare her fire mystic to burn any splinters attempting to pierce her flesh.

"You said no mystics, you cheat! You filthy cheat!" Etyne shouted with a laugh and lunged toward her once again.

"I didn't want to bleeeeed," she squealed when he picked her up again. Instead of flying, this time, she held onto his arm and used the momentum from his attempted throw to pull him with her. She jumped onto another crate and leapt from them to land her feet to his chest. He fell on his back, somersaulting backwards to prevent her from attacking him again.

Korteni and Livian had to keep running from one side of the cargo hold to the other in an attempt to dodge the captains about to collide with them. One of the lanterns was knocked over, and Korteni used her mystic to extinguish the flame before it could spread. "This is why I'm here," she whispered to Livian. "It's hour one, so you should probably try not to break any bones. I don't want to be the one waking up the medic," Korteni called to them.

"I'm already going easy on him," Brisethi teased.

He wiped blood from a cut on his lip. "Dammit, you're paying for this," he threatened and burst into motion once more.

Livian giggled, "He's mad now, you cut his pretty face!"

Brisethi dodged three out of four of his fast punches. The fourth found its target on her rib, causing her to double over. She prayed to the spirits it wasn't cracked and forced herself to counter with a tackle. She straddled him and grasped his muscular neck as tightly as she could.

Etyne burst into laughter. "You're never going to be able to strangle me, your paws are too tiny," he then used one hand to strangle her in return. When she released her grasp to pry his hand off of her own neck, he sat up, and then stood up, and threw her to the deck.

"Ouch," she painfully exhaled. She wanted to stand and keep fighting, but the thought of waking the corpsmen if they seriously injured one another kept her on the ground. Instead, she wiped the blood from her nose and caught her breath. She shared an aching look with Etyne.

"I honestly didn't think you were ready to fight again," he admitted. He stood over her, breathing heavily and stared at her with his hands on his hips. He tried to smirk but winced from the cut on his lip.

"You underestimate my fury," she grinned and held her hands up to him.

He took hold of them to help her stand. "I needed this. It's been awhile since I've beaten anyone up," he gloated. He touched and examined her ribs where his fist had earlier rammed into her.

She groaned from the tenderness. "Don't worry; you didn't break anything in me this time."

"The crates, however," Korteni pointed out. "Captain Nessel won't be happy with you two destroying his supplies."

Brisethi covered the crates with a tarp. "Shhh, no one will ever know-"

"'Sethi!" Etyne scolded. "I'm headed back up to the ready room. Don't damage anything else," he ordered.

Chapter IX

Sulica woke early the next morning and made a quick stop at the near-empty galley to grab a pastry. She wrapped it in a napkin and hurried topside. The deck was almost completely devoid of life, save the unfortunate sailors who had been scheduled for the roving watch. Her footsteps echoed slightly as she walked along the wooden deck to the fantail. Turning her collar up against the cool air, she settled on a couple of crates temporarily placed against the stack.

She bit into the warm, flaky pastry, savoring its sweet taste as she looked out across the railing to see the sun just barely beginning to rise over the mountain behind Vipurg. The sky slowly began to change from the near blackness to a mild purple. Sulica sighed happily, content to just be alive at that moment. She didn't want to think about what would happen once she reached Pahl'Kiar.

More footsteps could be heard approaching, and she instinctively leaned further back into the shadows. She recognized Ekani's form as he came into view, his profile barely visible. He removed his overcoat and tossed it on the deck at his feet. Moving rather quickly, he climbed up and over the railing slightly off to the side. Before her eyes, Ekani performed a clean dive into the water below.

Is he crazy? she thought in astoundment. Several minutes later, he returned, soaking wet, this time accompanied by Lieutenant Simtel.

"Are you crazy?" Simtel asked his friend. "I know you're nuttier than a squirrel, but are you genuinely crazy?"

Ekani laughed as he bent to retrieve his jacket. "The cold water sharpens my mind, and I'm going to need a clear head today." In answer to Simtel's unasked question, he continued, "I have to go to the embassy today. The Lantheuns have seriously considered our offer, and Vipurg could be a critical spot for transporting supplies."

"Great," Simtel grumbled, "Just what we need, crackpot scientists and bloodthirsty brutes."

"How is that any different from your crew?" Ekani teased.

"True enough, but I would rather go dress shopping than spend the morning at the embassy with those stuffy know-it-alls. No offense," he quickly added.

"Good," Ekani said with a grin. "Thanks for volunteering to take Sulica around town today." He began walking away, leaving Simtel at the fantail.

"I said 'no offense'!" he called after with a laugh.

Sulica contemplated just hiding until he went away then disappearing so he wouldn't be obligated to escort her.

"Whenever you're ready," Simtel said, startling her, "we can head on into town, so you can get your dresses." He turned and gave her his most charming smile.

A short while later they were passing through the large wooden doors into Vipurg proper once more. The sun had almost fully risen, and the day seemed to promise a little warmth. They traveled into the market quadrant, past the great lodge they had dined at the night before.

"What do you like to do?" Simtel asked Sulica as they walked past the snow-covered shops. "Besides talking to me, of course," he added confidently.

She rolled her eyes in response and thought about his question. So much of her time had been spent scheming up ways to survive that she could hardly remember anything that she did before. It seemed like her life before the Dominion training didn't even exist.

Sensing her discomfort, he suggested they visit his favorite place in the town. Shops lined the street with warm lanterns placed directly outside the door in order to allow potential customers to read the signs, even in darkness. At the moment, the lanterns were all mostly extinguished. Light, powdery snow covered the rooftops and lined the sides of the buildings, but paths had already been cleared for access. As they walked, Simtel translated the names of the most popular shops, cafes, and restaurants. He waved at some of the people who passed, greeting them kindly by name.

"How do you know everyone?" Sulica asked after the fifth incident.

"We pull into port here every so often," he replied casually.

He led her to a small corner store with a large wooden carving of a bear in front. Sulica paused and stared at the incredible details etched in the wood. The bear stood on all fours, its muzzle open wide, displaying all the carved wooden teeth. She reached out slowly, almost afraid to touch it.

Simtel suddenly grabbed her side and growled, "Careful, he bites!"

She jumped and whirled to face him, barely able to restrain the urge to punch him in the face.

He was doubled over in laughter, gasping, "Your reaction - that was priceless! I haven't had one like that in ages."

Her hands curled into fists, and she placed them on her hips for better control. She took advantage of his mirth and pushed Simtel's shoulder, sending him tumbling backwards into a pile of snow.

"Cold!" he gasped in a high-pitched voice, causing Sulica to begin giggling uncontrollably.

Sulica held out her hand to help him up. Acting like he was going to take it, he instead grabbed her forearm and pulled her into the snow pile with him. Between their laughter and struggle to get free from the snow, they seemed to sink further into it. Finally, they teamed up and used each other as leverage to get out. They brushed the snow off of their clothes, stomping their feet to loosen it from the boots.

Simtel straightened his uniform and attempted to regain his composure. "Well, I don't know about you, but I'm colder than an icicle in a freezer. How about a drink and a fire?"

They headed back to the lodge, which was significantly quieter than it had been the night before. Stone fire pits adorned the corners of the great hall, and Sulica found a set of plush chairs by an unoccupied one. She settled into it, sinking deep in the cushions. Putting her hands up to the warm flames, she felt the chill start to leave her fingers.

Simtel suddenly appeared next to her, holding out a steaming mug of brown liquid with white cream topping it. Sulica thanked him but regarded the mug skeptically. "It's not poison," he said, pointedly taking a sip of his before plopping into the chair next to her.

"Sure, but how much alcohol is in it?" He laughed easily, assuring her there wasn't any. She took a cautious sip, immediately burning her tongue.

"Well, it is hot," Simtel said innocently. After a moment, he leaned forward in his chair and said eagerly, "Tell me what it's like to grow up in Sariadne. Have you seen Ancient Kiar? Are there really dragons?"

Sulica was momentarily taken aback. "I would think it's the same as growing up in Pahl'Kiar," she answered slowly.

"Except for the mystics making your life easier than a drunk Beccilian."

She laughed at his unexpected word choice. "Mystics are a lot of work. We have to be able to keep them in check, or it could mean death."

Simtel scoffed, "Of course it does. Dragon spirits aren't easy to control." He noticed the bewildered look on her face. "Don't tell me you don't even know the story behind your own people."

Shrugging, she said, "I didn't have to pay attention in school. My father didn't care about marks unless it had something to do with money." Blowing on the hot drink, she was able to take a tiny sip. The chocolate drink immediately began to warm her insides.

"That is sad," he said. Then he set down his half-empty mug and clapped his hands together. "Time for a history lesson.

"Long ago, the dragons decided to give their dying spirits to the people beginning to inhabit Sariadne. The type of mystic a person had was related to the dragon and its abilities. The people were thankful at first, worshipping the dragons as the most powerful beings in the world. From there, the population continued to grow and expand, splitting into two major civilizations. But, as the years passed, the people began to forget where their gifts came from.

"Now, this is not a high point for my people," Simtel continued sadly. "The inhabitants of Kiar decided the dragons were too central to their way of life, and that needed to change. They tore down shrines and began hunting the dragons down. The dragons began to withdraw more and more, or they were mostly killed. Finally, the remaining dragons banded together and stripped the Kiarans of their dragon spirits, leaving them with just enough to live through the pain of it as a punishment."

"That's awful," Sulica said quietly, suddenly recalling the missing training division from her own expedition years before. She shivered, half-hoping dragons didn't really exist anymore, lest they enact vengeance against her people too.

A voice behind her interrupted, "Don't be telling her your tall tales."

"Vorsen!" Simetel said, "It's true, and you know it. That's why our eyes are the way they are, because we had mystics and lost them."

"It can't be all true," Sulica interrupted as Ekani came around to sit on her other side. "I know a half-Kiaran who has eyes like a full one, but he has full use of his mystics."

Simtel raised his eyebrows with a grin, "Yeah, what's his name?" he challenged.

Holding her head high against his disbelief, she looked directly at Ekani. "Etyne Vorsen."

-:- -:- -:-

The sailors of the *DSV Sovereign* moored her lines to the pier of the Southwest Naval Base just outside Ancient Kiar. Both moons lit up the purple sky above with their evening glow, threatening to outshine the orange sun upon the horizon. The normal hustle of the day had slowed to a crawl as the ship pulled in. The rest of the shipyard was relatively quiet.

Captain Sen Asel bid farewell to Captain Nessel, Lieutenant Sieter and Chief Kayula. She hugged Chief Korteni Pyraz, wishing her a safe journey on the way to the *DSV Reliant*. Sergeant Livian Reej gave her a salute and, after returning the salute, Brisethi shook her hand.

Etyne walked with her down the gangplank and halfway to where two base guards waited to escort Brisethi back to her division. He was saying goodbye to her again. "I'll see you in two years, 'Sethi. Write to me, and maybe I'll reply," he smiled.

"You better write back," she nudged his arm. "I'll mail you your frakshins when I get to my belongings."

"Please, don't," he told her. "I'd rather you thought of your compass watch as a gift."

She smiled at him. "If you insist, Etyne. Thank you." At the edge of the pier just before the mounted guards, she turned to him to give him a farewell salute.

He returned the salute and before she could turn away, he placed his hands on her arms and pulled her in. He held her close in a tight embrace, feeling her arms wrap around him in return. Regulations or not, he needed to give her the farewell she deserved. "You once stated that we were too good of friends for a formal goodbye," he whispered to her.

She squeezed him tighter at hearing him repeat her own words, written what felt like ages ago. "Why is this goodbye so much more painful?" she asked with a lump in her throat.

"I don't know," he exhaled, holding her tighter. "I'm guessing because we've never held each other like this."

I don't want to let go of you, she thought when sudden realization struck that she was content with his affection. They reluctantly broke away from one another in an effort to restrain the overwhelming emotions flooding their spirits.

"Or perhaps," he continued, "it's because the last time I said goodbye to you, it was almost the last goodbye."

"Well not this time," she stated confidently. Brisethi's heart ached at the thought that his spirit's lifespan was halved to allow hers to live on and had no way to repay him. She smiled sadly to him and began to walk away. After saluting the two guards, she mounted the horse that had been reserved for her two day travel to her division. She looked back to watch Etyne walking back up the gangplank to the *DSV Sovereign*.

"I love you, Etyne," she whispered to him, letting her words disappear on the breeze, knowing he couldn't hear her.

-:- -:- -:-

"What?" Where is Trenn? Who is that?" The rough Kiaran words dragged Ibrienne back into consciousness.

She squeezed her eyes shut to ward off worsening the pounding in her head. She tried to move her hands, but the rope binding them made it difficult. Resigning herself to lay still, she concentrated on the discussion taking place nearby.

"Stop giving me excuses," the same voice growled.

Ibreinne couldn't hear the mumbled reply. Slowly, she opened her eyes, blinking several times to clear her vision. Moving as little as possible, she looked around. From her position on the floor, she could see that she was most certainly not in the same room as before. Boxes and crates of varying size were piled all around her.

She heard footsteps and closed her eyes again.

"When does it wear off?" the voice asked, much closer.

"Any moment now," was the reply. She recognized it as the voice of the Kiaran who had trapped them.

Her eyes snapped open, immediately glaring in the direction of the second voice. The two Kiarans stood over her. Seeing her awake, the newer one picked her up and put her on her feet. He was not gentle.

"Where," he began, "is your friend?" His voice was low and dangerous.

Ibrienne kept her eyes on the second Kiaran and remained silent. She didn't see the first one's hand in time to dodge as it made contact with her cheek, hard. She staggered and almost fell, but the one who hit her pulled her close to his face and growled the question again.

From the corner of her eye, she could see the sorrow and shame expressed on the other Kiaran's face, and it angered her more. "He is no friend of mine," she spat. Droplets of blood mixed with her saliva on the man's face.

He tossed her back to the ground and walked away. "Mirako," he called behind him, and the other Kiaran hurried after. A door slammed after them, leaving Ibrienne in the near darkness.

Her cheek stung, and she wished she could have use of her hands. Channeling her mystic through her fingers had always made the process go faster. She struggled into a sitting position and leaned against a crate. Closing her eyes, she breathed in and out, concentrating on keeping an even tempo, just as Acolyte Roz had taught her. After several moments, she felt a numbing tingle in her face as it healed.

When it was through, she slumped down, completely exhausted from the effort. She leaned her head back, her eyes adjusting to the lack of light in the room. Methodically, she began to assess her situation.

Kanilas was gone, that much was obvious. She wasn't sure whether she ought to be relieved or irate. If he got away, then he'd know she was still in need of help, but with how untrustworthy he'd proven himself to be, she couldn't believe that he would actually try to rescue her. Her body ached from laying on the hard floor, and the pounding in her head had only subsided to a dull thud.

Maybe tomorrow will be better, she thought, repeating the words she so often had told Livian in the orphanage.

-:- -:- -:-

Ekani paced the carpeted floor of his cabin from his desk to the door and back again. The normally neat compartment was littered with clothes, papers, and books. Papers lay scattered all over the desk, letters from his father. Ekani had spent the better part of two days tracking down every letter he had received, searching for any mention or hint of a brother. He sat in the chair behind the desk, placing his head in his hands.

For as long as he could remember, it had always just been the two of them. His father never even dated anyone. Sometimes, Ekani thought he could recall a woman's soft voice, singing jibberish.

Suddenly, he stood and stormed to the door. His hand was on the lock when he hesitated. Reconsidering, he went to the bed and flopped down, ignoring the small jab of an object in his back. He closed his eyes, trying to think back.

"What the hell is wrong with you?" a younger Ekani yelled at Simtel. His friend's nose was spouting blood, and there was a nasty cut on his lip.

Simtel touched his face gingerly. "It probably looks worse than it feels." He tried to grin and winced instead.

"You realize your mother is going to kill us," Ekani said matter-of-factly, crossing his arms.

Shrugging, Simtel began the walk to his apartment. Ekani hurried to catch up to him. "Didn't think he could hit that hard," Simtel muttered. They walked the rest of the way in silence.

The street was mostly quiet. A few cats prowled around, hissing at the boys when they walked too close. The buildings in their neighborhood looked run down, as though a flood had covered them at one point, and the sun took a very long time to dry them. They stopped at a four-story brick apartment complex. Simtel's parents were the building managers, so it actually looked quite nice compared to the surrounding ones. Every year, the boys were enlisted to re-paint the trim and cut down the plants that tried to threaten to climb up the walls.

Ekani paused at Simtel's door. He turned to his friend, who suddenly seemed pale and much less confident than a few moments before. "Do you want help?" he offered.

Simtel gulped but shook his head. "Time to face the lioness," he said and opened the door.

Ekani went next door to his own apartment. It was dark. His father was still at work. Ekani lit the lamp and, ignoring the clothes tossed on the couch, went into the dining nook to sit by the wall, the closest to Simtel's living room.

The walls were thin, so he had no trouble hearing Simtel's mother screech, "Aderok, what have I told you about fighting!" There was a pause as he seemed to try to reply. "I don't care what the reason was, you have no business getting into scraps!"

"Would you just lay off me?" He yelled. "I'm tired of you hollering at me all the time!"

Ekani heard the door open and quickly tried to appear like he was cleaning the table. He looked over at his father and said brightly, "Hi, Pop, how was your day?"

Jiridian gave him a knowing look and nodded next door. "I heard Amora down the hall. Aderok was in trouble again?"

Ekani quit pretending to clean. "He got into a fight with three of the guys in class. I tried to help, but he wouldn't let me."

"You don't speak to your mother that way!" They heard through the wall. "Where do you think you are going?"

"To Vorsen's. I'm not dealing with this right now."

The dull thud of a door slamming met their ears. Moments later, their own opened and closed. Simtel stormed into the kitchen and grabbed a drink from the icebox. Sitting at the table, he cracked it open and said, "Suppose you heard all that."

Jiridian, not even phased, put his coat over the third chair. He moved to the other side of the room and began to pull out dishes to make their evening meal.

Ekani knew better than to say anything. Simtel needed the time to just sort out his own anger. "You're so lucky you don't have to deal with that," he said. "I bet your mother would have been just as chill as your father." Ekani glared at his friend. Suddenly realizing Jiridian was in the room, Simtel looked up and started to apologize.

"There is no need to apologize," Jiridian said with a sad smile. "If Ekani's mother could be here, she would be. You should consider yourself lucky to have both Amora and Darelek in your life." He looked down at his hands. "Being a parent is no easy task. The best anyone can do is whatever they can to make sure their child survives. A child has to push the boundaries to learn. Sometimes we forget what that was like."

Ekani opened his mouth to say something, but his father suddenly grinned at the two boys. "How about we visit your favorite food vendor? Or will you be able to eat with that busted lip, Aderok?" he teased. His tone was light, but Ekani could see the faraway look that remained in his eyes.

That evening, Ekani caught a glimpse of his father on his knees in his room. He held a box, and his shoulders shook. Ekani never told anyone what he'd seen.

A knock on the door brought Ekani out of his reverie. He ignored it, but the person on the other side was persistent. "It's me," he heard Simtel call out. "Come on, quit being an ornery badger or I'll keep badgering you."

Ekani smiled in spite of himself. He rolled off the bed and went to the door. Upon opening it and seeing Sulica standing next to his old friend, he began to close the door again. Simtel stuck his foot out. He gave Ekani a reproving look.

Sighing, Ekani let go of the door and stepped back, letting the two into the cabin. Simtel took one glance and grinned. "This is more like the Vorsen I know." Sulica remained impassive.

"Is there a reason you're here?" Ekani said, a little harsher than he intended. He noticed Sulica flinch slightly and regretted nothing.

"So you're upset that your father didn't tell you about Etane-"

"Etyne," Sulica corrected.

Simtel shrugged. "Whichever. Point is," he said to Ekani, "you didn't know. But it just so happens that you have a first-hand account of what your brother is like right here." He gestured to Sulica.

Ekani's face was stone. "You're the only brother I need," he told Simtel.

-:- -:- -:-

Lieutenant Vazeley saluted Captain Sen Asel upon her arrival at the desert camp with her two Dominion guards. After a quick debrief, the guards, along with the horse loaned to Sen Asel, departed the camp to return to Southwest Harbor.

She returned the salute then handed the navy officer the written orders given to her by Lieutenant Commander Jeksan and proceeded to greet her senior enlisted commanders. She wiped at the sweat beading on her forehead from the heat of the desert. She couldn't wait to change into her summer light-weight uniform, if she could locate it first.

"It's about time you returned, Ma'am, I'm so tired of Mr. Vazeley's ongoing sea stories," Sergeant First Class Kile teased. "Not to mention Master Chief Riquez and Chief Baderstoff's additional navy banter! I've been so alone and drowning in a sea of navy."

Brisethi chuckled at her stout sergeant. "I feel your pain, Kile, I really do." She mentioned to him her short trip on the *DSV Sovereign*, to commiserate in his pain of being surrounded by chatty sailors.

Upon reading the in-depth orders stating that Captain Sen Asel was not allowed to command the division without his supervision, Lieutenant Vazeley nodded, acknowledging his responsibility to her. "I think I can handle the duty of playing officer guardian to you for two years. Anything beats the desolate watchstanding at Post Four, briefing the colonel every other day on the vast amounts of nothing going on," he told her.

"I appreciate it, Sir," she replied, shouldering her pack. "Are the rest of my belongings on one of those wagons?"

He looked in the direction she pointed and nodded. "Chief, take her pack and help us with the rest of her stuff," he ordered, walking them to the canopy of horses and wagons.

The commanders tried not to stare at her smaller frame and oddly cut hair. They had read brief, vague reports of what she went through and couldn't imagine what she looked like the day she had been rescued.

Abyss snorted into Brisethi's hand when she greeted him, letting her stroke his face. "I missed you, too, old friend. Thank you for taking my father to safety," she whispered. Abyss bumped his nose against her shoulder.

Chief Baderstoff climbed into the wagon to search for the captain's other belongings. He handed her tent to the lieutenant then shouldered her pack of uniforms and gear to set her up at a suitable space in the sand near the command tent.

Sergeant Kile assisted the chief in propping her tent up to help her settle in. "Thank you, gentlemen," she smiled to them and crawled inside her small sleeping area. She dumped her bag of uniforms and traveling equipment, all of it smelling of campfire smoke and the outdoors. She swiftly changed into the airy red uniform trimmed in black cording and donned her hood. She straightened her collar device portraying her captain rank before stepping outside into the dry, bright desert air.

She joined the others in the command tent for the remainder of the afternoon to debrief them of her last two months away from Sariadne, leaving as much detail out as possible if only to suppress any thought to pity her. She commended the commanders when she learned that not one recruit had been sent home in her absence; in fact, the recruits had been motivated to surpass her standards in an effort to impress their captain upon her return.

Master Chief Riquez accompanied his captain around the camp to reacquaint her with the division recruits. Each of them gladly saluted her, welcoming her back. She returned every salute with a smile, overjoyed to see their faces and be reminded that she was in her element once again.

Brisethi instructed her enlisted commanders to have the recruits form up for combat training. She felt a strong need to ensure that each soldier could fend off the most basic of attacks from any bandit, pirate, or enemy soldier. The ten females in her division would especially receive her critical attention in attempt to effectively train them in offensive techniques.

"It's not enough to defend against the enemy," she shouted above the clatter of recruits practicing one of her new moves without the use of weapons. "You need to be able to take them out before they can touch you! If someone has the intent to harm you, they will stop at nothing to disable you. Take it upon yourself to prevent that harm by any means necessary!"

Brisethi eyed recruit Sergeant Talmin. She had caught on to the combat training faster than her fellow recruits, earning her quick promotions. She studied the recruit's moves, finding no error in her training. "Very good, Talmin. Have you had prior training in combat arts?"

Sergeant Talmin nodded. "From my uncle, Ma'am."

Brisethi brought her hand up to her chin in thought, "Carry on," she finally ordered. She strolled over toward the other commanders and rolled her shoulders. She picked up her sword and nodded to the navy officer. "Lieutenant, care to dance?"

"Yeah, sure," he lightheartedly replied and unsheathed his own sword. "I'll defend first?"

She nodded and drew back her sword at eye level, bending at her knees and preparing her muscles for the attack. In a blink of an eye she leapt toward her counterpart, forcing him to fall back instantly in an effort to deflect her sword. He had to keep stumbling backwards to dodge her ferocious attacks while simultaneously deflecting her quick strikes. He severely underestimated the rehabilitated captain.

He had finally managed to catch her sword hand and pry the weapon from her solid grip. Forcefully pushing her back, he caused her to stumble to so he could catch his breath. "Cursed spirits, Sen

Asel, did they enhance your body somehow?" Lieutenant Vazeley jested.

The enlisted commanders snickered among one another, not remotely surprised by her quick restoration. Chief Baderstoff was first to speak, "This is the tamed version of Ms. Sen Asel. You should see what she does to Captain Vorsen."

"What you army captains do in your alone time is none of my concern," Vazeley retorted while ducking from another vicious swing of her bare fist.

"You're terribly out of practice, Sir," she quipped, easing up on him.

"Only a tad," he stammered.

"Dammit, get over here, Master Chief," she ordered for a new sparring partner.

"Shit," Master Chief Riquez muttered under his breath.

The master chief was even more out of practice than the lieutenant, sloppily attacking her and slowing down within minutes. Chief Baderstoff stepped in to save his master chief of further humiliation. He deflected her every swing, advancing his own sword against her, forcing her to step back. A thin smile formed on her lips as she glared under her brow at the young chief. They burst into motion once more in an attempt to wear the other down.

"Gah, fuck," Brisethi stammered when she lost her sword. She ducked his swing and kicked upward, landing her foot on the knuckles of his sword-wielding hand. They were both without weapons now but continued to fight hand-to-hand. She leapt into the air in a quick spin, kicking at his torso.

The chief recovered quickly by throwing fists toward her abdomen but she blocked every one of them. She caught his final two swings in a tight grasp to pull him toward her knee. He flipped into her to avoid crashing his face into her knee and landed atop of her, holding her down by her neck. She swiftly wriggled her way from his grasp shoved him face first into the ground. Both had taken a moment to catch their breaths and wipe sweat from their faces.

"Well fought, Chief," she complimented him and helped him to his feet. He nodded his thanks and reciprocated the compliment.

Chapter X

It was dark again when Ibrienne woke. She had spent most of the trip in darkness, and she was growing accustomed to it, even finding it peaceful. During the day, people were always coming and going, disturbing her already uncomfortable sleep. Sometimes they would stop and throw food in it for her, but they usually forgot for days at a time. She soon learned to ration what little was given to make it last as long as possible.

Limbs aching, she stretched as much as she could in the container. It was large enough for her to sit or lay down curled up, but not enough for her to stand. As the days and nights passed, she could feel her body weaken. She was able to use her mystic to heal the splinters and scabs that formed, but even the strength to do that was dwindling away. There was no way to heal a starving stomach.

It was cool at night. She could feel a breeze come in through an open porthole, filling her nostrils with the salty air. Laying on her back, she stretched her arms up to the top of the box. Then she scrunched her upper body into one corner and put her legs in the opposite one. They tingled as the numbness left them. As she did every time she woke, she wondered how much longer it would be until they reached their destination.

Before setting sail, Ibrienne's captors had tried everything to get her to reveal where Kanilas had gone, including physical and mental torture. More than once, she had to keep herself from laughing at their ridiculous threats.

"When Sariadne falls, I will personally find every last one of your family and make sure their deaths are as painful as possible," one had said at one point. She had only stared blankly in return. When that didn't work, he resorted to striking at her repeatedly with a piece of coiled leather. She made an exaggerated show of the pain he was inflicting, when in reality it felt more like a minor pinch, so fast was her self-healing.

Finally, the main Kiaran gang leader had made an appearance for the first time since locking Ibrienne in the storage room. For several moments, he studied her. She was strung up between two columns, dirty and wasting away slowly. Finally, the man approached her, stopping in front of her face. "Do you realize," he said deliberately, "Trenn left you here to die? You are protecting a coward who lets a woman take his deserved punishment."

Ibrienne, who had shied away from conflict all her life, wondered how her friends would have handled the situation. Brisethi would have fought tooth and nail, burning everyone alive. Sulica would have demanded release and somehow would have gotten it. Korteni was too sly and quick to ever be caught in this kind of predicament in the first place, and even if she had been, she'd have chatted up the guards so quick they would have let her go.

A slow grin spread across her face. "At least he always had the courage to face me without binds," she said in a raspy voice that she could hardly recognize as her own.

The Kiaran backhanded her. She simply spat a spot of blood onto his tan shoes. "Which one is really the coward?" she asked as he turned away from her. She hoped his shoes were ruined.

Soon after, the henchmen came back and cut her down. She forced herself to try to fight, but her body was beyond weak. They merely laughed at her feeble attempts and unceremoniously placed her in the crate with a little bit of food and a flagon of water. No one had spoken to her at length since then, leaving her to her own thoughts. The solitude was poison to her. For years, she'd always had someone with her, even at the orphanage. Eventually, she came back to the idea that Trenn had truly abandoned her after she'd saved his life.

It weighed heavily on her mind as the ship continued its travel on the rocky seas. The sadness turned to bitterness. "I should have never even been there," she would mutter to herself in the darkness. Then the regret went further back. "I should have stayed in Sariadne instead of joining Sulica. What was I thinking?"

The next morning she was given her food ration, an abnormally large amount compared to her regular meal. She eyed it suspiciously after it was dropped in. The server said something in Kiaran that she couldn't quite catch, though it sounded like he was laughing. Her stomach growled loudly. Against her better judgment, she ate as much as she could until her swollen stomach was stretched tight. Suddenly sleepy, she curled up and passed out once more.

-:- -:- -:-

A few tense days later found the diplomatic vessel finally pulling into port in Pahl'Kiar. Sulica stood on the deck once more, apprehensively watching the city grow closer as the tugs pulled the ship into port.

The cityscape was full of tall buildings reaching far into the sky. Several looked to be even taller than the Citadel in Res'Baveth. Birds swooped all around the harbor, calling out to one another in loud screeches. The pier bustled with people of all nationalities save her own. As they approached, Sulica could see the pier divided into two by a large stone wall, extending into the deep water. On the left were multitudes of merchant and trading vessels. She could not see the right side from their position, but the tugs slowly brought their ship around the wall.

She soon realized that a cove protected the Kiaran military vessels on the other side. They were sleek, steel ships, dangerous-looking and powerful. As a diplomat, it only made sense that Ekani and his transport would be protected just the same as the military. Their ship was moored next to a semi-submersible, its plating so dark it was nearly black in color. Even in the morning, when there was activity in nearly all the other areas of the port, nothing seemed to stir on board the ominous craft.

Ekani and Simtel joined her. They were both in full dress uniform, blue jackets covered the gleaming white shirt beneath, and the trousers matched. Each leg had golden trim along the side. The shoulder boards on Simtel's were adorned with the outline of two golden circles while Ekani's were nonexistent.

When the ship was finally moored to the pier, the two Kiaran men escorted Sulica down the gangplank. Ekani took Sulica's elbow in his hand. She started to shake him off, but he gave her a look and she sullenly allowed herself to be guided through the throng of military men who were either preparing to depart or had just come home. She felt a twinge of homesickness as she witnessed the happy reunions. Small children screamed in delight at the sight of their fathers and happy shouts filled the area.

Ekani led her to the main entrance to the harbor, a large archway made of gleaming white stone. Something inside Sulica began to tingle. It took her several seconds to realize that it was her mystic. She took a deep breath and reached out with it, trying to soothe herself. *There are no other Resarians in Pahl'Kiar,* she tried to tell herself. Still, the nagging feeling lingered.

Suddenly she stopped in her tracks. Ekani tugged at her, but she didn't move. The world began to spin as she sensed another mystic, a familiar one. As it started to grow weaker, Sulica broke into a run in the direction she felt it coming from. Ekani and Simtel called for her, but she ignored them. She stumbled on the skirt of her dress and fell to her knees. Cursing the impractical outfit, she tried to stand again. Hands grabbed her, hauled her to her feet, and began to drag her away.

"No!" she yelled.

Ekani's face flushed as he gave Simtel an embarrassed look. They continued to pull the struggling woman out of the harbor amid stares. No one interfered, though, either due to the authority of the uniforms they wore, or because Sulica was not a Kiaran.

Angry tears stung at Sulica's eyes at her own weakness as she felt the familiar spirit slipping farther away. "Ibrienne," she whispered.

The drive to the Kiaran palace was very quiet. Sulica hadn't even allowed herself to be impressed by the motorized horseless carriage that was waiting outside the harbor for Ekani and his prisoner. Simtel asked Ekani if he would be alright then departed their company. She realized the kindness the two men had shown her was just a facade, a front to get her to trust them. She wanted to kick herself for her stupidity.

Her stony face was reflected in the glass window as she stared absently at the passing city. She could see her disheveled golden hair framing her face but couldn't bring herself to care enough to fix it. The feeling of Ibrienne's spirit hadn't left her.

After several more minutes of silence, Ekani finally cleared his throat and said, "What was that all about anyway?"

Sulica clenched her fist so tightly she could feel her fingernails dig into her skin. "Why didn't you let me go?" she countered.

Ekani sighed heavily. "Look at it from my view. The moment we were out of the military sector, you took off. That is not exactly reassuring behavior."

She considered his words, cautiously hopeful. Turning to face him, she felt her resolve melt away. His eyes seemed to be filled with real concern, despite the coldness with which he'd treated her on the remainder of their time on the ship. "Are there any more of my people here?" she asked quietly.

His brow furrowed in confusion. "There are a few Resarians in Pahl'Kiar, but all of them are housed in the palace for safety. That's where you'll be staying as well."

Our safety or yours? she asked silently. Looking out the window again, she began to pay attention to the streets they passed in case she should need to an escape route in the future. It was late in the evening by the time they reached the ornate palace gates. Despite herself, Sulica couldn't help but stare in awe at the gorgeous slate building lit by several glowing lights in the distance as they traveled up the long, winding drive. It ended in a loop surrounding a tall fountain directly in front of the entrance to the prestigious building.

A royal escort met their carriage. The uniform the escort wore was similar to Ekani's, minus the jacket. His crisp white shirt was almost blinding even in the darkness. He saluted as Ekani stepped down and offered his hand to help Sulica.

"The Emperor is expecting you," the escort said. "He would be most understanding if you wanted to freshen up after your long journey," he added with a pointed look at the woman.

Sulica, who hadn't understood all of the words but grasped the meaning, glared and opened her mouth to retort, but Ekani quickly interceded. "An excellent idea. Just a few moments should do the trick." He ran his hand through his jet black hair then leaned over to Sulica after the escort turned his back. "Remember, women are not the same here as your home," he whispered.

"Partially your home too," she hissed sullenly.

Ekani chose to ignore her and followed the other man up the sweeping staircase.

As austere as the Citadel was, Sulica found the Kiaran palace its complete opposite. Kiarans seemed to take great pride in their craftsmanship. Portraits of former prominent leaders lined the entry hall in ornate frames. She stared at each one as they passed, feeling as though she was traveling through time. The escort explained some of the pictures as they passed, introducing some as Presidents and others as Emperors. After the tenth or eleventh one, she finally asked why there were so many.

The escort paused mid-sentence and looked from her to Ekani in disbelief. Ekani flushed and said quickly, "Kiarans don't have the same lifespan you do. There have been many wars fought internally to determine who will rule and for how long."

Sulica felt momentarily embarrassed, but that shortly turned to indignance. *How was I supposed to know?* she fumed silently as they continued down yet another hall.

Soon they came to two separate doors marked in figures she recognized. Without waiting, Sulica hurried into the one for women. Marble counters and bright silver piping met her eyes. She half-reluctantly walked forward to the mirror. Her heart sank at the sight that met her eyes.

Eyes red, hair a mess, and her face streaked with a little dirt on one side, and so far from home, she almost began crying again from the sorrow she felt. After two deep breaths, she held her head high and stared obstinately at the reflection she did not even recognize. She scrubbed her face until it was pink and felt raw. The dirty water swirled in the sink. Immediately, she felt better than she had in weeks.

Sulica studied her hair for a moment, wondering how to salvage the style. It was a little thicker since leaving Lantheus but months of travel had given it an oily feeling she hadn't had since the Expedition. Finally, she took out the pins that were still struggling to hold it in place. She used water and her fingers to rake out the knots and twisted it back up onto her head, pinning it in place.

Her dress was dusty too, and there was a small tear in it from when she fell. Using her hands, she beat most of the dust out of the sweeping skirts and used a leftover pin to pierce the fabric together to hide the hole. Before leaving, she took another look at herself at the mirror. She smiled to herself reassuringly. No matter what else had happened, she was her father's daughter and would survive at any cost.

Taking particular satisfaction at the stunned faces of Ekani and their escort as she exited the room, she swept past them majestically, leaving them to catch up to her. A few moments later, they reached the end of the hall. "Please wait here while I announce you," the escort said and departed through the door.

Sulica rolled her eyes, already bored with the whole affair. Ekani tried giving her advice on how to speak to the Emperor, but she ignored him, picking at her nails. He eventually lapsed into silence, much to her relief.

Their escort still hadn't returned after several minutes, so Sulica began to walk around the enclave, examining the paintings. At some point, they had given way to scenic pictures rather than portraits. One depicted a beautiful blue lizard-like creature with fierce eyes and leathery wings flying in a bright sky, its body winding around and diving through clouds. "Is that-" she asked, trailing off.

"A dragon?" Ekani supplied as he stood beside her. "Yes. There are many who believe what Simtel told you about the Kiarans and the dragons."

Sulica suddenly recalled the burnt body her companions had found years before during the desert training. The memory of the charred bones made her shiver.

"Are you cold?"

"No," she said. She considered telling him about the encounter but decided against it. "Do you believe in dragons?" she asked instead.

"I believe they once existed, but they are long gone." He looked as though he was going to say more, but they were interrupted by the door opening.

"The Emperor will see you now."

-:- -:- -:-

Sulica could hardly believe her luck, standing in front of the mirror in the room she'd come to call hers. Her golden hair was long and shimmery. She felt stronger than she had in months, and her toned body fit smoothly into the clothes she wore, having filled out and toned up in all the places that had been so sickly-looking before.

In the past several weeks, she had been given as much food as she desired, mostly nutritious, and given the freedom to roam half of the palace, including the gardens, the library, and the training field. Never one for the books, most of her time was dedicated to physical conditioning. Her physical abilities came back to her like a long-lost friend, and she soon found herself bored with the solo routine.

Having grown tired of admiring herself, she set about roaming the halls. That was when she ran into Ekani, who had been away on leave for several weeks since he'd been in Lantheus for over a year and finally returned to the palace. Sulica hardly recognized him at first, his already tan skin even darker than before. He was in civilian attire once more, a button-up blue shirt with the sleeves pushed up and black slacks.

"Looks like you had a good vacation," she remarked after greeting him.

He gave her a lopsided grin. "I spent some time on the islands with my father." Then he was all business. "What kind of training have you been doing in my absence?"

She pouted briefly at his short demeanor and gave him a detailed account of her daily workout routine.

Ekani nodded approvingly. "What about your other training?"

Sulica raised her finely shaped eyebrows at him. "Who exactly was supposed to give me that other training while you were gone?"

His face briefly turned red. Wordlessly, he led her to the library. It was a large room with shelves of books lining every single wall and row. Light streamed in through the tall mosaic windows, casting colorful beams all around the room. In the middle was a large mahogany table where several books and scrolls were already laid out as though Ekani had anticipated her answer.

Sulica felt a headache begin to bother her when she looked at the spread. "Why does it have to be books," she groaned.

"There is much to learn from those who preceded us," Ekani lectured.

She rolled her eyes and flopped into the armchair on one side of the table. Ekani raised an eyebrow and picked up a book, tossing it in her lap. She glared at him then looked at the cover. "*The Origin of the Great War*," she read aloud then yawned. "I already had to learn about this in school." She put it on the table and picked up another. "Now this one looks interesting."

Secrets of Spiritual Mystics was in her hands. Then it was Ekani's turn to roll his eyes. "That one was Simtel's idea. I figured you might already know enough about mystics."

"But not all of them, and not how they all work," she said, browsing its pages.

Ekani looked at her thoughtfully. She felt his stare and looked up into his eyes. "What?" she snapped.

"I was just wondering if your abilities would be better if you were able to understand the mechanics behind them."

She shrugged, turning back to the book. "Possibly, but I'd have no way to test it. I haven't even seen another Resarian in so long, I'm not sure I can even still do it at all." She didn't like lying to him, but she was even more curious about his reaction.

Ekani looked alarmed. "The Lantheuns should have stopped before stripping your mystic. But I suppose we'll have to give it a try. Come on." He hurried back out of the library, leaving Sulica to catch up.

He was silent as he made his way through the halls, thinking quickly. There could be no way his first important mission would turn out like this, it was impossible. He felt so foolish for not checking her abilities before they arrived. But, he argued with himself, there hadn't been anyone around to check her against.

After they had traveled across the entire length of the palace, Ekani stopped at a heavy oak door guarded by two of the royal guards. They regarded Ekani suspiciously, but a quick conversation granted him access. He was about to enter when he turned to Sulica. "It's probably best if you wait out here," he said, avoiding her eyes. Without waiting for an answer, he passed through the door.

Sulica opened her mouth to protest, but Ekani was already gone. She didn't care for the disdainful way the guards eyed her, so she moved further back down the hall to wait for Ekani. It was then that she realized she had carried the *Secrets of Spiritual Mystics* with her. Unsure of how long she would be waiting, she sat down against the wall to read.

There are several different types of mystics, ranging from elemental to spiritual in nature. Additionally, there are varying degrees of power within each of the elements.

She skimmed over the rest of the chapter, much of which she had learned during her school days. Skipping ahead, she stopped at a chapter called Light and Dark, two that she hadn't heard of before.

Much of mystic use is based on balance of power. For every fire spirit there is a water spirit. Similarly, when a set of twins is born, they are uniquely gifted with light and dark mystics. Darkness cannot exist without the light, and the light is not light without darkness to compare it to.

Dark mystics can be manifested in a number of ways, but distortion and stealth are among the most common. They are primarily defensive spirits. In order to retain the balance, light mystics are generally offensive, manifesting in the form of solar-based powers such as blinding and light rays. They often have similar effects as fire.

When light and dark are paired, their strength is often unbeatable. However, they are also opposites in every sense. One is blessed by the spirits, while the other is cursed by the Gray.

Sulica leaned back against the wall, pondering the words. "If this is true," she said to herself.

"If what is true?" Ekani asked.

She looked up to see him standing nearby and quickly closed the book. Standing, she saw someone behind him. At first, the woman seemed to be around her own age. A closer glance revealed shadows and faint age lines on her tired face. She was bound in shackles and kept her gaze on the floor.

"Who is that?" Sulica asked.

"A test." He gestured for Sulica to follow him and went back down the hall, past the guarded door. Sulica noticed how the woman pressed herself against the wall as they passed the guards, as though trying to get as far from them as possible.

Ekani led them out of a door to a training field slightly smaller than the one Sulica had been using. It was large but still surrounded by palace walls on all sides. There was only one other exit. There were obstacles on one side of the field and a clearing on the other. Ekani paused in the middle of the clearing and faced Sulica.

"When I say go," he directed, "she's going to attack you. You will do what you need to do in order to stop her." He sent Sulica off to one side of the clearing while he took the woman to the other. Sulica couldn't help but feel like she was back in Sariadne doing combat practice. She saw him say something to the woman. At his words, the woman's head snapped up. Ekani stood a couple paces back and yelled, "Go!" while simultaneously releasing the woman from her chains.

The woman moved faster than Sulica thought possible. She sped toward her like a lightning bolt. Dimly, Sulica realized she should move. Her body barely got out of the way of the first attack. The other woman flashed by her then stopped on a dime and took off just as quickly. Sulica was too stunned by the woman's speed to remember to move. The fist that hit her was full of strength that shouldn't have existed.

Staggering from the blow, Sulica felt the anger in her begin to bubble. When the woman turned for another strike, Sulica sidestepped it and slammed into her with her own fist, but the woman dodged easily, moving with lightning quickness. They danced like that for some time, Sulica always a fraction too slow until finally she screamed in frustration just as the other was coming back for another round. She suddenly slowed as Sulica's scream pierced the air.

Sulica felt her power truly flowing through her for the first time in months. She looked at the other woman and realized with a start that she was Resarian. "Speed and precision," she said aloud.

Apparently the woman had realized what Sulica was and fell to her knees. "You traitor!" she screeched, her voice raspy, which made her sound like the harpies of legend. "Betraying your own kind! Spirits curse you!"

Ekani hurried forward, replacing the shackles. Sulica couldn't tear her eyes away from the tears pouring down the woman's face, couldn't block out the hatred in her voice.

"You liar!" she had turned her screams on Ekani. "You knew what she is and you set me up!" The woman tore at the chains on her hands until her fingers bled.

He grabbed the end of the chain and headed back inside the palace. Sulica followed him silently. The Resarian woman had fallen quiet except for the heaving sobs that wracked her body as they moved through the halls. Sulica didn't wait for Ekani to put the woman back in the room. She kept going down the hall, stopping only to pick up the *Secrets* book where she'd accidentally left it earlier.

She returned to the library, sitting at a window and staring out through the multicolored glass. Ekani's words from her first day in the palace replayed in her mind, "They are housed in the palace for safety." Her hands shook, and she clenched them tightly, pressing her nails into the flesh of her palm.

Someone cleared their throat behind her. "Go away, Ekani," she tried to say, but no sound would come out. Instead, she just kept her eyes riveted to the window.

"I'm sorry," the voice said, "that can't have been easy on you."

She finally turned to see Emperor Vimbultinir standing at the table. There was something she was supposed to do at seeing him, but she couldn't remember, so she continued to sit mutely.

The Emperor was a tall and powerful-looking man, younger than Sulica had expected him to be. His large, entirely gray eyes showed sadness and compassion. He wasn't dressed in the full imperial uniform he'd been in the first time they'd met. Apparently that was only for court days. Instead, he was dressed in simple brown trousers and a white open collar shirt. The clockwork insignia of the Kiaran empire shone on his belt buckle.

Moving closer to her, he spoke again. "Fighting your own is never an easy task."

Her head hung at the kindness in his words. "It never bothered me before," she said, so low he had to strain to hear her. "I was so focused on the end result that it never occurred to me that I was doing anything wrong." Images flashed through her mind of the Lantheun prison, Brisethi's piercing screams as the scientists stripped her spirit away to nothing. Sulica wrapped her arms around herself to fend off the shivers that threatened to overtake her.

"Perhaps what you need is a new focus," he said as though it were the simplest thing in the world. "For three-thousand years the Resarian Dominion has been at war with us, ensuring we never return to our homeland on Sariadne. They continue to practice sorcery and witchcraft against us, melting entire fleets and summoning demons just as their first emperor did at the Dominion's inception. If we continue to fall before them, no one will be able to stop them when they decide to conquer other nations. It's time we ally with the rest of Falajen to throw our deadliest war machines against them. You, my dear, are one of their deadliest war machines. Pahl'Kiar will prevail."

Her eyes narrowed as she stared at the Kiaran Emperor. He did not look at her, though. Vimbultinir's eyes were fixed on the window, but he seemed to be seeing much more than the courtyard below. "It is possible that right and wrong are justifications we use for our actions but have no true bearing on the outcomes of our lives. There are many shades of light and dark, Miss Nin. You would do well to remember that."

Chapter XI

Resarian Emperor of Sariadne, Arquistas Nal Enan, was never one to attend Four-Year Expedition Graduation Ceremonies. He had a continent to maintain and uphold which meant that attending a ceremony approximately every six months was out of the question. But this particular division had completed its expedition with a most honorable Captain, deserving of a commendation medal that had only been given out twice before.

Dominon leader General Riez Satnir, also a man too busy to attend every Expedition Ceremony, had taken the day off to greet the Dominion Officer that willingly halved his life to save another soldier one year ago. Both leaders wore their finest wardrobe and dress uniform. Even Admiral of the Dominion Navy, Sarina Onilak attended this ceremony in her finest uniform dress.

Captain Etyne Vorsen had not been informed that all three of Sariadne's distinguished leaders would be at the ceremony as he confidently called the commands to his division. He about-faced to the crowd of family members and his direct chain of command. He proudly stood alongside his three senior enlisted non-commissioned officers; Master Chief Denil, Sergeant First Class Tevor, and Chief Pyraz. Each of them were sharply dressed in their full formal black uniforms, trimmed in scarlet cording and gold insignia. His decorative rapier hung at his side while his flintlock pistol rested in its holster.

"Attention to the to the Dominion Creed!" Captain Vorsen shouted.

> *The spirit of our land resides in us*
> *through the breath of dragons.*
> *Our fire from the sky scarred the nations.*
> *From the scars of Sariadne, the Dominion was born.*
> *I will defend her from her enemy.*
> *I will die before I commit treason.*
> *I represent the antecedents*
> *who have passed their spirits unto us,*
> *And I will use such spirits to honor our nation,*

never against my brethren.

The words left her mouth like a sacred hymn as Livian pridefully repeated them with her fellow soldiers. The four years in the expedition went by quicker than she thought it would. Her last tedious year spent on the *DSV Reliant* had her contemplating commissioning with the Navy instead of the Army. There was so much more to do, dozens of distractions a day on a ship to keep her mind from wandering on what might have been.

"It takes an enormous amount of courage and mystic power to make the decision to save another spirit by sacrificing your own," General Satnir announced to the gathered crowd. "We train only our most gifted spirits of men and women to do just that in the dire times of need. They are not told that it is their duty to perform Soul Reclamation upon anyone, only that they have the power to do so. And so it is with great honor, on this ninth day of Tretiem, Forty-Three-Twenty-Nine, that I present to Captain Etyne Vorsen, the Medal of Courage, for his spiritual sacrifice," he concluded.

Etyne couldn't figure out why his eyes became watery but was too nervous to care otherwise. He never knew how to act when being recognized, especially with the second highest award that can be given to anyone. He remained at attention as General Satnir pinned the precious gold and white ribbon with a golden eight-pointed star surrounding an engraved ruby heart. He shook the other man's hand and they both saluted one another.

"I have met many fine soldiers and sailors in my six hundred years on Falajen; but I have met only one spirit who halved his corporeal life for another. Captain Etyne Vorsen; I hereby commend you with the Medal of Virtue, for bringing back from the nearly dead, another fine officer," Emperor Arquistas stated, placing the black and blue medal around Etyne's neck where the silhouette of a dragon molded from obsidian hung below.

Etyne was losing his composure at learning he was receiving the highest commendation from the emperor himself. As far as he was concerned, still having his best friend alive was the only reward he needed. The thought that she could have just as easily been dead when he found her haunted his mind and soul as he let the quiet tears fall from his eyes at the Emperor's embrace.

Cheers from the crowd broke out as the division was finally released for liberty. Admiral Tirinnis Sen Asel was quick to approach Captain Vorsen. He embraced the man who saved his daughter's life tightly, letting Etyne continue to lose his poise to grieve for what might have been, and for how his life will quickly come to an end. Naiana had no words either as she kissed Etyne on the cheek as if he were her own son. When Drienna Vorsen finally approached, sobbing at the sight of her brave boy, the Sen Asels offered their gratitude for the noble young son she had raised, and their sympathy for his sacrifice.

-:- -:- -:-

Livian Reej sat alone at her elegant table, waiting for her savory steak dinner. She watched as the rest of her division greeted their parents and siblings, telling tales of their time in expedition training and introducing them to their commanders. She remembered her days as a serving girl to the Dominion military personnel during their graduation, dreaming of being one of them. Now that she finally did graduate, it wasn't nearly as amazing as she once hoped it would be. She had no one to be proud of her accomplishments, no one to impress. Her self-satisfaction dwindled knowing that the four-year expedition was only the beginning.

Chief Pyraz broke away from the clutter of graduates and their families to join Livian at her table. "After dinner I can take you to the administration office and have you enroll into officer training. Is that still what you want to do?"

Livian nodded wordlessly. She was never one to make friends easily, and even worse at keeping them. She obviously couldn't consider the chief her friend, but she was still thankful for her presence, short as it was. Unfortunately, the sympathy that Korteni was attempting to give her was more annoying than it was helpful. She remained quiet in hopes the chief would take the hint.

When Korteni left the table to join her other commanders, Livian returned to picking at the appetizers and observing everyone else. The servers finally presented their meals; the only thing she had waited all evening for. She scarfed down the succulent culinary masterpiece then paused when she heard a familiar score from the symphony. She glanced over at the composer and froze. He was wearing the same white suit he had worn when the the Dominion Triad was their audience ten years ago.

Livian contemplated whether to wait for him to conclude the symphony and approach him, or to pretend she didn't see him and carry on with her life. She reluctantly surrendered to her soul and placed her head into her hands to wait for him.

The symphony concluded as the members began putting away their instruments. Livian's heart pounded when she made her way toward him. *What do I even say to him?* She thought to herself.

Elion turned to face her when he felt her presence. Both were speechless, but Elion was the only one to smile.

Livian's eyes fell on the metal collar around his neck. She knew it was the device that law enforcement used on Resarian criminals to suppress their mystics for as long as the collar was worn. Only three Resarians on all of Sariadne held the key to the collar; the Chief of Police, the Prelate of the Citadel, and the General of the Dominion.

"Um," Livian started, "you're on parole already?"

Elion brought his fingertips to his collar and nodded. "I have seventy years left to serve, but they allow me two evenings a week to continue composing."

Livian crossed her arms. "Did you train a woman named Sulica?"

Elion shrugged. "I trained a blonde woman but did not get her name. Her associate had paid for my services to help her."

"What did you think you needed with extra money? Our rent was paid for by the Dominion, they paid us a comfortable amount to live. Why did you do it?" Livian could ask a dozen more questions but the police officers nearby to take Elion back were encroaching on them.

Elion shrugged. "I no longer desired to be an acolyte, Liv. It's hard work spending a majority of your life meditating to the spirits to be able to train others, you know this. Isn't that why you didn't want to become one yourself?"

Livian was astonished at his indolent ideas. "Most jobs are going to take a lot of our time. You have no idea what I just did for the past four years - four years of no privacy, constant watch, dangerous obstacles, combat training, injuries - this list goes on! And *you* are whining about being an *acolyte*? You're pathetic. And I'm glad you were caught. Enjoy your next seventy years of not working." She quickly stormed off to allow the officers to take him back.

Though her eyes burned and her heart ached for what she once had with him, she finally had answers, such as they were. And with that, maybe a chance at a conclusion, for both of them.

Livian surveyed the administrative room of the citadel, idly chatting with the officer in charge of enrolling the graduates into officer training, re-enlistments, or lifetime reserves. She was fortunate to learn that the officer training would start in one month instead of having to wait six months for the next division to graduate so as to meet the minimum requirement of sixteen officer trainees.

"Navy officer or Army?" The lieutenant junior grade at the desk asked when filling out the paperwork for her.

"Army," she stated, no longer feeling the need of distracting, tedious ship life the Navy would have provided her.

"Do you need quarters now or after your month of leave?"

She didn't want to tell him that she didn't have any other place to go. "Now, please." The belongings she'd acquired during her service to the acolytes had been put in storage near the barracks during her training.

The navy officer opened a second log book to issue her the appropriate room. He handed her a key and wrote down the room number for her. Then he gave her the remaining papers stating her official orders with the time and place for her first day of officer training.

-:- -:- -:-

Etyne strolled through the halls of the Citadel the following morning in search of Major Paush. He knocked on the open door of his superior's office before announcing his presence.

"Vorsen, have a seat," the major ordered. He shuffled through papers on his desk until he found the ones he was looking for. He handed a small stack depicting orders to the half-Kiaran man.

"I'm going to a ship, Sir?" Etyne was confused by his ship detachment orders meant for navy officers.

"Your successful mission from the Lantheun Empire has earned your early promotion. You're needed on the *DSV Rogue* for advanced special forces training. Report to Rear Admiral Taussek after your month of leave," Paush explained.

"Aye, Sir," Etyne replied, feeling bittersweet about his new orders. Advanced special forces training on behalf of the Dominion Navy wasn't a duty that people chose. You were sought out and recommended by your superiors to the generals and admirals to endure the harsh training the officers were put through. The legends surrounding the mysterious ship came back to Etyne. The soldiers and sailors on the *DSV Rogue* were a resilient marine task force trained to undergo impossible missions in foreign lands. The orders were either accepted and the officer succeed, or denied and the selectee pushed into the lifelong reserves. Etyne folded his formidable orders and placed them in a pocket, unsure if he should thank the spirits or curse them.

"Congratulations on your promotion, Major," Paush shook his hand and saluted him. He then handed Etyne a small wooden box containing two collar devices to place on two of his uniforms. They displayed the gold rank insignia of major for the army.

Before returning to his empty apartment downtown, he stopped by his mother's small, stone and wood house for a surprise visit. With no one but herself and her son, Drienna spent Etyne's childhood working long hours to be able to afford their tiny home and the necessities. With Etyne on his own and doing quite well for himself, she no longer had to work as hard. But she still denied Etyne's offer to set her up in a more luxurious place.

"Spirits bless you, Etyne," Drienna embraced her son at her door.

"Hey mami," he hugged her tightly. He stepped back to look at her now that it was daylight and his eyes were empty of tears.

Though four more years had passed, she still had seven centuries left of youthful beauty.

"How long are you in town?" she asked, wiping motherly tears of joy from her cheeks for a second time.

"Only a month," he replied.

"You're getting bigger each time you come home." She patted his muscular shoulders. "I know you're hungry, do you want me to cook your favorite meal?"

"I would love it." Etyne could never turn down her offer of homemade flatbread stuffed with spiced meat and vegetables, layered with cheese and hot sauces. It was a recipe she learned from his father, whom he still had never met.

Now that he had a month to himself, and more than enough money to cover the cost, he asked her, "Mami, do you think you can take me to visit my father?" He put a bag of frakshins on the table.

She pried herself away from her cooking to look up at her son, ignoring the money. "Baby, are you sure you want to risk visiting Pahl'Kiar?"

He nodded. "I have a way with sneaking into places I shouldn't be in. I could hide you, too, if you don't want to risk deception as a non-Resarian."

Drienna considered his words. She began bustling around the small kitchen again. "On second thought, I'll send a message out to him and have him meet us in Pakayan Islands, instead. Would you rather we traveled there?"

Etyne grinned and nodded. "Yes, mami, anywhere is fine."

"When do we leave?" she asked excitedly, finishing the final touches of their lunch.

"I'll find us a ship as soon as we're done eating," he told her, grinning almost childlike at her when she placed his meal before him at the table.

Etyne and Drienna walked along the pier some time later, checking the schedules of departures from Res'Baveth to the Pakayan Islands. He thanked the spirits when one of the transport ships was scheduled to leave in three days. He reserved two seats for them and paid the ship's accountant half of the fare as a deposit.

They stopped at the mail house to have Drienna's letter sent to the secret address that diverted his letters to Etyne's father in Pahl'Kiar. With spirits' fortune on their side, the letter would arrive to him before they landed in Pakaya.

The city's main bell tower struck the twenty-second hour by way of eleven strikes in sets of two by the time Etyne reached the building of his new residence. The candle shop he lived above had filled his place with aromas from each candle. From sethi-pine tree and Mira'Shan blossoms to exotic tropical Pakaya fruit aromas, his apartment always left his clothes and linens with a new, pleasant scent. He picked up the letter the messenger had shoved under his door and finally unpacked the remainder of his expedition bags that he hadn't managed to unpack the night before.

He smiled to himself when the letter was from Division Sixty-Six. He opened it carefully and began to read the familiar terrible handwriting.

Etyne~

> *I regret to inform you that my division is still ninety-nine percent intact unlike yours when you lost, how much was it - nine recruits by year two? No one else has been sent home, nobody wants to leave. They love me too much.*

Etyne chuckled to himself at her boastful words.

> *We're about to board the* DSV Reliant *tomorrow. I hope I don't get tossed off the ship by some salty sailor. If I do, I won't tell you about it - you have more than enough ammunition against me.*

> *In other news, I haven't had a flashback in months. Lieutenant Vazeley and my enlisted commanders have been keeping a keen eye on me; unfortunately they're all terrible at fighting. You've raised my standards much too high as far as combat partners go.*

> *Well, I'll stop boring you with my uneventful division banter, Etyne. I miss you and hopefully I get to see you when I return if they didn't give you another recruit training command.*

> *~'Sethi*

Etyne exhaled loudly, half-regretting that his wistful thoughts of her hadn't yet dissipated. He hadn't seen her in almost a year and figured that if anything was going to happen between them, it would have happened a year or two ago. In all the time they'd spent together -- their initial four-year training expedition, the four years they had spent together in the Citadel, the two weeks in integration, and finally, their recent journey back to Sariadne -- she would have told him if she'd felt the same. Even as he held her vague letter in his hands, he struggled to put aside those feelings once again. The thought that they could ever be more than friends was impractical with his new orders of going out to sea for months at a time. Dominion life wasn't meant for young officers wanting stability; that came later with the higher ranks. Even then, it wasn't guaranteed.

-:- -:- -:-

Drienna Vorsen was giddy with excitement when boarding the civilian transport, *RSS Solstice*. The three day voyage across the ocean was one she hadn't experienced since Etyne was an infant. Drienna excitedly stood at the rail to watch the crew at work readying the transport vessel, just as she had the first time she left Sariadne.

She was the very young age of fifty -three years old when she first set sail to the Pakayan Islands. They were a legal trading ground between Resarians and Kiarans, known for its neutrality. It was there that she had met Etyne's Kiaran father, Jiridian Vorsen, who, at the time, was barely twenty-one.

Her low-income family had taken her with them to the islands to trade goods in hopes of making a decent profit. Jiridian was there on behalf of his noble family business. They had met while both were visiting the beach that summer, speaking to one another in common tongue. Their forbidden love story went on for two years until he could no longer afford to keep paying her way to visit him on the islands. When she told him that she was pregnant with twins, he paid for a final visit in Pakaya and stayed with her there for a year, even married her, to help tend to their infant boys. Jiridian's family had forbidden him to bring his little family to Pahl'Kiar to live among them - even cut him off from their family business. Since his kind was not allowed on Sariadne, they had no choice but to attempt to live together in Pakaya.

The second year was even harder than the first. Jiridian was unable to find steady work, and Drienna grew homesick. She didn't want to raise her babies in the corrupt, touristy, overpopulated islands. They made the dismal agreement to separate the boys, one raised in Res'Baveth with her, while the other was raised in Pahl'Kiar with Jiridian.

She always regretted having to leave, and most especially the heart-wrenching feeling of abandoning both her second son and her husband. She lived with the guilt and sometimes contemplated risking her life to leave Res'Baveth to live out Jiridian's final years with him in his own nation. Especially after Etyne joined the Dominion, she found herself wistfully dreaming of returning to her husband.

After three days at sea, Etyne and Drienna disembarked the *RSS Solstice* and took in the view of the crowded, busy tropical harbor. He carried both of their bags and led them to the resort where they would stay for the two weeks, awaiting his father. It was a modest establishment, fashioned after an ancient temple. Rooms had been built in an open square formation, leaving the middle open as a tropical courtyard pool. Intricate metal bridges crossed above the pool, connecting each floor to each other.

Drienna had been specific in her letter to Jiridian, detailing their temporary residence and the exact time she would remain on the beach each day.

Etyne sipped at the coconut flavored drink at the beach bar, watching the crystal clear waves splash lightly upon the sandy beach. It was their sixth day in the islands and Pahl'Kiar was only a two-day long voyage from Pakaya. Etyne's already tan skin had grown deeper in color as he spent his days swimming and hiking. The water was never very cold around the island. Drienna lay under an umbrella on the beach, reading a book.

A man approached her, causing Etyne to shift nervously in his seat. When he saw his mother stand and embrace the man, who in turn kissed the top of her hand, Etyne stood from the bar and cautiously approached the couple.

Etyne's indigo, long-sleeved airy shirt and beige, long shorts made him blend in with the rest of the islanders as a subtle breeze rippled his clothes. His heart pounded in anxiety, making him dimly wonder if this was the feeling Brisethi felt so often during her panic attacks.

Drienna and the sinewy man broke from their embrace and watched Etyne approach. She gestured for him to hurry with a happy open-mouthed smile spread across her face. She took his hand in hers when he finally reached them.

"Etyne, baby," she softly spoke, "Meet Jiridian Vorsen." Tears shone in her eyes, "Your father."

Etyne stood speechless for a moment, staring at the man before him. They were of similar height and build, but time had not been as kind to the man as it had to his still youthful-looking wife. His eyes were the same color of aqua without pupils as Etyne's. Finally, he summoned the courage to speak. *"Pa'teir,"* his voice nervously cracked with emotion when he spoke the word, father, in Kiaran.

Jiridian placed his rough hands on his son's face, nearly a mirror reflection of his own youth. "My son," Jiridian told him. "You look almost as I did when I was younger, and even bigger than your brother," he smiled. He pulled his Dominion warrior son close to him, embracing him tightly.

Etyne slowly returned his father's embrace before they both stepped back to examine each other more. Jiridian had strands of gray among his long black hair and fine lines on his tan face; an appearance that Resarians wouldn't see until their late seven-hundreds; one that Etyne would never have when he died before the age of four hundred.

"I have a brother?" Etyne said in astonishment after a moment's pause.

Jiridian gave his wife a mocked scolding look then grinned sheepishly. "I guess I have no reason to talk, your brother doesn't know about you either."

They gathered up Drienna's things and walked to the resort to talk in the comfort, to catch up on the thirty-two years of Etyne's Resarian-raised life.

Chapter XII

"Dadi," she softly called his name after a brief salute.

Admiral Sen Asel scooped his daughter up in his strong arms, unable to believe she was standing before his eyes once more. Naiana Sen Asel joined the homecoming, embracing both of her loved ones in her small arms.

Tirinnis still held his daughter tightly, "I read the reports as soon as they came in, 'Sethi, I'm so sorry for everything you had to endure."

They finally broke away from the familial embrace in somber silence. "It was two years ago, Dadi, I'm fine now, please don't be sad," she smiled to reassure both of her parents. Brisethi's expedition ceremony was about to begin the fine dining event in celebration of the graduation.

Brisethi guided her parents to their table then allowed herself a moment to greet the families of her recruits; fully qualified soldiers and sailors. A smile of personal satisfaction and achievement spread across her face at retaining ninety-nine military personnel through graduation. It was a feat that only an estimated one out of every fifty divisions could accomplish. A division had yet to finish at one-hundred percent. *If only that damned Jiken hadn't fucked things up*, she thought bitterly.

"Ma'am," a small voice reached her ears, dissipating her sour thoughts.

She turned and smiled at Sergeant Sherice Talmin. "Is your family here?"

Talmin nodded nervously to her paragon. "Will you come meet them?"

"Of course, lead the way," Brisethi obliged.

Brisethi greeted the young soldier's parents, thanking them for raising an obedient, intelligent and agile spirit. "Your daughter stood out among her fellow soldiers," she ended.

"Captain," a familiar voice beckoned her.

She looked behind her and smiled widely at newly promoted First Sergeant Vilkensen along with his wife and two children. After returning his salute she took his hand in hers. "What a pleasant surprise, how have you been? What brings you to a random ceremony?"

"Sergeant Sherice Talmin is my niece," he grinned with pride, clapping a hand warmly on the young girl's shoulder.

"That explains so much," Brisethi grinned. "She has your tenacity."

Not wanting to spoil the evening by asking about her recovery from Lantheus, he sought out a different topic. "Have you been keeping contact with anyone else from my division? Crommik, Pyraz, Vorsen?"

She nodded. "It's been a year or two but we exchange letters now and then. I was told that Crommik was given orders to assist in the final touches of the *Dreadnought*."

"A deadly spirit for a deadly ship," Vilkinsen added. "Pyraz will most likely be added to the ship's roster with her impeccable hydro-mystics to power the mighty beast. Your division had quite the unique combination of talents."

She sat with him at his family's table to continue Dominion banter and catch up on the nine years since her graduation from recruit training. Despite the opinion she'd had of him during her first year in training, she found deep respect and admiration for him shortly after. She realized that he'd demonstrated more perseverance and strength through their trials than any other commander she'd known, officer or otherwise.

"It's about damn time Division Sixty-Six showed up," rang another familiar voice in her ears.

Her heart skipped a beat from the sound of his voice. She stood immediately to face the man she could always lose herself over. After exchanging a salute, she embraced him, once again disregarding uniform regulations.

Major Etyne Vorsen held her close, despite the strict and severe training he had endured on the *DSV Rogue* the past year that should have screamed for him to release her. "We're just asking for a reprimand," he spoke in her crippled ear.

Brisethi reluctantly pulled away to meet his eyes. "What brings you here, Major?" She polished his already shiny collar device.

"*You* bring me here, of course," he replied as if she didn't know any better. He caught himself lost in the way her dress uniform hugged the curves of her body once more, most of her lower hair grown back and tucked away in a bun behind her head - and her genuine smile, still able to captivate him. He forced himself to greet First Sergeant Vilkinson to pry his eyes off of her.

"Oh my, they awarded you with the Medal of Courage *and* the Medal of Virtue?" she asked, happy that he was commended as she straightened his ribbons. "They gave me the Revenant Commendation Medal for coming back from the dead," she grinned, puffing her chest out.

Etyne smiled as he handled the precious silver dragon silhouette dangling from a blue and gold ribbon on her chest. "I see that and it suits you well."

"Are you stationed here?" Brisethi asked him after they bade a quick farewell to the first sergeant to walk back to her parents' table.

"Yes and no? I'm on a ship, and this is the homeport, but we're out to sea a lot," he sighed.

"On a ship?" she arched a brow.

"I'll tell you about it later," he said. He greeted the Admiral with a salute and her mother with a handshake.

"Mr. Vorsen, again, I can't thank you enough for the courageous act you performed in rescuing my daughter. How can I ever repay you?" Admiral Sen Asel hugged Etyne as if he were his own son the same as he did a year ago.

"If you ever need anything at all, please don't hesitate to ask," Naiana said earnestly, embracing him as well.

Etyne blushed at the familiarity of Brisethi's parents. "I would have done it for anyone, Sir, Ma'am. Knowing it was my best friend that needed me, I'd half my life again to keep her in it," he replied, giving her a genuine smile.

Brisethi's heart ached at his words as she wordlessly placed her hand on his arm. She wished she could give his life back even if it halved hers in the process. They sat down at the table to partake in the fine meal before them, moving the conversation forward onto other things.

"How is the *DSV Rogue* treating you, Vorsen?" Tirinnis asked.

Etyne suspected that the admiral had to have known about the secret missions that the stealth ship was tasked with. He chose his words carefully. "Well, it's definitely a challenge, Sir," he admitted. "We've had three successful missions already, and I'm still considered a trainee." He subconsciously straightened the several medals and ribbons on his dress uniform portraying the number of achievements he'd earned in just the past year.

"I'm so envious," Brisethi told him. "I wonder where my orders are sending me." She then winced, "Ugh, I have a medical examination in the morning to see if I even get orders."

"With any luck they'll deem you unfit for further duty. Then you can finally settle down," her mother lightheartedly said.

Brisethi had to bite her lip lest she allow her rage explode. In her kindest tone of voice she finally replied, "Yes, Mami, let's just disregard all of my hopes and dreams and do what would make *you* happy. Someday, I'll stop being a disappointment to you-"

"'Sethi, that's enough," her father interrupted. "Naiana, stop discouraging her. Let her be happy while she's still young," he said with a chortle.

"And risk almost losing her again? I nearly lost both of you, how can you be so inconsiderate of my feelings?" Naiana replied.

Tirinnis glared at her to quiet her tone and took a rather large gulp of his alcoholic beverage. Brisethi knew that she and her mother were the reason he drank so much and felt a twinge of guilt.

Etyne picked at a stray thread in his uniform to distract himself from the family conflict. It was awkward moments like that which made him almost content that his parents were forced to live separately.

Brisethi stood from the table. "Thanks for coming," she mumbled to her parents. "I'll come visit in a few days," she told them. They ended the night with their farewells. At the last moment, Brisethi threw her arms around her parents again, not wanting to end their reunion on a sour note.

Etyne walked by Brisethi's side toward the Citadel to retrieve her packs from the expedition. He carried the bigger one for her to the carriages. "Are you going downtown? I'll ride with you," he offered.

She nodded and told the carriage driver her address. "How long are you in town, then?"

"I leave in two days," he told her.

"Of course you do," she sighed. There was never enough time for them. She still had no idea of how to repay him for giving up half of his life to her and hoped that by spending more time with him, she could find a way.

The half-hour long ride to their buildings was quiet, the two friends exhausted from their busy day. The carriage halted in front of Brisethi's building as she shuffled around her bag for her key.

"Let's have dinner tomorrow night," he suggested while they stepped out. "Do you remember where I live?"

She nodded with a smile.

"Come over when you're done with your day at the Citadel," he told her and shouldered the bigger of her two packs.

"What if I'm done before noon?" she asked with amusement.

"I'm on leave, I have nothing going on," he replied, walking up the stairs with her to her residence.

"What if I'm not done until hour twenty-three?" she pressed and unlocked her door.

He pursed his lips in thought. "I'd be a bit sad, but I'll stay up."

She let out a small chuckle and saluted him farewell. "See you tomorrow."

-:- -:- -:-

Brisethi answered the usual medical questions to the army officer giving her the examination. After an hour of physical, mental and spiritual evaluations, he wrote her off as fit for duty.

Brisethi grinned widely, thanking him and donned her uniform back on. She ran out of the infirmary and rushed a few halls and stairs up to her superior's office.

She knocked on the door and announced herself.

"Captain Sen Asel," Major Paush smiled to her and removed her file from his drawer. "I take it you passed?"

She smiled and nodded, "Yes, Sir. What have you got for me?"

He handed her the orders that had been assigned to her. "After your report on the people of the Aspion Empire, General Satnir has considered your words and wants you to start training in politics."

Brisethi's smile faded as she looked up from her orders. "Politics, Sir?"

"Diplomacy, peace talks, treaties - how to speak like a dignitary," he reiterated. "You're going to train in the palace for the next three years. Afterward, you'll have earned your next rank and be on your way to Beccilia."

She was uncertain as to why the word 'politics' sounded so grueling to her. The word 'dignitary', however, piqued her interest. This was one step closer to her ambitions of influencing leaders of the world. The sound of palace work sparked her curiosity as well. "Beccilia," she repeated to herself. "Thank you, Sir," she shook his hand after being dismissed for her month of leave.

-:- -:- -:-

"Is that a kitten?" Brisethi barged into Etyne's apartment when he opened the door and immediately dropped beside the tiny black bundle of fur.

Etyne nodded and smiled at her. Her layered, burgundy hair was scented of blossoms. The chestnut-colored long-sleeved coat hugged her form, contrasting her black leather pants. When she looked up at him he diverted his eyes to the kitten. "He needs a home. I spotted him the other day looking for his family and when he was still alone last night, crying in the alley, I took him in, bathed and fed him, but I can't keep him if I'm out to sea more than half the year at a time."

"What's his name?" She cuddled the little kitten.

"I don't know, I didn't ask him," he joked.

"You're so stupid, Et- oh my spirits I love him - I'll take him in." She hadn't found this much happiness in an animal since the days she'd spent with Abyss. "I have orders to stay here for three years, he'll keep me company. My mother can use his company when I go to Beccilia." She tore her eyes away from the little kitten and handed him her orders, proud that she would be spending her days in the palace.

"That's impressive, 'Sethi." He handed the orders back to her after reading them. "I feel sorry for your trainer - having to reform someone like you into a cold-hearted politician," he paused for a moment, "On second thought, you're mostly there."

She stifled a laugh as she placed the kitten back on the ground, "He smells like candles, like your place."

"Why are you smelling him? Is that a thing to do with kittens?" He was overjoyed that she had accepted his request to spend the day with him, especially after spending the past year among mostly males on the *DSV Rogue*. He could never quite find the right balance among both genders to keep him from losing his mind.

"Yes, especially after you told me you washed him. His tiny fur is soft on my nose," she then picked him up to put him against Etyne's face. The kitten let out a high-pitched 'meow'.

He reluctantly nuzzled the kitten with his forehead if only to keep her smiling. "You're so odd. What are you going to name him?"

She pet him one last time before standing. "He looks like an Edewat."

"Ee-de-what?" he arched a brow, earning a stern look from her as if he should know better than to question her.

"Do you have a sandbox for him?" she asked.

Etyne nodded and pointed to the corner. "Take it with you."

"Ohhh, you hung all three of them up?" Brisethi was distracted by her own paintings displayed on his wall. She gleamed that he had kept every one of them she had painted for him.

"Of course - they're a great conversation starter when friends are over," he said. "It's nearly hour thirteen, did you want to pick out dinner down at the market with me or is Edewat going to steal all your attention?"

She chuckled and pulled out the compass watch he had purchased for her two years ago to show him she still treasured it. She checked the time then realized he had just said it. "Of course, let's go."

He guided her to his favorite vendor that sold exotic spices and produce imported from Micinity continent. His mother had passed her recipe of his favorite meal to him so that he could cook it himself for his friends.

The sound of the bell tower reminded Brisethi to ask Etyne a question. "Have you ever tried to eat a clock before?"

"Um, what?" he asked in return, not sure if he heard her correctly.

"It's very time consuming," she replied, trying to hold in her laughter. "Especially when I went back for seconds!"

Etyne resisted the urge to laugh until he caught sight of her grinning face. "Ah, you got me again with the childish joke," he chuckled, shaking his head.

Before purchasing fresh meats, they stopped at various other stores to pass the time and catch up on the last two years, teasing one another, laughing at crude or childish jokes, and comparing their second tours of *DSV Reliant* where Brisethi swears she behaved herself.

Back in his apartment they shared spiced tea and started a game of cards they picked up which was Sariadne's version of Fates of the Enchanted. Brisethi examined each card's artwork before picking a deck she wanted to use against him.

"I met my father last year," he randomly stated while testing his set of dice.

She had been mid-sip of her tea before the shock hit her. "Etyne, that's wonderful. Where? How?"

He recounted to her his adventure with his mother to the Pakayan Islands and the overwhelming emotions he'd felt when meeting him. "I also have a twin brother," he mentioned.

"Spirits, that's amazing! Are you going to meet him?" She asked excitedly.

He shrugged. "I don't know, we're strangers, raised in adversarial lands. I do plan to visit my father at least once a year, though, now that I have his address."

"But...we're forbidden to..." she smiled slyly at him when he brought a finger to his lips in a gesture to keep silent. "On the islands, you mean," she winked.

After a few rounds of their new card game, Etyne made his way to the kitchen to start their dinner. Brisethi followed to help cut up vegetables and continue bantering about the rules of their card games, his secret missions he couldn't reveal to her, and their opinions of the *Dreadnought* still awaiting commission.

Etyne poured a glass of wine for each of them before presenting his culinary specialty to her. She smiled gratefully and cut into the smothered, stuffed flat bread of meats, chopped vegetables, melted cheese and spices. She let it cool down on her fork before taking a bite.

Etyne took a bite from his meal before asking, "Is it good?"

"It's delicious," she declared, shoving another bite into her mouth before continuing. "You realize now this is what I'm going to expect you to cook for me every time you come back to Res'Baveth."

"Not if I visit you first and make you cook me something," he teased.

She shrugged, "I make a fierce chicken dumpling pie."

"Can't wait to have it," he smiled.

Brisethi helped him clean up the dishes when they finished their meal, helping themselves to more wine. He didn't want her to leave and discreetly started packing his bags to ready his next deployment in the morning. When she looked at the time on her compass watch she readied herself to take leave of his home for the night, picking up Edewat in her hands.

"Do you have anywhere to be in the morning?" Etyne asked from his bedroom when he saw her picking up her coat.

She shook her head, "I'm on leave for a month."

"Then you have no reason to rush home now?"

She eyed him suspiciously. "I figured you needed to finish packing and get enough rest."

"Stay with me," he nervously requested, "for my last night in the city."

Her heart and body screamed yes, and her mouth nearly formed the word, but her mind recalled his history with past lovers and her own terrible relationship with Joss. She was terrified of becoming just another temporary thought to him and feared treating him like Joss. She had to force her voice to kindly reject. Her heart would thank her later.

"Etyne," she hesitated from her pounding heart, "We both know this would destroy us...not to mention the Uniform Code of Dominion Regulations forbids us to..."

He arched a brow. "'Sethi we've spent plenty of nights sleeping next to one another and we're very much still best friends," he attempted to dodge her rejection.

Brisethi sighed in relief at his innocent request feeling humiliated for misconstruing his words. She should have known that he couldn't possibly be low enough to care for the type of victim she was. "Cursed spirits, Etyne, the way you worded it made me think..."

He chuckled before she could finish her sentence. "You should know by now that I have too much respect for you to treat you in any other way." He removed his packed bags from his bed when she walked into his room.

She noticed an envelope had fallen to the floor and picked it up. Ordinarily, she would have handed it back to him, but she saw her name on it. She snuck it into her coat pocket before Etyne had turned his attention to her.

She placed Edewat on the bed and proceeded to remove her boots. "I'm scared that you'll crush him," she said through a yawn. She crawled onto his bed and under the blanket where she could discreetly remove her outer clothes. Although her scars were small, they were visible enough that she felt she would forever hide them.

"He'll know when to move," he gave the kitten a soft pat on his head. Letting his day clothes fall to the floor Etyne snuffed out the lantern lights and found his way next to her. "Thanks, 'Sethi," he quietly told her.

"For what?" She cuddled Edewat next to her as she leaned her back against Etyne's. The hyper kitten was not ready to sleep and wondered around the bed instead of staying with her.

For not allowing me to ruin this, he wanted to say. "For your comfort," he instead whispered.

Chapter XIII

Second Lieutenant Livian Reej hastily walked through the library to get to her favorite spot before anyone else could take it. She didn't study often; she had no need to when she could remember most things she cared about. When she did study, she preferred to be on the balcony of the library's second floor. The library was located on the fourth floor of the Citadel, and she often found herself staring out at the view of Res'Baveth more than actual studying.

She frowned, sighing loudly, upon seeing that someone else had taken her seat at the only table. She was about to return inside when the student sitting there called after her.

"There's three other chairs at the table, you know," the female Ensign told her.

Livian knew Ensign Yulana Terrez from her class but rarely spoke to her, or anyone else, during their first year. Reluctantly, she walked over to the table and heavily placed her books down. They sat in silence for the first hour of studying until the fall storm clouds blocked the sun, threatening their comfortable climate.

The Ensign looked up at the gray sky. "I hope it snows already. What's a crisp fall day without snow?"

Livian scowled at her. "Why would you ever wish that upon us? I hate the cold."

Ensign Terrez smirked and lit a small flame in her hand. "I don't have a problem keeping warm."

Livian rolled her eyes at the display. The woman's gray eyes and ability to summon fire reminded her of a certain unstable officer she once knew. Yulana Terrez, however, had shiny black hair that fell in long waves.

Yulana studied Livian's tousled blonde hair before speaking to her again. "You clearly weren't in Division Sixty-Three with me; how did your expedition training go? Anything exciting happen?"

Livian exhaled loudly at the interruption of her attempt to study. "Yes, actually, lots of things. The biggest event being that I took a trip to the Lantheun Empire, saved my incapacitated enlistment officer, watched my captain commit the Soul Reclamation on her, traveled to the Aspion Empire, was nearly killed by the crazed after effects of her stay with the Lantheuns, then boarded the *DSV Sovereign* to return to my usual expedition training onboard the *DSV Reliant*."

Yulana's mouth was halfway open in awe. "You're the one who helped retrieve Captain Sen Asel? She's a fire mystic like me! I've wanted to meet her ever since hearing about what she did during her recruit expedition so that I can ask for exclusive training on how to summon lightning and lava the way she does," she said, the words spilling out excitedly. "The acolytes couldn't get me to learn it," she sadly told her.

"The woman is crazy, I would stay away from her if I were you," Livian reiterated.

"Crazy *gorgeous*, you mean. I only saw her once in passing with that half-Kiaran fellow - oh he was your division captain?" Yulana asked.

Livian nodded. "He's a good person. I don't even notice that he's half-Kiaran anymore."

"What about Sen Asel? Is she nice? Mean? Boring?" Yulana persisted.

Livian sighed. "She's freakish and odd - I wanted to get away from her as soon as possible. Captain Vorsen is my mentor, though, and I'm sure he still keeps in contact with her. I can ask him for an introduction of her for you if you're that interested-"

"Would you really?" Yulana interrupted. Her previous perception of the snobby blonde girl had suddenly changed to one who might just be decent enough to befriend. "I'll buy you dinner for a week if you can make this happen."

Livian was a devout cheapskate when it came to how she spent her money. Saving a hefty amount of frakshins by allowing someone else to purchase her food for a week was something she couldn't pass up. She held her hand out to Yulana. "Make it two weeks and you have yourself a deal."

Yulana shook her hand, smiling.

"If you're a fire mystic, why did you choose Navy instead of Army? You're going to set your own ship on fire," Livian almost smiled when talking.

"I want to see the world and the Navy goes everywhere. You're just going to defend Sariadne for the next nine hundred years, have fun with that," Yulana teased, closing her book to appear more interested in chatting, rather than studying.

Are all fire spirits always so...charming? Livian asked in her head when reminded of Elion and even Captain Sen Asel the first time she met her, before she had allowed her dignity and self-worth become stolen.

-:- -:- -:-

The air felt heavy with anticipation as Sulica silently moved along the street. Her mouth was dry, and her heart thudded so loudly against her chest that she was sure it would be heard. Slowly, she gestured to her team to move forward. Three dark shapes passed her quickly. Two stopped at the door while the other moved further along to ensure their security. The fourth member of her team stayed behind as a rear guard.

The two at the door, Azuda and Neiko, hurried at their task. One oiled the hinges while the other set to work picking the lock. When they were done, the door swung open slowly. They moved inside, crouched low to avoid being seen. Sulica and the other two followed.

Furniture was piled haphazardly all around the room. At the far end, they could see a strip of light streaming out from under the door. The group continued to move slowly, avoiding the obstacles laid out all around. They stacked up on either side of the door. One of her team, she couldn't be sure who, reached out for the knob. Sulica nodded, and suddenly it was thrown open.

The five of them rushed into the room, throwing themselves at any person standing inside. With surprise on their side, they were able to quickly subdue most of the enemy force. On one side of the room, Azuda was struggling to get the best of her target. She finally threw her weight backwards, causing the target to get off balance. Moving fast, she swung up onto his shoulders and dug her knee into his back, pushing his face into the ground.

He came up gasping. "Uncle, uncle!" he yelled.

Sulica strode over to the man and ripped the mask from his head. At seeing who it was, she threw her hands in the air and walked away. "Seriously? Another test?"

Azuda looked down at the unmasked man and quickly jumped off.

Coughing from lack of air and the dirt in his mouth, he rose to his knees slowly. "Sorry," he choked out.

Sulica rolled her eyes while Azuda handed Aderok Simtel her water. "What gives?" she said angrily. "Haven't I proven myself yet? Haven't we shown that we have what it takes?"

Simtel stood slowly and reached halfway around, causing his back to pop. He sighed in relief. "Y'all are going to have some stuff to teach me by the time this ordeal is through," he said, rubbing his neck. His wholly blue eyes met Sulica's as they flashed angrily. Simtel just smiled. "Hey, I'm with you. I don't know how much more my guys can take."

Sulica's team helped the others get to their feet and recover. The two groups left the old shack together, heading back to the palace for the debrief and a bath. Neiko and Potin were yammering away excitedly with some of Simtel's group, reliving the takedown over and over. Sulica's anger continued to build while they walked until it reached a boiling point. Simtel seemed to sense her anger and refrained from speaking directly to her.

When they reached the palace, she let the others go ahead of her. She took a deep breath, clenched her fist, then punched the ground next to the walkway. When she drew her hand away, there was a small crater in the grass. Feeling much better, Sulica followed the others into the palace to the meeting room. Sulica recognized Ekani's figure facing away from the door as she entered. Forcing herself to remain calm, she leaned against the wall while the rest took their chairs. Simtel too, she noticed, remained standing. After a few moments, Ekani turned, holding a large scroll in his hands.

When he looked up, his eyes locked with Sulica's. There were dark shadows under his eyes, as though he hadn't been sleeping. His face was haggard, and she could see the pain in his eyes every time he moved. She felt the rest of her anger fall away into guilt as she studied him. Ekani didn't even seem to acknowledge her presence one way or another after that.

He spread the scroll onto the table in front of him. Two of the group took hold of either side to keep it from rolling together again. "Today," he began in the same steady voice Sulica had awoken to years before, "marks the end of your training." He paused to let the cheers die down.

"I have for you, your first mission. It is not easy."

"We don't do easy!" called out Simtel.

The faintest smile appeared on Ekani's lips. "It is an extraction. The rebellion has continued to tax our already limited resources, but we recently found out they are using kidnapped Resarians to further their cause." He pointed at the spread before him. "This is a warehouse on the eastern side of the city. We believe they are keeping the Resarians here. You will bring back as many as you can, preferably alive."

"What of their mystics?" one of Simtel's team asked.

"You won't have to worry about that," Ekani replied, staring straight at Sulica. She met his gaze, determined not to look away. Ekani broke the contact first, proceeding to lay out the plan of attack and detailing the position of both Simtel's and Sulica's teams. He dismissed them when they were done, making a feeble attempt at a joke regarding how much they all stank.

"Try sitting in a fish house most of the evening and see how good you smell," Simtel grumbled. He and the others filed out of the room, but Sulica hung back to talk to Ekani.

Several moments passed before he noticed her, so absorbed was he in the scroll as he made sure he hadn't left anything out for the mission. Finally, he felt Sulica's eyes on him, and he looked up. seeming not at all surprised to find her still there.

"Are you alright?" she asked, dropping all pretenses.

He sighed heavily and sat down. "It has not been an easy time."

"I'm sorry," she said quietly.

"Don't." His voice was sharper than he intended. Sighing again, he amended, "I'm exhausted, and it's taken a toll on my...spirit." He gave a small chuckle. "It's still so weird to say that." Meeting her eyes again, he continued, "But the moment I discovered it, I felt more whole than I ever have in my entire life."

The genuine smile he gave her tugged at her heartstrings. She ached at hearing the pain and joy in his voice. Not trusting herself to speak, she simply nodded.

Ekani leaned back in the chair and closed his eyes. "You could have been fried, you know. I might have killed you."

"But you didn't," she said playfully.

"Barely."

"You needed to see for yourself. I just had to prove it to you."

"You mean prove me wrong."

"That was a bonus," she laughed. She crossed her arms and leaned against the wall again.

"Thank you."

"For what? Your parents should have told you years ago. Then it wouldn't be so painful."

"If he knew, my father would have. My mother must have assumed that being raised in Pahl'Kiar would prevent my mystic from presenting itself. And it would have if you hadn't read that book."

"You would have figured it out eventually," Sulica said, shifting uncomfortably. She had waited nearly a year before revealing to Ekani what she had learned about light and dark mystics and what Etyne was capable of. Curious to see if it was true, she constantly pressed Ekani to try to summon his mystics.

He had denied it at first, of course, but she did not let up. One day, after a particularly rough combat session, she bitterly told him that his mother had likely given him up to his father because he had no spirit. It was then that Ekani's fury manifested itself in a solar ray that burned so hot and intense that it singed Sulica's hair as it shot toward her while she was walking away. It was only by pure luck and Ekani's complete inaccuracy that she survived.

From then on, they secretly worked together to develop his mystic and strengthen her own, no longer requiring the use of the Resarian captives for her practice. The months of training had improved his accuracy and abilities, but years of disuse made it extremely difficulty for his spirit to regenerate, often taking days for him to recover enough to face Sulica again. The first time it happened, Ekani was unconscious for a full day. Only Sulica's immediate reaction of suppressing him kept him alive. She had stayed by his side the entire time, not daring to leave for fear he'd slip away in her absence. The guilt continued to consume her, and she remained ever watchful for the moment he might push himself too hard in their training.

Sulica watched Ekani's chest move slowly with every breath he took before realizing he'd fallen asleep in the chair. Smiling to herself, she quietly left the room and headed for her own quarters. As she prepared for bed, she racked her memory for anything that could help Ekani's transition. In the cool darkness of the room, Sulica thought about her own realization as a suppressor.

She had been so disgusted with her mystic during pre-Expedition training and again during. Kanilas Trenn had been the one to pry into what the training acolyte told her. When she told him that he asked what her career intentions were, Kanilas was curious. Resarian law enforcement trained with certain unique mystics if the right spirit applied. He realized that, whenever a particular spirit manifested, the acoyltes would work with the law enforcement to train the suppressors amongst them. Despite all his investigation, their identities were always kept classified lest Kiaran intelligence found its way into the city. Quick to seek out his delinquent childhood friends, Kanilas with his silver tongue found a disgraced acolyte willing to guide Sulica into furthering her powers after their graduation.

Her sharp eyes had noticed the hesitation in the acolyte's voice after he searched her spirit upon meeting. "What is it?" she demanded. "You know something."

The acolyte licked his lips nervously. "I really shouldn't-"

Kanilas whispered something in his ear that made the acolyte's skin pale. Taking a deep breath, he told them that Sulica had a mystic that could cause an upset in the scales of balance.

"What is it," she said icily, tired of his stalling.

"It is known as suppression," he answered, eyes on the ground. "The ability to prevent others from using their mystics the way police officers do."

She and Kanilas exchanged a wide-eyed look. "How does it work?" she asked.

The acolyte proceeded to reluctantly instruct Sulica in the use of suppression but warned that it ought to only be used in the most dire of circumstances. She began to practice. It felt good to have some form of offense, even if it was a kind of defense.

The first time she'd used it on another person, Kanilas volunteered. When her spirit reached out to restrict his, she could see the terror in his eyes and reveled in it. Even when she'd used it on Brisethi, Sulica had felt the thrill of being able to render such a powerful spirit useless.

Then Lantheus happened. Even after nearly three years, her senses were still haunted by the horror that befell them there. When she saw the same terror in Ekani's eyes the instant she suppressed him that first time, there was no more thrill. Only sickness.

-:- -:- -:-

Ambassador Milia greeted Captain Sen Asel when she entered his office. He was sitting behind a large solid wooden desk, covered in papers. He had been her exclusive diplomacy trainer for the past year and wanted to put her abilities to the test. "I think you're ready," he grinned.

"Ready for what?" she asked suspiciously and eyeing the lanky, balding man.

"Yes, let's test you. Come," he ordered, ignoring her question and stood. He exited his office with Brisethi at his heels.

"Where are we going?" she asked as they entered a grand corridor of the palace she had never seen before. Again, the Ambassador refused to answer. She followed him up a sweeping staircase and down a final corridor before they approached an ornate, grand set of doors. He knocked on it twice. Brisethi's heart sank when she realized where they were.

"Milia, please tell me this isn't where I think-"

"Shh," he hushed her.

At the sound of a stern voice commanding them to enter, Ambassador Milia pushed open the massive doors and casually walked in, his elaborate layers of robes swishing behind him. Brisethi's heart pounded at seeing the prestigious Emperor of Sariadne and the intimidating General of the Dominion at the end of the room at separate massive desks. A third desk was unoccupied, where the Admiral of the Navy, Admiral Sarina Onilak, normally worked.

"Your Eminence," Milia proudly announced his presence and halted before the two of them. "I present to you, Captain Brisethi Sen Asel, Military Envoy on behalf of the Dominion."

Brisethi was struck with panic and anxiety. She took a step forward, bowed her head, and lost her voice. She looked up at Emperor Arquistas Nal Enan who had stood and walked from behind his desk along with General Riez Satnir.

"Your Eminence," she stammered, "pleased to meet you."

"What the fuck is this, Ambassador?" General Satnir scorned Milia with his deep voice.

"Are you seriously trying to address me right now, Captain?" Emperor Arquistas asked the young, trembling female. He was tall, with long black hair and steely cerulean eyes. She tried not to stare but had never seen him before and fell silent in shock.

General Satnir stood taller than his emperor but had a shaved head and dark brown eyes to accentuate his dark brown skin. He had more girth than the emperor and his arms were as thick as Brisethi's thighs. They were the most reputable, well-dressed men she had ever met, and ten times more fearsome than her father.

She was speechless as the two leaders verbally ripped her apart for her wasted year of training on how to speak to her eminent superiors. She had no words to stand up for herself and she dared not interrupt either of them as she kept her empty stare on the windows behind them. After what seemed like an eternity to Brisethi but was no more than four minutes in reality, the emperor and the general halted their verbal assault.

"We need a strong and powerful representative of the Dominion, not a child!" Arquistas demanded with finality and returned to his desk.

"I asked for a confident officer, not a stammering private! Remove yourself from the presence of the Emperor!" General Satnir shouted.

Once they were through the double doors, Brisethi leaned against the corridor wall, hands trembling. She couldn't help that tears of humiliation were beginning to trickle down her face as her mind replayed the encounter with the two highest ranking men on Sariadne. Had the formidable Admiral Onilak been in attendance, she surely would have fainted.

Milia covered his grin with his hand to keep from laughing. "You handled that only slightly better than my last trainee."

She glared at him through watery eyes. "Why would you do this to me? I wasn't ready, you know I wasn't."

He finally let out his laugh. Despite his mirth, he wasn't mocking her. "How else are you going to build your nerve if not by having those two break you down first?"

"I can't do this," she wiped her face. She wasn't nearly as imposing and influential as she thought she would be.

Milia patted her on the back, speaking as though she were a wounded animal. "'Sethi, they do this to each of my trainees on their first year, it's just an act! Didn't your drill instructors treat you like this in your expedition training?"

She nodded. "Yes, but I was prepared for that, and they weren't the leaders of the Dominion!"

"Then you would know that they're not really this mean; they know who you are and want you to succeed. By this time next year, not only will you have more confidence to greet them, they're not going to bite your head off, either." He smiled to her. "Even if you're still nervous, they will simply correct you."

She placed her hands on her head, massaging her scalp, "I have a headache, now. This stressed me out so much, I can't believe I failed so hard."

He chuckled once more. "It happens to the best of us," he reassured her.

Brisethi had been relieved for the rest of the day to let her clear her mind of frustration and humiliation. Thinking fresh air might do some good, she left the Citadel as quickly as she could. She hadn't seen the harbor in months and took the opportunity to visit it before the threatening gloomy clouds brought a snow storm upon the city. Though, she wasn't a sailor, she admired the warships so long as she didn't have to live on one.

The chilly air helped her push the awful encounter to the back of her mind. She strolled through the harbor, watching the flags wave from the masts and the sailors and civilians milling around the docks. Her eyes caught sight of a small, stealthy frigate in port. "Pardon me, how long has the *DSV Rogue* been here?" She asked a passing shipyard worker.

"She's been here at least three months, Ma'am; dry-docked for maintenance and repairs when she took damage from a Kiaran warship," the kind man replied.

"She was attacked?" Her heart sunk in fear.

"Aye, but the injuries were minimal. Whole crew is alive and accounted for," he said, hurrying to soothe her obvious fears.

Fear turned to worry as it consumed her spirit to know that Etyne hadn't contacted her when his ship had been dry-docked for the past few months. Her mind ran through all the possibilities, and she wondered if he was simply billeted to another ship the moment they docked.

Without even bothering to stop by her home to change out of her uniform, she rushed over to his building, hoping to the spirits that he wasn't home. She climbed the stairs to the second floor, walked to his apartment door, and lightly knocked. The familiar smell of scented candles from the shop below flashed memories of her last visit to him. *He better not be home*, she thought while her heart pounded as fiercely as it had earlier that day in the presence of the Dominion leaders.

His door opened and there he stood, almost surprised to see her. "Sethi, hey," he stammered. His chest was bare, and she could see faint scar lines criss-crossing his torso that hadn't been there the last she'd seen him.

Brisethi resisted the urge to throw her arms around him. "How long have you been home?" she innocently asked, her relief mixing with the crushed sensation that he didn't tell her.

Etyne invited her in, knowing this was going to be a complicated discussion. He found a shirt to wear before continuing. "Since Sessjemir," he hesitated.

"For three months," she whispered. "Were you not allowed to see me or something? I know it's been a year, but we're still close, aren't we?" Her eyes searched his for the answer.

"Sethi, I need you to understand something," he started in the kindest voice he could portray, breaking the gaze, "if I had seen you the first night I arrived as I initially planned, you would have been the *only* person I would have seen for the past three months. We are inseparable when we're together, which isn't a bad thing, but it's not in the way I'm in need of right now." He chose his next words carefully while returning his eyes upon hers. "Sethi, I've been on a ship with mostly men for close to nine months; and before that, it was another eight months and before that, I was on an expedition for four years!"

Etyne looked down at his hands, unable to face her as he said, "One of my comrades introduced me to his sister's friend when we arrived and - well do you get what I am saying or shall I elaborate?" He tried to grin to turn it into a joke but could already feel the anxiety coming from his friend.

"I...get it," Brisethi quietly said. She realized that she was holding him back again, just like their time in officer training. However, she was dismayed that he no longer thought of her in the way his unsent letter had portrayed. Her heart thudded painfully, her face flushed and her ears hissed at the thought that he had found somebody else to take her place so easily.

"What about me, Etyne...?" Her voice trailed off as she lost her courage to ask him in more detail when a lump in her throat formed.

"I was going to come visit you the week before I left, after I visit my father next month," he said, stumbling for words. Mentally, he began kicking himself, knowing that she would have eventually seen his ship in port and at some point the conversation had to happen. "I know it sounds selfish, but-"

"No, Etyne, I mean, what about *me*?" she softly asked and placed a hand on her chest. "Do you feel nothing for me in that way? Have I become repulsive to you?" she asked, not wanting to let the tears fall again for a second time that day.

He swallowed the guilt of shunning her from his life for the past three months to be with someone else. "Sethi, I once asked you, a year ago, to stay with me for a night - I wanted something *more* with you. But you rejected me, even attempted to state an article of the UCDR - which, by the way, only applies to personnel in the same immediate command. Regardless, I shrugged it off by saying that I meant it as friends. Do you think I really shrugged it off, though?" He raked his fingers through his hair out of frustration. "Do you *know* how difficult every single night that you have ever slept in my bed at the Citadel, or in a faraway resort, or by my side on the top of a river boat; and most especially, in my bed the last time we saw each other - can you even *begin* to know the pain that has been for me?"

Hearing it so evident in his voice broke her resolve, and the tears fell from her eyes. "Etyne, I was *frightened!*," she declared, stamping her foot. "Every woman I have known of you to be with - Marinelle, Kara, Serythe - you've let those relationships just die! You don't even remember their names, they mean nothing to you! I didn't want to mean *nothing* to you!" Her voice had grown progressively louder as she spoke until she was shouting.

Etyne remained silent, shocked that she had felt this way, that she was screaming at him from her own frustrations. He wanted to avoid her eyes full of sorrow and anger, but could only stare at the very paintings she created hung on the wall behind her. It was as if they were both caught in the chaos of her destruction. In an act of desperation, he considered bringing up the way she treated Joss for most of her life. He wanted to mention to her that he didn't want what they had. But he feared it would only prolong this misapprehension of one another, that firing back with her dreadful past was not the civil way to save their suddenly fragile friendship.

"How could you possibly think that I would want to be just another fling to you?" she asked, her voice quiet and breaking. She didn't want to look at him anymore. She stormed out of his apartment and slammed his door. She never meant to be dramatic, but fire was meant to be destructive and the only way her spirit knew to move.

I could never regard you as a fling, Sethi, you will always mean the world to me, he thought, wishing he'd had the chance to say it to her. Etyne fell heavily on his couch, considering the events that had just unfolded. Brisethi's rage was a fire he couldn't easily extinguish this time. She needed to fizzle out on her own to think about their misinterpreted treatment of one another.

The words she'd yelled had struck a chord in him, and he felt the despair at her perception of how he treated the women from his past - that he couldn't take a relationship serious. He never thought to let her know that one of them made him choose between her and Brisethi or that he had chosen his best friend over continuing a relationship with Serythe.

If he'd known how she thought of him, maybe he could have approached her better the year before. Etyne cursed himself for pushing Brisethi away and feared she might never open back up to him. He was profoundly confused at what cataclysm could possibly be raging in her mind. All he wanted at that moment, was for her to come back, forgive him, and allow him to finally tell her what he'd kept to himself for years. He didn't want to go another year of not seeing her without her knowing.

She ran through dark alleyways to take a shortcut to the city's botanic gardens. The leaves of the trees were shedding hues of orange and yellow leaves as large flakes of snow crashed into each of them. Now that she was out in public, and in uniform, she forced herself to regain her composure and found a cold stone bench, dusting away the freshly fallen snowflakes. She took a deep breath and removed the letter she had carried with her every day from her uniform coat pocket. It was the letter she had stolen from Etyne the last time she saw him.

It was dated a year after their two-week long integration, the month she had been taken to Lantheus. She read his words one last time.

Sethi~

Could you possibly be any more cryptic in your next letter? I tease, of course. I'm at a loss on how to respond to your recent message, however. I only hope I'm not misconstruing any of your words. I can't promise that in two years we'll still have this mutual blissful feeling of one another, but seeing your face, your smile, hearing your laugh; it all stirs up emotions I try very hard to suppress. They are feelings and emotions that I can't even write out, but would rather tell you in person. I suppose we'll find out when we see each other in a couple of years if what we had was real. Spirits guide you a safe expedition, Sethi.

~Etyne

How could she assume that he still thought of her that way after all those years? After finding her rotting away in a disgusting environment? *I...misconceived my place in your life,* she thought. But it was time for her to move on, just as he had. She had two years left in diplomacy training until they shipped her over to the Aspion Empire. Her tour there would bring new friends, new adventures, and new duties to bring her one step closer to her life's ambition.

With finality, she conjured a scarlet flame and incinerated Etyne's letter, his lost feelings of her, into ash.

Chapter XIV

When she fit the last small sack of candies and treats into her bag full of books and small toys, Livian Reej rushed out of her quarters, along the hall, down a flight of stairs, and out of the double doors of the Citadel. She hastily walked to the carriage where Yulana Terrez patiently waited for her classmate.

"Did you grab all of the pastries and cookies?" Livan asked while piling their bags inside.

"Yes, I even resisted the urge to eat one!" Yulana told her, climbing into the carriage and sitting across from her. She rubbed her arm through her overcoat to warm up.

"They smell delicious. The kids are going to love them! I'm so glad the rest of the class helped out with this," Livian said with the slightest hint of excitement in her voice.

"Oh hey look, it's snowing," Yulana placed her head against the carriage's window to get a better view.

Livian groaned at Yulana's dismal weather forecast.

"Of all the days to snow, this is the perfect holiday for it, lighten up!" Yulana playfully chided her friend. Yulana smiled at her when she glanced in her direction. Ensign Yulana Terrez had spent the first half of this special day with her parents and brother on the outskirts of Res'Baveth. She promised to spend the second half of the day with Livian. Yulana had spent every other one of her off days with the introverted, carefully self-guarded woman since befriending her the year before.

The two Dominion officer trainees unloaded their goods from the carriage when it arrived at their destination; Res'Baveth's orphanage. Although the two had frequented the orphanage on a monthly basis, today was a particularly important for the people of Sariadne: the celebration of winter solstice. Winter festivities were held in various districts of the city while families and loved ones partook in gift exchanges in thanks to the spirits of the northern skies for their gift of extended life and mystics.

The home had been rebuilt a few streets away from the original. It was three stories tall, even larger than its predecessor. The first time Livian saw it, she feared the enlargement was because there were more orphans than before, but she was pleased to learn that the donor had requested more and larger play areas for the city's lost children. On that day, the home's windows were decorated with paper leaves and snowflakes - products from Livian and Yulana's visit the month before.

The two young women hurried up the steps. "Happy Solstice Day, kids!" Yulana shouted when they barged through the door of the orphanage with bags full of gifts.

Seven anxious children screamed in delight and ran to greet the familiar officers with joyful hugs. Caretaker Melyca greeted the two recurring guests, thanking them for lifting the spirits of the children's home on the familial holiday.

Livian began handing out the festively wrapped bundles to each of the seven children. Her spirits lifted at seeing that the amount of homeless children had dwindled in the recent years as more adults adopted and the war seemed to stall procreation for the time being. She knelt down when she handed the final gift to the half-Kiaran girl of only age six. Her big green eyes without pupils revealed the smile hidden behind her gift.

"Thank you, Liv," the little girl politely told her as she began unwrapping it. Her face was bright with joy at unveiling a stuffed animal in the form of a puppy, much like the one Livian had when she was a child. Around its neck was Yulana's Dominion Navy issued neckerchief to add their personal touch to it.

"Do you like him?" Livian asked. Seneca was one of her favorite children, not only because she was more intelligent than the others, but she was also the most well-behaved. She was also concerned that the little half-Kiaran would struggle as the outcast among the group once they were old enough to realize her physical differences. Not every Resarian accepted half-Kiarans in their society as her mentor, Major Vorsen, had to find out through his young life. And growing up without a family was difficult enough.

"I love him, Liv, what shall I name him?" Seneca asked, hugging both the plush and Livian.

Livian looked over at Yulana then back down at the little girl, pushing her dark thoughts aside. "Well since he's kind of a sailor with that neckerchief, the Kiaran word for 'Ensign' is *Valku*. Just a suggestion." She patted the plush.

"*Valku*," Seneca repeated decidedly..

The door to the orphanage opened when Livian's and Yulana's instructor, Lieutenant Maclout along with a fellow Citadel instructor, Commander Sooza, walked in loaded down with trays of hot food.

"Spirits bless you all for taking the time out of your special day to be with us," Melyca spoke through joyful tears. She assisted the two new guests in setting up the dinner table, dodging excited children running around with their new toys.

"It's the least we can do," Yulana replied. "It takes an even bigger heart, though, for someone in your position to care for those who have no one else."

Livian's heart ached at the thought of her own caretaker who had been lost in the fire. She was the closest thing she had to a mother. Having nobody else genuinely care for her throughout her young life made it easy for Livian to treat others with disregard. And when those she had been remotely close to had befriended her, they were quick to abandon her. Livian's outlook on life wasn't a pleasant one. At least, it wasn't until the day Yulana pushed her way into her life a year ago. But just as the other temporary friends had come and gone, so too, would Yulana once they completed officer training in two years. Shaking her head, she pushed out the dark thoughts, reveling in the happiness around her.

After the small feast had ended, officers helped the caretaker bundle the children up for outdoor festivities. The botanic gardens was their district's festival venue for the day as they walked the few blocks through the snow. The gardens were filled with colorful stringed lanterns, festive decorations, fire pits and vendors selling warm beverages to the patrons. Snowball competitions and ice sculptures were set up throughout the labyrinth of naked trees. The constant snowfall enhanced the feeling of the celebrated shortest day of the year for Res'Baveth.

Livian shivered when a small breeze broke through her thick, uniform coat. With her fiery mystic, Yulana warmed the air around them while they walked away from the crowds and the musical band to find the other ice sculptures scattered about the garden. It was only the sixteenth hour of the day when the light behind the clouds began to diminish, enhancing the vibrant colors of the lanterns all around.

"This is definitely my favorite holiday," Yulana stated, captivated by the ice sculpture carved into an ancient ship.

Livian scoffed. "I prefer summer solstice. The sand castle building and surfing competition is more to my liking," she explained.

"You just like staring at all of the shirtless men," Yulana teased, brushing aside strands of her black hair that fell in her face.

"When have you ever known me to care about a man's physique?" Livian asked.

Yulana rolled her eyes, once again confused by Livian's cryptic retort. Shrugging at Livian's last question, she removed a small satchel from her coat pocket and handed it to Livian.

Livian held the satchel in her hand. "Your gift is in my room, I didn't want to shove it in my pocket. I got you a card game that you can take on your sea deployments that resembles the one I found in Essenar."

"Oh, with the fancy dice?" Yulana asked excitedly.

"Yes," Livian smiled. There were times that Yulana reminded Livian of Chief Korteni Pyraz more so than Captain Sen Asel. She turned the satchel upside down as a brass pendant of an anchor embedded with a single gemstone fell into her hand. "'Lana it's beautiful," she finally told her, removing the pendant from her current necklace to replace it with her new one. She gave her friend a hug in thanks for the gift.

Yulana wrapped her warm arms tightly around her shivering friend. "I figured you won't forget me as fast when I'm out to sea if you have a constant reminder around your neck," Yulana told her.

Livian reluctantly pried herself away from Yulana's warm embrace. "I won't forget my only friend that easily."

"What about that Pyraz girl you told me about? Or your mentor? Are they not your friends?" Yulana asked.

Livian shrugged. "I haven't heard from Pyraz since the expedition ceremony and Major Vorsen is only that; my mentor. Which, by the way, he finally replied to my letter about you wanting to meet his friend. He told me that he's not exactly on speaking terms at the moment with Sen Asel."

"Oh no, did they break up?" Yulana asked.

"I don't know, I didn't ask. I don't think they were actually ever lovers - they're both sticklers about the Uniform Code of Dominion Regulations," Livian replied. "Regardless, I've grown accustomed to being without friends. As much as I enjoy our time outside of class, I know we'll go our separate ways in a few years." She braced herself against the wave of sadness.

Yulana frowned. "Well, yes, because the Dominion will send me to a ship. That doesn't mean our friendship has to end-"

"It does and it will," Livian retorted.

"You're still bitter after all these years, aren't you?" Yulana asked in regards to Livian's vague backstory.

Livian sighed. "I really need to stop telling people about that-"

"It's a good thing to let it out, Liv. As painful of a reminder that it is, you will eventually be able to tell your story without watery eyes," Yulana said. "I'm not telling you to move on, but I am telling you not to judge others by what one man did to you."

"It's not you that I'm afraid of, Yulana. I do like you, in a lustful sort of way," Livian admitted. "But I just don't have the energy and love to give to anyone. I'm afraid of hurting you."

Yulana tightly held Livian's hands and met her cerulean eyes, contemplating heavily on how to respond. Part of her wanted to confess that she only wanted something physical as well, while the other part of her hesitated for multiple reasons, one of them being the UCDR. Because of Livian's reticent nature, Yulana had been unable to fully interpret any of her words or gestures. Summoning her courage, Yulana placed her warm hand on Livian's cold face and replied with a pounding heart, "Liv, I don't need your love. And if ever you do have some spare energy, well you know where I live."

Livian closed her eyes and welcomed the warmth Yulana's hand. Within seconds, Yulana felt Livian's lips press upon her own.

Chapter XV

The *DSV Rogue* remained dozens of miles south of the Pahl'Kiar, hidden among the marshy islands under the distortion shields of Etyne and three other similarly gifted Resarians until Etyne and his select group boarded a smaller vessel.

Etyne remained crouched at the bow of the watercraft, observing the murky swamp. Willow trees and vines crowded over in a canopy, blocking anything left of daylight. He felt the nudge of Lieutenant Brannod Cullin.

"The last letter my sister wrote said that you hadn't written to Balia. Was she not your type?" Cullin asked in a quiet tone of voice.

Etyne sighed. "This probably isn't the time or place for discussion," he said, glancing briefly at his task group.

"Ah, come on, Majah, we can use some light bantah while Gerad here *slowly* rows us ta shore," replied their newest officer of the *DSV Rogue*, First Lieutenant Jenibel Teer. The crew had been relieved that they took on two females at their last homeport, lifting the spirits of the old crew.

"I very much do not need to be a part of ship gossip," Etyne replied sternly.

"Too late fa' that, in'it?" Teer muttered, nudging Lieutenant Junior Grade Quttel. He stayed reserved of her quirkiness.

Etyne swiftly turned to scorn Gerad. "Would you row faster, Sergeant?"

"Ey, we've no idea wot could be lurkin' in t'is swamp. 'Ave *you* ever been 'ere, Sir?" Sergeant First Class Gerad replied, scratching the red hairs of his chin.

Captain Deseria Holt sat up from her relaxed position at the aft of the boat, brushing aside several braids of her hair, black as her eyes. "Gerad, honey, don't take any of the Major's sass. If your little arms are tired I can take over for you - let mama show you how to row a watercraft full of strong Dominion soldiers and sailors," she pridefully told him.

The rest of the crew struggled to stifle their laughter.

"Right, right, let's all pick on the only enlisted person on the boat!" Gerad replied.

"Ahem," the mostly silent Master Chief Perrit coughed, reminding Gerad that he wasn't alone.

"Aside from you, 'course, Mast' Chief," he quickly amended.

"So, Balia is a no?" Lieutenant Cullin pressed on, raking his blonde hair.

Etyne crossed his arms in disbelief that these were the finest, most tactical Dominion personnel in all of Sariadne and glared at his gloomy surroundings. "There's someone else," he reluctantly admitted. Perhaps it was the swamp that changed his mood, or the amount of time he had spent with the six men and women of his task group, that had shifted his mindset to consider them his companions. Everyone on the *Rogue* knew everyone's personal life, such was the life of a small ship's crew.

"Ooooh, do go on, Seh," Teer added, grinning widely at her commander.

"There's not much else to say; I lost my chance with her," Etyne somberly replied, surprised at himself for opening up to his crew.

Teer itched at her ash blonde hair, twisted on either side of her head until it met in the bun behind her. "I'd say the usual, 'ah, she'll come around', but given we're out here for spirits know how long, she'll more 'n likely move on," she said with a chuckle, earning a scowl in return.

"Thank you, Teer, that's very encouraging and I'm so glad you're here to boost our morale," Etyne sarcastically replied.

"I do wot I can, Seh," she winked. "B'sides, you're so brash 'n serious oll the time, she'll surely find someone t' make 'er laugh."

"You're not talkin' 'bout wot's her name ah you?" Gerad asked, halting his rowing.

Etyne remained silent while Lieutenant Cullin nodded his head in answer to his question.

"Who is she?" Teer whispered to Gerad, making no real effort to keep her voice low.

"Dammit, girl, you know you ain't gotta chance with our commander, you tryn'a get him in trouble?" Holt shook her head disapprovingly.

"Roight, she's a beau'iful Cap'n 'o works at t'e palace wit 'air as fierce as gahnet. She wos in my div'sion in exped'tion trainin' wit t'e Majah 'ere," Gerad replied.

"Wot did he jus' say?" Teer asked.

"Boy, was that even Resarian you were speaking?" Holt teased his deep, inner city accent.

After relentless whispered banter, the crew made it to shore, trudging along the mud and marshes of the humid area. Birds chirped among themselves and geckos sped out of the path as the seven Dominion Special Forces members made their way out of the swamp and into arid desert. Night fell upon them as they raced against time to rush into the city to rescue the captive Resarian.

"Quttel, do you sense anyone?" Etyne asked to the healer of their group.

Lieutenant Junior Grade Quttel inhaled sharply, scanning their vicinity of Pahl'Kiar for any hint of a Resarian spirit. "There are two about a half a mile northeast," he quietly replied.

"Sounds like our captive and a suppressor," Cullin whispered.

Etyne nodded. "Head in, I'll go clear the way," he ordered.

In less than a minute, Etyne was in a dilapidated building of a bandit crew, led by none other than a Resarian man with suppressing mystics. Seventeen bandits jumped to their feet when Etyne appeared behind the suppressor, throwing him face first into the ground. He held both wrists of the man under his knees while his dagger was firmly pressed against the side of his neck.

"I thought I felt another spirit, but you were too quick for me to suppress," the leader calmly spoke.

"Release the girl and I may consider sparing your life," Etyne stated.

"Your Dominion words mean nothing to me. Kill me, and my men will end you and still have the girl," the suppressor replied, struggling to breath under Etyne's weight.

Etyne only needed to stall three more minutes for the rest of his task group to show up. Killing the suppressor would endanger the girl's life. Etyne glanced at the young girl, locked in a cage meant for animals. She was younger than he expected; a girl of not yet ten winters. Her poofy, black hair, dark brown skin, and angled features bore a striking resemblance to to Captain Holt. Her round, chestnut eyes stared at Etyne, a mixture of hope and fear.

"Killing you will allow the girl and me to release our mystics on your crew," Etyne calmly replied, certain the young girl hadn't yet learned to summon mystics.

The suppressor laughed, "Do you even know what her mystic is?"

"Do you know what I can do *without* mystics?" Etyne retorted and, at hearing the rapid footsteps of someone in the alleyway, he cut the man's throat and quickly vanished.

Etyne appeared in front of the girl's cage and summoned his shield mystic around them both just before the remaining men opened fire on them.

Holt was the first to enter the building, releasing her precision mystic as she rapidly pulled several sharp metal arrowheads from a satchel, aiming them at the center of the group of men. Each arrowhead, under her guidance, found its target in the eyes of each adversary, crippling and bringing them to the ground in shock and pain. Etyne took on the other five men, distracting them until the rest of his crew arrived to finish everyone that was willing to fight.

Etyne wiped blood off of his face and walked toward the two women tending to their recovered Resarian. He watched as Holt held the little girl closely, kissing her forehead.

"I thought I'd never see you again, baby," she choked out the words, stroking the girl's hair to comfort her.

"She's your daughter?" Etyne asked, crouching down next to the reunion.

She wiped the joyful tears from her face and nodded. "She was taken away from her home four weeks ago by her own damn cousin."

The rest of the task group stood in triumphant silence, awaiting Etyne's order. "Let's head out before the Kiaran guards decide to pay a visit to investigate the commotion we just caused," he ordered.

-:- -:- -:-

The morning sun broke through the scattered clouds, shining upon the weary Dominion Task Group. Gerad took hold of the oars and summoned his energy rejuvination mystic to power them all back to the ship. Captain Holt sat with her daughter, praying once again to the spirits for their successful mission. She could feel the members of the crew glancing at her, wondering how and why her daughter ended up in the Pahl'Kiar.

"You don't have to tell us all, not now, anyway" Gerad broke the silence first. "Wot's her name?"

"This here is Ulara," Holt replied. "And like very few of our kind, she discovered her use of mystics just last year, sparking a lucrative opportunity for my greedy good-for-nothing nephew. According to my husband's letter, my nephew abducted her and sold her to the Kiarans."

The crew remained oddly silent. Etyne walked from the bow of the watercraft to the aft where they sat. He knelt down in front of them. "May I ask what her mystic is? The leader of the group we vanquished led me to believe she wasn't a destructive spirit."

Ulara looked up at her mother when the Major spoke. "Go on, honey, show my boss what you can do. We're a little curious of his mind," she chuckled.

"What?" Etyne arched a brow at her last sentence. He looked down when Ulara held her hand out to him. With skepticism, he took her hand in his, waiting for something to happen.

The girl's slight frame swayed slightly. "You're sad," Ulara stated with total innocence. "You broke each other's hearts before even giving them to one another. You have never been sure of anyone in your past but you were so certain of her-"

Etyne withdrew his hand from hers. "You're a confessor," he smiled, trying to stay polite to the little girl despite his unnerved spirit.

Ulara nodded.

"Major Vorsen is heartbroken," laughed Lieutenant Brannod Cullin as the others joined in on the laughter. "Was that really the only thing going on that little head of his?"

"No, but it's the strongest emotion in him - that's how confessors work. They read what someone is trying to hide from everyone else," Ulara's mother replied. "Kiarans pay well for suppressors and confessors; any spirit that isn't destructive, really."

"Thanks for the trap, Holt," Etyne said snidely to Deseria and made his way back to the bow of the boat.

"And thank you, Sir, for leading us," she winked to him.

The *DSV Rogue* returned to Res'Baveth for only three days for replenishment and the safe return of Ulara Holt to her father. At the break's conclusion, they returned to the vessel for their next mission.

Rear Admiral Taussek ended his dismal lecture of what his crew of twenty-nine sailors and soldiers would expect for the next two years. They would not return to port, or any other port, until their two-year mission was complete.

"So did you tell her?" Lieutenant Cullin nudged Etyne as the crew was leaving the briefing.

"She wasn't home," he replied shortly, not wanting to discuss his life at the moment.

"You leave her a message at least?" Cullin prodded again.

"No, I didn't have one written out for her. Some things are just better left to die out so new things can thrive - like plants that break through igneous rock and flourish," Etyne retorted.

"Igneous is bliss, eh? Maybe these next two years will break you and the rest of us. We'll all come back as new men!" Cullin exclaimed.

"Speak fa' ya'self" Teer added. "I plan t' remain a woman."

"Are you sure you were a woman to begin with?" Cullin teased.

"Are ya tryin' to get me to show ya my knocka's? Is that the only way ya can get a woman to let ya look at her? Or are ya trying to see if I have bigger balls than ya?" she crudely replied.

"Shut up, all of you," Holt calmly told them. "We're here."

The crew of the *DSV Rogue* rushed onto the top deck to have a look at their home for the next two years. Most of Falajen dismissed the idea that the continent even existed. Legends told of men and women stepping foot into the Gray and never returning. And now, Etyne, along with his task group, would have to survive the next two years without the comfort of resources and home.

-:- -:- -:-

Ambassador Milia Kon sat at the small table for two outside the cafe, waiting for his trainee. He found it odd that for the first time, Captain Brisethi Sen Asel was running late. Her favorite pastry he had ordered for her was cooling off as he frowned upon his pocket watch once more.

"Milia, sorry I'm late," Brisethi announced, taking her seat across from him.

"Is everything going well for you, 'Sethi? I was growing worried when you weren't here fifteen minutes before the hour as you usually are," he chuckled at her incessant military-trained punctuality.

"I had the strangest encounter. I was well on my way here thirty minutes ago. I took out my compass watch to see if I had time to stop by the harbor - something I do every now and then - and my clumsy hands dropped my precious compass watch when I missed my pocket!," she dramatically explained.

"No! How could you! That device means the world to you!" Milia added, conceding to Brisethi's flair for drama.

"It gets worse - it rolled off the bridge and into the river!" she winced, placing her hands on her head in dismay.

"'Sethi, noooo!" Milia shared her sadness.

"I ripped my uniform coat off, getting ready to dive into the river when out of nowhere, this little girl comes up to me and says, 'I'll get it for you, Ma'am.' She was the sweetest little thing, two poofs of black hair on the top of her head," Brisethi explained, taking a bite of her pastry before it went stale. She quickly ordered her favorite hot beverage of choice to the server then continued her story. "She was already playing with her friends in the river so it didn't bother her to dive back in and retrieve my compass watch. Upon handing it to me, however, she held my hand for a moment and said,

'I've seen you before.' I smiled and told her she mostly likely has because I'm usually running around the market looking for specific ingredients every time I make dinner for you and Sycris.

"Anyway, she then says to me, 'No, Ma'am, I've seen you in someone else's mind. You're 'Sethi.' Upon hearing her say such spine-chilling words, I ask her, 'Who are you? What do you mean?'" Brisethi took a break to sip at the sweetened spiced tea the server had delivered.

"'Sethi hurry, tell me, I'm very intrigued!" Milia excitedly replied, genuinely interested.

"The girl then says, 'I am Ulara Holt. The man who helped my mama to rescue me in Pahl'Kiar let me read his mind. And you were in it.' And of course, I am standing there still holding both of her hands in both of my hands, stunned, taken aback, all of those synonyms, Milia, my spine shivered!" Brisethi took another sip of her tea.

"You met a confessor!" Milia added. "They're about as rare as suppressors. Whose mind did she read?"

"She wouldn't tell me the name, because of her promise to her mother that she wouldn't use her mystics for such gossip but I know who it was, who else rescues Resarians from Pahl'Kiar that knows me? She then said something along the lines of, 'His heart aches for you, and I can see that yours does for him. Please stop torturing one another and try not to lose your compass watch again. It's a physical embodiment of his spirit within you and that's why you love it almost as much as you love him.' And then I hugged her and I gave her about twenty frakshins for saving something priceless. She wants me to tell him she said 'hey' the next time I see him," Brisethi concluded.

"My spirits, 'Sethi, you haven't talked about him in a while. The only man you ever talk about lately is Edewat, and I can only pretend to care so much about how long he meows at you when you sing to him," Milia retorted. "We need to find you a nice man or lady, 'Sethi. I worry about you sometimes."

Brisethi mockingly scowled to him before taking another sip of tea. "You know I haven't had a craving of desire since the Lantheuns defiled me four years ago."

Milia gave her a concerned look. "I'm sorry, I sometimes forget that's the reason you shun affection."

"Oh, look who I've stumbled upon, the Dominion's finest doing what they're best at - nothing," Milia's husband said from behind him.

"Sycris, nice to see you, too," Brisethi said warmly. She stood to gently hug the civilian merchant.

"I just came by to wish you spirit's grace upon your second meeting with Emperor what's-his-name, Admiral someone and General whoever this evening. You look as stunning as usual, let's hope they're more distracted by your burgundy locks than your stammering voice," Sycris teased.

"I won't be stammering today," Brisethi replied more confidently than she felt.

Chapter XVI

The day of the extraction mission dawned bright and clear. The air was crisp with the promise of snow. Ekani analyzed the conditions and made some adjustments in the plan to account for snow, in case it did come that evening. So much depended on the success of the mission and ensuring that it was never revealed that the Emperor had sanctioned a rescue for Resarians.

When he was done, Ekani took a deep breath, momentarily enjoying the wintery sun on his face. He stared out across the cityscape, marveling at the sight before him. Light sparkled through the air breaking through the clouds that were trying to block it. The balcony outside his room was useful for getting a few private moments in before facing the day. Since the discovery of his mystics, the sun in particular seemed to help rejuvenate him. He resisted the urge to test the power that he could feel flowing through him, not wanting to accidentally become incapacitated for the mission that night.

Ekani relocated to the lanai for his morning routine of scanning reports from the diplomatic staff. From the corner of his eye, he could see shapes moving nearby. He tensed momentarily before realizing it was Sulica's team getting some early morning training in. After a while, he couldn't focus on the reports in front of him and moved closer to the training field.

Sulica was standing off to the side, watching. He joined her silently. Azoda was at one side of the field with her back facing the others. Intermittently, she would turn around quickly, trying to catch the rest moving closer to her.

"Really?" Ekani said incredulously, "You're having them play Tocal?"

Sulica smiled without looking at him. "It's good for practicing the sneaking skills."

They continued to watch as Potin tried to tap Azoda on the shoulder right as she was twisting around, causing Potin to jump back in surprise. The rest of the group began laughing as Azoda squealed and shouted "You're out! You're all out!"

"Why aren't you out there?" Ekani asked, grinning at the antics.

Sulica shook her head vehemently. "I am so awful at Tocal," she said. "Besides, it's good for them to get the sillies out before a mission."

Ekani looked at her long and hard for a moment before suddenly laughing harder than he had in months.

"What?" she asked, wondering if he'd gone insane.

"You," he said, gasping for air. When he recovered, he continued, "These are Kiaran government trained special operatives, and you're talking about them having the sillies."

"Oh." She gave him a brilliant smile. "Do you disagree?"

He glanced out at the team running the length of the field chasing after Azoda. "Not at all."

-:- -:- -:-

That afternoon, Ekani gathered everyone in the conference room once more to complete the final preparations. Sulica stood in the corner again, surveying everyone. Nervous energy emanated from Simtel's team as a couple of them paced and chatted with each other. Her own team, dressed completely in black so as to blend in with the shadows, was calm and collected. Sulica gave Ekani a pointed look.

He shook his head then called for attention. The room quieted. "We're going to be leaving soon. Does everyone understand their part?"

Dereso, a large-built Kiaran man with a lisp raised his hand. "Why I got to be the driver? I wanna kick rebel ass."

Simtel clapped a hand on his shoulder while glaring at the rest of the team to stifle their snickers. "Come on, brother, you're responsible for making sure we get out of there in one piece. You got the most important part. Just don't mess it up."

Dereso seemed mollified. "I won't." He puffed his chest out. "You be proud when we done."

They assembled by the gates and departed in groups of two or three. Ekani had told them to take different routes and transports to the target building on the outskirts of the city. Sulica's team had exchanged their black clothes for the bright-colored ones that were in high fashion, but, like her, they still wore the skintight clothes on underneath their garb.

"This is ridiculous," Sulica muttered to Simtel and Ekani as they left, the last of the group to depart. She was wearing a long dress with a large ruffled black skirt and a bright blue bodice tied tightly. The sleeves were also long and puffed to hide the long sleeves of her black shirt. With the setting sun, she would be grateful for the extra warmth. On her head she wore a black velvet top hat with a veil. Ekani believed it would help prevent people from staring at her eyes. With her bright hair, she could not have passed for Kiaran.

"You look fine," Ekani said shortly, focusing on finding the others in front of them.

"Just 'fine'? Come on now, Ekani, that's no way to compliment a lady!" Simtel hurried in front of Sulica and bowed to her. "My lady, you look prettier than a glob of butter melting on a stack of wheat cakes."

Sulica laughed as he offered his arm to her, reminded of their journey through Vipurg. "Don't push me in any snow piles this time," she joked.

"Only to save your life," he replied as though it were the simplest thing in the world. He had chosen to wear his normal civilian attire - a white collared shirt with a necktie and a crimson double-breasted vest with black trousers. Over it, he sported a long, black wool coat.

Ekani was similarly dressed, only with a dark blue vest and a tan overcoat. "What a way to help her blend in," he remarked, still on the lookout.

They continued walking for quite some time, passing other people on their way to do the shopping or running errands. "Everyone seems so normal," Sulica said under her breath.

"Well, what did you expect?" Ekani gave her a look. "Didn't you do the reading I told you to?"

"Look!" she said excitedly, pointing. "It's starting to snow."

"Nice avoidance," Ekani mumbled. He smiled in spite of himself at the wondrous look on Sulica's face. She stood still, staring at the sky turning pale pink as the sun began to set. "Come on," he said gently after a minute, "we have to keep moving."

They continued on their way, taking a trolley car most of the journey. No one even glanced twice at them playing the part of a young trio out about town. Several blocks from the target building, the three stopped at the fishery that had been the site of their last exercise. Sulica shed her fancy clothes, stowing them in a crate. She stretched and breathed deeply, "I infinitely prefer pants to skirts," she said then giggled.

The two men looked at her strangely. "Ten years ago I would have never imagined myself saying those words," she explained.

Ekani rolled his eyes. The three waited for the last rays of day to disappear. "Are you ready to go?" Ekani asked.

Sulica moved to a door on the opposite side of the open room in response. Ekani nodded to her and left with Simtel through the same way they had entered. Sulica slipped out the other door and quickly moved through the shadows to the rendezvous point. As she approached the meeting spot, she slowed and looked around her very carefully. There. Subtle movements in the darkness gave away her team members as they assembled at the spot. She paused to scan the area for any other movement before finally joining the others. They nodded at her, but none of them spoke a word.

The group moved into position outside two of the warehouse doors. Sulica had to swallow her doubts and nervousness. She nearly threw a prayer to the spirits before catching herself. So much of this depended on Simtel's team mirroring her own. Sulica reached out cautiously with her mystic, searching for Ekani's. A momentary panic hit her when she couldn't feel his presence, but she quickly reasoned with herself that it was possible he was not in range. Breathing deeply and closing her eyes to concentrate, she pushed the limits of her power, feeling it begin to pain her. A slight tingle met her reach, then another and a third. She felt one more, and her eyes snapped open.

Forcing herself to remain calm, she gestured for the team to move ahead. Potin and Neiko worked the doors open, cringing when one made a squeaking sound as it moved inward. The team paused for a couple of minutes, waiting to see if there was any reaction. When nothing happened, the team moved inside. They were in a small, dark room filled with stacked furniture covered by sheets and a thick layer of dust. A door on the other side of the room was propped open, allowing a beam of dim light to spill in. Sulica gestured, and Azoda crouched, moving towards the door. She moved slowly until she was out of sight. After a few moments, Azoda's hand was visible, two fingers held up.

Neiko looked back at Sulica from his position. He was nearest the door. Sulica nodded, and he slipped out behind Azoda. A few minutes later Azoda reappeared, waving the rest of the team forward. As they walked by, Sulica noticed the bodies of two guards lying motionless. She made a face and moved her hand to indicate them. She and Potin moved them out of sight.

They continued to move through the offices of the warehouse, taking great care to make sure each was clear before moving on. They finally reached a large dark room filled with crates. There was a staircase at the far end with a light shining down it. Sulica halted her team and reached out with her mystic. She had to remind herself to remain cautious as she felt for the four Resarians.

Her team moved forward into the room until they heard a scuff on the ground. Each froze in their positions for several long moments. Sulica peered around the crate and watched as the barely visible group moved in the next row over. They stopped by the crate nearest the stairs. Sulica motioned for her team to move up next to them.

One of them seemed to sense her and turned as they approached. Sulica could barely make out Ekani's face in the darkness. He nodded to her and double tapped the shoulder in front of him. The motion moved forward through the line, indicating the other team had joined them. Ekani moved to the front of the group, and Sulica took his spot.

They all headed to the staircase. When they were inside of the light, each person put on protective eye-wear. Ekani held up three fingers in full view of everyone and slowly put one after another down. He bolted up the staircase with the rest of the group behind him. The door to the office at the top of the staircase was open, allowing the team to rush through it into the room. An ultra bright light suddenly filled the room, and Sulica instantly reached out with her mystic to suppress the Resarians' mystics. To be safe, she shut down Ekani's as well. Meanwhile, the rest of the team quickly took down the three armed rebels, none of them had been able to put up a fight between being caught off guard and the blinding light that hit them.

The room was cluttered with desks and papers. At the back of it was another door. Sulica rushed past a kneeling Ekani and burst into the next room. The light from the main office spilled in, revealing two cells. Three bodies shrunk back from the door as soon as it opened, but the fourth lay immobile. Sulica's eyes quickly scanned the features of the first three then they came to rest on the fourth, in a separate cell. Though the fourth's back was to her, Sulica could not mistake the familiarity of the spirit.

Letting out a strangled cry, Sulica moved to the cell and grabbed a hold of the bars. "No," she whispered. "It can't be." She released her hold on the one mystic.

She was dimly aware of footsteps behind her. The clink of a key in the lock brought her out of her disturbed reverie. As soon as Neiko had the other cell door open she held her hand out for the keys, her gaze still locked in front of her. He handed them over wordlessly, and she fumbled with putting it in the lock, tears blurring her vision. She finally got the cell door open and fell next to the body. She rolled it over onto her lap and brushed the long, tangled brown hair away from Ibrienne's face.

Sulica pressed her fingers to Ibrienne's throat, muttering, "Please," over and over. Ibrienne's pulse was weak, but it was still there. Not realizing she had been holding her breath, Sulica breathed out in relief. She held her hand out behind her, and someone gave her a container of water. Cradling Ibrienne's head, she tipped a little bit into the other girl's mouth.

Ibrienne stirred slightly. "No more," she said in a voice that was barely more than a whisper. Her eyes opened for a few moments then closed and re-opened. She squinted, barely able to make out the face above her. Finally she croaked, "You're late."

Sulica felt a sharp pain in her chest, and she held Ibrienne tightly. "I'm here now. You'll be safe now." Even as the words left her lips, she wondered how true they were.

Chapter XVII

Sulica made her way up the stairs two at a time. She ran down the halls until she reached the wing where the four Resarians were quartered during their recovery.

Although the initial flight from the warehouse had been relatively easy, except Neiko prying Sulica away from Ibrienne to carry the Resarian woman to the car and the somewhat unexpected snag in Simtel having to carry an unconscious Ekani, the first several weeks had been anything but simple. Three of the captives were cautiously grateful of their rescue until they realized where they were going. Sulica had to keep them suppressed for days until they began to assume that they could not use their mystic. While their malnourished bodies regained strength, Ekani visited with them often, to persuade them to join his cause. Sulica, with Ekani's assistance, had convinced the Kiaran government that Resarians could and would be far more beneficial as team augments rather than prisoners.

Ibrienne, on the other hand, remained unconscious for over a month. The physician told Sulica that Ibrienne was on the brink of death for days. Another week, and she probably would have been lost.

Sulica was outside training with Ekani and one of the rescued Resarians, Davik, who had decided to help out of nothing other than the feeling of indebtedness for saving him, when word reached them that Ibrienne had awoken. With a quick apologetic glance at Ekani, she took off for Ibrienne's room.

Skidding to a halt in the hall, she paused, took a breath, and walked inside. The room was empty. She could see the covers on the bed rumpled from where Ibrienne had lain. But she was nowhere to be found. Sulica reached out with her mystic, searching for Ibrienne's and fearing the worst. She felt relief flood over her when she found it. She took off in the direction she believed Ibrienne to have gone. After climbing three flights of stairs and hitting a couple of dead ends, she finally saw Ibrienne in the garden on the top floor.

The other woman moved slowly, kneeling to smell every patch of flowers she passed. She wore a ruffled green skirt, with a black loose-fitting shirt. Given the state Sulica had found Ibrienne in, she was amazed the woman was able to walk at all. Then again, she considered Ibrienne's healing ability, as powerful as it once was.

Ibrienne seemed to notice that she was not alone. She turned and regarded Sulica coolly before turning back to the flowers. Her relief at finding Ibrienne after a few years since that initial contact in Pahl'Kiar's harbor slowly faded. After several minutes of silence while Ibrienne wandered around the garden, Sulica grew impatient.

"So you have nothing to say?" she finally spoke up.

Again, Ibrienne stared at her with an icy gaze in her once kind blue eyes. She opened her mouth then paused, as though considering her words. "Should I thank you?" The voice that came from Ibrienne's mouth was not her own. It was scratchy, hoarse, and rough. Sulica shivered at the sound, and Ibrienne gave a chilly smile. "Thank you for dragging me into your criminal world, for playing me into betraying a friend." The words tumbled out, as though she had waited a very long time to say them. "Thank you for associating me with the likes of Kanilas, who betrayed me just as you did. Thank you for subjecting me to years of torture on subjects I knew nothing of. But no, they did not believe me because of who I was linked with."

Sulica shrank back from the verbal assault, though Ibrienne did not yell, probably incapable of even raising her voice. The guilt that had been sitting with her since Lantheus resurfaced. "I tried-" she began to say.

"Don't." Ibrienne cut her off. "No matter what you say, it will likely be another lie, another trap." Her harsh tone disappeared, replaced by weariness. "Just leave me alone. You've done enough." She turned away and moved to the next patch of flowers.

Biting her lip, Sulica walked backwards toward the door back inside the palace. Her hope of redemption was chipped away more and more with every word that Ibrienne said. She stood at the door, not wanting to leave but terrified to face the monster who had taken her friend's face. As she watched, Ibrienne picked one of the beautiful yellow hibiscus flowers and held it to her face. The sun broke through the wintery clouds and illuminated Ibrienne's face, which had been hidden by shadows for weeks. Scars streaked the young Resarian's face, from her eye down her neck. There were probably many more hidden beneath the clothes.

Sulica shivered, remembering her own torture experience. "I'm sorry," she whispered. "What do you want?" When Ibrienne gave no response, Sulica turned and fled.

Ibrienne heard the door slam at the other end of the garden. She sighed and walked to the edge of the garden. Lilac bushes were in full bloom near the short wall, despite the cold, thanks to the Kiaran technology. Taking a deep breath, she could feel heat all around her, and the scent of the beautiful flowers filled her nose. For the first time in many months, she smiled. Ibrienne stepped onto the ledge and stood there for a long time. Images of every horrible person who brought pain upon her, both physically and mentally, flashed in her mind. She inhaled deeply and tried to think of the few good people left in the world, whom she no longer had contact with. She gazed at the various terracotta rooftops of the city, then glanced down below at the empty alleyway. *I no longer have purpose,* she hopelessly concluded.

Ibrienne closed her eyes, and, still holding the flower, she fell. *Peace,* she thought in answer to Sulica.

Sulica took off as fast as she could, away from the rooftop garden, away from the training area where she might be seen by Ekani, away from the lanai. She hid on the far side of the palace grounds, tears streaming down her face. A boiling hot anger began to fill her. *I paid my dues too. I am trying to make up for it.* Rushing back up the winding staircase, she re-entered the garden and raced to the wall.

A hand closed around Ibrienne's wrist. She didn't move, and neither did the hand. It was a loose grip, just enough for her to know it was there, but not enough to catch her if she chose to step off. "You should let me go," she said.

"If you really wanted to, you know I couldn't stop you," a voice said, striking a chord of familiarity in her. She remained still, wanting to hear it again. "Did you really survive and fight all that time just to do this?" The timbre wasn't quite right, but that didn't matter to her.

Ibrienne glanced down and behind her, catching a glimpse of the coal black hair and bright eyes. Her vision swam in front of her, mist obscuring her view. She was standing on the shore, but everything seemed darker and felt off somehow, like looking through a screen. To the side, she saw Etyne, surrounded by a group of other Resarians - she could tell by the sense of their spirits - battling what appeared to be a large shadow. Everything was silent, not even the clang of the weapons could be heard. A huge paw reached out from the shadow, claws extended and swiped at Etyne. She cried out, swayed and fell.

Sulica reached the edge of the garden where Ekani was kneeling, cradling Ibrienne in his arms. "Is she...?"

He looked up at Sulica and tried to smile reassuringly. "She's alive." He couldn't hide the confusion on his face and revealed, "When she saw me, it was odd... Like how you were during your flashbacks, almost. Except..."

"Except?" Sulica pressed.

"She started to disappear." They looked down at the very solid woman laying on him. Ekani then studied the anxious expression on Sulica's face. "How much does she mean to you?"

With a sharp look, she said, "What kind of question is that?"

"Just answer."

"I owe her more than my life is worth," she said quietly, kneeling next to them. Sulica took Ibrienne's hand, terrified of what might have happened if Ekani hadn't shown up.

He watched as Ibrienne began to stir and made a decision. "You need to get her out of here," he said urgently but quietly. "If she does this again in front of the medical staff, they won't ever let her go." Ekani explained his plan. Sulica realized he was right, but she didn't like it.

When Ibrienne was semi-conscious, they escorted her back to her room, where Sulica insisted she stay with Ibrienne and keep watch over her as she was no doubt worn out from the exercise before she was ready. "How dare you let her out with no assistance?" she had shrilly chastised the staff before following Ekani into the room, shutting it behind her.

Ekani left soon after Ibrienne woke. Sulica stood her ground against her former companion's icy words. When that didn't work, she requested a pad and paper then lapsed into silence and finally into a fitful sleep. All the while, Sulica stayed by her side until late that night, when Ekani returned to the room with a pack filled with food and clothes. He carried an additional set of clothes in his arms. Sulica woke Ibrienne and bade her to get dressed. Groggy as she was, she did not protest. Ekani made sure to turn away.

When she was ready, the three of them slipped out of the room and quickly made their way to a door used mostly by palace staff. Once outside, Ekani handed the pack to Sulica then strode towards the gardens, rather than the grounds entrance that Sulica led Ibrienne to. When they reached the gate, Sulica pushed the pack into Ibrienne's arms.

"There's food, clothes, and money in there," she whispered. "They won't come after you. We'll make sure of it."

"Why?" Ibrienne asked.

Sulica glanced around, not wanting to dawdle. "I'm not the same person I was when we separated. You're a beautiful soul, and I should have never got you caught up in this, this mess."

Ibrienne studied the woman in front of her. The Sulica she knew had been confident, brazen. This one was cautious. Maybe she was different. "Who is he?"

"Etyne's twin brother," Sulica answered. "And he'll be in danger if you don't go now." She disabled the alarm on the iron wrought gate, pushing it open for Ibrienne to walk through.

When it closed behind her, Ibrienne turned back. She pulled a paper out and handed it through the bars to Sulica. "I don't know if I'll make it, or where I'll make it to. Can you make sure this gets to Livian Reej?"

Sulica nodded, taking the paper.

"Spirits be with you," Ibrienne said, though it felt more like a curse than a blessing. She walked away, disappearing into the night.

Sulica watched her go for a moment, glanced down at the letter in her hand, then hurried away from the gate, shoving it in her pocket. She did not return to the palace, but went to the garden instead, where Ekani was waiting for her. He asked if it was done, and she nodded.

They walked around the garden in the cold night air, their breath appearing in front of them like steam.

The streets nearest the palace were devoid of any activity late at night. Ibrienne glanced up at the night sky, the way she had many nights before. The docks would provide the fastest way home, but she wasn't even sure if that's where she wanted to go. Even if she did make it back to Res'Baveth, she would likely be arrested for her part in capturing Brisethi. Her thoughts travelled back to the scene of Etyne battling the shadow. Instinctively, she pulled the hood up over her head and began heading south.

(END)

About the Authors

Ginger Salazar and Jasmine Shouse are United States Navy veterans. Both natives of Colorado, they met while stationed in Hawaii, bonding over their mutual love of video games and writing and began work on what would become *Sethi's Song*.

Ginger lives with her husband and cats in Denver. She enjoys drawing, playing video games, science fiction shows, and metal music.

Jasmine lives with her husband, three sons, and greyhound in San Antonio, TX. She loves reading, doing puzzles, and playing Xbox.

Made in the USA
San Bernardino, CA
17 February 2018